THE INFAMOUS STORY OF RETRO BRITE
Copyright © 2023 by Felicia Jones

ISBN 979-8-9864995-6-7

Cover Design by Brittany Evans

Edited by Represent Publishing

THE INFAMOUS STORY OF RETRO BRITE

THE INFAMOUS STORY OF RETRO BRITE

FELÍCIA JONES

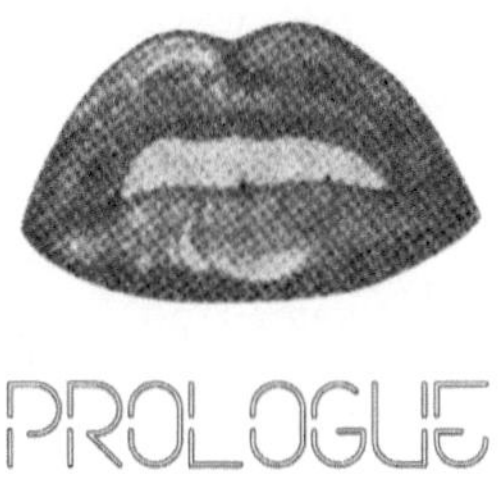

PROLOGUE

What is fame?

Most people know it as being well-known or talked about by lots of people, but they have no idea. Some people are born into it, while others bring it upon themselves. Whether you can admit it or not, we all like attention and fantasize about what it would be like to live a lavish lifestyle. It's a part of who we are. I mean, come on, who wants to be remembered as an ordinary person? The average person takes about 216 billion steps and 672 billion breaths, hoping every step leaves footprints, and with every breath, remarkable words are spoken. Even though this may be true for most people, it isn't for me. Most people my age would want this. Kids are all the same, right? I mean, I think fame and attention would be nice, but what're the chances of something like that happening to me. A regular high schooler from a small town. I never thought any of this would happen to me. I am the type of person that sits idle in the background. Most people think it's better to say, "Wow, I can't believe I did that" rather than, "I should have done that." And let's just say, I've had my,

"Wow. I can't believe that just happened." Though . . . I'm not sure if I wanted something like fame.

Listen to my story and make your own decision.

A STAR IS BORN

1

I WAS SITTING in history class, the last class for the day, gazing out the large window as usual. *Just a few minutes until the weekend*, I reminded myself. This was my senior year, and I promised myself this year was going to be the best one yet. Just three more months until graduation. I couldn't wait for all the free time and concerts scheduled; the perfect combination of awesome. I had one earbud in my ear; rock music buzzed. I tapped my pencil against my desk, which had a heart shape engraved into the wood. The gum I had been chewing since the beginning of class was now a tasteless, bland glob.

"Leon, what's your opinion on this?" a stern voice announced. I felt the many eyes of my classmates as the typical background noise of chatter died down. My chair scraped against the tiled floors as I straightened my posture. Mr. McKinney's stare was intense. He must have been calling on me for a while now.

Time to deal with the reality of school life.

I jumped back to my senses and retorted, "Do you think we really care about this? It's Friday. Time for the weekend." I lifted my hands and slapped them against my desk. It didn't matter what he wanted from me in these last few minutes of class.

What could he possibly try to teach us in such a small amount of time? Just let us pack up to leave.

"Well, this is more important than the weekend or that silly little band you all have been talking about," Mr. McKinney fired back without missing a beat. I expected him to stumble over his words, but I guess he was getting used to my snarkiness.

"Silly band!? It's not just any band; it's Retro Brite, one of the best new bands of this decade!" my friend Kim exclaimed, standing out of her seat.

"Miss Evans, sit down, please!" Mr. McKinney urged her. His round face was now the color of a tomato.

Most of the students were whispering, smirking, and giving nods of approval. Mr. McKinney shot them a look that made them shut up within seconds. His fist was clenched and placed on his forehead. This was routine in this class: I rarely pay attention, he calls me out, and I say a smart comment. Either that or the entire class doesn't oblige to his rules.

The bell sliced through the silence. Everyone rushed out of their seats to claim their freedom. Mr. McKinney rambled about some assignments, but everyone had already exited the class. The hallway filled with laughter and excitement about the weekend. Pieces of paper were crumpled up on the blue and yellow checkered floor. Lockers clinked open and closed and the smell of cheap perfume lingered in the air. Kim and I made our way to the student parking lot to catch up with our friends.

"Leon!" Landon yelled. He then cut through a group of students to give me a bear hug. His muscular arms held me tight. He was wearing athletic shorts and a t-shirt; gym was his last class of the day. His normally loose, curly brown hair was wet and slicked back. His olive skin was sunburned. He must have been outside for a couple of hours.

"Dude, I can't wait to go to the Retro Brite concert tonight. It's practically all I can think about." Kim bounced on her toes.

Her converse sneakers crunched against the concrete as her over-sized flannel shirt dangled off her narrow shoulders.

"Me either," I said. "It's gonna be a fun night! And thanks for taking the heat off me in class," I cackled. "Mr. McKinney was over it. I'm surprised he hasn't quit yet."

"Anytime. I can't believe Seth let you get the day off. I thought you said he was a hard ass? You'll finally be able to rekindle with your twin brother! Aren't you excited?" Kim smiled as her shoulder-length auburn hair swayed in the wind.

"Yeah, I had-got off. I covered someone else's shift, and he said he owed me a favor. And I guess it would be cool to see them live." My hands were clammy. My friends didn't know that I still haven't called off. I need to stop doing things last minute. If Kim knew I hadn't call out yet, she would be upset. She's been talking about it for months.

Why couldn't I just tell the truth? I couldn't ruin it for everyone. But it was okay. I was not going to get fired. I've been there for a couple of years. And we're understaffed right now.

"Wow, you got off even though it's your weekend to work?" Landon said, scratching his head and squinting his brown eyes.

"Yeah, crazy, huh?" I said.

I wish I would have called off. If only I had been more responsible and not used my time off already. I could guarantee I wasn't the best employee or student. I already used up most of my sick days, and all my paid time off. When I would call off, I usually snuck back into the house while Aunt Mel was at work or hung out at Jetstream Hill, a park where high schoolers in Crestview hung out at. The only reason I wanted to go to the concert was to spend time with my friends. And not too many performers come to Crestview, anyway. I could admit Retro Brite's first album was a massive success with many great tracks.

But after that, their music and branding went downhill. Since the band had become popular, everyone noticed how the lead singer Vince and my looks were uncanny. I mean, way too similar to where many people thought I was him. At first, it didn't faze me and I enjoyed the attention, but after they realized our similar looks were a coincidence, they seemed to lose interest in me. People would ask if we were related and wondered why we looked alike. Their faces would go from interest and surprise to disappointment and disbelief. And after their disappointment, I'd go back to being Leon Halloway the III.

Retro Brite coming to town was a big deal, not only to my friends but also to everyone in the town. This was because I'm from Crestview. A town most people haven't heard of on the east coast with a population of 7,000. A majority of the people have lived here their whole lives, including me. It was a place you wanted to escape as soon as possible. There were no good job opportunities or higher education. Crestview once had an impressive lumbering industry, but that came to a halt many years ago. Now the options were to work at a mom-and-pop shop or own one.

Retro Brite was a band whose tickets always sold out fast, or they performed exclusive private shows. The band, for the most part, performed in much bigger cities. Every year during spring or summer, the band had a huge tour where an exclusive amount of people could win tickets and get backstage passes. This year, the band was having a look-alike contest, which would allow the winner to get a cash prize of $2,000 and back-stage passes. I really didn't care much about the contest, but the money would help my aunt and uncle a lot. I have lived with my aunt and uncle since I was 9 because my parents died. Money has been tight lately and they could use the extra cash.

"Don't worry, Leon. We can easily win this contest. You're practically twins." Kim reassured me by squeezing my shoulders.

"I don't think so; they look alike, but he must capture the

essence of who he is. The hair, the walk, the attitude," Landon argued.

"Really, Landon . . . Leon and Vince are practically identical," Kim lashed back.

"Yeah, but is he ready for the questionnaire? Has he been practicing?" Landon asked.

"Yeah, I have," I said while scratching my head. During the contest, the contestants would be asked various questions about Vince. I have been practicing, but only because Kim kept on reminding me about it. And I only did it for a few minutes a day.

I hope this all went smoothly. My friends would never let this go if I messed up.

"Come on, Landon. I'm sure he's been studying," Kim said.

Kim and Landon started to bicker, which was normal. He argued with Camille way more, anyway. Camille was another friend in our group. She was the loud, fun party girl and the most popular out of the four of us. Her and Landon were dating and argued about the littlest things. Kim and Landon have been friends for many years. They grew up next door to each other. They fought like siblings. I've just learned to ignore it and keep on going, but somehow, I always got dragged into it. Kim huffing her breath and Landon with his exaggerated hand motions. They both stopped arguing for a second and made unavoidable eye contact with me. I knew what was coming next; the words I dreaded to hear.

"Right, Leon?" they questioned at the same time. I hated choosing a side, especially when it was over stupid arguments like this. So I gave them a blank stare and shrugged my shoulders.

"You always do that," Kim whined. Her golden wide-set eyes were closed.

"Look, let's just meet up with Camille at Su Castillo."

Su Castillo was the local Mexican restaurant in our town. It has been the weekly hang out spot for my friends and me for years. And has been a staple in Crestview. It was the perfect spot for everyone to hangout at from kids like us to middle-aged soccer moms gossiping. Every other day, we met there at 4:30 pm after school. I often got tired of the mundane life of this small town, but going to Su Castillo was always a good time.

Kim climbed into my car without any further remarks while Landon walked toward his Hyundai Elantra. Kim was the only one without a car and was always hitching rides from everyone. My 1997 black Honda Civic shouldn't even be called a car, but more like some old hooptie. The gray cloth seats were now neon blue from fruit punch being spilled. The scent of French fries was embedded in the car. In the back seats were video games and movies I bought from Borrowers, the store I work at. The AC blew humid air; the headlights were too dim, and the windows creaked while being rolled up. I never had the luxury of my parents buying me a shiny, somewhat new car, like most of the students at my school. Especially since my aunt and uncle have been struggling financially. A lot of kids around here drove new Nissans and Kias, making my car stick out like a sore thumb. At least my car had some form of charm and many memories with my friends.

Even though Kim and Landon were in the middle of feuding moments ago, as soon as I turned on the radio, I let out a deep breath.

Walking into the restaurant was relaxing every visit. Su Castillo, meaning "your castle," was supposed to make you feel just like royalty. There weren't too many nice restaurants in Crestview, but this one tried to have a luxurious feel. The rural castle interior transported its guests to Mexico with a courtyard. It was a beautiful two-story castle. The wide-open space and chipped, painted checkered floor always made me feel like I was in a fairytale land.

When we entered, a waitress escorted us to where Camille was sitting at our designated table: a small booth in the corner with vinyl seats that made a scratching noise when you moved. She squealed with excitement as we sat down like she hadn't seen us, even though we just saw her earlier at school. She hugged us and grinned as we sat down. Camille gave Porter a smooch on his cheek. Her glossy lips left a shiny mark on his cheek. She was already munching away on tortilla chips. It was times like these that made all the stress of life go away. Whenever we came here, everyone was suddenly in a better mood, like a love spell was cast upon us. I wished these moments were infinite. On Friday evenings, the restaurant was lively. Families sat waiting on wooden benches lined against the wall. The children screeched and their feet pattered against the floor. A Mariachi band was playing. The trumpets shrilled, the violins were melodic, and the guitars were resonant. The music was always great here; it was hard not to clap and dance along.

"So, who's pumped for the concert?" Camille announced with a big grin that exposed the purple brackets on her braces. She danced along to the music in her seat.

This comment led to a big eruption of conversation. We have been so excited for this event. My friends had all the details down to a science. Especially Kim. *Well, almost everything. I still hadn't called out and there was no way I was telling them. I hope no one brought up work again.*

"Let's go over the plan again, so we are ready for the contest," Camille said. "The next few months are going to be amazing. I already started planning our graduation party!" she said. Camille was the only one in the group that was into partying. She would often plan them or dragged the rest of us to them.

Besides me, Landon was the most laid back of the group. Camille, on the other hand, was the life of the party, but also helped me tame Kim and Landon's outbursts.

"Let's go over contest rules and facts about Vince," Kim explained this, for the millionth time, looking at pictures of Vince on her phone.

"Okay, so the contest will begin at 7:15 pm. All contestants must pay a $35 fee prior to entering. Which I will be taking care of," Kim said, placing her hand on her chest. "The contestants will not only be judged on their looks but also on their knowledge of the lead singer of Retro Brite, Vincent Continolo," she read with great speed.

"Yeah, yeah, we got this." Camille nodded toward her while brushing her dyed blond locks to the side.

Did we? Knots formed in my stomach. I stirred around my plate of rice and chicken. I nibbled on my food. I couldn't believe I have to enter this contest. My friends and I were splitting the money, but I needed it the most. Kim would go off and become a great photographer, Landon would open a successful business, and Camille would become a party planner. And there was me, dressing up like someone who was more successful, famous, and richer than I'd ever be.

If there was anyone who knew the most about bands, it would be Kim. She knew pretty much all the gossip and had a wide knowledge about Retro Brite.

"Mm-hmm," said Landon, wiping salsa from his mouth. He was leaning on the table with his eyes half-shut. He was tired of her talking, but didn't say anything else.

"This is going to be the best night ever," Camille gushed. "I can see the money in our hands!" The silver bangles on her wrist jangled as she waved her hands around.

Everyone at the table chuckled in agreement.

"Anyway," Kim cleared her throat. "What's his favorite color?" Kim asked, looking at me.

"Blue."

"What shade of blue, though?" she pressed.

"Navy," I mumbled. *Was there really a difference? They're both blue.*

"C'mon, Leon, you can't half-ass these," Kim pleaded. "Now, what's his dog's name?"

"Granny . . . something."

"Ganymede!" she snapped. "Ga-ny-mede!" She clapped the syllables for emphasis. I couldn't help but laugh at her anger.

"We had Astronomy together. I know you know how to pronounce it!"

Joke was on her; I didn't remember anything from that class. I have hardly retained anything from any of my classes. Currently, I was sporting a D average. What made her think I remembered some random space term? I did kind of remember the dog's name, though, and Vince's passion for navy blue, among other random facts. But, since she made me study something, I had to give her some form of hell.

"Oh, also—" Kim fidgeted with her phone before shoving it in my face. Her thumbs moved at lightning speed. I already knew what was on the screen, so I turned my head and tutted my lips.

"Look!" she demanded. "This is how you have to cut your hair."

"Nope," I replied.

"You already look just like him, but this will take you to the next level. Do it!"

"Don't you mean *he* looks just like *me*?" I countered.

"Actually, he's older than you, so you are the copycat." Her small lips were twisted in a smug smile.

I folded my arms and leaned back in my seat. I remembered a time when Kim thought my hair was cute. Now, she was begging me to shave it off. Not that I cared; it was only hair. But it was funny how feverish she was getting about this dude. She didn't even know him, yet she has me imitating him for a chance to maybe meet him.

"I'll think about it," I told her. It took all my strength to not crack a smile at her frustration. I admired her passion. I was still looking for the thing I was most passionate about, but the fact she got so worked up about a stranger irked me.

"If we wanna win this, you have to dress completely different. That means skinnier jeans. Oh, and I already ordered some temporary tattoos that look just like his." She showed me fake tattoos, which to my surprise looked somewhat convincing. One of them was a moth with a skull on its head and it had a long tail. "And you must get rid of this." She scratched my small wiry mustache with her index finger.

I swatted my hand at her. "No, I'm trying to grow it out," I said, turning away from her.

"Vince has a clean-shaven face."

"Fine," I mumbled. *I also couldn't care less about my mustache. I just wanted to see Kim squirm.*

"You have to practice his walk and his voice," Kim said. "Landon, show him."

Landon stood up and slouched, making his 6" frame smaller. He began to stagger his walk, trying his best to mimic Vince's 'cool boy' demeanor.

"Hey, what's up?" he deepened his voice.

"Now, it's your turn." Camille motioned for me to stand up.

I shook my head. I was not embarrassing myself in the restaurant, and this was stupid.

"Come on!" Kim chimed.

"No. No way." I sighed loudly.

"Fine. Just practice when you get home. I'll send you some videos and pictures." She folded her arms.

"So," Camille piped up, "we will meet up at the concert hall at 7."

"Yes, we have to be there an hour early for the contest," Kim said.

"You mean, you three have to be early," Landon said as he pointed to Kim and me. "I already have seats. I'm not standing around for an hour for no reason. The concert starts at 8."

Kim slanted her head in complete disbelief. "We also need to be in line, like, as soon as possible to get a chance at the merch."

Landon motioned toward his shirt, a white tee with the iconic rosy lip mark that defined the band. He pulled on the shirt, making the image warp. "I already have their shirt!" He laughed.

"No, the exclusive stuff." Kim's voice was strained. We all

liked Retro Brite, but Kim was a super fan. I think everyone would agree that you could divide Kim's life into two stages: pre-Retro Brite and post-Retro Brite. She was the first of the friend group to hear about the band, and now, we couldn't go a day without her mentioning something about them or inserting one of their lyrics awkwardly into conversation.

I couldn't be too annoyed. Their music was more than catchy to me. Their first album actually hit home more than I could ever let Kim know. I listened to it daily when it came out. Hopefully, they would play songs from it tonight. They were now on their third album and had made many new songs and grew their fanbase. It was cool to see a group this well-known perform, but honestly, I just wanted to have a great night with my friends and escape my boring life. It was almost not a possibility with my family's tight budget. It was a huge surprise when my aunt presented me with a ticket and a great seat next to my friends. She and Kim must have conspired to make that happen. And for that, and because Kim has been my friend since 5th grade and all, I was going along with this crazy look-alike contest.

"I could go without waiting," Landon said, yawning. "I'm going to get some homework done before the actual event I paid money for starts. Have fun standing around to spend more. See you guys later." Landon walked out of the restaurant without another word. Landon was the most studious of us, a 4.0 student. I knew he was telling the truth about cramming school work before the concert.

Kim waved him off and turned to Camille. "Well, you ready to go?"

"Um." Camille shot me a glance, but I broke eye contact. She had to stand up to Kim's manic behavior on her own. "I guess I don't have anything else to do." She sounded like she was struggling for an excuse, but just settled for the truth. Camille grabbed her leopard printed furry jacket and put it on.

"Cool," Kim chimed. That was the most cooperative remark

she got from one of us the whole conversation. "And you!" She turned to me. "See you at 7 with a fresh cut."

"I told you. I said, I'll think about it." We locked eyes in a stare out, one of many we had when poking fun of each other. I couldn't hide my smile this time and broke into laughter.

There was a moment of relief in Kim's eyes before she replaced them back with a stern glare. "Just come looking correct, 'kay?"

"I mean. Who knows." As we left the table, Camille and Kim started their own conversation.

"Let's get some snacks to sneak into the show," I could hear Camille plead.

"I got snacks in my backpack. We'll be fine," Kim told her.

"Not the cheap dollar store stuff," Camille scoffed.

"Should we even sneak snacks in? What if they get taken away?" Kim asked.

"It'll be fine," Camille said.

"Fine. You're so bougie," Kim said. She jumped into Camille's car and waved bye to me.

"See you at 7." The girls zoomed off.

I arrived home to the sound of my aunt in the kitchen. She often cooked and baked to relieve her stress. And now, I was adding to the stress by lying about work.

This would just make things worse. It would be fine; I should stop worrying. I exhaled.

Our kitchen was small and cozy. The three of us often bumped into each other, moving about. The daffodil tinted wall-paper was peeling off. A small circular dining table was placed near a cabinet. The rickety chairs were mismatched because they were thrifted.

"Where have you been? I've been texting you. Are you hungry?" she asked in one breath.

"I was with everyone at Su Castillo. Sorry, I didn't text you," I apologized. "We meet up there every day at the same time," I mumbled.

Did she forget? I know she had a lot on her plate. She did so much for me. All of the cooking and cleaning and has been taking extra shifts at the diner.

"You're right. I'm sorry. But I would still appreciate it if you answered me." She ran her hand through her short salt and pepper curls. "I was worried. I even made your favorite," she told me while draining the water out of a pot of pasta.

The savory scent of garlic flew from a pot of tomato sauce that was on the stove. Aunt Mel always went above and beyond for me, and I was lazy and did the bare minimal. She opened the dim fridge and grabbed a head of lettuce. I caught a glimpse of the packed lunch in a brown sack that I forgot to take. She put all that effort into making it for me, and I forgot it again.

"How was school?"

"Same old same."

"Well, I hope that history grade isn't the same." She gave me a dour look.

My grades were horrible, especially in Mr. McKinney's class. He always went on random tangents and never finished class on time.

"Don't worry, Aunt Mel, I will."

School was the last thing on my mind.

"Your uncle won't be home till Sunday." My uncle was a truck driver. Lately, he had been on the road so much that I haven't seen him. It's mostly Aunt Mel and me. "So, are you excited for the weekend and the concert tonight?" she asked.

"Yeah, I can't wait." I forced a smile, despite still having to call off sick from work. Maybe I should just tell her the truth. She picked up more shifts at the diner to pay for the ticket. And she had the ticket for a few months. I should've at least called off earlier and been more responsible with my vacation hours, but skipping work to sleep and play video games was more appealing at the time.

"I know your friends are superfans, unlike you, but you'll have fun, anyway. The amphitheater just opened. I heard it's nice. And Retro Brite is the biggest act to perform there so far." Aunt Mel gestured; she often did while she spoke. The long shifts and hot plates did an obvious number on her scarred hands.

"Yeah. Thanks for dinner. I'll eat later." I bent down and wrapped my arms around my aunt's small frame.

When I walked into my bedroom, I noticed the dirty clothes and books that had been dispersed across my room were now in the hamper and placed on my bookshelf. A hamper of freshly folded clothes was in front of my dresser. I took my shoes off and jumped into my unmade bed. I never made my bed and didn't see the point in doing so. It was going to get unmade, anyway.

I glanced around at my band and movie posters that lined my dark blue walls. I sighed, recollecting my thoughts from today. If I told Aunt Mel about work, she'd be mad about the money. If I just called off, she'd still be mad at me for lying. I was always in situations like this. If I was going to lie and go to the concert, I should at least give this my full effort.

I sat up from my bed and walked over to my desk. Papers and my untouched textbooks were stacked up into a tower. I lifted my laptop from underneath the clutter and opened it. I pulled up videos and magazine interviews with Vince, beginning to study the videos of his mannerisms, laugh, vocabulary, and more. After a while, I withdrew a deck of flashcards Kim made for me out of my backpack.

Okay, when was Vince born? I paced around my room while biting my thumbnail. *April, no, that was not it. Come on, this was an easy one. June 30. That was it.* I chuckled as I flipped the card over, revealing I got the answer right.

A few minutes later, I opened another tab on my browser and began searching for hair salons that could give me Vince's signature look. I scrolled past hundreds of expensive looking salons until I reached one that looked affordable. Hopefully, I'd be able to get my hair cut and get dressed in time. I got up and grabbed my phone to check my texts. The group chat was in full effect.

Kim and Camille were super hyped about the concert. Landon didn't join in the conversation. He took studying so seriously.

I glanced at my alarm clock beside my bed; it was only 5:30 pm. Kim insisted that I got to the venue at 7:00 pm. I guess I should call off now. I dialed my boss's number. I should've done it earlier today. I was too nervous. But it's fine. I've called out last minute before, so he should believe me. It's Friday evening, and Retro Brite is in town.

I tucked my dry lips inside my mouth as I wondered if any of my other coworkers called off.

"Hello. Seth, I don't think I'm . . . going to make it," I whimpered in a raspy voice.

"Look, Leon, we're understaffed today. So I'm going to need you. Two people have already called off."

Really?

"I know, but I think I'm coming down with the flu." I tried my best to sound convincing.

We both were silent for a few minutes. *Damn, I think he knew I was lying.*

"Okay, fine. I'll see you tomorrow, hopefully," he obliged.

I hung up the phone and exhaled with relief. Finally, that part was over. I hoped it all worked out. I should stop lying and being irresponsible. I said goodbye to my aunt and hopped in my car on my way to the mall.

Crestview Mall was packed just like every Friday evening. A bunch of teens and families were scattered about, laughing and having a good time. I never went to the mall unless one of my friends dragged me along. I got most of my clothes from online thrift stores, or whatever my aunt and uncle gave me. It was not like I was missing anything, anyway. The stores were boring and generic. They didn't offer any pieces that were unique or eye-catching. Everyone in this town pretty much dressed the same; in t-shirts, shirts, and jeans. The food at the food court was bland and overpriced. The tables were often dirty, and the smell of grease and coffee wafted through the air.

Plastic shopping bags crinkled as a group of young girls passed me.

I turned into True Alchemy. It was a mixture of pop culture, hipster, and alternative clothes. The poor lighting and loud grunge music probably distracted customers from the high prices. The store was small and was crowded within a few minutes. People continued to file into the narrow store, blocking the exit. T-shirts of various TV shows and bands cluttered the walls, including a couple of Retro Brite; which Kim was a proud owner of already. Cheap earrings, nose rings, and other accessories dangled from a rotating rack. I went over to a pair of black skinny jeans and peeked at the price tag. It was $60. I crumpled the pants back onto the table. Even though Kim gave me some money for clothes, I still couldn't fathom paying that much.

A short store clerk with fiery red hair approached me. "Need some help?" she yelped over the music.

"No, just looking. Do you think this is something Vince from Retro Brite would wear?" I yelled back.

She giggled. "So, you're entering that lame contest."

"No . . . yeah, but this whole thing is my friend's idea." I tutted my lips.

"Sure. Don't sweat it; you're not the first one to come here. And I guess it will work, but he gets all his clothes custom made."

"How do you know that? I mean, the band is lame, right?"

Why was she acting like she disliked Retro Brite? Mostly everyone here around our age liked them.

She playfully shook her head and walked over to a rack of jeans, then to some graphic tees. "Try these." She handed me a pair of ripped black jeans and an oversized hoodie with Kanji on it. I went into the dressing room and squeezed into the snug fitting clothes. The tight jeans were already making indentations on my calves. I looked in the mirror and grimaced. I mean, it's definitely different from what I'm used to. I guessed it would work. It just sucked that I would be wearing this the entire night.

But I was still gonna try my best to have a good time. And at least I didn't have to pay. I changed back into my clothes, paid, and left the store. Hopefully, Kim would approve of this outfit.

Now it was time to head to the hair salon, which was next to the mall. I entered A Cut Above. A guy with a man bun standing at the front desk greeted me. Although the salon had affordable prices, the white and gold decor gave it a high-class feel. In the waiting area, white leather chairs with gold details were near the entrance. The man guided me to a stylist. Fragments of hair were sprawled on the black floor. The sound of hair dryers hummed. I got situated in a salon chair and showed the hair stylist a picture of Vince.

"I've had a few clients today that wanted that same style. I'm heading to the concert tonight. It's all my daughter has been talking about." She spoke slowly, with long vowels. I nodded in agreement. She soon got to work cutting my medium length curly hair. I let out a deep breath as I heard the razor buzzing in my ear like wasps, and my corkscrew curls fell to the floor.

Well, I hope it was worth it.

"Okay, all done." She spun around the chair to face a large gold mirror. I gasped in disbelief that it looked nearly identical to the picture, except it was a little shorter. I rubbed my upper lip, which was now bare.

"So, what you think?"

"Umm . . . it's nice," I said. It was *awful.* I hated having short hair and always grew my hair out.

As long as Kim approved of it, it'd be worth it. At least it was similar to Vince's hair. Maybe if I styled it differently, I would like it better.

"If you win the contest, I get a cut of the earnings." She smiled.

"Yeah." I chuckled, trying to get out of the salon ASAP. I looked at my phone; it was now 6:10 pm. I needed to get back home.

As soon as I paid and left, I pulled my hoodie up on my

head. Maybe I could make it work. I should have listened to Kim and started getting ready way earlier. I sped on my way home.

I showered, got dressed, and tried to salvage the haircut. When I came out into the living room, I was welcomed back by my aunt, who was vacuuming the living room.

"You look amazing, Leon!" she shrieked, admiring my outfit.

"Thanks."

She handed me the ticket, grinning. I thanked her again, but my lies still lingered in my mind.

"Be careful at the concert. Retro Brite's crowd can get rowdy." Her eyes were now serious.

I've had this discussion many times with my aunt. Every time they have a concert, at least one person gets injured. The last concert, people were trampled, getting thrown off stage and fighting.

"Don't worry, there's extra security at this show."

"Well, don't stay out too late; you have to work tomorrow."

I resisted the temptation of huffing my breath in annoyance. I knew she was looking out for me, and that I've put a lot on my uncle and aunt, but sometimes I hated the pressure they put on me.

"Okay, see you later." I hugged her, and then I texted my friends to let them know I was on my way to the amphitheater.

FIRST EXPOSURE

2

I DROVE with the windows down; the wind whooshed in my ear, drowning out the sound of the radio. I hummed along to a song by Painted Dog, the band that was going to open for Retro tonight. I was excited that they were going to be there. They were a newer band. Driving to the theater, I started to get excited. I realized that this would be the first big show I've been to. The other concerts I'd gone to were local performers that had free shows or charged a couple of bucks.

Ten minutes later, I was at the new concert hall. The parking lot was packed. Cars darted in and out. Hoards of thousands of people were already lined up outside to get in. I barely found a parking spot. When I got to the back of the line, I heard a group of familiar voices and a hand on my arm.

"Over here, Leon!" Camille said before she led me to the middle of the line. A few concert goers frowned at me for skipping ahead in the line.

"Your hair!" Kim exclaimed as she rummaged her fingers through it.

"Surprise." I wiggled my fingers.

"Didn't think you would do it."

"You're definitely gonna win," Camille said, nodding at me.

"Do you guys think I can sneak this in?" Camille asked, revealing a couple of snacks tucked under her oversized hoodie.

"Yeah, they're just going to just check our bags. Don't worry," Kim said. "I finally get to test out my new camera." She smiled as she kissed the side of the camera.

Kim was obsessed with photography to the point where she carried her camera everywhere. She had just got that camera as a gift from her father, who was also a photographer. It was cool how passionate she could be, but sometimes her wanting to capture every moment was annoying. It was also neat to see her following her father's footsteps; I could never do that.

We waited and waited. Kim kept reassuring me that I would win the contest while Camille blathered about how fun tonight was going to be. Every time the line moved up, my excitement grew. I surveyed the other people in line, noticing a couple of other guys dressed in similar clothing as me; despite this, they did not look very similar to Vince. *Were they also entering the contest? They probably were, but they looked a little older than me.* They looked like they were in their early twenties, like Vince.

"Look, take a picture of me in front of it," Kim hooted, pointing at the giant marquee that read: 'Retro Brite' in bold letters. Camille grabbed the camera and snapped away. Once she was done, Kim quickly placed the camera securely around her neck.

When we reached the front of the line to hand in our tickets, we stepped inside the glass double doors of the theater. It was vast and regal. Walking inside transported us into a whole new atmosphere that felt different from any other place in Crestview. This venue was hands down the nicest place I've been to. The cold air immediately made the hairs on my arm stand up. Mellow atmospheric music played in the background. Layered chandeliers were suspended in the ceiling. The wall panels were tufted in a dark rich green velour.

As we waited in the security line, I leaned against the black safety rope barriers. When we strolled through a metal detector to get our bags checked, the security rummaged through Camille and Kim's bag, but found nothing to confiscate.

"I told you it was gonna be fine. Now we don't have to pay for snacks," Kim whispered.

"I thought we would be the first ones here. We're an hour early," Camille said.

"Yeah, me too, but I need time to get the merch," Kim said, holding her fist up in the air.

"It's okay. I know we brought snacks, but the popcorn smells go good." Camille ran to the concession stand. Kim and I followed behind so we didn't lose her.

After a few minutes of munching on overpriced popcorn, Kim glanced at her phone. "It's almost 7:15!" Kim patted me on the shoulder.

"Time for the contest!" the girls screamed as they guided me over to a sign that read: 'Retro Brite Look-alike Contest'.

A woman was sitting on a stool at a table. "You look like you're entering the contest. So fill out this form with your info and I'll be back to collect it. And there is a $35 fee. You will be called into a room to be judged and interviewed." She gave me the form. Kim handed her the cash.

I wrote my name, address, and number on the paper. *An interview?* I wonder what they would ask us. Aren't all the questions about Vince? My palms grew sweaty. My oversized hoodie clung to my body. Suddenly, all the trivia questions I studied popped into my mind, but I couldn't recall the answers to many of them.

I exhaled. Why did I even care about this stupid contest. *The money, of course*, I reminded myself. *Get it together*. I was hoping this would only take a few minutes and I could rejoin my friends quickly. I gave her back the paper.

"I'll show you the green room."

"Good luck, Leon." Kim and Camille said their goodbyes as

the woman rushed me off into another room. The room was small and cozy. It was decorated similarly to the lobby, with dark green curtains. Gold wall sconces were mounted to the walls, giving the room a warm glow. A burgundy oriental rug covered the floor.

"Wait in here and feel free to help yourself to any refreshments." She motioned to a full spread of any snack food I could imagine. Cookies, chips, and candies filled up a table against a wall.

Two other guys were sitting on a green couch. *Where was everybody else? Maybe we were just the last ones for the contest.* My stomach began to turn. I had a weird feeling about this.

I placed a few cookies and candies in the pocket of my hoodie. Maybe Camille and Kim would like these. I sat down on the couch next to the two guys. One man was tall, wearing black ripped jeans and a white anime graphic tee. The other guy had a green streak in his black hair and was husky.

"How long have you guys been waiting for?" I asked.

"I don't know. It's been a while," the husky guy answered with a cookie in his hand.

"We've been the only two in here so far."

"What!" I shouted. The guys just shrugged their shoulders.

"It feels like way longer than that," the tall guy said.

A few more minutes of small talk, then the same woman walked in. "Okay, Max, we're ready for you." The husky guy stood up and followed her through another door.

I tried to munch on the snacks as time passed, but my stomach was in knots. I kept crossing and uncrossing my legs in anticipation. The lady re-entered the room and took the tall guy through the other door. My hands were clammy. I couldn't be the only one who thought this was strange. The other guys had seemed so relaxed about this situation.

Where were the other contestants? I thought the contest just started. There was no way Kim would let me be late. I thought more people would enter to win the backstage pass and money.

I waited alone for what seemed like forever. *Could this be over already?* I slouched against the armrest of the couch. I wondered what my friends are up to. Why didn't the other guys exit back through this door? I pulled out my phone to look at the time. It was 7:40 pm. I texted my friends to pass the time. Kim was talking about how amazing the new merch was and was asking me what was going on. Camille was wondering when Landon would arrive and worried he would miss the beginning of the show. Luckily, the show hadn't started yet.

Moments later, the security lady walked back in. "Last but not least, Leon."

I followed her through the door into another room. This one had a stage. It looked like a rehearsal space. Rows of theater seats formed an oval shape around the stage. The lady took me to two metal folding chairs in front of the stage.

"Okay, you will be interviewed and judged by Audrey." She smirked.

"Audrey! . . . really." I didn't think I would get to meet someone from the band yet. I sat down in a folding chair. My friends would be freaking out right now. I exhaled loudly.

Audrey waltzed into the stage room. Her heeled shoes clicked against the floor in tandem with my heartbeat. She crossed her legs as she sat from me. She had long flowing pink hair, wore a leopard print mini dress, and chunky platform shoes. She was more petite than I thought she would be.

"Nice to meet you." She extended her hand. Her nails were adorned with rhinestones. I shook her hand, and she pulled me in for a hug. The scent of vanilla lingered on her skin. She had this glow about her. A presence that made anyone take notice. My gaze was fixated on her every move.

"So, are you from here?" Her upturned amber eyes twinkled.

"Y-yeah," I stuttered.

She chuckled. "Relax, don't be nervous." She smiled sweetly. "What's your favorite track on the new album?"

"Umm . . . 'Outsiders.' I just love it. I listen to it every day," I said. My eyes shifted away from her for a brief moment. I only listened to their music a lot when they made the first album. Kim usually had it blasting while we hung out. But I could admit I enjoyed that song.

"I love it too, especially when we play it live. You look just like Vince," she giggled. She glanced from side to side as if there were other people nearby and whispered in my ear, "The best contestant so far."

I was probably blushing; heat radiated to my cheeks. I always thought she was pretty, but in person her beauty was unmatched. *Damn, I need to pull myself together. I wondered if she was like that with all the contestants.*

"So, do you play any instruments or sing?"

"A little, I fiddle around. I had guitar lessons when I was younger," my voice squeaked. This felt so surreal to be talking to her so casually. When would she ask me the trivia questions? Not like I could manage to recall anything now, though.

"So, how tall are you? I know it's kind of random."

"Um, 5'10"."

We were silent for a few seconds.

Audrey's eyes were now studying me. "Just like Vince. So—" as she began, a security guard interrupted.

"Sorry, we're out of time."

Audrey and I both stood up. "It was nice to meet you," she said, tucking one of my stray hairs back in place. My heart was fluttering. A guard walked toward me.

"Keep the details of the interview to yourself. We will notify you about the results. If we find out about any details being leaked, you will be disqualified," the guard instructed me.

I nodded in agreement. I was then led back out into the lobby. The interview was so bizarre. It seemed more like she was scouting or interrogating me. I couldn't believe I met Audrey and I couldn't mention it to my friends. This was my first time meeting a celebrity. I always told myself that I didn't care about famous people, but that was actually cool. But I would never mention that to my friends.

I found Camille and Kim in the lobby next to a merch stand. Kim was already holding a few t-shirts and posters. She currently had my whole paycheck in her hand.

"Hey, Leon!" Camille yelled. Her pupils were dilated.

"How was the interview? Who did it? What were the questions?" The girls began talking at once.

"Did they say the results!?" Kim asked. "Which one do you want?" She held up a t-shirt. "You like this one." She put the shirt down and picked up another one.

"Nope. They said they will notify me and told me not to talk about the interview." Everyone sighed.

"You can tell us," Camille pouted.

"If we get to meet them, can you imagine how cool that would be?" Kim said.

"Maybe later. Let's just find our seats first." I quickly changed the subject. "Where's Landon?" I asked, raising an eyebrow. So much had happened; I forgot he wasn't here yet.

"He called saying he's on the way. Ugh, studying on a Friday night. Who does that? Why can't he wait till Sunday like the rest of us?" Camille curled her thin lips at the mention of his studying habits.

I led my friends into the large concert hall theater. Plush retractable chairs fanned out in a circular pattern around the stage. Gigantic LED screens hung on both sides of the stage while lanterns shined brightly from a large truss. We squeezed our way through the crowd to a few rows from the stage. The place was packed; it was a sold-out show, according to Kim. Despite the amphitheater being massive, the seats quickly filled.

"Put this on." Kim shoved a shirt toward me.

"So, you buy me one expensive shirt just to wear it for about an hour, and now want me to put on another one? I'm supposed to look like Vince. He wouldn't wear his own merch."

Kim glared at me, which was something she did often to

make me comply. Kim wasn't the type of person to take to take 'no' for an answer. And she put a lot of effort into this event. So I might as well take the shirt. I put the shirt over my undershirt without saying another word.

"Now you're one of us." Camille grinned broadly. Pieces of popcorn were stuck in her braces.

Minutes later, the auditorium lights dimmed as the stage lights grew brighter. The main singer of Painted Dog, Arin, stepped up from behind the stage. The crowd roared. My friends followed suit and started to cheer.

A couple minutes later, someone squeezed by us to sit down.

"Landon!" the girls screamed.

"I had to study. Sorry." He sat next to Camille.

"So great of you to join us, Socrates," she joked.

Arin waved to the fans and grabbed the hand of a guy near the stage. He walked up to the mic with his signature black and silver electric guitar. Arin was known for his unique fashion sense and he always changed his hair. That night, his hair was cut short, dyed blonde with black roots, and faded with a geometric design. He wore black jeans, a black t-shirt, and a black leather jacket that had patches of different fabrics. The patches were red and black checkered, cheetah print, and silver studs. The jacket would be hideous on anyone else but him.

"We're Painted Dog. What's going on tonight, Crestview!" he bellowed. The rest of the band came out a few seconds later, ready to play.

As the first song started, the auditorium filled up with a peaceful ambient electric guitar riff.

"I love this song!" Kim cried out, swaying to the rhythm. She had her camera out snapping away. Camille and Landon were bobbing their heads.

This week had a rough start, but it was totally worth it. It was a great performance. When Painted Dog finished playing their opening set, applauds and screams erupted from the crowd. The band left the stage.

"They were amazing," Camille yelped.

Yep. And soon the moment we all been waiting for was finally there.

About twenty minutes later, thick smoke rolled onto the stage. "Let's go, Crestview!" Vince yelled.

Vince and his bandmates took the stage. The crowd howled like a wild pack of hyenas. My face lit up as he walked on stage. I glimpsed at Kim, who had the biggest grin on her face. I couldn't wait to see the performance and hoped they played their song 'Endless Things'. It was my other favorite song on their first album back when I enjoyed their music more. This was going to be great. My first concert was already off to a great, start minus the weird contest.

Vince was dressed in ripped black shorts and a navy blue graphic tee. Jamie, the drummer, was wearing a simple flannel shirt and shorts. Porter, the bass player, in jeans, a t-shirt, and sneakers. And lastly, Audrey, in a silver sparkly jumpsuit thing. Her pink hair was now in two buns. Jamie clicked his drum sticks together and started the beat. Audrey took center stage. Her presence was magnetic. I literally couldn't take my eyes off her. The melody of her and Vince singing together often puts me in a trance. We were close enough that she even made eye contact with me briefly. I glanced at my friends to see if they had noticed, but they were too entranced. It was almost as if I was the only one in the audience. Everything moved in slow motion despite my racing heart.

The next song they played was a more upbeat dance track. The crowd erupted once again; dancing, clapping, filming, and screaming. No one was sitting in their seat. Everyone in the crowd was singing along to the lyrics. At that moment, it felt like all 4,000 of us were connected. We all knew every single lyric. Strangers became acquainted with smiling, laughing, and dancing with each other. I started to jump up and down. Kim, Camille, and Landon followed suit. My blood was rushing. It felt like electricity was flowing through my body. Sweat poured from Vince's face as he shuffled across the stage. Audrey's hips and shoulders moved in circular motions. She danced alongside Porter, who was smiling at her and swaying his bass as he played.

Suddenly, everyone was pushing and grabbing each other. Next thing I knew, a group of people lifted me in the air, passing me through the crowd. I tried to get back with my friends, but through the massive crowd, I could not see anything. I felt a rush of adrenaline as I crowd surfed. My breathing was shallow and my head spun. I was completely engulfed in that moment. I felt free. Security guards infiltrated the crowd; they yelled and grabbed people, forcing them to put me down. I continued to jump up and down with the crowd where they dropped me. My heart raced; this was the most fun I've had in a long time.

"Hey, watch it!" an angry voice yelled. I looked to my left to see Charles, my coworker. "Didn't you have to work today?" he yelled over the crowd.

"No, I was off. What about you?" I bellowed back.

"I called off. Told him I had an emergency. You know we rarely get days off. You probably did the same thing. I know you're a slacker."

"Whatever, man. It was nice seeing you." I raised my hand up in a wave. I had to get away from him; I could barely tolerate him at work. I shuffled through the crowd and made my way back to my friends.

"That was so cool. Unbelievable!" Landon yelled.

"I know, right. I just saw Charles."

"Ugh, Charles. He's so annoying," Kim replied, swaying her head back and forth.

The rest of the night consisted of laughter and dancing.

"This was the best night ever," Camille cried as the concert ended.

"I will never forget this night. A mosh pit and everything. I even got a little beat up." Landon rolled up the sleeve of his shirt to reveal a purple bruise.

"You're so brave," Camille teased as she hugged his side.

"You want a matching one?" He punched her arm playfully.

"I wish we could hang more." Camille looked over at me. "But you have to go to work tomorrow," Camille said.

We walked out into the large parking lot. All of the fans were still full of energy; talking and hanging around. Kim was still excited and wouldn't stop recapping the performance.

"This was so cool. We had the best seats. We were so close I could feel Vince's sweat on me!" she exclaimed.

"Yeah, the performance was better than I thought it would be," Landon said.

"What do you mean by that? Of course they would be great," Kim said.

"He's just playing around Kim. Everyone knew it was going to be an awesome performance," Camille said.

"Yeah, I wish we could hang more, but Camille is right. I have to rest up and be up for work in the morning," I said.

"Let's just hang for a few more minutes," Kim said, stomping her foot on the asphalt. "Check out the pictures I took. They came out so good."

"Sorry, I have to head home," I said backing away from the group to my car.

"See you later, Leon." Camille and Landon walked toward his car.

"I'm riding with Leon." Kim followed me to my car.

"We should go to more concerts." Kim grinned from ear to ear. I smiled back for a few minutes, but it faded at the thought of coming home to my aunt after lying to her. I could see her now, excited, wanting to hear every detail of my night.

It was now 10 pm. The sky was flashing with silver stars. We drove with the radio humming and the windows rolled down. The humid air caused my curly hair to stick to my forehead. Kim had her foot hanging out the window.

"What's wrong?" Kim frowned.

It seemed like minutes ago I was on top of the world. Having the best time in the world with my best friends. Now, I have to face reality; my lies would eventually catch up with me. But this wasn't the first time.

I told her everything.

"She might not be that mad. And if you need the money for the tickets, I can—"

"No, thanks for everything, Kim, but you always help me, and I still owe you." She furrowed her brows.

"Leon—" she interceded before I could say anything else. Kim and her family had always been there for us and our financial struggles. From dinners, to trips, and gifts.

"Okay, but I'm here if you need me. She won't be mad forever."

"You're right." I scratched the back of my neck as I pulled into Kim's driveway.

"Thanks, Leon, for everything." She hugged me tightly.

"See ya."

I drove into my driveway to see the porch lights on. My stomach turned and twisted; my aunt was definitely up. I walked into the living room, and she was sitting down on the loveseat in her robe. Her eyes were puffy from lack of sleep. I tried to dart up the stairs as if I didn't see her sitting there.

"Leon," she called out. I stopped at the bottom of the stairs.

"Your boss called."

"For what—"

"Leon, I know you called off. He was checking to see how you were feeling. I can't believe you lied to me." Her voice began to tremble.

"Your uncle and I saved up to get you those tickets." Tears filled her brown eyes. "Leon, you have to be more responsible. What else have you been lying about? In a couple of months, you will be graduating. That's even if your grades are good enough." She paused to look up at me. "You'll be on your own. Have you thought about that? You can't rely on your uncle and me forever."

I sat down on the couch across from her. "I can get more hours at work or find a side gig," I pleaded with her.

She sighed deeply and rubbed her temples. "This was supposed to be a nice surprise. It's your senior year, and we thought this would be a nice graduation gift. I told you to let your boss know months ago. And what if your boss doesn't let this slide? I would appreciate it if you paid us back."

"Look, I'm sorry. All my friends wanted me to go, and I couldn't resist. And I'm going to pay you back."

"You still didn't have to lie to your boss, and especially your uncle and me."

I hung my head down, ashamed to look her in her face.

"Goodnight," she replied with no emotion. Her house shoes dragged against the wood panel floors as she moved up the stairs.

I went up behind her and went to bed. I tossed and turned all night, thinking about everything: the fun night, the interview, the mosh pit, and the lying.

Was it worth it? I don't know.

DOWNHILL REAL QUICK

3

My alarm buzzed, waking me up at 7:30 am. I rubbed my eyes; I had thirty minutes to get ready for work. I needed to rush to try and make it on time today. Maybe Seth would be so surprised by my punctuality and ignore last night. I had barely gotten any sleep with my mind thinking about what happened last night; the good and the bad. Hopefully, today's shift would be fast and smooth. The sun cut through the blinds, making my headache and my eyes cringe. I reached over, stopping the alarm, yawned, and stumbled out of bed.

My bathroom was always a mess due to the fact my dirty clothes stayed next to the laundry bin. But it was now clean due to my aunt. I felt bad that within a few hours it would be messy again. The walls were painted a taupe brown and a painting of a seashell hung on the wall. The bathroom had a beach theme, but all the decor was from the thrift shop and mismatched like the kitchen. The room was compact. It felt like the toilet, sink, and the tub/shower were crammed into the room. Looking into the mirror, I noticed how tired my brown eyes were and how messy my jet black hair was. I showered and put on my normal work attire; khaki pants, a black t-shirt with the logo of the second hand shop I work at, and black sneakers.

When I made it to the kitchen, I saw my aunt standing over the stove cooking bacon.

"Morning, Leon," she said, glancing over her shoulder.

"Morning."

"Hurry up and eat. You don't want to be late." My aunt placed a plate in front of me.

"Sorry about last night," I said. "I'll make it up. I promise."

My aunt looked away. I could tell she was still angry. I couldn't remember the last time she was this upset. But when she was, she wouldn't make eye contact with me and would give me short snappy responses. I wish I could take this all back. If only I would have done the right thing a couple of months ago.

I gulped down my food, said goodbye, grabbed my jacket, and headed out the door. The sun peeked through the clouds, giving the sky a warm yellow glow. A lawn mower roared as the grass was being cut. My neighbors were already up doing yard work before it got too warm.

Minutes later, I pulled into the parking lot to see my manager, Seth, smoking a cigarette. Seth was probably the worst manager ever. He got paid more for doing less. He mostly sat in the break room on his phone or told others what to do while doing nothing.

"Finally!" he exclaimed after he exhaled a wave of smoke. "I thought you were going to be late."

"Nope, I'm on time, Seth." I wagged my finger in his direction.

"Barely," he scoffed, removing the cigarette from his pierced lips.

I entered the store, exhaling sharply. I hoped Seth and Garrett could give me another chance. *From now on, I'd be a better employee,* I told myself. No more being late, and I definitely couldn't call out anymore. I needed to prove to my aunt and uncle that I could be responsible.

During the mornings, it wasn't too busy. On Saturdays, the afternoon was when most of the customers arrived. Borrowers was a second-hand shop. The store was spacious and had a slight musty smell to it. On one side were metal bookcases filed in rows. As I walked through, the smell of dry, old paper lingered. A few customers were fanning through pages of books. A boy sat on the floor reading a book. His back was facing one of the bookshelves. The other side of the store had shelves of video games, movies, and bins of vinyl. It was quiet, except for a few murmurs here and there. The back had home goods, clothing, and knickknacks.

I proceeded to the break room. It was the place where the employees kept our belongings and relaxed. It wasn't the most relaxing place, though. The floor was covered in dirt and food. It looked as if it hadn't been swept in months. I inhaled spoiled food as I walked by the fridge. A small TV hung in the corner of the room. No one really watched it; maybe because there were only public access channels. After I placed my things in my locker, the store owner, Garrett, spoke with me.

"Leon, you're back at electronics today," his gruff voice instructed.

"Yes, sir," I grumbled.

Garrett strolled away, his beer gut bouncing while he moved. As much as I liked electronics, working it was a pain. Most of the customers were rude and were unaware of our return policy.

As Charles approached me, I frowned. I was hoping he didn't come in today. I looked the other direction and fiddled with a display on the counter. *Maybe if I looked busy, he would go away.*

"Hey, man, you didn't finish the markdowns on Thursday," Charles said.

"Um, that's cause that was the project Garrett assigned to you." I raised an eyebrow.

"But we're a team, right?" He leaned against the counter. His dark blue eyes probed me.

I sighed and motioned for a customer to come to my counter.

Charles often was instructed to do things and tried putting the work on me and our other coworkers. He always had an excuse for his lack of effort. Without a doubt, I wasn't the best employee, but compared to him, I was the employee of the month.

The day was going smoothly until one of our unruly regulars, Mrs. Smith, entered the premises. As I saw the portly redhead middle-aged customer, I scowled. "Damn it," I whispered.

I looked at my coworker, Sam, who quickly escorted another customer to her register to avoid talking to her. *How could she do this to me? What about those shifts I covered for her?*

"Hey, welcome to Borrowers. How can I help you today?" I smiled with fake enthusiasm.

"Um . . . yes, I would like to return this DVD; it does not work," she said, not using her inside voice.

"Okay, what seems to be the problem?" I raised an eyebrow.

"It just doesn't work and I want to trade it for another movie," she explained.

"I understand, but is the DVD damaged? What was the issue with the item?" I asked, trying to reason with the woman.

"No, I just put the DVD in and it won't play. How many times do I have to say it?" She threw her chubby arms in the air.

"Excuse me, but you did not explain why the DVD did not work. May I see the DVD?" I sighed and slapped my hands on the counter.

"Here!" She shoved it toward me.

I inspected the disc, but nothing was wrong with it.

"What's the problem?" she blurted out.

"Umm . . . I don't see one. Maybe there is a problem with the DVD player or device you used to play the disc."

"Nope, it's a brand new DVD player. Geez, you guys are never helpful." She wrinkled her freckled nose.

I then looked at the cover of the DVD that read 'Blu-ray'.

"Do you have a Blu-ray player?" I asked.

" . . . I don't think so, but how am I *supposed* to know that? Like they should have them marked regular DVD or Blu-ray," she remarked like she just thought about something original.

"Sorry, ma'am. It does." I pointed to the 'DVD' cover, which clearly read 'Blu-ray'.

"Oh . . . well, I didn't ask you." She became flustered and grabbed the DVD—I mean Blu-ray. "I want to speak to a manager. You're so rude to customers." She walked away, giving me a nasty look.

Seth gave me a glare as he went to assist Mrs. Smith. After she left, Seth approached me and called Charles over.

"We need to talk," he said, taking us to his office.

My stomach dropped. *Maybe we were hashing out the past and he was giving me another chance. No need to worry*, I thought.

We crammed inside the tiny office space, which smelled like old coffee and was covered in dust. We sat down across from him in cushy armchairs. I rolled my shoulders, sitting up straight.

He cleared his throat. "Listen, guys, lately you both have not been performing well. Horrible customer service." He looked at me. "Coming in late and calling off." He glanced at both of us.

"Mrs. Smith is always rude. I think I handled the situation well." I squinted.

"I know, but the customer is always right. Always. You could have done better. And Charles, you should do the same. Telling customers you just started working here is not an excuse to get out of helping them. And I can't forget 'taking' supplies and merchandise." Seth eyed Charles.

Charles looked at the wall. "Someone was stealing?" he spoke in a low tone. "T-that was just some stupid rumor. Ashley told me it was Sam. You heard about it, Leon, didn't you?" he spoke, narrowing in on the wall.

I shrugged.

"I'm afraid I have to let both of you go." He tapped his fingers on the wood desk. My stomach churned. A bitter taste formed in my mouth. *What! Aunt Mel would never let this go. This was all a nightmare and I would wake up soon.*

"Go where?" Charles asked.

"You guys are fired," he replied.

"But I can do better. Can I speak with Garrett?" I asked. My eyes darted from Charles to Seth.

"No, we already came to this decision," he replied.

My heart sank in my chest. I needed this job; this was just the icing on the cake. My aunt and uncle were really going to be upset. I closed my eyes.

"Look, sir, just give me one more chance. Everyone deserves a second one." Charles's voice cracked as he pleaded. He tugged on his long straight hair.

"This is more like the third or fourth for the both of you. I've got to get back to work." He left the room.

After collecting my belongings, I sat in my car in the parking lot for a few minutes. *Did this really happen?* My hair was clenched in my fist as I rested my head on the steering wheel. I didn't know what to do. Back to coming up with excuses, or I could just tell the truth. I could blame it all on the customer or that Seth doesn't like me. My aunt wasn't one for excuses, though. She was all about accountability. She'd see through it all and know it was my fault.

I banged my hands on the steering wheel. Glancing at the time, It was 2 pm. There were only two hours left to finish my shift. I stared at the clock in my car; I couldn't come home too early. I could tell her Seth let me go home early since we were slow. *Yeah, she'll believe that.* He often did that, anyway.

"He let us leave early," I practiced out loud, looking into the dirty sun visor mirror. My voice broke and cracked as I spoke.

Charles approached my car and tapped on the window. *What does he want now?*

"You could have had my back in there," he exhaled.

"What could I have said?" I shrugged.

"You know I didn't steal anything. This is all your fault. You should have said something."

"My fault?" I placed my hand against my chest.

"You know what. Never mind." He waved his hand, dismissing the conversation, and walked to his car.

Did he really just blame me for all of this?

I started the car up and drove in silence until I reached home. My mind was racing. In the driveway, there was a red van. It must be Aunt Sharon. I snickered. Another family member I had to lie to.

Aunt Sharon and Aunt Mel were my father's sisters. She came to visit for dinner often. Aunt Mel was always in a better mood and relaxed when she was with her sister. I walked in the door and immediately heard the roaring of laughter and the smell of food wading through the air.

"Leon!" Aunt Sharon called out in excitement. I hadn't seen her in a couple of weeks. She was an ER nurse and had been busy with work.

"How's work and school, honey?" her nasally voice rang out. She gave me a hug.

"It's fine, I guess. Trying to keep my grades up. I'm off work tomorrow." I smiled, knowing deep down I was lying again. I needed to stop before I got caught again. I didn't want to add to the tension between Aunt Mel and me. I sat down at the table.

"You're home early, aren't you?" Aunt Mel questioned.

"Yeah, some of us got to go home early. Seth let us leave," I said while gulping down a glass of water.

"That's nice of them. I was thinking about stopping by today. Joey's been bugging me about some video game he wanted for his birthday," Aunt Sharon spoke.

I'm glad she didn't. Joey was Aunt Sharon's son. I often got stuck babysitting him.

Aunt Mel tutted her lips. *Was my answer not convincing enough?* I shuffled in my chair. The raggedy chair scraped against the floor.

"Anything funny happen at work today?" Aunt Mel asked.

"Umm . . . Ms. Smith showed up today." I stirred the food on my plate. Both of my aunts giggled.

"She should be banned by now!" Aunt Sharon yelped. My aunts have known Ms. Smith for many years. Our families went to the same church and her sons went to school with me. We often talked about her many antics. Everyone in town knew Ms. Smith as the annoying lady that complained about everything.

"Do you guys remember that time she came in the diner and ordered spaghetti and complained that the noodles were too short. Crazy, right?" Aunt Mel chuckled. We laughed for a couple of minutes. *I should change the subject before they find out about me getting fired.*

"What about you guys? Anything interesting happening at the ER?" I asked, folding my hands on the table.

"You don't wanna hear about my boring life. And nothing we can talk about at dinner." She waved her hand in my direction.

At that moment, I wanted to hear about anything else but work and school.

"So, Dan will be back soon. We should all have a family dinner. It'll be my treat," Aunt Sharon gushed.

Aunt Mel smiled.

I half-smiled, knowing he would be furious that I got fired.

Uncle Dan had just returned to work from a work accident. He pulled a muscle in his back from lifting boxes off of a truck. His employer considered him an independent contractor, meaning his injury did not get covered by worker's compensation. His recovery took a few months and caused us to accumulate debt. Aunt Mel was taking up more shifts at the diner and she was exhausted. Since my uncle was back to work, my family was supposed to be more relaxed. Now I just ruined it.

But does it really matter? My life seemed so meaningless. I lost both my parents at a young age; I lost my job, and I'm stuck in this crappy town.

"You look just like Lee," Aunt Sharon smiled.

The room grew quiet, and we smiled, thinking about my father. My aunts often reminded me of how much I looked like my father and laughed like my mother. I remember Dad and I driving around blasting rock music. We would sing at the top of lungs with the windows down. I wish I could thank him for my good taste in music. If he were here, I think he would like Retro Brite and Painted Dog. He would probably want to tag along. And I remembered laughing for hours with my mother. She was one of the funniest people ever. Ever since they've been gone, my life has felt at a standstill. It all seemed meaningless. It's not that I didn't love or appreciate my aunt and uncle. I just wondered how my life would of been if my parents were still here.

The rest of the dinner went great. Everyone was in a good mood, talking and laughing, so I decided to keep my mouth closed and pray the truth didn't slip out.

Sunday was a slow, easy day. I basically sat around mentally preparing myself for getting back to my old routine for Monday morning. I paced around the house, thinking about everything that had just happened. It tried getting my mind off things by watching TV and playing video games, but I couldn't shake those thoughts. Friday night was one of the best nights ever, but I had to ruin it by not calling off early enough. If I had, everything would have been fine. As much as I hated my job, I still would have had it.

My phone buzzed with a text from Kim:

Did you win the contest?

Nvm, don't tell me. How did it go with your aunt?

I still don't know the results. Everything is okay for now.

I decided not to tell her about my job. I couldn't. I wanted to, but I didn't want to admit to my lies again. I know it seemed like a small silly lie, but my friends would be upset. We told each other almost everything. I closed my eyes and drifted off to sleep.

The sun peeking through the curtains made me cover my eyes with my blanket.

Ughh, it's Monday morning. This weekend went by way too fast. I need this day to go by fast.

I wanted to tell Aunt Mel I didn't feel well to get out of school. Knowing Aunt Mel, she would give me some medicine and still insist I go to school. I'm already on thin ice, anyway. I'm up on time for once. I might as well go to school, so I got dressed and headed downstairs.

"Morning," my aunt beamed. "Do you work today?"

"Y-yeah," I stuttered.

I had to tell her the truth, but now wasn't the time, and I'm not sure if it ever will be. I'd have to find something to do before heading home.

As I headed for the door, Aunt Mel stopped me. "Eat before you go!" she told me.

"I'm fine—" I waved my hand at her.

"Leon, you're going to be hungry," she said.

"Okay, I'll just have a bagel," I said, grabbing it from the kitchen counter. I then left and headed to school.

I pulled into the parking lot and met up with Camille and Landon.

"This weekend was so unreal," Camille gushed for the

millionth time. Her blonde hair danced in the wind as she swayed her head from side to side.

Landon jumped out of his car to greet us. We waited for Kim to get off the bus. When she arrived, we went into the school entrance. Bleach immediately filled my nostrils. *Aww, the smell I missed so dearly.* The hall was crowded and chatter filled the hall. My friends followed me to my locker.

"Did you win?" Kim's face morphed into a clownish grin.

"Still no word of it yet." I shrugged my shoulders.

"I want to be the first to know," Kim said.

"I think you won; just wait and see," Camille said.

"Well, I got to get to class and study before this quiz." I changed the subject as I slammed my locker and walked in the other direction.

"Leon, studying," Landon chuckled. "Since when?"

It's true, but I really did need to improve my grades. That was one way I could remedy everything with my family. I was not as lucky as Landon to be a gifted student. He already knew what college he was going to, and he had hopes of taking over his father's business. I could never follow my father's steps. I'm Leon Hollaway the III. I'm nothing like my father or my uncle.

My father was one of the most charismatic and funniest person I've ever met. He was hardworking and studious. He wanted to become a doctor and help people. The death of my parents was something that I thought about often. The event had changed my entire life. Since I was very young, I don't have many memories of them, and as time goes by, they become even more faint.

I went through my day trying my best to pay attention in class and do well on my quiz. However, my mind was still racing. The bell rang, signaling it was time for second lunch. The cafeteria was packed with students conversing. I sat at my friend's usual round table in the middle of the cafeteria. There were large trash-cans with wheels on them overflowing with trash. Posters placed on the walls, showing various clubs and activities. Plastic lunch trays scraped against the tables. A sizzling piece of pizza singed the roof of my mouth. I kept on eating, anyway. The aroma of ketchup and french fries floated around the cafeteria.

"So, how was your quiz? Did you ace it?" Camille questioned.

"Probably not," I sighed. I leaned on the table. *Could this week be over yet? Could everyone stop questioning me?*

"What's wrong, Leon?" Camille tilted her head.

"I lost my job," I mumbled.

"What!?" they all yelled in unison.

"What happened?" Landon asked.

"I had another incident with Mrs. Smith. And I called off too many times," I replied.

"What did your aunt say?" Camille's eyes were wide.

"She doesn't know yet. I told my aunt we weren't busy and they let us leave early. And I lied about being off. So I could go to the concert." I shoved a fry into my mouth.

"So, when are you going to tell your aunt and uncle the truth?" Landon asked.

"I don't know. Maybe after I bring up my grades. Or I could look for another job, get hired, and tell them I decided to leave Borrowers."

"More lies." Landon shook his head. "Your gonna have to face it, man."

Landon was right, but I'm tired of him acting like a saint and like he doesn't lie to his parents. It seemed like lately I was the center of most of my friend's conversations. *Could they stop asking me questions?*

My phone buzzed; thank goodness. I reached for my phone, which sat on the table, but Kim grabbed it before I even had the chance. She put the phone on speaker and grinned.

"Hey, Leon, I need you to pick up your little cousin, Joseph, after school, before you head to work." It was Aunt Mel.

I grabbed the phone from Kim. "Okay, sure thing. Talk to you later." I hung up, slamming it on the table.

"Why can't someone else do it? I mean, I don't mind every once in a while, but it keeps happening." This is the second time in a row I had to pick Joey up.

"I don't know; maybe they have jobs?" Landon snickered, scratching the side of his face. "No? Too soon?"

The girls shot him a stern look.

"Yeah, it's true." I nodded my head. "Is your dad's store hiring? I need to find a new job quick as possible." I raised an eyebrow at Landon. Landon worked at his dad's hardware store.

"We had someone leave. I can see for you, man."

When the final bell rang, Landon and I walked out to the student parking lot. Most days, I was excited to leave school, but today, I'd have to go back to lying.

"You can hang out at my place. My parents will be gone if you need a place to go until your shift is over," Landon offered as he got in his car.

"Thanks for the offer. But I'll just hang around. Drive through town," I said, getting into my car. I buckled up and drove to Sandwood Elementary School to pick up Joey.

On the way there, I got a call from an unknown number. *It's probably a telemarketer.* I placed my phone inside of the cupholder. At the school, buses lined the front of the building, and I pulled into the parking lot around the side of the school. Children screeched with joy as they were being walked out school by their parents and teachers. I walked into the main office, and Joey came running toward me and gave me a big hug.

"Leon!" he yelled, and I hugged him back. It was nice to see Joey. I felt more relaxed.

I checked him out of the office, and we got in the car. I looked at my phone before leaving the parking lot; I had three missed calls from the same mysterious number. *Hmm, they didn't leave a message, so I couldn't have won the contest.*

"How was school?" I asked Joey, looking at him in the rearview mirror.

"It was fun." He grinned from ear to ear.

He began talking my head off like most little kids do. Telling me about every detail of his school day from the playground, lunch, and the classroom.

"That sounds great." I smiled. I enjoyed hearing about Joey's day; it took my mind off things. I remembered when I was that young and full of life. The phone rang again from the same number. This time, I answered.

"Hello, Leon. It's Charles."

"Hey . . . "

Why was he calling. He was the last person I wanted to see or hear.

"Look, since we both lost our jobs. I've been thinking."

"Who are you talking to?" Joey's tiny voice chimed.

"Shhh. Be quiet," I hushed him.

"So, I have a way for you to make some extra money. You interested?"

"What do you have in mind? It can't be anything crazy . . . or illegal," I huffed.

I should have hung up the phone. Charles was never up to any good. But the extra money was enticing.

"Meet up with me, and we can race. Winner gives the others their paycheck."

"I don't know. It's definitely illegal. And I'm with my little cousin."

"Come on, man. Just bring him along. Meet up with me at Jetstream Hill."

I sighed, rubbing my eyes. *I've got to find a way to pay my aunt back for the ticket.* "Sure. I really need the money more than anything."

"Great. See you in a few."

Did I agree to this even after everything that has happened? We could get in trouble if we got caught. Charles has gotten in trouble for racing before.

This wasn't my first time racing. My classmates and I often challenged each other. However, I was never a winner due to my busted car. But today was different. I might have a chance against Charles. I had to get back at him and win this money.

"What's going on?" Joey questioned.

"We're just going on a little detour. I'll take you home in a minute."

I shouldn't of involved Joey in this.

"This doesn't seem right." His voice raised.

"No, no. We're just having a little fun." I smiled at him. His eyebrows raised, and he pursed his lips.

"Can I have this?" he asked, picking up one of the video games I had lying around the back of the car. "I asked Mom for it, but she said I'm not old enough to play it." He pouted.

"Sure. Sure." I lied to calm him back down. I had just bought that game. I, for sure, wasn't letting him keep it. Aunt Sharon wouldn't let him play it, anyway.

Jetstream Park was lush and hilly. The park had many meandering paths. Oak trees of varying heights traced along the paths. Metal benches near tall shady trees were often occupied by teens who had nothing to do but kill time. They often skipped school and raced cars. Flower beds and shrubbery surrounded a large lake where geese and ducks swam. Not far from the lake were a few pavilions with picnic tables. Bright green leaves fell from the trees. Ducks squawked. They were probably fighting over a piece of food. The park was surprisingly empty.

Charles and I met on top of the largest hill. My beat-up hooptie of a car versus his beat-up minivan. *This would be good.* We both lined up at the start of the road. He rolled down his window. I rolled mine down as well.

"What's going on?" Joey asked again. "Is this a race?"

"You ready for this?" Charles yelled, revving up his engine. I nodded my head and revved up my engine.

"What's going on, Leon?" Joey asked.

"Shh!" I hushed him.

Charles took off in the lead. I sped up, passing him. We sped along the winding road. The tall oak trees shaded us from above. Birds flew overhead, going from tree to tree.

"Woah, this is fun!" Joey screamed. "Go faster!"

I sped up even more, and we yelped with excitement. *We were still in the lead. I couldn't believe it. The money was mine.*

A few seconds later, Charles passed us. My car was so close to Charles' I could reach out and touch it. My car swayed around the curves as I sped up.

"Faster, faster!" Joey screeched. Our hair flowed in the wind. I peered in the rearview and saw Joey grinning. His chubby, round face was flushed. We were in the lead again. *Yes.*

Suddenly, I lost control on one of the winding paths. Everything happened in slow motion. Joey's laughter turned to crying. His small voice was shrill. We were heading for a tree. I attempted to steer away, but it was too late. My heart pumped out of my chest. The tires screeched. A loud bang pierced my ears. Glass shattered. Our bodies propelled forward and back in an instant. The airbags popped out. A chemical smell filled my lungs. The front of the car was buckled against the tree.

Everything was still and quite, besides Joey sobbing. I saw blood, but wasn't sure where it came from. My breathing was heavy. *Was Joey okay? How could I do this?*

I woke up in a hospital bed. My body was stiff and ached, and my vision, while blurry at first, sharpened. The room was frigid. The AC hummed, and footsteps echoed in the hallway. I glanced around the room; I was alone. A small leather chair was in the corner and a TV was mounted on a wall near the window. While the curtains were shut, a gray-blue light faintly peeked through. It was probably evening. My left arm had an IV inserted into it. I looked down at my arms and noticed I had a few reddish-purple bruises.

Footsteps grew louder outside the room. The door opened; it was a nurse and Aunt Mel.

"You're up now," Aunt Mel exhaled.

The nurse informed me not to worry, and that my injuries were minor scrapes, bruises, and cuts.

When the nurse left, Aunt Mel started to sniffle. "Why do you continue to lie to us?" Her voice was muffled as she buried her face in a pile of tissues.

"I just couldn't bear telling you guys I lost my job—"

"Racing. You could have gotten killed. And Joey—" she began wailing louder. She was right; I should have never brought Joey into this. "Sharon is in hysterics right now!"

"How is Joey?" I asked.

"He's fine, but he's scared to death. He has a broken arm and rib. You guys are lucky to be alive, Leon. Do you know how irresponsible that was!? You could've died, just like Lee! . . . " she stopped speaking. Her eyes were red and her voice trembled. My eyes welled up.

We were lucky to even be alive. I had a few bruises, but Joey, on the other hand, had a broken arm and rib. They would never forgive me for this. Everything went to shambles so quickly. It could of ended badly just like it did for my parents.

"How are we going to pay off these bills. Do you ever think, Leon?"

"I—"

"No, you don't. You have always been hardheaded, but these past few weeks, you have been acting very selfish."

"How much is it? I can find a new job."

My aunt sighed. She got up and began to walk away. "I'm going to check on Joey."

I hung my head down in silence. *How could I fix this? Think, Leon. Think.* Nothing came to my mind. *How could I be so reckless and involve Joey like that? I was so exhausted that nothing came to mind.* Maybe my friends would have solutions.

A ringing interrupted my thoughts. I looked at the small table beside the bed. It was my phone.

Who was it? Talking to someone was the last thing on my mind. The caller ID read: Muse Agency. *Was this from the band? Did I win?* Relief entered my body, and I reached for the phone.

A female voice answered.

SECOND EXPOSURE

4

I GASPED as I answered the phone. It was Audrey. I couldn't believe it was her. Her voice sounded just as angelic as the day I met her.

"Hey, Leon, looks like you won the contest!" she yipped.

I was in disbelief, especially after everything that had been happening. I was completely speechless.

"Leon, are you there?"

"Yes, I'm here," I finally sputtered out.

"So, will you be able to meet us around 3 pm tomorrow? We found this cute cafe in town."

"Yeah, of course."

"Okay, I will text you the details and you will get the check tomorrow as well. Oh, and congrats on winning."

"Sounds good. I'll see you guys tomorrow."

"Oh, and just you alone. You're the winner, after all! Don't tell anyone; not your family, friends, no one."

So, was this the meet and greet? Why couldn't my friends come? This whole time everything had been a secret. My skeptical thoughts vanished at the thought of the money.

I hung up the phone and grinned, but my excitement was broken with my aunt, who now had Joey in tow.

"Who were you talking to?" she questioned with her hands on her hips.

"Audrey, from Retro Brite. I won the contest—"

"What if it's a scam, Leon?"

"It's not. I'm meeting them after school tomorrow. And of course, I'm giving my share of the money to you."

She calmed down at the mention of the money. "Fine, just text me and send me a picture when you get there. And even if you get the car fixed, you won't be driving."

I sighed; she wanted a picture. I guess it made sense. And I wasn't allowed to drive indefinitely. I get it though. I messed up badly. I wanted to ask for how long, but she was already aggravated enough. My trust with my family was on the thinnest ice at that moment.

"Fine," I hissed.

We got in my aunt's car to take Joey home.

"I'm glad Leon's not driving this time, Auntie," Joey said.

I slumped down in my seat my seat. *I don't blame Joey. I was so stupid.*

The rest of the ride, I was silent while my aunt continued to comfort Joey.

◎

The road was pitch black. It was raining heavily. A man and a woman were driving down a vacant road. The radio was static and crackled in and out. Rain pattered on top of the car. They smiled at each other. They were on their way home from somewhere. I wonder where? The rain intensified and thunder roared, shaking the ground. The man suddenly lost control of the wheel, veering off on a dirt path, crashing. Smoke violently drifted out of the car. Glass burst in the air like confetti.

I jumped out of my sleep and sat up on my bed. I haven't had that nightmare in a while. It was probably the accident that triggered it. Since my parents died, I've had nightmares about car crashes on and off.

After calming my nerves, my regular morning routine continued, except now I had to take the bus, even after begging my aunt to drive me to school. I hopped on the bus and the body heat of the packed bus felt like walking into a sauna. I sat toward the back near the emergency exit doors. The bus was quiet. In the mornings, everyone mostly slept, trying to get a few more minutes of rest before school. A few stops later, Kim got on the bus. The electronic doors closed sharply, and I waved her over. Kim looked surprised, but sat next to me. I reached up to pull down our window, letting cool air in.

"I'm glad you're okay." She squeezed my shoulders tightly.

"Me too."

"So, it looks like you'll be riding the bus with me. How much was the damage?"

"The front was the only thing that got dented, but the cost to fix the car and the hospital bill is a lot."

"We can raise money by making a Helping Hand page for you." Kim pulled out her phone, ready to set up the profile. Kim was always coming through with good solutions, but I don't think my aunt would be fond of this idea.

"No, I'll just have to find another job," I huffed. I wanted to tell her the good news, but Audrey made it clear to keep the details of the contest private. "I'll work something out," I reassured her.

The final bell signaled releasing us from school. Kim and I got into Camille's car. They were both headed to Landon's place, and Camille was dropping me off at home.

"Are you sure you can't stop by for a minute?" Camille asked, pulling into my driveway.

"No, I still need some rest from the accident and I have a lot of homework to catch up on." I reached behind my head and scratched my neck.

"Here he goes talking about 'homework' again." Camille used finger quotes.

I hope they're not becoming suspicious.

"Plus, my aunt doesn't want me going anywhere," I added as I got out of the car.

I walked in and headed straight upstairs. Audrey said to meet at Sunshine Cafe. I looked up the directions of the restaurant, and *whew*, good thing it was in walking distance. I'm surprised my aunt or friends haven't mentioned this place before. It was near our house and it seemed like a place they could relax after work.

I took a shower before heading downstairs. My aunt was sitting down watching TV. I zoomed past the living room to the front door.

"Leon, make sure you send me pictures when you get there. And come straight back home."

"Okay," I mumbled.

The cool breeze sent chills through my body. I strolled to the cafe, thinking about everything. I wish I could tell my friends that I won. I know Kim would be ecstatic. This was her dream. I walked into the brightly lit cafe; the cafe was appropriately named Sunshine Cafe. Flowers and plants hung on the muted yellow walls. I sat down in a small wicker chair in front of the cafe and waited. Dishes clinked against tables. The scent of coffee was heavenly. People were chatting.

A few minutes later, Audrey, Jamie, and Porter entered the building. Jamie and Porter were laughing and smiling. While Audrey had a serious face.

"Leon, so good to see you." She hugged me before taking off her large designer sunglasses.

"I'm Porter." He extended his hand and introduced himself like I had no clue who he was. Jamie did the same. We got seated at a table and all started to look over the menu.

"Did you tell anyone?" She stared at me intensely.

"Um . . . " Aunt Mel's face popped up in my mind. "No one," I laughed.

Audrey twisted her lips. I cleared my throat and shifted in my chair. "So, how did you like the show?" Audrey asked.

"It was great. My friends and I had a great time." I looked around the table and noticed that Vince was missing.

"Is Vince coming?" I asked. I mean, he is the lead of the band, and the reason why I'm here.

"No, he's not feeling well, but he said congrats and he would like to meet with you sometime later," Porter answered.

Why would he meet me later. I'm sure they have a busy schedule. Once he's feeling better he'll have to go back to work.

We made small talk for about ten minutes while we waited for the waiter.

"You're in high school, right?" Porter asked.

"Yeah. It's my senior year."

"That's exciting. What are your plans? Going to college?" Jamie asked.

"No, not really. I'll be in Crestview." The inflection in my voice dropped.

"Let's talk about something else. School's boring." Audrey grabbed a menu from the table and buried her face in it.

The waitress came over shortly after. "Are you guys ready to order?"

"Yes, finally." Audrey frowned as she ordered her food. "I want the chicken salad, no onions, or tomatoes." She closed her menu and set it down with a thud. Everyone else ordered, and the waitress walked away.

The cafe was so nice. I could see myself and my friends coming here sometime. However, Su Castillo was our go-to place. Whenever someone suggested a different restaurant, we would return to our usual place.

"You have scratches and bruises on you, man. You okay?" Porter asked.

"Um, yeah," I hesitated. "I was in a car accident. It was all my fault. The car's damaged badly."

"So, the moment you have been waiting for." Audrey cleared her throat as Jamie and Porter drum rolled on the table. The silverware and cups rattled. *Did she really not hear what I said? It's okay, as long as I get this money.*

"The check." Audrey pulled out the check.

I grinned as I put the $2,000 check in my wallet. Even though my share of the check was only $500, I was still excited. The money would not be enough to cover much damage or debt.

We continued to have small talk about our favorite musicians, artists, and life in general. The conversation was going well. I was in shock at how down to earth and friendly Porter and Jamie were. They seemed like they were genuinely interested in my life. It felt like we were becoming friends.

"I can't wait to leave this small town. Ugh. No offense." Audrey wrinkled her nose up.

I hated living here, especially since I've been here my whole life. A small town with not much to do. Most people my age tried their best to leave here. Everyone did the same things and saw the same faces. It was like we lived in a boring, continuous loop. So, I took no offense.

"It's not that bad. I kind of like it," Jamie said.

"Yeah, but I'm a city girl," Audrey added.

"I've been here my whole life and would love it more than anything to travel." Audrey's eyes lit up as I spoke.

"Then you should come to our show next week."

Porter and Jamie looked shocked for a second. My heart began to flutter. *Audrey was inviting me?*

"Really?" I tilted my head.

"Yes. And again, don't tell anyone." She pointed her finger at me. "What's your Sonder username?"

Sonder was a social media app everyone my age used and raved about. I'm not very fond of social media. I usually went on for a few minutes to see what my friends posted and logged off.

"ItsjustLeon. I can't come with school and my family. And why can't I tell anyone?"

"We want to keep things low-key just between you and us," Audrey said.

The waitress came back with the food.

"I'm starving," Audrey said, swiping the salad out of the waitress' hands. She began munching on the lettuce like a wild animal. For her being so girly, she ate like a pig. The rest of us thanked the waitress and began eating as well.

"Don't worry about any of that. The show will be Friday night. I just want you to come. So you can get the full experience this time," she explained, wiping salad dressing from her mouth.

"Yeah, Vince would like to meet you. I'm sure he will be better by then," Jamie said.

We finished up the meal and paid. Porter left a tip for the waitress while Audrey complained about the service.

"Well, it's nice meeting up again. If you decide to come to the concert, message me on Sonder. We'll put aside a ticket for you."

We all exchanged hugs as we left. I couldn't believe it that just happened. I wanted to go to the concert, but I highly doubt my aunt would let me. Audrey was really adamant about me coming alone and not telling anyone. Jamie and Porter were exactly how I imagined: cool, friendly, and down to earth. Audrey, on the other hand, was brasher than I thought she'd be. When she interviewed me, she was charming and sweet.

The whole experience had been so surreal. I've never met a celebrity before. My friends wouldn't even believe this.

SHOWTIME

5

THE REST of the week passed by just as mundane as usual. It was really hard not to tell my friends, and even my aunt, about the concert. However, I did tell them I won the contest. I'm not sure Audrey would be happy about that, though. But I couldn't keep it a secret any more and I didn't want to keep the prize money to myself. Kim was estatic; she jumped and screamed at the news. Camille and Landon were in shock. We all talked about what we wanted to do with our share of the money. Kim wanted to go to another concert, Landon wanted to save his, and Camille wanted to go shopping.

The sound of a wind chime came from my phone. The notification alerted me that I got a message on Sonder. It was from Audrey.

Hey Leon, you still wanna come to the show?

Yeah of course

Glad to hear. We'll have a ticket for you and
only you

Audrey sent me a digital ticket. Now all I had to do was sneak out without being noticed, get a taxi to the bus station, and go to the show. This should be pretty easy, considering my aunt went to bed pretty early and I could control the security system from my phone.

I paced back and forth in my room. I couldn't get caught. I'd already put my aunt through so much and my uncle would be coming home soon and he would be upset. But this was exciting and gave me a rush. How many people casually get to hang out with famous musicians? My life had been a little more inter-esting lately.

"Leon, dinner's ready!" my aunt called.

We sat down. She had already called me to come down twice, but I was nervous and kept thinking about the concert. She told me I couldn't go anywhere and here I was planning to sneak out. A plate of chicken, potatoes, and green beans was set in front of me.

"So how's school been?"

"It's great." I nodded, shoving mashed potatoes in my mouth.

After small talk about school and my aunt's day at the diner, dinner was finally over, which was a relief. My aunt was about to gather the dishes, but I grabbed them for her and cleaned up. She was surprised, but didn't question it. She went into her room at 7 pm and turned on the TV. I went back into my room and waited for about an hour just to make sure she was asleep. At 8 pm, I crept down the stairs. They creaked as I stepped down each one. I managed to make it out the front door and followed my usual routine of setting the house alarm. I walked a couple of blocks away before calling a taxi. It took around 35 minutes for one to arrive; most people in Crestview didn't use taxis often. I got in the back seat and sank down into the worn-out leather.

The streets were mostly empty except for a few cars lined up outside someone's house. Some people stood outside talking; music played softly.

Ten minutes later, we were at the bus station. I got off, got my ticket, and headed on the bus. The bus was empty, with only a few passengers. The 1-hour ride felt like an eternity. Finally, off the bus, into the station, and back into another taxi to the show venue. Good thing I had enough money saved for travel. I checked the time. It was now 9:00 pm. Right on time. The venue was not as packed as their previous show. It was a small lounge and bar. I was surprised the venue in my small town was nicer.

A wave of heat hit me as soon as I walked up to the door.

"ID and ticket, please?" a bouncer asked. I shuffled through my wallet and handed him my ID/ "Oh, Audrey told me about you. Come on." He waved me through and pointed to a room not far away.

A group of onlookers mumbled. *Wow, it's so cool how Audrey told him about me. I get VIP treatment.* I shifted my way through the bar into the dressing room. The bar was small; it smelled like cigarette smoke and sweat. My shoes stuck to the floor as I walked, and the furniture appeared worn out, like it hadn't been replaced in years. Booth seats wrapped around small circular tables. Exposed light bulbs draped from the ceiling. I wasn't sure if that design was done on purpose or not. The lights flickered on and off. A guy was on a small stage singing and playing an acoustic guitar. He played a bluesy tune while I walked into the dressing room and saw Audrey and Porter sitting down in makeup chairs. A hairstylist was curling Audrey's pastel purple hair. Her hair was pink when I last saw her. *I wondered how often she changed her hair color.*

"Excuse me!" the stylist shouted at me.

Audrey waved her hand at her, motioning for the stylist to calm down. "Have a seat. There's someone I would like you to meet." As she finished her sentence, a slender man got up from a seat in the corner of the room.

"Hi, I'm Jeffrey. Retro Brite's manager." He shook my hand. "I'm so glad you won the contest." He grinned. Jeffrey was a middle-aged man who looked like he would never listen to Retro's music. His smile suddenly faded away and his face became more stern.

"Porter, go see if Jamie is ready," Jeff asked. Porter didn't say anything and just did what he was instructed. The stylist also walked out of the room.

"Vince is not going to make the show tonight," Jeff said.

"Why not? I thought I was going to finally meet him?" I cleared my throat. *What was going on? Was he really ill?*

"This might sound strange," he held his palms out to keep me from interrupting, "but we need you to go out on stage as him."

My heart beat out of my chest. *Was he serious, or was this another dream?* I began shaking and biting my lips as a wave of anxiety hit me.

"Yes, Vince won't be here, and we need you to replace him." He looked at his watch. "In ten minutes. You'll do it, right? You know all the lyrics? Just lip-sync." He rubbed my shoulder, but instead of comfort, it only added to my worry.

"W-where's Vince?" I stuttered. *Why me? They could have just canceled the show.*

"He's really sick. He's in the hospital. And we can't perform without the star."

Audrey gave Jeffrey a glare.

"The star?" she hissed.

"Why can't you cancel . . . ?" I shook my head in confusion.

"He is the frontman," Jeff said like that added to any validity.

Audrey sprung over with a dressing bag. "Put this on in the next room."

I took the bag. *None of this could be real. It was all a fever dream that I would soon wake up from and get ready for school.*

"Go on, get dressed." My body became stiff; I was unable to move, but Jeffrey shoved me into the dressing room. I put the clothes on without noticing what I was putting on or how I looked.

Jeff and Audrey knocked on the door a few moments later and entered.

"What happened to your face? Was it from the accident?" Audrey examined the scratches on my face.

Why was she asking about the accident like I didn't tell her the other day? Well, she was barely paying attention when I told them.

"Yes," I replied.

"You were in an accident? So glad you're okay, Leon. Woah. I can't imagine." Jeff exhaled and gave me a small smile.

"Oh, nothing a little makeup can fix." Audrey cupped her hand around my face.

I yanked my face away from her, just as I was ushered out of the room again into a makeup chair.

"I'm just doing a little eyeliner, concealer, and powder. Vince's signature look," the stylist from earlier said. Even though she said it was a little makeup, it felt like a lot. The makeup caked on my face. It was dry and itchy. It was my first time wearing makeup and I did not enjoy it.

"Finally, the hair. The most important part." She tousled my curly hair into a mess. "Done."

I examined myself in the mirror. *Woah, I really did look like Vince.* I thought I looked ridiculous.

"It's time!" Jeff exclaimed.

"What do I do?" I panicked.

"It's okay, Leon." Audrey stared into my eyes. "Just lip sync, air guitar, and dance a little. Don't worry, I'll be singing most of the time, anyway. Just stand next to me."

Jamie and Porter entered the room.

"Ready for show time?" Porter bounced on his toes.

"Yeah," I replied, looking at the floor before glancing down at my outfit. I wore black ripped jeans and another graphic tee. It was very similar to the outfit I wore to the contest.

Jamie appeared just as nervous or even more than I was. He began shaking.

"Is he okay?" I asked them.

"Yeah, don't worry about him." Audrey brushed it off.

Jamie took out a Ziplock bag of pills and took a few. *Was he okay? Does he take does daily? I wasn't aware that Jamie was a pill user. A lot of kids at my school were into them, but I only heard stories about them.*

"It's like Pringles. You can't only have one. Take one and you're addicted," Audrey sneered.

Porter opened his mouth; his tongue pushed forward like he was about to speak, but he didn't.

"This way." Audrey led us to the stage door.

I heard the crowd outside the door screaming with joy. Although, the sound of my heart beating was much louder. I was petrified; unable to speak or move.

"Coming to the stage is Retro Brite," a voice announced. Audrey took the lead.

"Come on," she gritted her teeth, grabbing me by the arm.

"Just take a deep breath," Porter told me. "Don't be so nervous."

I walked out the stage door behind Audrey, who was beaming from ear to ear. My eyes grew wide. The crowd erupted with even more excitement when we stepped up on stage. I scanned the crowd. There were only probably only 100 people.

Why was Retro Brite playing for such a small crowd tonight?

I could do this; there weren't many people.

Kim did say they felt more connected to smaller audiences and liked going back to past venues to perform again. Blue lights shined on us. Audrey took front and center with me a few feet away. I stumbled on some cords on my way to my spot on stage. Porter held his bass and Jamie on the drums.

"Who's ready for tonight?" Audrey yelped out in a cutesy voice. Everyone screamed.

"I love you, Audrey," a man from the crowd screamed. Audrey simply looked at him and giggled.

I grabbed my guitar—Vince's guitar. *It felt so weird. Was I even holding this right?* It had been a while since I played a guitar. I only knew basic chords. The song 'Outsiders' started playing. *Good, a song I knew and only 'harmonized' in the chorus with Audrey.* I had already thought Audrey illuminated the stage from the audience seat, but she was electrifying when I was right beside her. She wore a black leather blazer dress and thigh-high black boots.

I could barely concentrate. But I managed to fumble my fingers around the fretboard. Her angelic voice, subtle but sexy dance moves, the way the audience couldn't take their eyes off her was intoxicating. Audrey's eyes scanned the audience, and she smiled, making eye contact with them the whole song.

They whistled and howled as she danced. *Here came the chorus. I couldn't mess this up. I was pretty sure someone would know I wasn't Vince.* I felt the pressure of 200 eyes watching me. *How did performers do this every night?* The chorus began.

"She makes every word come to life," I lip-synced. Another skill I'm not used to doing.

Was it convincing enough? The crowd howled along with the lyrics. They were swaying and held their phones up. A girl got close to the stage and tried grabbing my foot. I hopped away before a bouncer yanked her back.

The crowd cheered and seemed to enjoy the performance. So, it must not have been that bad, or maybe they were too busy watching Audrey. The next song played, and I was the lead vocalist. I stepped up in front of her. The crowd hooted, easing my nerves a little.

I already made it through the first song. I could do this.

The song was way more upbeat than the last one. I was bobbing my head and singing along to the track as heavy drums kicked in and the baseline grew more intense. I jumped up and down, the energy from the crowd yelling and singing the words consumed me. It was exhilarating. I felt more alive than ever. It felt so good to be seen as someone talented and liked by so many.

At the end of the concert, I was soaked in sweat while Audrey still looked completely intact, like she just came out on stage. *Was this even real life? Did I just perform as Vince? It was kinda fun. In my life, I would never have people cheer and admire me like he did.*

"Woo, thanks for a great show tonight," Audrey yelled. The crowd went wild, screeching like this was the best night ever. It was amazing, but I couldn't imagine doing this every night.

We went back to the backstage room. I could still hear the audience yelping.

"That wasn't so bad, was it?" Audrey smiled.

"The crowd loved us," Jamie added.

"Give us a minute." Jeff looked at Porter and Jamie, who retreated from the room once again.

"Just a little bit of training. And he will be a star in no time," Jeff exclaimed.

"Training?" My eyes widened as I took two steps back.

"Yeah. Come with me on Monday. We can have you prepared for the next show. And we have a radio interview, photoshoot, and a rally to go to."

Why would I go with them? This was a one-time thing I got roped into doing.

"What!?" I couldn't process his words.

"Yeah, Audrey told me you would love to travel. Come with us." He opened his arms widely. "You have to. Vince is not getting better anytime soon. And we need you. There's nothing to lose here. Anything you want, we can provide; money, clothes, cars . . . " He gave me a small smile. "Plus, we are starting our overseas tour soon." His smile widened.

Overseas. I've always wanted to travel abroad but never had the funds or time. This might be my only chance.

I fixed my gaze on Audrey. She was leaning against the wall, nodding her head, encouraging me to agree.

"But I want my regular life back."

"Do you really?" he smirked. He reached into a manila folder with my name on it and pulled out a form.

"We can give you a new one. All of your debt is gone. A new car. No more school." He stood close to me, making vivid hand motions to paint the imaginary.

"What will my family think? I can't not go to school."

Jeff held his stomach and chuckled. "Money can fix everything." He twirled a finger in a circular motion. "I can write you another check," Jeff said, reaching into his pocket, pulling out a pen and checkbook.

"Yes!" I blurted out.

"I just need you to sign this nondisclosure form. Hope you kept your promise thus far and haven't said anything."

I nodded my head. There was no way I would say anything else, but now I was legally obligated. I scribbled my signature without reading the contract.

I couldn't believe I agreed to this. What exactly did it mean? When would Vince be better? How would my family and friends believe this? How much money were they willing to give me or my family and friends? This was so surreal. Couldn't they find someone with actual talent? I'm going to be a part of a band. Not just any band, but Retro Brite?!

"We'll be in contact. And don't worry about your ride back. We will take care of it. You're part of the family now." He gave me a warm smile.

Was there a way I could still back out of this. Was my life gone?

"You did great. Glad you're part of the team!" Audrey beamed.

"Okay," I muttered as I walked away. I heard Jeff called a security guard, and a guard was immediately next to me.

"Ready to go? The car's out back," the security guard asked. I nodded my head, and he walked me through some back doors that led out to the parking lot. A mob of fans screamed. I flinched as they tried to get close to me. Another security guard was holding them back. *There were quite a few of them. This was more terrifying than performing. I wondered if they were at the show or if these were the fans that couldn't get a ticket.*

"Get back. Get back!"

Cell phones were flashing and recording.

"Let me get a picture!" A girl reached over a rope barrier, leaning in toward me. My body tightened. I rushed into the black SUV. *This was crazy. I know a lot of fans could push personal boundaries, but I was not expecting this to happen so soon.*

I looked at my phone clock. It was well past midnight. I wondered if my aunt had gotten up or noticed I was not home. The thought alone was more frightening than performing and acting like a superstar.

"You're way better than the last one," the driver stuttered.

"What?" I shouted.

"Um . . . the show was great." He tried to change the subject.

Okay. Did I just hear that? Nevermind, I must just be tired. I closed my eyes and laid my head against the window.

The car halted what felt like moments later. We were in my neighborhood. I didn't remember telling the driver, Audrey, or Jeff where I stayed. It must be from the form I filled out at the contest. I thanked the driver and stumbled out of the car. My body was so sore it felt like cement. I rubbed my tired eyes, and the driver waved bye.

Good, my aunt's car was still in the driveway and the neighborhood was quiet. The wet grass squeaked and crunched as I walked. It was still uncut and about ankle high. I could hear my aunt saying, "I told you to do it last week."

I need to stop being so lazy.

I walked toward the front door, but I hesitated. Instead, I turned and walked toward the fence. It was easier to sneak back in through the back door. I could use the spare key under the doormat. The fence creaked, and my heart beat faster. I slipped through the fence, tiptoed to the backdoor, and fumbled under the doormat, trying to find the key.

Whew, I sighed with the key in my hand. I turned the knob and entered the house; the cool air gave me goosebumps. I crept up the stairs and into my room.

DOPPELGANGER

6

THE NEXT MORNING, I woke up to loud upbeat music playing and chatter in the living room. Did we have guests? We rarely had anyone over besides family.

I entered the living room to see my Uncle Daniel sitting in his Easy Boy recliner. Uncle Dan's recliner had indentations from him sitting there. It was his special seat that no one was allowed to sit in. However, when he was away, I would often relax in it

"Hey, Leon," he bellowed. "Not staying out of trouble, I see."

Great, He was home already?

"Did you mess with my chair?" he groaned as he jerked the broken handle. The chair was thrifted, like most everything in the house. The handle was broken before he left, but no matter what, I always got blamed.

"Dan!" my aunt scolded from the kitchen. "Come eat, boys."

I wasn't glad he was back, but maybe my aunt would be less stressed. She was the one always giving me extra chances. Looks like I might be out of them.

I slouched down at the table in front of my plated breakfast.

"Sit up," Uncle Dan's husky voice instructed. I huffed, but

did as instructed. "So, have you at least brought up your grades?" he started again.

"Yeah," I answered back softly. *Hopefully, I could improve before the end of the term. I needed to start studying for real.*

"You better start looking for another job. That prize money won't cover everything." My uncle's baggy eyes stared into mine.

He was right, and Landon texted me about a job at his dad's store. But if only they knew how much I could make from impersonating Vince.

"I have a new job at Landon's dad's shop," I announced.

"You working at a hardware store?" His face was blank while he scratched his balding head.

While we ate breakfast, my aunt also questioned me.

Was it that hard to believe I was working at a hardware store? I guess it was. I don't blame them. I don't know anything about hardware.

I groaned and rubbed my temples. As we continued eating, they carried on talking about what happened at work. *Thank God.*

◉

Monday morning, I walked to the bus stop. I got on and took my seat. The bus pulled up to Kim's stop shortly after. She made her way to the back of the bus and sat next to me.

"I can't believe you won the contest," Kim said for the millionth time.

"Yeah, me either."

"I can't find any information about you winning online. They usually post everything online. Maybe they want to keep it a secret," Kim told me. She was on her phone, scrolling through posts online.

"Yeah, it was tough competition," I said.

"Not really. Your outfit was so good. The other Vince's could never," she said.

The rest of the ride, Kim chatted about her family, music, and TV shows.

The bus stopped in front of the school; Landon and Camille greeted us as we stepped off the bus.

"So, my dad said you can come in for an interview today." Landon smiled.

"That's great, Leon! I'm sure it'll go well." Kim smiled.

"Well, I guess. My uncle doesn't think I'm a good fit for the job." *I probably was not, but I was happy to have another chance.*

"Oh, is he back yet?" Camille asked.

"Yeah, unfortunately for me. But he's there for Aunt Mel now. And he's up to date on everything that's been happening." I placed my hands in my pockets.

"Well, at least you might have a new job now." Landon clapped his hands.

"Yeah, but it's going to take forever to repay my aunt and uncle." I sighed. *Even with my $500 share of the prize money, it wasn't enough to fix the car or repay my aunt for the concert ticket.*

"I'm sure you'll get the job. I can help with interview questions!" Camille said.

"No, it's okay. Thanks for offering," I said.

There weren't many job opportunities in Crestview. Even when I graduate, I won't be heading to college because I can't afford it.

"Well, hopefully I get hired," I said, while kicking a piece of gravel in the parking lot.

We said goodbye to each other and proceeded with the day.

Finally, 5th period; Mr. McKinney's history class. *I'm so ready to go talk to Landon's dad and go home.* I sat by the large window, opened my textbook, and leaned my head on my desk. *This should go by fast.* I closed my eyes and drifted off. I was thinking about how I could be starting a new job. *What time would I have to be there? Would he interview me like everyone else? Would he be easy on me? Camille was right; I should of practiced. I have to pay attention and prove my uncle wrong.* The chatter of my classmates drifted away. Everything went black.

"Leon Holloway, you're getting picked up," the sound of the intercom rattled me out of my sleep. I tried to regain my composure and act like I wasn't asleep. Standing up, I straightened my shirt and grabbed my things.

"Alright, Leon, have a good day. And don't forget the assignment," Mr. McKinney said.

"See ya." I left. I don't remember the assignment. I must have already been asleep.

I headed toward the office. *Why was I getting picked up early? I don't remember having any appointments anywhere. I rarely got to leave school early.* I walked into the office.

"Leon, your uncle is here to pick you up," the receptionist said.

Why would Uncle Dan come pick me up? This was his first time being at school. He was usually on the road all the time.

"Hey, Leon, let's go." I glanced up to see a tall, blond-headed man. Definitely not my uncle. My mouth was agape . . . Jeff?

"Come on, Leon, we don't want to be late to the dentist," he said with a toothy grin.

"Um . . . okay." My voice shook a little. *How did he know this was where I went to school? I didn't tell any of them.* I laughed and followed through the corridor.

"What are you doing here?" I whispered.

"Just being a good uncle. There's a place I want to show you. I want to take you to Muse."

We were outside in the parking lot. *Muse? Was that the name of the agency Audrey had called me from earlier?*

"How did you know where I go to school? And why would they let me go with you? They never met my uncle."

"You are full of questions," he chuckled. "Get in. You're a superstar now." He opened the passenger side of a black Mercedes with tinted windows.

"Where are we going?" I buckled in.

"Where stars are made."

"Hollywood?" I guessed. He chuckled at my answer. "And do I get paid like you said I would at the lounge?"

"Nope, you will see. And of course. I keep my word. Listen to this new track; you need to start learning the lyrics." He connected his phone to the stereo. An upbeat guitar track was playing.

It wasn't too bad. I nodded my head along to the rhythm. I got lost in the music playing, and by Jeff's random rambling, that I barely noticed we were driving along a winding dirt road. Gigantic pine trees towered in the sky. The view in front of me was not visible. But I wasn't afraid of what was ahead. It had to be better than what was behind me.

Man, where were we, though? We were pretty far from the town. We must of been driving for about an hour now. Jeff pulled into a deserted field. *Were we even still in Crestview? It was a pretty small town, but I didn't go out much. So I wouldn't know.*

"Where the hell are we?" I said, looking up at the aircraft hangar that was now in front of me.

"Going on a little field trip!" Jeff screeched playfully.

"Are we getting in that?" My body stiffened.

"Oh, it'll be fun!" He opened the car door and yanked me out.

We walked toward the small plane. My heart sank to my stomach. I've never been on a plane before, let alone to many different states. My family would always travel by car because of the cost of airline tickets.

"Where's the pilot?" I asked. My voice shook.

"You're looking at him right now, baby!" Jeff slapped the nose of the plane.

"Um, are you sure?"

"Yep, I'm a certified professional." He jumped into the driver's seat.

Jeff's lanky body was cramped inside of the cockpit. He

patted the passenger's side, and I got in. I was a little afraid, but still wanted to see what was next. I bet it was better than being stuck back home. We then fastened our seatbelts. Jeff flipped on a couple of switches, and the plane began moving along the dirt path, gradually increasing its speed. I clenched my eyes closed.

Next thing I knew, I felt a dropping sensation. *Were we in the air?* I looked out the window and saw large puffy clouds.

"Not so bad, is it?" Jeff cackled.

I nodded, even though I was still terrified. My ears began to pop and my stomach flopped as the plane ascended and descended. I gripped onto the armrest and was gasping for air. I started to hyperventilate and closed my eyes.

"Calm down," Jeff told me.

After a couple of minutes, the flight became much smoother. My eyes were still closed most of the flight, the engine hummed, and Jeff was still talking. I don't remember much of anything else.

"We're ready to land," Jeff said.

The plane slowed down and jolted as the wheels hit the runway. We got out of the plane, and my legs wobbled as I stepped on the runway. I was glad to be back on the ground. We walked into an airport.

"Where are we?" I asked.

"You'll see."

The airport was small and secluded; most of the people there looked like they were mechanics or flight students. There wasn't much but a small lounging area with a few reclining chairs and vending machines. Warm yellow light emitted through the large terminal windows. Specks of dust suspended in the air.

We left the airport and got into another black SUV. I had so many questions, but didn't dare to ask. I knew Jeff would just ignore me or say something cryptic.

Where were we going next? Would Audrey and the others be there?

We drove and drove, passing buildings, stores, and houses. People were going about their normal mundane routines:

crossing the street, shopping, and working. Then there was me, stepping into a world of unknown, pretending to be someone else.

As we drove, civilization became more distant. We were now in another wooded area and stopped in a field. In front of us was a large metal gate, and further up was a tall metallic gray skyscraper.

Woah, I've never seen one before. It was breathtaking.

The building had a unique contemporary design and was at least 40 stories high. The top of the building was covered by feathery clouds. It was hard to see where the top ended. Crestview didn't have many buildings like this. They were mostly worn down and old. My mouth was agape and my gaze was fixed. I sat so close to the windows, my breath fogged up the glass. The windows in the building looked so tiny. I couldn't imagine being that high up.

We pulled up to the gate.

"What is going on?" I asked. *What type of talent agency was this? It was in the middle of nowhere. Maybe I shouldn't of agreed to this.* I looked back at the dirt road.

"Shut up. We're almost there," he hissed as he approached a speaker by the gate. *Why Jeff was now less playful and becoming angry? Anyone would be confused and questioning in a situation like this.*

"Yes, sir, we're here," Jeff said, and the gate opened.

Who was he talking to? Was this a good decision? I wonder if my friends would look for me? Was it too late? I should have thought about that before getting into the car. He drove through the gate and into a parking garage. A few more black SUVs that were identical to the one I was in were also parked there.

"Okay, are you going to tell me anything?" I whined.

"I'll explain in a minute. Just stay quiet until then." He got out and opened the door for me. "Follow me."

The contrast from the dark parking garage to the brightly lit building burned my eyes. I followed Jeff through a corridor until we reached a white marble desk. Inside the room, the walls were white, and the floors were also white marble. Behind the desk, bold silver letters read 'MUSE TALENT AGENCY'. A pink succulent decorated the counter, giving the space a pop of color. Near the counter was a set of U-shaped steps with white paneling. My eyes inspected the room. This place was so clean I couldn't imagine it ever being dirty.

The AC in the building was so strong that I wrapped my arms around my chest. The room had a clean neutral smell to it. I really wasn't able to describe it. A woman dressed in a plain gray pants suit sat at the desk. Her hair was slicked back in a neat bun. Pinned on the collar of her suit jacket was a silver 'M' emblem. Her face was dewy and bright as she peeked up from her desktop.

"Hello, Mr. Spencer. This must be Leon." She smiled as if this was a regular meeting or a doctor's office. She handed Jeff a file with my name on it.

"Welcome to Muse Agency!" Jeff wiggled his fingers. He was now back to his more playful demeanor.

"This is the agency?" I raised an eyebrow.

A talent agency in the middle of nowhere. We walked through another hall; a group of young adults around my age sat in chairs lined up against the wall. They appeared to be uncomfortable and confused, like me.

Were they in the same position as me? Why was that woman acting like this was a regular audition?

"I don't know if I have the right look," one girl discussed with the boy sitting next to her.

Jeff stopped in front of a door and punched in a code. The door beeped and opened. I walked to his spacious office, which was adorned with pictures of celebrities. *His clients, I suppose.* Audrey's picture was the largest and in the middle of the wall. The shining star. I recognized a few more faces, a couple of actors, other small bands, and singers. He had a pretty impressive clientele, but were those the real people or phonies like me?

His desk was neat. Books and paper were meticulously placed. On the desk was a photo of Jeff, and what seemed like his parents and his brother. They were all smiling, but no one really appeared to be happy. Their eyes looked solemn and lifeless. They were well-dressed in matching sweaters that looked like cashmere. I bet they owned vacation homes on the beach, or maybe even in other countries. I couldn't imagine being that wealthy. *Was that his younger brother? What did his parents do for a living?* All the decor in the room was also white, just like the lobby. *This place was so neat it gave me an eerie feeling.*

"Sit. Give me your phone. Now." He snatched it from my hand as soon as I took it out of my pocket.

I sat down and looked him directly in his eyes, demanding answers. "When will I start getting paid?"

"Soon. I promise. We have so much to discuss." He drummed his thin fingers on the desk.

"What if I change my mind?" I looked away.

"Too late to get cold feet. You're a natural, anyway."

"Really?" I spun my head back in his direction. *I rarely got told that I was good at something. Even if he was lying, it was nice to hear.*

"Say goodbye to your phone forever." He placed it inside his desk drawer. "It will soon be deactivated."

It didn't bother me that much. Kim and Camille would be devastated about that, but my phone was outdated anyway.

"You're here for media and musician training. You'll be at this facility for a few days. This first day is mostly an introduction and training for interviews."

"So, how long will this take? I'm not good at school stuff." I slumped down in the chair.

"Just listen." He extended his hand out. "It's nothing hard. You already performed as him. This will be easy."

I hoped so. The thought of sitting in a classroom made me shudder. How big were these classes? Would I have to study?

We sat in silence for a few minutes as he typed on his computer.

"Okay, follow me. Time for your introduction class." He got up and guided me to a room a few doors down the hall.

We entered a small lecture room. A few other young adults were sitting, spread out across the room. A woman entered the room also dressed in a gray pants suit with the same 'M' pinned to her collar. Her hair was also in the same style as the lady at the front desk.

"I'll be watching," Jeff told me as he walked out the room.

Were there cameras here? I looked around the room. *No cameras were in sight. Maybe he was watching from the glass window behind us.*

The classroom was also all white. It looked totally different from the typical classrooms I sat in. The chairs were egg-shaped, and the desks were quite spacious. Tablets were embedded onto the desks. Weird looking headsets were also placed on the tables. At the front of the classroom, there was a projector hanging from the ceiling and a strange treadmill-like apparatus.

What were those things? Crestview High's technology was years behind. The instructor smiled widely and motioned for me to sit down. I picked a seat near the front next to a girl with dark hair. The seats were very comfortable. I scanned the room. The other students appeared to be around the same age as me. *Were they happy to be here?* A girl in the front row grinned like it was the first day of school and she was reunited with her friends. A boy, a few seats from her, was leaning on his desk. He bounced his leg up and down. He clearly wanted to be somewhere else.

"Okay, everyone's here. Welcome. Don't be alarmed. This is going to be a pleasant experience," she drawled out her sentences. "From now on, you'll be referred to by your new names. 'Star names', as we like to call them." Her voice was so smooth and soothing, it almost made me forget about the strange new environment I was in.

"You stars are grouped together because all of your famous

counterparts share the same social circle and will most likely have to interact with each other in public." The lady shifted her weight and began walking around the room. Her heels clicked loudly against the floor.

"Vince, you and Mila are childhood friends." She glanced at me and the girl with the dark hair. She wore her long hair in a ponytail, and she was dressed in a white tee, jeans, and an army green military jacket.

"There are files downloaded on your tablets. These files contain information that varies from basic to complex. Such as favorite films, colors, responses in interviews, and a list of their close relationships."

A folder opened on my tablet. I searched for Mila's name and tapped on the file. Mila Kyung. 19 years old. Originally from Atlanta, Georgia. A singer-songwriter, dancer, and model. Now residing in Los Angeles. Has known Vince Continolo since childhood. Her mother is a filmmaker and her father is an accountant. She has two sisters who also dance and act as well.

I looked through the list and found the file about Vince's parents. Hollie and Thomas Continolo. Hollie and Thomas resided in Las Vegas. Hollie was an esthetician and Thomas was a doctor. I scrolled down to see a picture of them. They were hugged up, smiling from ear to ear. They appeared to be genuinely happy. Hollie had a small coil afro and Thomas' hair was buzzed low and balding in the center. It was strange to see his parents. I haven't heard anything about them before. Vince and I looked so similar; I thought maybe our parents might share similar features as well, but they didn't.

I scanned to the bottom of the list. Omar Haidar. 22 years old. They had a falling out over the years and have been seen fighting and bad talking each other on social media. A guy with short, curly dark brown hair shot me a look. He must be Omar. He had a scar above his right eye. His brown, deep-set eyes were intense.

I sunk down into my seat. *I couldn't believe I had left school just to go back to school.* The instructor introduced the other people in the room and their relationships. I did not recognize who anyone in the room could be a double for. I rarely kept up with celebrity gossip, but Mila did look familiar. I probably saw her on some show—oh, I saw her on the soap opera *Under The Sun*. I watched it every week with Aunt Mel. The show was a guilty pleasure of mine. I wouldn't dare bring it up to my friends, but the intense over-the-top plot lines had a way of sucking me in.

I scanned through more of Omar's detailed profile. Omar was a young fútbol player that got injured and now decided to take on a career as an actor and model. Omar was known for his quick temper and fighting. Vince and Omar became enemies after Audrey broke up with Omar and started dating Vince. Omar and Audrey had a toxic relationship. Rumors of cheating and domestic violence.

Woah. I wonder what Vince's role was in all of this drama. I scrolled further down to see images of some of the drama on Sonder.

FAN

Can't stop listening to Retro Brite's new song.

OMAR

Meh.

Another post showed an excerpt from an interview where he insulted Audrey:

My idea girl would be someone who only talks about makeup and fashion. Someone that isn't spoiled and only thinks about herself.

AUDREY

Only thinks of herself?

Now that I thought about it, Kim did show me this.

"Don't be afraid to get acquainted, but remember, you're being monitored at all times," the instructor interrupted. "You will also have time to study your new families. You will be interacting with them on a regular basis. Some of you guys did not cooperate the first time and are here again." The instructor side eyed Omar. *Here again. Did not cooperate? What did he do?*

The students in the room began to chat. I turned to Mila, who had a pout on her face.

"So, what do you think?" I asked.

She shrugged. "What do you mean? It's awful. I want to go home. This isn't what I imagined." She adjusted her dark long locks behind her shoulders.

Did she choose to come here? Was she misled? Was she forced?? At least I wasn't the only one that was confused and didn't want to be here. I shifted my focus to the other students.

"I'm so excited. I can't believe I get to be Bethany," a girl with a pixie cut screeched.

"Do we actually get paid?" I heard another girl say.

Good question. Jeff said I was, but I feel like I can't trust him.

"Is anyone else ready to go home?" a guy said, turning to a group.

The instructor cleared her throat; we stopped talking.

"So, each of you will have more in-depth training before your first major interviews. The most important rule is to play it safe and say as little as possible." She continued with the lecture and made us role play some scenarios.

"Vince, how long were you and Audrey together?" she asked me.

Why did I have to go first?

"Um . . . I actually don't like talking about my private life." I sighed. Not sure of how to answer.

"Great answer, just be more confident," she instructed me. I exhaled.

"Mila, how does it feel to finally get your big break and

dance in Elora's new music video? How is she on set?" she asked, standing in front of her.

"Umm . . . it's great to be involved with so many great projects. And no, she's great—"

"I heard she can be intense and a diva," the instructor interrupted.

"No, not at all," Mila giggled. "Everyone on her team is humble and down to earth."

"Okay, that was a good response. You all have to learn how to take the pressure from pushy interviewers. Remember to take your time with your responses and know what's off limits." She paced around the room; her focus on the entire class.

"Now let's work on getting the body language down. Everyone put on your headsets." Most of the class followed suit. A few of them, including me, hesitated.

What was I about to see? Was I about to play a game? This place was weird. I put the headset on. *Was this those VR headsets that people have been talking about lately?*

A female voice spoke. "Congratulations, you have been chosen to impersonate Vincent Continolo. Let's watch a few clips to perfect his accent and body language."

The screen was white and had subtitles of what she was saying. Moments later, a clip of Retro Brite in an interview popped up.

"Listen and watch closely."

"So Vince, what's the best part of touring?" a man asked him.

"Well, um, like, it's definitely goin' to other places. Seeing the fan." Vince was laid back on the sofa and his legs were crossed.

"Notice here how he says 'like.' Vince often uses this filler word. And notice how his legs are crossed and how relaxed he's sitting. It's okay to exaggerate these things when practicing.

Vince is also originally from the south. So, take your time when speaking to perfect that southern draw and remember to drop the 'g' from the end of words."

This was interesting and creepy at the same time. It reminded me of when Kim and Landon made me walk like Vince. This was going to be easy. It was way more fun than learning about some dumb history fact or math equation.

She gave me more examples, such as how Vince often used the words 'man,' 'dude,' and 'really.' How his eyes would widen when he was excited. How he often spoke with his hands and shrugged his shoulders. How he would shuffle across the stage or when he laughed, it was often a deep belly laugh. And how he acted on red carpets and with fans. This continued for what seemed like almost an hour.

"Okay, class, pay attention up here!" the instructor yelled. We took off our headsets. "Anyone want to get in front of the class and demonstrate what you've been learning?" She scanned the room. A few hands flew up. "Okay, how about you Mila?" she said to the girl with the dark hair who didn't have her hand up.

"What!? Me!" Mila replied.

"Yes."

"Um . . . how about someone that volunteered?" She motioned to the students that had their hands up.

"Yes, but why don't you give it a go?" the instructor asked.

Mila scoffed and went to the front of the class.

"Okay, class, Mila will give us a demonstration. Please step on the treadmill. This exercise will demonstrate what it is like to be around a mob of fans."

Mila stood on the treadmill and put on a VR headset.

"We'll be watching it as well," the instructor added in.

Suddenly, the image of a street was projected on the white walls. Mila walked on the treadmill, observing the view. Moments later, a group of screams erupted. She strolled down the street, and it seemed like she was in awe.

"Mila, we love you!" said a girl, walking toward her.

"I'm a big fan!" said another.

"Hey, sign this!" a guy said.

The street was now busy with tons of people. She was surrounded. A security guard was there, but he struggled to keep them back. The street grew more and more chaotic. Mila started jogging on the treadmill, trying to escape the horde of fans. She was panting.

"Sign one more, Mila!" a voice yelled. Mila ripped off the VR set as she slipped and fell off the treadmill. The class gasped loudly.

Was she okay? I'm glad I didn't have to do that. I gripped the edge of my desk as Mila laid on the floor.

"It's okay, class. This exercise is intense and takes time to get the hang of," the instructor explained. The class was now hushed and fixated on Mila. Another student rushed over to help her up. The instructor shooed them away. Mila gradually got up and sat back down.

"She's fine," the instructor said. I heard a few whispers and mummers. "Now let's continue class."

For the rest of the class, we talked about more tips on how to handle press and watched examples.

"Okay, that's it for the first class. We'll start again early tomorrow. You will now be taken to the cafeteria and lodging area."

Three guards entered the lecture hall. "Line up!" one of them yelled.

Without hesitation, all of us formed a line. They frisked us down, making sure we did not have anything on us. We walked into a large cafeteria. The floors were gray tiles. The walls were white with neon purple light strips lining the corners. The room was more vibrant than the other ones. Geometric shaped lights hung from the ceiling. There were buffet tables filled with food from any culture you could think of, from Italian, American, Japanese, and more. *I have never seen this much food before.* The rich smell of food made my mouth salivate; I was starving. I haven't eaten in hours.

"Sit next to me." Mila grabbed my arm, and I sat down next to her. She had a plate full of pasta and another full of sweets.

"So, what do you think of this place? When did you get here?" she whispered closely, looking around the room cautiously.

"Um, I just got here not long ago. I don't know. It's okay. How about you?"

I was starting to lose track of time. It felt like I had been here forever.

"Okay?" she raised her thick eyebrows. "I've been here for a day. They scouted me at the mall. You see Omar?" She pointed in his direction. "He's already been here for a week, but since he's been misbehaving, they had to isolate and sedate him. If we act up, we will be here longer until we finish the program." She started to look nervous. Omar was sitting hunched over alone at a table not far from us. He had a plate of food, but was not eating. He only stirred the food around on the plate.

They found her at a mall. Were they pretending to scout for models? Looks like she was forced to come here. They sedated Omar? Why didn't he follow along with the program? How long was it?

"They found me at a concert. I was promised money." A guard glanced in our direction. Mila backed up from me and continued to eat her food. I couldn't tell if the food was delicious or if I was just hungry. But everything seemed pretty good.

"We'll talk later." She rubbed my lower back. After that, the rest of our dining went by silently.

When lunch was done, more guards entered the room. "Everyone, get up, now!" the guards rattled.

My fork dropped in a clank against the plate as I stood up. Everyone else followed suit.

Omar got up slowly. A guard grabbed him from the back of his head. *Hasn't he learned his lesson yet?*

They moved us out of the cafeteria and into a hallway, then to an elevator. The guards stood between us to keep us from talking to each other. We ascended many floors up. Mila and Omar were on the other side of the elevator. The guards blocked my view of them. The elevator was huge with glass windows, and I glanced outside as we went up. The green grass below became a speck. My stomach twisted. *It finally hit me I was no longer home and there was no telling when I would be back. Or if I will.* The elevator beeped, and the doors opened. The guards stepped off and led us down a hallway that looked similar to a hotel.

"Guys, come with me," one guard told us. I lined up with the rest of the guys. We walked down the hall and he began assigning rooms to us. He pushed me toward a room.

"Everyone stay in their rooms until the morning wake up call!" another guard yelled.

"I'm not staying here. I wanna go home!" a girl from across the hall screeched. She tried to run, but a guard tased her. Her body fell limp across the hall. I jumped back against the wall. *Was she okay? I better listen to everything they say.* One guard picked her up and placed her in her room. I shuddered. *I guess these guys weren't harmless. I thought they didn't have any weapons.*

Mila's room was next to mine. I was pushed into my room. When I turned on the lights, I saw it was decorated like an ordinary teen boy's room. The walls were a navy blue. Vince's favorite color. Retro Brite posters were on the wall. A bulletin board with a collage of pictures was hung up. There were pictures of Vince and his bandmates. And a couple of him and Mila. Mila and Vince were at the beach, hugging and smiling. *I miss Kim, Camille, and Landon. Reminded me of hanging out with them.*

Dark curtains blocked out the sun. I turned to see a desk with a picture of Vince. He was smiling in between a man, woman, and boy. I've never really seen his family before. I heard Kim talk about them, though. I opened the drawers and the closet to see an assortment of clothes Vince would wear. They were full of many graphic t-shirts and jeans. I opened the blackout curtains to see if there was some sort of view. The light was so bright; I squinted my eyes. There was a sliding door that led to a screened in balcony. I stepped out. It felt like forever since I had some fresh air. I took a deep breath and looked out the balcony. We were so high up that all I could see was the big vast sky and patches of trees.

What was this place? When would I get the money and go back to my family? What's up with Mila and Omar? How does she know all of this? I stepped back inside and sat on the bed.

There was a TV on a dresser. I wondered what we were allowed to watch. I turned on it on; the woman from the front desk appeared on the screen.

"Welcome to the agency. Here you have access to all the information that can make you a star." Jeff and some other agents, I suppose, walked into frame. "You can learn everything from modeling, acting, singing, and most importantly, charisma," she spoke in an overly enthusiastic voice.

Lord, you would think they had a better budget and used some of their own advice. Are they actually trying to help us?

"Next, let's learn some techniques to always be camera ready." Her voice beamed, but her eyes were dead. She was still dressed in the gray suit with her hair in the slick backed bun.

I wondered how the employees felt about this job. This was so strange. And it became evident I couldn't leave.

I turned the TV to a different channel before she could carry on. A loud static noise came from it. The screen was black and white. *Of course, they wouldn't let us watch anything else. What the hell was going on?* I turned off the TV and decided to take a shower instead. As I took my clothes off, a piece of paper fell out of my jacket pocket. I didn't remember carrying anything with me; plus, the security should have found it.

I unfolded the napkin, and it read:

MEET OUT ON THE BALCONY LATER. I WILL GIVE
YOU A SIGNAL. DON'T WORRY. GET RID OF THIS. —MILA

What was she going to tell me?

I shredded the note up into millions of tiny pieces and flushed it into the toilet.

Was someone watching me in this room? I searched around the bathroom. No cameras were to be found.

After my shower, I laid in bed. The room was pitch black and not a sound could be heard from inside the building. It was a little peaceful, but eerie at the same time. A soft thumping noise came from the wall. I turned my body in the opposite direction in my bed. I heard another thud, but this time, it was slightly louder. I crept out of the bed, hearing the noise once more. Was it coming from outside? I pulled back the curtains and stepped onto the balcony. I looked to the right of the next balcony and saw a dark figure.

"Hey," it whispered. *Who was it?* I was sweating. I wanted to scream, but held it in. The figure was petite. It was Mila. My eyes adjusted to the darkness. She was wearing button downed pajamas.

"Don't worry, the camera's audio can't pick us up here."

Then why was she whispering? Was this a set up? How could I trust anyone?

"How do you know that?"

"Omar told me. He knows a lot about this place." She was leaning against the screen.

Why would we listen to someone who has been kept captured for misbehaving?

"Look, we should try to get out of here. Even if we go through with the program, we won't have our normal lives back. Our friends and family. We can choose our futures," she said.

I know this place is strange, but the agency might be the only chance I have for a brighter future.

"It's just me, my aunt, and uncle. I'm too much of a burden on them, anyway. I have no future." I sighed.

"Don't say that. I'm sure they're wondering where you are now. I know how you feel; my mom was a dancer and forced me to take lessons even though it's not my thing. I was just a normal college kid looking for some extra cash and they saw me." Her voice softened even more. It was easy for her to say. She was in college and on her way to create a nice life for herself. "It created a wedge between us. But if we don't leave, we will forever be living in someone else's shadow. Their truth." A moment of silence passed. "They're taking advantage of us. Do you think they will pay us? And let us go back to our families after what they are doing to us?" she spoke louder. Her green eyes sparkled.

"So what's the plan?" I asked. *Maybe she was right. Something was up with this place. Nothing made sense.*

She moved a little bit farther from the screen.

"Omar said that there's an elevator that leads downstairs to tunnels. We can get out and bypass the fences above. Omar said he opened the door, but got caught before exiting. We can leave tomorrow night. Omar will create a diversion, and we can run for the elevator. He gave me the code."

"And if we get caught, we get locked up in the basement and become the next Omar, and we will stay here longer?" I asked her, pressing my lips together.

Was she crazy? There was no telling what could happen. If we complied, we at least could rejoin civilization. Or a fake version of it. What if they killed us? How many chances did they give Omar?

"Okay, I'll do it," I sputtered out. *This place was starting to creep me out. I needed to get away from it, and Jeff.*

"What, really?" She tilted her head up. "Tomorrow night, we rush toward the elevator; Omar and the others will help us."

I agreed to her plan even though I'm frightened of what could happen. But I'm willing to risk getting in trouble. I head back in, nervous, scared, and excited for tomorrow.

BREAKING FREE

7

LIGHT SUDDENLY EMITTED into the room. The curtains automatically pulled back. The TV turned on with the same secretary lady speaking. I woke up, gasping for air, and threw the covers off me. My heart palpitated, and I was covered in sweat.

"Welcome to Muse Agency. This is your morning wake up call. Get ready for a day full of excitement. Classes will begin in twenty minutes. A complimentary breakfast will be provided."

I got up and stretched my arms. *This kept getting stranger. This place was confusing. One minute we were hostages, and the next, we were in a nice resort.*

On the armchair in the corner was a pair of athletic shorts and a t-shirt. They were gray, just like the outfits the staff wore. *Hmm, was that always there? If not, who placed it there? Was I safe here? If someone came in, I'm sure I would have heard it.* I proceeded to get dressed. *I hated working out. I hoped that was not what we're doing. I felt like I was back in gym class.*

The door unhinged, and a man entered with a meal tray. He uncovered the lid, displaying an omelet, ham, potatoes, and orange juice. The meal looked amazing, but I didn't have much of an appetite. *Was this place as bad as Mila said it was?*

"They'll get you in a few minutes. Enjoy your meal." He left without saying anything else.

I nibbled off the plate. I wondered if our plan would go well. *This was so risky. There was no telling what could happen. Could I really trust her?* The door flung open. It was one of the guards from yesterday.

"Come on, time to go," he said, grabbing me by the arm. I tried to yank out of his grip, but I was still taken down the hallway with a few other people.

"Time for a light workout, kids." A short woman emerged from the elevator. "Come on, get to running!" She blew a whistle, jogging in place. She wore a gray tracksuit with an 'M' logo on the front. Her hair was slicked back into a bun like the other women employees.

We all began to shuffle into a light jog down the hallway.

"Let's take the stairs," she said, guiding us toward the exit.

After jogging down four flights of steps, I was already out of breath. I glanced around to see if my peers were doing just as bad. *Everyone else seems to be tired as well. So at least I'm not the least athletic one in the group.* The instructor opened a door to a workout faculty filled with treadmills, weights, and other equipment. I exhaled deeply. *There was more. I didn't think I'd make it through.*

"Okay, you, and you, get on the treadmill!" she yelled, pointing at me, another guy, and a girl. They scrambled toward the treadmills, huffing.

Even though I was exhausted, I got on the treadmill. I ran for what seemed like hours. She antagonized us as we worked out. My legs felt like jelly.

"Don't you want to look the part? You're a star now. Gotta lose a few pounds if you want to be like Vince," she sneered at me.

I knew that I was a few pounds heavier than Vince, but was it really that noticeable? No one would care. Sweat poured down my face as I ran. My heart was pumping out of my chest. I desperately wanted to stop, but was too afraid of what might happen. I was about to faint.

After the grueling workout was over, we were sent back to our rooms to freshen up and get ready for more classes. I was so sore and could barely walk without any pain. I took a shower, got dressed, and laid back in bed. I rested for what seemed like twenty minutes. The door unhinged once again; startled, I sat up on the bed.

"One last step to complete the look." A man with a mohawk and a couple of guards entered. He was holding a pin with a needle in it.

"What? Please leave me alone right now!" I pleaded. I tried to bury myself under the covers. *This had to be a hallucination. Maybe I was just dehydrated.*

No one responded to me; the guards ripped the blanket off me. The cold room made me shiver. They pinned me down, and I heard a sharp buzzing noise. My skin was burning like I was being stung by bees. I squealed in agony. The pain increased as a needle moved across my arm and chest. I tried wiggling my way out of their arms, but it was no use. Tears ran down my face as I stared up at the ceiling.

"Stop moving, or else," a voice grunted. I complied and stayed as still as possible.

The buzzing stopped. I looked down to see Vince's iconic moth tattoo on my forearm and a medium-sized skull in the middle of my chest. They wrapped it up quickly before I could inspect it further and left the room. I was shaking while I sat on the bed. *When would this torture end?*

Minutes later, I was lined up once again with the rest of my new classmates. Mila waved at me from across the hall. She also seemed slightly distressed. *What did they do to her? It couldn't be as bad as working out or getting tattoos.* I half-smiled back, but a security guard stepped in front of me, blocking my view of her. Omar was walking down the hall with two guards holding his hands behind him. I started thinking about the escape plan. *Would it work? How many times did Omar get caught? Would he come through? Was he trying to escape again? Why would he trust us?*

The first class of the day was with her. She spoke more about our stars and I got a chance to skim through the profiles more. It was hard to pay attention because I kept thinking about the plan.

I read through Vince's roommate's profiles:

Arabella was a social media influencer, and she dated Porter. She was a brunette with a short bob cut. Her hair was chocolate brown, and her eyes were smoky gray. In the picture, she was taking a selfie in front of a full-body mirror. She was small and wore jeans, a white blouse, and some heels. She was smiling widely. Her teeth were very white; I could tell she whitened them.

Calix was written above a picture of a guy with a blonde fade. He was an actor. *Strange name; I never heard of it before.* He had sepia-colored eyes, a sculpted face, a refined nose, and russet brown skin. The picture appeared to be a professional shot.

Elena was a model. Her picture was in black and white. It looked like one of her campaigns. Her dark hair blew in the breeze as she wistfully looked over a cliff at the beach. She was statuesque and elegant.

Their profiles weren't very helpful. I wished they gave me more information about their personality. It was going to be hard to act like Vince around them. Maybe he wasn't that close to them. I knew I wouldn't be able to remember their names. I was better at remembering faces. After the class, she gathered us back into the hallway for the next class.

"Good afternoon, I hope you all are doing well. You all will be split up into groups based on your new occupations. Musicians over here, actors over there, and dancers there." She pointed toward three different guards, and we began to split up. Looked like I wasn't with Mila or Omar this afternoon.

I stood next to three guys and two girls. The guard put us into the giant elevator. He used a key card and hit the button for the 7th floor. We stepped off the elevator and were greeted by a man. He seemed kind of young, like he could be in his late twenties. He was short and was dressed in ripped jeans and a white tee with shaggy hair above the ears. He seemed like a normal guy, and I was a little relieved to see him.

"Hey, today you will be learning about stage presence and how to imitate your rock star. We will also go over basic instrument skills and theory," he told the group while opening the door to a stage room. The medium-sized room had guitars, drums, and keyboards.

"Have a seat." He motioned.

I winced as I sat cross-legged next to some guy on the carpeted floor like we were back in elementary school. My body was still sore from the workout.

"You're lucky to be Vince. He's so cool and well-known. I have to be Dustin," he whispered while the instructor was talking.

"Who?" I whispered back, confused.

"From Painted Dog? The bass player?"

My heart began to pitter-patter. *They just opened for Retro a couple of nights ago. Was that him or the real Dustin? Was Dustin sick like Vince?*

"Did you perform with them yet?" I asked.

"No, but I will be with them for a photoshoot soon. "I'm Trey. Wow, what happened? Is that a tattoo? I heard some other people got them too." He grabbed my arm, even though it was still taped.

Really? I wonder how they reacted to it.

The instructor cleared his throat and glanced in our direction. *Look at me not paying attention in class like usual.* The teacher handed me a guitar.

"Let's go over basic chords and techniques. And Dustin, here." The instructor handed him a bass.

For a few minutes, everyone tinkered around with their instruments and practiced basic skills. The room was filled with ruckus. Horns blared, piano keys pounded, and guitars ringed. Only a few of the students knew how to play their instruments. The room was so loud I could barely hear my own thoughts. I have played guitar but only knew the basics. I gave up once things got more challenging.

"Okay, now let's get on stage and learn how to get the crowd motivated. First, I have videos for you guys to watch and imitate of your star." He passed a tablet to everyone; mine had video clips of Vince.

Vince jumped around and did his signature shoulder shimmy. He was very energetic on stage, but not too much to where it took the focus from Audrey. Dustin volunteered to get on the stage first. The instructor turned on a backtrack of a Painted Dog song. Dustin grabbed the bass, swayed to the music, and pretended to fret the guitar. He was confident on stage, making great eye contact with us, and lip-syncing perfectly.

"More. More! Feel the music," the instructor stood up and yelled. "You guys have to be more authentic, believable. You look like a kid playing dress-up," he yelled more. His nice demeanor quickly faded away.

Did they really expect us to know what to do?

The instructor got on the stage, grabbed the bass, and pushed Dustin out of the way.

"Like this. Don't worry about talent. It's about feeling. You can learn that later. Become the music. You are the music." He moved his shoulders to the beat and did a two-step movement. He bobbed his head back and forth. Stepping from side to side.

Dustin's face dropped, and he quickly sat back down on the floor.

"That's how it's done. And you have to execute it by next week." He shook his head disapprovingly, as if we had had more time to prepare for this. "Vince, you're up next." I glimpsed around the room, forgetting that I was Vince for a minute.

I could do this. I already performed as Vince in front of many people. Now, I was really Vince. I had the tattoos. I was working out. It was official.

"Yes, you. You're named 'Vince.'" He used finger quotes. "We don't have all day!" he yelled.

I got up, picked up the guitar, and took my place on stage. My palms were sweating and my vision became a little blurry. *Why was I so nervous about a mock performance?* As soon as the drums kicked in, I felt at ease. I threw my head back and moved to the beat. I air guitar to the rhythm perfectly and began shuffling my feet. My eyes were closed with my head tilted back. I was becoming the music. When I finished my performance, everyone was silent, including the instructor. He slowly clapped his hands.

Was this good or bad?

"Finally, someone who puts in some effort," he said sarcastically. "Better, but it still needs some work."

I took a deep sigh of relief. At least he wasn't that hard on me. *Maybe I could go through this process. If I was good at something, I should keep doing it, right?*

The rest of the day continued. Each class was just as intense as the first one. Instructors with harsh criticism, meeting new doppelgängers, who were mostly B-list or C-list stars, and guards watching us and leading us from one room to another like cattle. It was starting to become tiring and overwhelming. At least the classes were more interesting than regular school.

Throughout the day, I had so many new questions, but still no answers. *Was Mila right? What were Jeff and the agency's true intentions? If I did get paid, would the money be worth it? I wondered if my friends and family were worried about me. Were our families looking for us? I would give anything to be back home with them, but we would be out of here in no time.*

The guards herded us back into the cafeteria for dinner. I sat next to Mila again. She appeared different; her long hair was no longer in a ponytail and was shoulder length. She wore a pair of leggings, a t-shirt, and sneakers. *Had she been working out, too? Mila was a dancer.*

The cafeteria was mostly quiet. Everyone seemed on edge, and they didn't want to say or do the wrong things. People sat with their heads down, avoiding eye contact. Whispers and murmurs were here and there, but the most audible sounds were forks scraping plates and the chomping of food.

I looked around the room, then leaned my head closer to Mila. "So, how was your day?" I spoke softly, trying to keep my mouth closed.

"I guess it was good, considering the circumstances." Her green eyes were puffy.

"Where's Omar?" I glanced toward where he was seated the other day.

"I don't know. He might be on punishment or something. The plan is still going on tonight after dinner."

The plan. I shuddered. *I hope it went smoothly. I was ready to go back home, but where was Omar. This could horrible without him. What if he doesn't go through with the plan? If we got caught, what would happen?*

Mila picked up a bread roll and discreetly stuffed it into her jacket pocket. "I've already been stocking up." She grabbed more food.

This was crazy. Even if we did escape, where would we go? And that little amount of food won't help us much. It was pointless to escape, but I also didn't see a point in staying here and being Vince. Would Jeff still pay me?

The rest of dinner was silent, but I was used to it. I've had many silent dinners with my aunt and uncle due to my bad grades or behavior over the years. Dinner concluded, and we were escorted back to the hallway. As soon as I walked near my room, a loud shriek erupted from down the hall. It was Omar. Multiple guards flocked to his room. My heart pumped rapidly.

Mila ripped her arm away from the guard holding her. She glanced at me for a second. I felt so scared, but the adrenaline hit my body, causing me to sprint behind her. The security seemed alarmed and caught off guard. They began bustling behind us.

I didn't even know what the plan was exactly. Did she know what to do?

"Come on." Mila waved me into the elevator.

A guard was right behind me. I slipped through just before he could grab me. An alarm sounded off, and guards were talking to each other on walkie-talkies. She pulled out a keycard and hit the basement floor.

How did she manage to get that? I was sure she would have gotten caught. I stared at myself in the reflection of the glass windows. *Woah, I looked even more like Vince. Did I slim down already?* I looked down at my stomach. The elevator sped to the lower floors. The blurry green grass became clearer. The elevator dimmed as we made it to the basement floor.

"Don't worry. As soon as the door opens, just make a run for it. There's an exit nearby," she told me while grabbing on the railing and leaning forward.

The elevator beeped, and the doors opened. Mila's black hair flowed as she sprinted out of the elevator. I followed her. The basement was damp and smelled like mildew. It was pretty dark, besides a few floodlights that lit up the hall. We ran straight down the hall. Footsteps thumped behind us. My legs ached as I ran as fast as I could.

We could make it. As soon as that thought came into my head, a guard swooped in from the right and tackled me. I wiggled, trying to break free. He gripped me tighter. I thrusted my right arm out from underneath him and elbowed him sharply in the face. Blood sprayed out of his nose. He grunted in pain. I continued to run down the hall as Mila kicked a guard near her in the shin, causing him to drop to his knees.

"Almost there, Leon!" she huffed.

An intercom speaker came on. "Mila and Vince, please don't resist. There's no way out of here."

Mila and I tilted our heads up for a brief moment to see where the noise was coming from.

It was a woman's voice that I had never heard before. *Was she in charge of this place?*

Mila kept running and easily dodged the guards. *It was like she had done this before. Why was she so good at fighting them off?* The blaring of the alarm rang in my ears as we made our way closer to the end of the hall.

Mila pointed to a large metal door. "Here it is." She typed in a code.

Omar must of given her the code. I thought she had only been here a little longer than me. The door croaked as it popped open.

"Let's go." She waved her fingers.

Brisk air flowed in. The sound of birds chirping announced our freedom. Footsteps behind us broke the immersion. As we ran out the door, a security guard grabbed me. He slammed me against the wall and placed his hand around my throat. Mila turned around. As she ran over to help me, more footsteps were behind. A group of guards materialized before our eyes.

"Go, we're outnumbered. They will get both of us," my voice choked out.

"I'll see you!" She glanced back, then sprinted toward the unknown terrain.

"Get her!" a group of men shouted.

They burst through the door after her. *She probably won't make it far. I might see her again tomorrow; hopefully.* The guard slammed me against the wall again. I became winded, barely being able to breathe. He placed handcuffs on me.

"Don't move anymore." He grabbed me by the back of my hair and dragged me.

We went down the hall back to the elevator. He pressed a button that took us below the basement. We stepped off onto a floor that was even darker and muggier than the one before. The dim lights buzzed and flickered. We passed by rusty brown iron-barred cells.

My body quivered at the thought of being locked up and more isolated than before. *Where was he taking me? I thought we were already on the lowest floor.* He threw me into a cell. There was a dingy mattress, an old TV wired on the wall, and a rusty toilet. Tears formed in my eyes. I leaned against the cement walls. The coolness of the walls felt good to my warm, sweaty body.

Could this experience get worse? Why did I involve myself with Mila and her plan? I crumbled into the thin mattress and tried to sleep. I kept hearing footsteps, coughing, and iron doors sliding open. Maybe I wasn't the only one down here. *Was this where they took us for misbehaving? Was Omar or Mila here with me?*

◉

The room was still dark. *Was it morning now? There was no way to tell. The TV didn't turn on like it did in the other room.* The door cranked open and the rustling of the bars alarmed me. I saw the woman from the orientation, Jeffrey, and a guard.

"Rise and shine," the woman said sarcastically. "Can't believe you and Mila pulled that stunt yesterday. Don't do it again."

"Mila . . . is she okay?" I mumbled.

The three of them paused for a moment.

"She will be," the woman said, but I didn't feel reassured about it.

They took me out of the cell in handcuffs once again. *I wondered what I looked like right now. If it was anything like how I felt, then I knew I looked horrible.*

Back in the elevator and up to the upper level of the floor we went. They pushed me into a classroom, and the woman stepped inside too.

"Behave for my class. Don't want another merit, do you?" Her shoes clicked against the tiles.

The class filled up with no sight of Mila or Omar.

Days passed, but it felt like I'd been here for months. More mock interviews, press junkets, fan Q&As, and red carpet events. Every morning, I woke up to a long grueling workout and weigh-in. Over time, I grew endurance, and the workouts became a little easier. But there still was no Mila or Omar. I wondered if they were locked up in the basement, or if they ever had been. I questioned whether or not I should try and look for them, but was afraid of getting caught. I had to make it out of this program.

One morning, the TV flickered on. "Today is the last day, students. All of you have done great and we wish you well on your new journey."

I rolled my eyes. At least I could get out of here. The door opened, and it was Jeff and more guards.

"Time to go back home. Or to your new home, as I like to call it." Jeff and I were soon back in another black SUV.

"So, when will I get my first check?" I asked.

"Soon. Stop asking." He flashed me a toothy smile.

I sighed and sunk into the seat. We drove for what seemed like forever, only seeing shades of green and blue.

REUNITED

8

HOURS LATER, the colors began to change. We drove into a cityscape. It looked like I was even farther away from home. Cars zoomed in and out of lanes, horns blared, and pedestrians crossed the street. I have never been to a city this big and lively. Jeff and I pulled up to a hotel. *Was this another place for me to stay captive in, or was this for a show or something?* We went inside the garage and into an elevator. The lobby of the hotel was nothing extravagant or special. It was nice, but I expected it to be more luxurious. The floors were white tiled. A few guests lounged at tables.

"The rest of the band will be here," Jeff told me as we walked into the lobby. The staff greeted us. They looked delighted to see us. It was clear that they recognized us, but they didn't mention it.

"Oh my gawd, it's Vince!" a group of teenage girls flew over and began to swarm me.

"Take a picture with me!"

"I can't wait to post this online," one cried.

Another latched her arms around me, snapping photos. This

was already overwhelming. *They didn't even ask.* I looked to Jeff for comfort, but he just grinned.

After being mobbed by the fans, we entered the penthouse suite floor. Jeff unlocked the door with a keycard, and we entered the luxury suite. It had a full-sized kitchen, bar, and lounge area. In the kitchen, there was every type of breakfast food known on the planet. Pancakes, eggs, bacon, and so much more. *The room was nicer than I expected, considering how the lobby looked.*

I sat next to Jamie, who did not stop eating to acknowledge me entering the room. Porter sat on the couch near the kitchen. He was preoccupied with the TV. I helped myself to the food on the table. I felt more relaxed here. No more being held captive. I was now going to live a life of ease and luxury. I didn't deserve it, though. I didn't work hard like Vince to earn this. As soon as I took a bite of eggs, Jeff followed me into the kitchen.

"Don't want to gain any more weight after all that hard work." He patted my stomach.

I grimaced at the thought of the grueling workout and having to keep it up. *Come on, I wasn'tt even eating that much.*

"Hey Vince, how was everything? Feeling better, I see."

Jamie finally acknowledged me. Oh God, what should I say? Vince has a slight southern accent. I can't forget that. They'll know I'm not him if I don't speak like him.

"Okay, get a move on, kids." Jeff clapped his hands loudly. *Good thing I didn't have to answer.* "We are already running late for the rally. Then we have a fundraiser to go to."

"What rally?" I nearly spat out my food.

"The rally for Mikko . . . " Jamie stopped eating for a second.

I shrugged my shoulders.

"The candidate for the mayoral election," Porter said. He had a look of puzzlement too.

I needed to focus more on acting like Vince. If he was confused, I could blame it on being sick. But who was Mikko? Was it Mikko, the pop singer? He sounded familiar. I think I heard a few of his songs. Why would he go into politics?

"Here is the speech for the leading man." Jeff handed me a few index cards. "Memorize this. It's not a lot."

"You weren't going to tell me about this last night or on the way here?" I asked. I swiped the cards from him. *Did he always do things like this last minute? Was he a bad manager?*

"We were so busy." He walked away toward Audrey's room and started to bang on the door.

"Get up, Audrey!"

"Ughh!" she hollered.

Audrey waltzed into the kitchen with a fluffy pink robe, slippers, bed head, and puffy eyes a few minutes later.

Wow, she looked completely different without all the makeup she wore. I mean, not bad, just different. I gazed at her in disbelief for a few seconds; Audrey's eyes caught mine.

"What, never seen a girl before?" she asked, agitated, and pulled her robe closer to her body.

"No, you just look different," I said. The guys snickered.

"Guys are just so stupid. Do you think girls' eyelids, lips, and faces are magically colored?" She grabbed a plate from a nearby counter.

"Okay!" Jeff clasped his hands together. "Be in the lobby in ten."

"In ten!?" Audrey shook her head.

Everyone finally made it to the lobby, but not in ten minutes more like thirty. And surprisingly, Audrey was not the last one to get ready. While sitting in the lobby, a couple of squeals erupted from the entrance. *Once again, where was Jeff? He rushed us to get ready, and he was not here himself.*

"It's Retro. They're sitting right there!" A group of girls howled.

"Vince is so cute." A girl rushed over with her phone. *Not again.*

"Selfie!" another announced. The lights flashed on my face, and I squinted my eyes.

"Sign this." Another girl handed Jamie and me a picture of the band. "Yeah, I can't believe we just bumped into you guys."

I rolled my eyes. I wanted to say, *Really? You carry that picture of the band in your purse all the time?*

A few minutes later, Jeff came into the lobby. *He should have been here before us.* I shook my head. This whole situation was a mess. *Maybe he was just running a little late. No need to be alarmed.* It was hard for me to imagine Jeff working for MUSE agency. Most of the employees seemed more organized and put together. Every single day that I was there, it was managed like clockwork.

"Sorry to interrupt, girls, but we have to go." He moved his thumb in the other direction.

"Aww!" they whined in unison.

We followed Jeff to a raggedy van. It was a faded blue with the paint chipped off it. The van smelled like rancid food. This reminded me of my old car. *My reason for doing this,* I reminded myself.

"The destination is only a few minutes away. So we won't be that late," he reassured the group.

Everyone was chatting away. Porter and Jamie sat behind me, chuckling, while Audrey's attention was glued to her phone. I could tell Porter and Jamie were close. They were talking non-stop. I bet they had so many great stories and jokes from traveling on the road. It made me think about my friends. I rolled down the window to let the cool morning breeze hit my face. The van was warm; the AC must be broken. Porter stopped talking to Jamie.

"Come on, Vince . . . what's wrong? You still not feeling well?" Porter asked.

"Yeah, man. You're so quiet," Jamie said, wrinkling his brows.

"No, everything's cool. Just relaxing."

"Nervous about the speech?" Jamie asked me, while leaning against the seat in front of him.

The speech. I panicked and pulled the notecards out of my pockets. Audrey giggled and turned to Jamie.

"Calm down, Jamie. You're not the one giving the speech. You can save your Xans for later." She winked mockingly. Another low blow at Jamie and his addiction. *Did she even care?*

"Audrey!" Porter and Jeff scolded her.

"Well, it's your fault. You started it, Audrey." Jamie pinched his mouth.

My eyes started to widen with interest, but I regained my composure before anyone noticed. *Really? Audrey was the one to give Jamie Xanax? I didn't know any of this. It was hard to imagine them not getting along because of the various interviews Kim showed me. It was kind of of intriguing and entertaining to be part of the drama, but I had to act coy.*

"For the last time, I didn't make you do anything. It's not like I shoved it down your throat." She folded her arms and stared out the window.

I shook my head and went back to studying the index cards.

"Out loud," Audrey's voice rose playfully.

I began to speak, but I was cut off quickly.

"Sound more confident," Porter told me.

"Yeah, like you mean it," Audrey teased.

I sighed deeply. "Y'all are lucky I'm even going through with this crap."

The other three stared blankly. *I should've kept my mouth shut. Why did I say that?*

"Don't be like that, man." Porter rested his head against the seat. "You got this. It can't be that hard."

"Just don't make us look bad," Audrey warned me.

"Audrey can do it, right?" I asked, folding up the note card.

"Just do what I tell you. You'll get paid this week." Jeff leaned back and whispered.

I highly doubt that. He had been dancing around the topic for a while now.

The rest of the ride, I tried to remember everything that was on the index card. *Ugh, I hated public speaking; I never was good at it. The bands comments of: Don't make us look bad. We're a close-knit group, blah, blah, weren't helpful.*

We arrived at the venue. It was a large beige brick building that read: City Hall. The parking lot was packed with a sea of people. People were holding blue and red signs that read: Elect Mikko Kouchi. They sported matching attire. The van pulled up into a parking garage. Two men dressed in button-down shirts opened the doors.

Hmm, one of the men looked familiar . . . It was the same guard at the concert hall. He must be a part of Retro's security crew.

"Let's get going," Jeff said.

We followed him into an elevator and were ambushed by a few fans when we entered the building. They screamed, recorded with their phones, and ran over to us. Security quickly diffused the situation by blocking a girl dashing toward Audrey. Another girl came toward Jamie, but a familiar security guard shoved her back. She fell face first on the tiled floor.

Was she okay? No one seemed to help her. I felt a little bad for her, even though she was getting too close to Jamie. I looked over my shoulder, and she got up and hurried to her feet. *At least she was alright.*

"I love you, Jamie!" she cried, tears filling her eyes.

Jamie smiled at her warmly and continued walking while Audrey stared at them blankly.

Wow, that was a little harsh. Did she even care about fans? Maybe they were used to this type of behavior. The guard took us to a small room.

"Oh, snacks!" Audrey excitedly ran to a table with little sandwiches on it and grabbed one immediately.

"Audrey, remember your diet. You only have 500 calories and

you already went over the limit at breakfast. No more for you." Jeff snatched the sandwich from her fingers.

"But I'm hungry," she pouted and whimpered like a toddler.

Why was he controlling what Audrey ate? Was he only doing this to me and her? What about Jamie? It was awful to see. Audrey wasn't the nicest person, but she didn't deserve that.

"Okay, guys, everyone get ready to perform. Vince, you got your speech ready?" Jeff asked.

A woman with short, dark hair entered the room. "You guys are going on in ten minutes."

Audrey, Jeff, and Porter looked enthusiastic, cool, calm, and collected. Of course, they were. I sighed; they've been through this before, and all of the stakes were on me. Jamie, on the other hand, seemed nervous like before.

Why couldn't someone else make the speech? Why were they even supporting Mikko? So many questions, and no one was willing to give answers.

"Don't be nervous. Just be yourself . . . Le-Vince," Audrey paused and thought about what to call me. The other two band-mates erupt with laughter.

"Shut up, you two." She furrowed her thin brows as she glared in their direction.

"Who's Leon?" I laughed playing along.

"It's so hot in here. The heat must be getting to me," Audrey said while she glared at me.

Man, the only positive thing out of this experience so far was no school. Now it seemed like I was right back there with a bunch of adolescents pretending.

Audrey and the boys were arguing about something else again.

Jeff stopped talking to the short-haired lady and tried to pull us back together. "Let's just focus on the task at hand. Vince, do you know the speech?"

"Yeah," I huffed.

"And don't worry, you guys are playing the same set we

been playing this tour" He smiled as if being happy fixed everything. Jeff's smile was like a band-aid; it made you feel better at first, then, when you ripped it off, it stung and reminded you of the pain.

"I only played through the set once," I mumbled under my breath.

"You did better than we expected. Plus, a backtrack is playing," Jeff said.

They didn't seem to get it.

I should just leave right now; it's not like they are threatening me. I was out in the real world now, not at the agency where I was being watched closely. There were security guards, but they seemed more concerned with keeping fans from getting too close. I could make a run for it. *Should I?* I glanced at the door behind us. My gaze was caught by a husky security guard. I panicked and looked away. I bet if I ran they would catch me. Though, we were in public; they wouldn't tase me like they would back in the agency.

Running away was a bad idea. I shifted my focus back on what was happening.

The event manager lady popped back into the room. "Everyone ready?" Her laugh lines crinkled on her face.

I shuffled out of my seat and walked to the door.

"Cheer up. Be confident!" Audrey told me.

The two security guards and Jeff led us into a huge conference room. So many people were here. There were hundreds of them; people of all ages were in attendance. A few people in the audience cheered for our arrival. They howled and screamed as they held up their signs.

A woman stood on a stage. "Okay, we have a few words from lead singer Vince of Retro Brite!" she announced.

Jeff and the rest of the band were seated a few rows from the stage. I walked up smiling, but my hands were trembling. She handed me the mic. *I think I memorized everything.*

"Umm, hello! Good morning," the mic screamed as I spoke. I

stopped and glanced at Audrey, who was eyeing me intensely. "I'm here today to support Mikko. I know he is the change we need to see in this city. I know he won't stop until every citizen receives what they deserve. Until everyone is able to get the education, jobs, and health care that is needed. Mikko is an artist with a unique vision that can help this city tremendously. Thank you!" I exhaled loudly.

I was glad that was finally over. I saw Audrey and the others applauding, so I must've done okay. I sat back down next to Audrey.

"Not bad; you're getting the hang of it," Audrey whispered.

Mikko took the stage. He was wearing a sequined button-down shirt and black pants. I couldn't believe he really was campaigning for mayor. He was way too young and was only using this opportunity to propel his career.

"Hey, everybody, it's an honor to have all of you here. And my favorite band and supporters." He waved at us. I cringed. *We're his favorite of all the musicians and bigger groups?*

"I promise to do my best. This city needs a strong leader, and I believe I can make that happen." Everyone clapped at his weak speech like he just said something outstanding.

After a few more speakers, we got on stage to perform our set. I didn't recognize any of the speakers. They were probably locals. Everything went well, though. I guess those stupid training sessions really paid off. *I was starting to get the hang of it, and I felt like a real performer.*

After the event, we exited the building and hung out outside, where people were gathering around, talking, and there were some tables with snack foods.

"That was great. Everyone, keep it up!" Jeff told us. "Now, it's time to mingle." He danced playfully.

Great, now I was stuck going to a party with a bunch of rich people I couldn't relate to. Audrey, being a social butterfly, was grouped up with a couple of girls.

I walked over to the snack bar and began to munch. Jamie followed me while Porter mingled.

"We are not party animals like them." I pointed to Audrey and Porter.

He nodded his head in agreement. "Yep. Audrey's the life of the party." He grabbed a drink from the table.

"Do you think Audrey's been acting different lately?" I tilted my head.

"Well, a little. You two have been arguing more than usual. She's probably just stressed," he spoke in between sipping his drink.

"Yeah." I nodded. I wondered what their arguments were about. *Was it petty drama like in the file I read about?*

"But unfortunately, we're contracted for three more albums. Remember when they told Audrey about the contract and she was so pissed? I don't know why she's worried; she's the star of the show, and we are replaceable."

My heart jolted at the mention of us being replaceable. *Wow, this was crazy. He really doesn't have an idea of what's going on. He had to know. If so, why did Porter and him act so unfazed?*

I nodded my head, taking in the new information that was just spilled. Jamie took out a cigarette and began to fumble around in his pockets.

"Give me a light." He held the cigarette out. *Did Vince smoke? I pretended to dig around in my pockets. I didn't remember that detail, but there was so much in his file.*

"Sorry, man. I don't have a light."

"I gotcha." A slim brunette walked over.

"Thanks, Mila! We can always count on you." Jamie held the cigarette up in appreciation.

Mila looked a little different than I remembered. *Was this her, or an understudy? If not, I was glad she was okay.*

"Of course." She glanced at me. "You look like you've seen a ghost." She giggled.

"Yeah, I'm still in a state of shock from Mikko's outfit," I joked.

"Same. I have something to tell you. Can we talk in private?"

"Awe, I can't be in on this?" Jamie poked his lip out.

"Nope, this is between besties," Mila sang.

She whisked me away from Jamie, and we went over to a secluded lounge table with a giant umbrella shielding us from the sun.

"Are you okay?" I asked.

"Yeah, it's me. A little traumatized, but okay." Her eyes widened. "We have to expose these people. We were so close last time. There are people that will believe us."

I sighed; not this again. Mila was a nice girl, but she needed to work on the execution of these plans.

"Like a conspiracy theorist?" I shrugged.

"Exactly; we just have to find them. After our last stunt, it's going to be much harder. Maybe I can take my agent's phone. She's always laying it around."

Right on cue, a woman with a curly afro ran toward us.

"Speaking of her." Mila threw a hand up.

"I've been looking all over for you. There's someone I want you to meet." Mila's agent looked at me. "Hi Vince, see you later at Mikko's party tonight." She took Mila away.

At this point, we were basically puppies on leashes, being guided and told where to go and how to act. Jeff quickly did the same and brought me back to my bandmates.

"Do I have to attend this party later tonight?" I looked at Jeff, hoping he would say no.

"Yes, we all do," Audrey answered before Jeff could say anything. "It's Mikko. An up-and-coming star. The party is going to be huge."

"I don't know. I might sit this one out," Jamie said.

"It's just a party, and I already hooked up your meds if you need it."

"Leave Jamie alone. It isn't funny. And it's just a party," I spat back at her.

I was aggravated, and I also didn't want to go to this party. If it's just a personal party, and not for an event, I just wanted to sleep. I was exhausted.

She looked surprised and appalled. I've had enough of her bullying and making fun of Jamie. It was tiring to see her pick on him and I was surprised Jeff or Porter didn't say anything. I recalled Kim telling me about how Jamie's been struggling with anxiety ever since the band blew up and their work schedule has been crazy.

"It's not just any party. Do you think I like coming here with these fools?" She motioned toward the sea of people. "It's called networking. You may be the frontman, but I'm who everyone remembers when the lights turn off. I'm the one transitioning from music to film and to fashion. You guys don't have the range like me."

"You make everything about you. We're a group!" Porter yelled back.

"Exactly why we should all go." She turned around to walk away.

"Guys, calm down. We can figure this out after the fundraiser. Let's go. You're making a scene." Jeff finally intervened.

A few attendees were now looking in our direction. They're probably wondering what all the fuss was about.

"You guys need to keep it together. Especially in the public eye. PR is going to have a field day with us if you don't simmer down," Jeff snapped. His friendly face was cold.

I kind of felt bad for Jamie and Porter. It seemed like they had to deal with Jeff and Audrey's crazy behavior on a daily. From the outside looking in, Retro seemed like a tight-knit group of friends, but I guess every group of friends had arguments and falling outs. I could say the same for my group. Kim and Landon have gotten into intense fights where they stopped talking for weeks. Over the years, my friend group has gotten smaller. I supposed people outgrow each other and change. Maybe that was happening with Retro Brite.

"Tell that to Miss Audrey," Porter said. "You didn't use to be this way. You changed, Aud."

Could they stop arguing? I suspired loudly.

"I didn't change. But what needs to change is your attitude," she snarked back.

Jeff intervened another time. Jeff couldn't control their behavior. *Maybe he wasn't as scary and threatening as he puts on. Or he was keeping face in public and I haven't seen his wrath.*

As the day went by, Audrey's facade of being kind and beautiful started to vanish. After a brief argument, a much-needed moment of silence, we filled the van.

"So, who's ready for the fundraiser?" Jeff's voice went up a few octaves. He really was asking like a few minutes ago we weren't trying to bite each other's heads off.

"Sure, what's it about?" Porter asked.

"I briefed you guys about this a few weeks ago." Jeff shook his head. "Audrey, do you remember?"

"I don't know . . . something about kids . . . hurricane relief. Whatever it is, it makes me look good."

At this point, the rest of the group was over her antics and ignored her.

"No, it's for helping endangered species." Jeff sighed deeply. "You guys need to pay attention to me more." He shook his head.

"Oh, I love animals!" Jamie cooed.

"It's a photoshoot campaign," Jeff added in.

"After this photo shoot, we're free for the rest of the day!" Porter threw his hands in the air.

"We are going to Mikko's party and partying like real rock stars. Remember!" Audrey shrieked and made the rock symbol with her hand.

"You know it." Porter smirked, placing his leg on the back of Audrey's seat.

This was going to be exhausting. I sighed, burying my head into the headrest and zoned out. The sun grazed over my face.

Jamie looked nervous once more and sunk down into his seat.

The van grew quiet. The only thing audible was the humming of the air conditioner. A ringing noise emitted through the van speakers. Jeff hit a button on the steering wheel, answering the call.

"Hello," a harsh voice said through the speaker. "Jeffrey, I've been trying to contact you for a few days now."

Jeff groaned. "Sorry, I've been busy—" he started.

"Too busy for your own mother?" she scoffed. "You know our annual gala is around the corner and the whole family will be in attendance," she said. Her harsh voice was now smooth.

"Mom, I'm busy!" Jeff shouted. I chuckled to myself as Jeff spoke with his mother. It was funny to see his mother nag him. It made him appear even less threatening.

"We're all busy, Jeffrey, but we put things to the side. Your brother is already running the firm. And you choose MUSE over us."

I wondered what type of business his family had. *Did Jeff ever want to run it himself, but his parents thought his brother would be better at it?*

"I'll see what I can do." Jeff hung up and turned the radio on. He didn't say anything to us and we also kept quiet.

Suddenly, Audrey looked up from her phone. "Hey, Jeff, do you still have Vince's phone? I'm tired of being the only one to interact with fans," Audrey asked Jeff in a whisper.

Why would they trust me with a phone? I could call the cops immediately. Dude, I wondered how many celebrity contacts he had.

Jeff shuffled through the pockets of his baggy pants. He pulled out the latest model smartphone and handed it to me.

Was this really his phone? Why would Jeff have it? Was it taken when Vince was at the hospital? Was it his original phone or a new one with the same data? I wondered how many messages I-he missed. Would I even know how to work this? My phone was very old and raggedy. Where was Vince?

"Don't get carried away. I can see everything you're up to. And I will limit your privileges." Jeff gave me a stern look.

Really? He bugged the phone? Why even bother giving it to me? Why can't someone from our team take care of my social media accounts? Wow, a dozen missed calls and hundreds of online notifications. Some calls from his parents and a couple of friends.

"Now that you have your phone back, I need you to interact with the fans," Jeff said as he took his hands off the wheel for a second.

"Why do I have to do it?" I asked, scratching my head.

"Because—" Jeff began. He glared at me in the rearview mirror.

"Fine, I'll do it," I muttered. "Let me make a warble message."

The account logged in automatically. Warble was a popular social media app like Sonder. Many people posted about their day and joked around on it, some have even become internet famous on the app.

I warbled:

> On our way to a photo shoot, I can't wait for you guys to see it!

I started going through his contacts. *Cool, he had a text from Arin from Painted Dog and a few C-list actors.*

"Having fun, nosey?" Audrey whispered discreetly to not alarm Jamie or Porter.

"Yeah . . . I guess this is sort of cool."

"We will be there shortly," Jeff announced.

Five minutes later, we pulled into a parking garage.

"So, what kind of animals will be here?" I raised an eyebrow in Jeff's direction.

"I don't know. I just know they're endangered. Just go with it; you're natural by now." He dismissed my concerns.

"Who cares!" Audrey said, throwing her arms in the air. Audrey was good at putting on a façade in front of everyone.

I sighed. *I guess that one semester of drama class really paid off.* We entered the facility, and a woman greeted us.

"Welcome, Retro Brite." She clapped her hands. "I'm Stacy. Follow me to the dressing rooms. The makeup artist will be with you in a few minutes."

We smiled and followed Stacy's direction. As soon as she left the room, Audrey's smile evaporated.

This was cool. We could hear a soft hooting noise. *I wonder what animal was that?*

"Uhhh, I hope we can get this shoot over. I don't want animals crawling all over me." She shuddered.

"Then why would we agree to do this?" I extended my arms. She shot me a glare.

"Aud, calm down." Porter tried to instruct her.

"You guys always gang up on me," she said. They argued for a few minutes. Porter said that Audrey complained too much, and she made everything difficult. *He wasn't lying.*

"We do what we're told, Vince," Jamie's soft voice cut through the bickering.

"That makes no sense . . . we should be able to speak your mind."

Porter shook his head and exhaled for a minute.

"You should know the ropes by now." Audrey smacked her lips.

I was so confused. I could understand not wanting to support Mikko, but wasn't this photo shoot a good thing?

Three women and a man entered the room and introduced themselves. We got ushered over to makeup stations. I tried to break right and sit next to Porter, but Jamie interceded and plopped down next to him. Now I had a front-row seat to hear her complain. I attempted to tune out Audrey but the whole time all I heard was, "Ouch," "I don't like that," and "Are we almost done?"

After a long, grueling hour and a half, we were ready for the shoot. The four of us stepped onto a lush green set decorated with trees, shrubbery, and four wooden chairs placed in the middle. The photographer walked in. He was a bearded, medium statured man.

"Hi, I'm Francis, the photographer," he said with a thick, indistinguishable accent. We assumed the position in the chairs. "Bring out the animals," he said.

A zookeeper stepped out. "Keep your voices down and don't make any sudden movements," they explained.

I was now getting a little nervous. These were wild animals that could potentially harm us. Audrey sighed. She wanted to be done with the shoot.

They placed an orangutan on Audrey. It became acquainted and wrapped its arms around her neck. Audrey jerked in fear.

I snickered, but regained my composure. *It would be hilarious if this orangutan ripped her face off. But I could understand her fear. Thank God, I wasn't holding it.* In Crestview, there wasn't a zoo. So being this close to animals was new and frightening to me.

"Keep calm," the animal keeper told her.

"Okay, look straight into the camera, look caring and heart-felt," Francis bellowed. "Save the animals. The rainforest," he continued.

I guess all was going well until . . .

"Eeek! She peed on me." Audrey tossed the orangutan to the ground. I jumped back. The animal trainer swooped up the orangutan before it reacted, and Audrey ran off.

Jamie darted behind to consult her.

Wow, could anything go right?

"Shake it off." Francis started to shimmy. "We don't need them; the real stars are here." He pointed at me and Porter. *Was he saying we're better than Jamie and Audrey? She would freak out more if she heard that. I thought Audrey was the darling in the group.*

Another trainer then brought out a tortoise and sat it in front of us.

Porter and I finished up the remainder of the shoot. We proceeded back to the dressing room and saw a frowning Audrey and an annoyed Jeff. He was scolding her.

"You looked so unprofessional. This was a big opportunity for the group."

"Who cares about these animals?" she snorted.

Why did they even deal with her? I shook my head. Audrey was very talented, but there were other people just as talented as she was. Porter and I walked over.

"Don't worry about her. You know she just hates this type of stuff." Jamie chuckled.

What doesn't she hate?

"Yeah, dude, we're going out tonight. Don't worry about her." Porter patted my back.

"Yeah!" I said with fake enthusiasm. This could be fun, but with this group, there was no telling what could go wrong.

Back at the hotel, Audrey was on video calls with her friends, coordinating her outfit, while Jamie was talking about not going and Porter was convincing him to go. Afterward, we all got ready. I came into the living room where Audrey was dressed in a tight fitting jumpsuit.

"That's what you're wearing? Umm . . . it will have to do." She scrunched up her face. Her voice was flat and dry.

There was nothing wrong with a simple pair of jeans and a t-shirt. I was not changing.

"I already called our ride." She left the hotel room without waiting for anyone else.

Jeff pulled me to the side and leaned close to me. "Have fun tonight, but not too much. Don't do anything drastic. Blend in."

"I'll try not to cause a scene." I rolled my eyes and crinkled my lips.

"No, listen. You want your money, don't you?" he spoke slowly.

"Yeah—"

"Don't want to go back to that dark cell, do ya?" He rubbed my back.

I shook at the thought of going back to the agency and that dark room.

"I'll behave, I promise." I nodded.

The thought of going back to the cell was unsettling. My stomach twisted in knots thinking about it.

THE PARTY

9

A BLACK LUXURY SUV pulled up. This was absolutely better than that ragged old van. The driver welcomed us as we took our seats. Once again, Jamie and Porter were together in the back, and Audrey and I were near the front. I was a little glad I got a break from Jeffrey, but I think Audrey might be worse. I was pretty sure she would make a good substitute.

The SUV weaved in and out of traffic, and cars honked left and right. We arrived at a large, gated mansion, surrounded by vibrant green hedges. There were cars parked in a cul-de-sac driveway. The party was already in full effect. I could hear loud rap music playing while we were still in the car. Audrey reached out the window and pressed a buzzer at the gate.

Mikko answered, "Hey, I was waiting for you guys. Thought you wouldn't make it." His voice was muffled by the music.

"Wouldn't want to miss it!" Audrey yelped.

When we walked toward the mansion, I stepped onto the soft cushy carpet-like grass. I was in awe of how manicured the yard was compared to mine at home. This was what luxury felt like.

I would never experience something like this in Crestview.

Audrey took the lead up to the door and rung the doorbell.

A tall blonde girl opened the door and squealed. "It's been a minute. Glad to see you!" She hugged Audrey tightly.

The girl gave us a small wave. She let us in and showed us the living room. The house was crowded with people dancing, drinking, and gossiping. There were at least 50 people just in the living room. The guests at the party might've been some well-known models or actors, but as I quickly scanned the room, no one jogged my memory. A dance track started to play. The music was deafening; the bass boomed in my chest. Everyone started howling and dancing more energetically. We walked to the center of the living room, and it started to reek of liquor and smoke. The living room decor had a medieval vibe; the walls were a dark hunter green and gothic-styled scones hung on the wall, giving the room a dim ambiance. Classical paintings surrounded us. The people in the paintings were either engaged in battle or were eating and drinking. The wooden furniture seemed old and had flowery designs cut into it.

This place was massive; it had to be at least a $1 million. I was curious how many rooms there were. This was probably my first of many mansion parties.

"I'll be here with Asha and Mikko," Audrey said, breaking my concentration. "Have fun and don't embarrass me." She left us like a parent dropping off their kids.

I wondered if she ever hung out with Jamie or Porter. Not that I was complaining about her absence. I hung my head low and jammed my hands into my pockets while leaning against the wall.

"Cheer up! At least Jeffrey won't be here. It't not a fancy event, you can relax!" Porter yelled over the music. "Come on, man. Let's dance." Porter moved closer to a crowd of people dancing, and danced along to the techno pop track.

Jamie shook his head and walked away.

"Come on, Audrey's not here to make fun of our terrible dance moves," Porter said. "Loosen up. Here, let me get you a drink," he continued. He was shuffling his feet and moving in circles, dancing his way to a nearby bartender stand and grabbed a shot.

Jamie followed us to the bar and gulped back the shot within milliseconds.

How old were the band members? I couldn't recall if they could legally drink. I just know that I was a little younger than Vince.

"One for you, too, Vince. It's a party!" Porter cheered.

I usually didn't drink, but after all the crazy things that had been happening, I could really use one. I just had to get over my PTSD of the last time I had drinks, and the memory of how Aunt Mel wasn't too happy. I took the shot. It went down smoothly and didn't burn my throat, unlike the cheap liquor I had before. A warm sensation tingled throughout my body. Jamie threw his head back and rolled his shoulders; he was already more relaxed. He started to dance with Porter, and a random girl came over to them and danced with the group.

Good, now that they were occupied, I could see if Mila was here.

"I'll be back, guys. Just gonna have a look around."

"Come back for more shots!" Jamie yelled back.

I scanned the large living room again. No sight of Mila. I went into the next room over, which was the kitchen. I saw Audrey, Mila, and the blonde girl, Asha, talking.

Did Audrey know Mila was a replacement like me? My heart pumped. *Had Audrey spoken to the real Mila. Was she okay?*

Audrey had to know we were from the agency. Jeff probably filled her in on everything. I wondered who this blonde girl was. She might be a Warbler or some other social media influencer.

"Hey girls, what's going on?" My hands fidgeted in my pocket. *I didn't want to be at this party, and I definitely didn't want to upset Audrey or Jeff.*

"Nothing, just scoping out the party. Chatting." Audrey looked unenthused to see me again. "Come on, Asha. Mikko has to show us something." She grasped Asha's hand.

"I haven't had the chance to meet him yet." Mila walked in the direction of the other girls but was promptly stopped.

"Oh, it's a secret project he's been working on. I'll let you know when we're finished," Audrey grumbled before leaving.

I waited for the girls to be out of earshot. "So, what did you guys talk about, and who was that blonde girl?" I asked Mila. Or who I thought was the one from the agency.

She looked and spoke like the one from the agency. I didn't know much about the real Mila, so I had nothing to compare them. I hoped it was her.

"Um, hello to you too," she chuckled. "Just boring stuff, the party, Asha's life. She's a kid of a celebrity. She's not really an actor, singer, or anything."

"Little Miss Nepotism." I laughed.

"Basically." Mila took a sip of a drink.

I followed Mila back into the living room.

"Let's go upstairs and see if we can find anything interesting," Mila suggested.

"Why? Jeff told me to keep a low profile." I leaned in closer to her.

"We're just looking around. Nothing to worry about. There's so many people here, we'll blend in."

Was she serious? Even though it was risky to sneak around, I was curious to snoop. I wanted to see every crevice of this mansion; to get a feel of what it was like to be rich.

We walked past the living room area and found a set of stairs. She sprinted up them, and I followed slowly behind. A couple of people were leaning against the railing above. We went behind them and quickly ducked into one of the rooms. It was a bedroom; not sure if it belonged to Mikko, but it seemed so. The room was kitschy, with a bunch of different knickknacks. License plates from various states hung on the wall. A dancing hula girl bobblehead sat on a bookshelf. The stuff reminded me of the types of things that were sold at Borrowers. *Aww, back when things were more simple.* A black and white cat clock swayed its tail and rolled its eyes back and forth. *I had only seen those clocks on TV before.* Its tail and eyes were now moving in tandem to the beat of the music. The more I focused on its large eyes watching me, the more I felt bad for snooping. I felt like the cat was going to out us as imposters.

"Look at all these clothes!" Mila rummaged through the walk-in closet.

Tons of bomber jackets, jeans, colorful prints, and a couple of designer clothing. His style was all over the place. I left the closet and looked at his bookcase. Interesting reads like: *How To Get What You Want: The Guide To Being Charismatic, Dark Magic,* and many other strange and narcissistic titles. Well, at least the majority of the books still had bookmarks in them or looked pretty much untouched.

Mila walked out of the closet and opened up a nightstand. "Jackpot!" She pulled out a joint, and a lighter, and lit it.

"Put that back. We need to be more stealth," I cautioned her.

She shook her head in disapproval and passed me the joint. "It's okay. Here."

As I inhaled and exhaled, it felt like a weight had been lifted off me. Like I wasn't a doppelgänger replacement at some strange party with someone I barely knew. It felt like I was back home with my friends hanging out. I wasn't opposed to smoking marijuana. My friends and I smoked on occasion.

"Look at this strange literature." I held up an occult book.

Her eyes widened, and she snatched the book out of my hand. "None of this is real. Magic?" she tutted. She leafed through the book. "Love spell. Charismatic spell. Take the blood of a sacrifice—" she stopped and laughed at my widening eyes.

"I don't believe in this stuff," Mila informed. "But it doesn't seem bad, just stuff about candles and chants." She passed the joint back to me. "But the rumors are pretty common in this business, right? I've heard of some people using spells to attract lovers, fortune, good looks, and charisma," she said, her jade eyes looked into mine.

"Really?" I shrugged. *What was she even talking about? She must've heard about that on some sketchy blog.*

"What's going on here, kids? Are you stealing?" a slurred voice bellowed, barging into the room. Jamie was drunk.

"They stealing!" he turned around, yelling down the stair railing.

"What!?" I heard a voice say.

Mila and I scrambled to put everything back into place. "Jamie, no one is stealing! Just looking around a little. Be quiet," Mila shushed him.

"Okay, try this. It's goood!" he cheesed, pushing a red plastic cup toward my face.

"No, I'm good." He shoved the drink at me again, causing it to spill on me a little. "Okay, okay," I obliged and took a few sips of the drink. *At least, it was good.*

Jamie stumbled out to the balcony again. "Hey, guys! I'm Jamie from R-Retro Brite. I hate this band. Don't listen to our music!"

People took out their phones, recording Jamie's outburst. Jeff was going to be furious. *What would he do to Jamie? Maybe Jeff would just give him a warning like he's been giving me.* I guessed this wasn't the first time he had too much to drink. *What should I do?*

"Oh, and Audrey? She's the worst control freak ever. So fake too."

Mila grabbed Jamie to stop him, but he continued to rant.

"Stop it!" I shouted.

"This night is the best!" he yelled.

Porter ran up the stairs and grabbed Jamie. Someone else stomped up the stairs behind him; a short guy dressed in skater clothes.

"W-were you guys really stealing?" the guy asked. He was standing close to my face. His breath had a strong liquor smell.

"No, we weren't, just looking around," Mila retorted.

"God, I told Mikko to hire more security." He rubbed his temples. "Jamie, you need to watch your mouth," the guy said.

"Look, he doesn't know what's happening," Porter defended him as they walked off. Jamie had a dazed looked on his face.

"Well, let's see what Audrey thinks." The guy smirked, and he walked down the staircase.

"Where are you going?" I questioned. Mila and I chased after him. "Jamie didn't mean anything. Look at him; he is clearly drunk," I tried to reason.

"Well, let's say that to Audrey and Mikko's faces," he said.

"Who are you!?" Mila yelped at the guy.

"I could say the same to you guys. I'm a close friend of Mikko's. That's all you need to know."

Was he really a close friend? Or was he just saying that? If he recognized Jamie, why wouldn't he recognize Vince or Mila? He was probably lying about that, too.

He quickly pushed through the crowd, passing through the living room and kitchen. We passed a couple of other rooms and went down a narrow staircase.

Where was he taking us? I looked at Mila, and she shrugged her shoulders. A door was cracked on the basement level. We saw Audrey, Mikko, and that one girl from earlier . . . Asha, in the dimly lit room. They were chanting something, but it was stifled.

"What the hell is going on?" Mikko's friend looked shocked. His eyes were as wide as flying saucers.

"If you were a good friend, maybe they would have included you in this," Mila whispered aggressively.

He scowled at Mila.

What the hell was going on? Was I seeing what I thought I was seeing? I thought all of that stuff in that book was a lie. I should have learned to never be surprised by anything, but crazier things kept happening. Maybe it was some sort of play or game. I had a few drinks, but I'm not drunk enough to be buggin' out.

Asha lit a candle.

"Now time for the sacrifice," she said, passing a large goblet. Audrey grabbed the goblet. Mikko's 'friend' moved in closer to hear. He leaned forward against the door, causing it to creak. Their eyes darted up like missiles hitting a target.

Audrey's beautiful face distorted with anger. "What . . . get out of here!" she yelled.

"How did you get down here? Who left the door open?" Mikko slammed the door and locked it.

His friend started banging on the door. "They were trying to steal your stuff, man!" he continued to knock on the door, but to no avail, nobody answered.

Mila and I stood back from the door with our mouths agape and eyes widened.

"Oh, and Jamie was talking bad about you, Audrey!" He gave Mila and me a smug smile, knowing he would get a reaction out of Audrey.

The door flung open so fast, I thought the hinges broke. "What did he say?" She tapped her long talons against the door.

"Audrey, don't worry about them. We need to finish," Asha called her.

"Nope, I can't let this slide."

"He said you're a control freak brat. He told everyone," the guy said.

"He was drunk and didn't mean it," I countered.

"Did I ask you?" she spat at me. I'll be damned if some junkie embarrasses me and airs out my business." She charged out of the room as if it were on fire.

"You embarrass other people all the time!" I yelled.

She ignored me and marched up the stairs.

Mila, the random guy, and I followed Audrey back into the living room. Jamie and Porter were huddled with a group on a couch. Jamie was laying his head back into the cushion. Audrey snatched Jamie by the collar; he gasped.

"Look, I shouldn't have invited you here. When it comes to me, keep my name out of your mouth unless I prompt you. Jeff will hear about this!" Her face was red; spit flew from her mouth.

"What? Hey, Audrey. I haven't seen you all night," Jamie slurred.

"You still found the time to talk about me. You know what? "I'm calling you guys a ride. All of you." She eyed me, Mila, and Porter down. "I just wanted one night without you guys trying me."

"You made us come," I told her.

"Yeah, it was a mistake. You guys can't even act right at a small party. And award season is coming up. You're lucky Mikko isn't mad about you guys snooping around."

"What were you doing?" Mila asked.

"What were you guys doing?" Audrey lifted her brows and walked away. "The car will be here at 10."

I was glad we were leaving the party. However, I wondered what Jeff would think about what happened.

Would he punish us?

HOME SWEET HOME

10

"Wake up, Vince. We're going to be late."

"For what?" I mumbled, pulling the covers over my face.

"We have to catch a flight back home," Jeff said.

Why didn't Jeff mention this yesterday? He was literally the worst manager. I slowly rose from bed, like a zombie. My eyes were dark and puffy; my hair bunched up. I chugged a glass of water on the nightstand and proceeded to get ready.

Even though I was exhausted from the party last night, I still managed to be the first person dressed. I sat down in the living room to wait. Porter walked out sluggishly, followed by Jamie, who sported dark sunglasses and a baggy sweatsuit.

"Okay, Audrey, we are waiting on you." Jeff sighed deeply. He then looked over at the three of us. "I heard what happened at the party. You guys have to control yourself better." He glanced at Jamie, but he was slumped in the couch. Jeff pulled out his phone and opened up Warble, playing a video of Jamie at the party.

"I said that? Audrey will never let this go," Jamie muttered.

"No, and neither will I. You have to shape up. Do you want to get sent to rehab?" Jeff asked.

Why hadn't he sent Jamie to rehab before? This clearly had been going on for a while. Where would they even send him? I hope wasn't a place like the agency.

"No. I promise it won't happen again. I don't need to get sent anywhere," Jamie said. He rubbed his temples.

"Porter, you too," Jeff said.

"Me? What did I do? I de-escalated the situation," Porter said with his hand on his chest.

"Not enough. The videos should have never happened. And Vince and Mila were rumored to be stealing," Jeff said; his gaze fixed on me.

"No, we didn't take anything," I said. My voice squeaked as I spoke.

"Any news about Audrey's cloak and dagger party?" Porter snickered.

"What?" Jeff twisted his face up. "Audrey does a lot of weird things. But magic? You were probably drunk last night," he said.

There was no point in bringing that up. For some reason, I could tell Jeff favored Audrey more than the guys. *Why were they so afraid of Audrey?*

Audrey finally entered the room with all 5 of her suitcases filled with clothes I'm pretty sure she didn't even wear. She cleared her throat, "Can one of you guys be a gentleman?" she said, struggling with one bag and throwing it to the ground.

Porter, Audrey, and I got caught staring at each other for a few minutes until Jeff broke the ice.

"I'll take the bags." Jeff took the bags before the situation could escalate any further.

When we arrived at the airport, paparazzi crowded around us. The flashes started as soon as Audrey stepped out of the car. The lights were blinding, and we covered our faces, running into the airport. Fans tried to swarm us, but security came through pushing them back.

"Take a picture." One girl walked alongside me, recording a video.

Poor Jamie; not only was hungover, but he looked anxious and terrified. The fans finally backed off as we were guided through our terminal and to the runway where our jet was. It was pretty cool that I got to ride on a private jet. I just hoped Audrey didn't act dramatic anymore. Maybe she'd be too tired and sleep the whole way. Though, she didn't look as tired and worn out as the rest of us.

I stepped on the jet and made my way to a cushioned seat in the back before the guys could. Now they were stuck being closer to Audrey. *Thank God.*

As quickly as I sat, I jolted up. It just occurred to me that we'd be flying. It was only my second time. Luckily, this one was bigger than the small plane Jeff took me on. My heart pumped quickly, and I closed my eyes, breathing deeply. My family never flew because of the high ticket prices. So every trip we could afford to go on, my uncle would drive us. *It would be okay.* I continued to breathe.

"Um, where are the snacks, Wi-Fi code, movies, and drinks?" Audrey already commenced the complaining.

"Damn, can you wait to sit down!?" Porter let out an exaggerated sigh.

I hope they would shut up. I was literally about to have a panic attack again. I squeezed my eyes shut, feeling like the air was becoming thinner. I folded my legs into the leather seat. Their piercing voices made my head ache.

"Damn, Porter, can you mind your own business?" Audrey said.

"Audrey, the snacks are already on board. I'll get them in a second," Jeff mumbled. He was tired of Audrey, like everyone else.

The pilot stepped aboard. "I'm so happy to be your pilot today. Could we maybe get a quick picture before the flight? My daughter is a huge fan," he said.

"I already sat down," Audrey said.

"Um, yes, sir. We're happy to have you as well. They'll take a picture after we land." Jeff chuckled. The pilot nodded and went into the cockpit.

Everyone was finally quiet as we took off. Everything was going smoothly until we ran into some turbulence. I started shaking and hyperventilating.

Jeff came over and patted my shoulder. "It's okay, Vince. Just breathe," he told me.

"Someone's acting like Jamie." Audrey said.

That joke was getting really old. Could she say something else?

"Look at the view." Jeff opened the small sliding window, revealing the outside of the plane.

The clouds were massive. The sight of the puffy clouds and blue sky began to calm my nerves. I exhaled and the muscles in my body started to relax.

"Vince, I swear you've been acting weird lately. Never seen you act like this on a flight before," Porter questioned.

"I'm okay. Still not feeling well," I reassured him.

When I finally relaxed and closed my eyes, the jet had already landed. We were forced to take a picture with the pilot before we stepped off. Nobody seemed thrilled about it. Audrey half-smiled and tried to walk away as soon as the camera flashed. Jamie was slumped over. Porter's eyes closed in the photo. And I tried to get over my newfound fear of flying.

We exited through the airport and back into another van. Massive palm trees sprung up along the road; this was my first time noticing them since I got to California. After hours of being stuck in traffic, we made it to our home in the hills. The three-story house was unlike anything I had ever seen before. There wasn't anything like it back home. The exterior had large glass windows on each floor. Stairways from the outside connected to each floor through the balconies. It looked way too massive for just the four of us.

That was right; I forgot the band had roommates. What were their names again? I pondered. *I'd figure it out.*

The humidity of the West Coast caused my clothes to stick to my body. A few trees surrounded the house and a wooden black squared vertical fence outlined the yard. We were not in Crestview anymore. The van dropped us off in front of the house, and the door opened at once.

"So good to see you guys. Welcome home!" A small brunette with a bob hugged us. She looked like the girl in the selfie pictures in Vince's file.

"So glad to see you, Port." She laid a large smooch on him. This must have been Porter's girlfriend.

"I ordered everyone's favorite: Chinese takeout!" Her voice rose.

"So glad to be home." Audrey pushed through the door and stretched her arms out.

We entered the spacious living room, which was pretty much bigger than any room in my home. The high ceilings made the room feel more open. A bulb-shaped chandelier hung from the ceiling; a fireplace was embedded into a wall; the walls were a light blue with lilac undertones. There was a large, gray U-shaped sectional sofa with a matching ottoman. A medium-sized glass coffee table was in the middle of the sofa.

Wow, this place was decorated nicely. I wondered if they did this themselves or if they hired someone. It was strange to see everything matching, unlike the furniture at my house. This house was amazing, but I didn't understand why Vince lived with these fools. If I were him I would want to get my own apartment. He was possibly staying with them because everyone was splitting the rent. *Yeah, that's the reason I'm going with. Or Jeff forces them to live together.*

I wondered how much each of them pay. According to Kim, last year the band made close to $1 million on their first tour, but who knew. I looked around the living room once more and noticed it was a little messy. I guess that was expected with so many people living together. A pair of shoes peeked out from under the sofa, and Ganymede's toys were trailed around the room.

"So, is Elena home?" Audrey asked the brunette.

"No, probably partying. You know her." Porter's girlfriend placed a plate of Chinese takeout on the living room table for Porter.

Great, I had more people to pretend to know and I barely remembered their names from the file. This would become exhausting . . . I was an introvert. I was so used to just my small, tight-knit friend group. And everyone else was an acquaintance.

Audrey grabbed a plate and sat on the floor in front of the table with her legs crossed. Jeff, who I forgot was in the room, sat down for a minute.

"I'll see you guys on Tuesday. Tomorrow, you guys relax and take a breather. Then, we have to talk about the new album and award season," he said. Everyone said bye to Jeff as he left the house.

Today was Monday. At this point, I had forgotten the concept of days of the week. They all just meshed together. At least we got a day off. I'd most likely sleep the whole day and recharge for what was coming next.

A dog busted into the room. *This must be Ganymede. The dog that Kim told me about. I guess her useless facts weren't so useless in the long run.* He ran up to Porter, Audrey, and Jamie and began to lick their faces.

"He was so good while you were gone," the brunette said, smiling at me. "Oh, I'm so glad you're back," she said, picking her phone up and aiming the camera at Porter.

"Not this right now. I just got back in and I can't enjoy myself." He covered his face with a napkin.

"We haven't done a vlog in a while and my views have been down," she said.

"Because you're boring," Audrey said, rolling her eyes.

"Shut up!" she hissed back.

"No, I'm tired of our relationship being put online constant-ly." Porter exhaled.

She ignored his comment and continued to film. "Hey guys, Porter just made it back home. I'm so excited." She smiled thinly. "Say hi everyone. We're having dinner with the roomies." She panned the camera to us quickly, and Porter waved.

Man, being a well-known musician and filming your personal life must be exhausting.

Ganymede kept backing away from me and whimpering. *Did he notice that Vince and I had different scents? I hoped no one else noticed his strange behavior.*

"Come here, boy," I said, patting my knees. He looked away and ran into the kitchen. *Stupid dog. I wasn't much of a dog person, anyway, so I was not that offended.*

"I'm not really that hungry." Jamie got up and walked up a flight of stairs.

"Um . . . me too." I got up, straightening my shirt. I followed Jamie up the stairs and walked into the room by Jamie's.

"What are you doing in Porter's room?" he questioned.

I laughed. "Wow, this is Porter's room? I'm so tired," I said.

I had a feeling that would happen. This house was so massive. I had to figure out where everything was without others noticing.

I slid past Jamie as he entered his room. There were two more doors at the end of the hallway. One of these had to be Vince's room, or it could be one of the other inhabitants of this house. *Let this be the right room.* I walked in to see blackout curtains. The same picture of Vince and his family I saw at the agency sat on his dresser. I was so relieved.

I guess I knew where the saying, 'Be yourself, everyone else is taken' truly means now.

I unpacked the small duffel bag Jeff had for me when I was at the hotel. The room didn't look too much different from the room I was held hostage in at the agency. *How had they put so much detail into it? Did someone from the agency snoop into his room? Was it Jeff or one of the instructors?*

Near the dresser was a TV and connected to it was the new video game console that just came out. It would take me forever to save up for one. I picked up a controller and gripped it in my hand, admiring it. I wanted to test it out, but I was too exhausted. I laid down and drifted off to sleep.

A loud banging sound emitted from the door. I stretched my arms above my head, and the door flung open before I could answer it. A man with a receding hairline and a woman with a curly short afro entered. The couple from the picture. *Did they have to come now?*

"Get up, honey," the woman said, annoyed.

"Your mother and I have been calling and texting nonstop. The least you can do is answer," the man rambled on.

"Mom?" I rubbed the sleep out of my eyes. *That word felt so foreign to me. I haven't said that in years. And now I had to act like these strangers were my parents; the two people that I missed the most.*

"Yes, you look exhausted." She ran her fingers through my knotted up hair.

"Get dressed. We ordered breakfast for you guys," the dad said, leaving the bedroom.

I got up to leave the room, and the mom moved closer to me. "You look so much like him," she examined me.

"What!?" I choked.

"Yeah . . . Vince," she said.

"You know?" I asked.

"Of course. Thanks for taking over. He's been so sick. He's better now, but still not 100%," she said.

They knew. And they were okay with this? Why couldn't they wait till he was at 100%? What did it matter if he was resting for a couple of weeks? Did they care about money and attention that bad? Could they be making money off me being Vince? I haven't got paid yet. I felt for Vince. My face twisted with confusion.

"Don't worry, only us, Audrey, and Jeff know. Your secret is safe with us." She held her finger up to her lips.

They then went downstairs to the kitchen, and I hopped into the shower. I knew I would have to meet people close to Vince, but I was not expecting it to happen so soon. *I had to play it cool and be neutral. These were his parents; wouldn't the roommates know if something was off? I could just blame it on Vince's mysterious sickness, but did he have a good relationship with them? Were they strict stage Hollywood parents?* I only knew a little about them from the classes at the agency. *Oh, could this be over already?*

I joined them at the table after my shower. Audrey was in pink fuzzy pajamas. Porter was at the counter fixing a plate. Porter's girlfriend and the guy with the blonde fade sat on the barstools at the counter. I remembered him from the file. *He was an actor or a model.* Another girl with dark wavy hair was also in the kitchen. *Was she Elena?* I remembered seeing her face, but I was not sure of her name. She had a round face, dimples, and tawny eyes.

Vince's parents sat across the table from me. I had my fingers crossed that having his roommates here would make this less awkward and I would be able to talk less. The dad sat down with a plate of bacon and eggs. The mom sipped some orange juice.

"So, have you been feeling better?" his mom asked.

"Yeah, but we've been so busy," I said, avoiding eye contact.

"We didn't know you got back home. Jeff told us," his dad replied.

"And we couldn't visit you in the hospital. You had to get injured overseas when my passport was expired. We're so worried," the mother said, running her hands through my hair.

What! Where was Vince? How long had he been sick? I did not recall the last time the band was overseas. I'm sure Kim said something about it and I wasn't listening.

"Sorry about it. We're working on a new album, award season performances, and—"

"I heard you went out to a party. You need to rest. Did you drink a lot?" his mom interrupted.

"He was so drunk," Audrey said, looking up from her omelet. *Really, Audrey?* I wasn't drinking that much. What was the point of lying? She was just trying to get under my skin and make me more uncomfortable. My eyes rotated to the back of my head.

"You just got back from the hospital. You can't be reckless with your condition." The dad shook his head.

"She's just joking." I waved my fingers in her direction.

"Why would she joke about your health and well-being?" the mother asked.

Well, because she was Audrey and we were all a joke to her. She even joked about Jamie's anxiety, like she was collecting points for a free smoothie. I bet she poked fun at all of the roommate's personal issues. I gave Audrey a glare, but she wasn't looking.

"Well, your brother's graduation is coming up soon, and he'd love for you to be there," his mom told me.

"Yeah. I would love to come, but lately things have been crazy." I stuffed a piece of French toast in my mouth. I couldn't wait for them to leave. *Should I come up with an excuse to miss the graduation?* "You know award season is coming up," I said again.

"Yeah, I hope you guys finally get a win. And make me your plus one," She giggled.

Great, now I had to take her to one of the award ceremonies. It had to be one that was classier. Could you imagine partying with your mom? The thought of me partying with Aunt Mel sent shudders down my spine.

They continued to talk about their jobs and other things in their life. When breakfast was finished, they decided to leave. *Thank you.*

"I'm glad you're back, man," the guy with the blonde fade told me.

"Yeah, me too," I said.

"You didn't miss much," he said.

Audrey placed her glass in the sink and went up the stairs to her room; to practice witchcraft, I presume.

"So, what have you been up to?" I asked.

"Going to auditions. Oh, and I have a pilot coming out, remember?" he said.

"Oh, yeah, I can't wait for it." I grinned. *I finally got to put my lying to good use.*

"You guys need to start washing the dishes!" the guy with the blonde fade yelled, looking at the dirty dishes pilling up in the sink.

I finally got to meet Elena. The party girl that Porter's girlfriend mentioned last night.

"So, any plans for your day off? It was nice to see your folks again!" Elena said, getting off the barstool. She spoke loudly and too fast.

"No, no plans. Just staying at home. Sleep, TV, video games."

"So, how much of the new album did you guys write?" She grinned at Porter and me.

"Not much, just a few concepts and ideas for the cover," Porter answered.

It was interesting to hear about the new music. I wondered what the new album sounded like. Would it be their typical alternative rock sound like their first album, pop rock like their second, or would it be something completely different, or a fusion of the two? It was cool that I got an inside look into their music and the recording process.

"Give me a hint!" she said, giggling loudly. Her laugh sounded like she was choking.

Oh god. It was so annoying.

"Nope, not yet." Porter turned around.

She pouted and poked her lip out.

"So, what are you going to do today?" I asked her.

"Nothing. I have a huge shoot campaign tomorrow," she answered. *That was right; she was a model.*

"That's awesome. Well, I will see you guys later," I said, walking up the stairs to Vince's room. Ganymede was outside the door. I opened the door to let him in, but he still stayed outside. *He knew I wasn't his owner.*

I walked into the room, turned on the TV, and sat down on the bed. I was going to relax, but I saw Vince's computer on the desk. I couldn't resist. I had to look and see if there was any information I could find. Maybe an email or message from Audrey, or I could go on the internet and search on my friend's social media accounts. I just hoped that this computer wasn't bugged like the phone.

I powered up the desktop. The password and desktop profile icon appeared. *Now I had to think of what he might use as a password. Maybe it was his birthday?* I typed in his birthday. The text box shook, indicating that was the wrong answer. *Dang, what else could it be?* I thought about all the information and facts Kim had given me, and the stuff I learned at the agency. I tapped my fingers on the desk. I tried typing in Ganymede. The computer unlocked. *I didn't know Vince was that much of a dog person.*

The desktop loaded up. There were photos of Vince, some of his friends ,and him on tour with the band scattered on the screen. I opened up his pictures folder to find more. He had pictures from all of his travels. There was a picture of him and Audrey kissing in front of the Eiffel Tower. I almost forgot that they once dated. I could never imagine him with someone like her now that I've got to know her. There was another one of Jamie and Porter that looked like they were in Japan. Seemed like traveling was one of the cool opportunities a famous person could have.

I exited out of the pictures folder and I clicked on the internet browser. His email account automatically popped up. He had tons of messages from Jeff, friends, and potential business partners. *Should I answer some of them?* I wondered if they were suspicious as to why he didn't answer them yet. Some of them had been days, others were weeks old, unanswered. I also saw some emails from his medical insurance. *Why didn't Jeff or someone else from the agency answer the emails?* Maybe Vince was actually sick. Maybe he could have had a history of health problems. This was probably the perfect alibi for me to replace him. The agency thought no one would notice, and hopefully no one would.

I typed Warble into a search engine. I found Kim's page. She didn't seem to be posting much. But her posts were the usual. Things about music, specifically Retro Brite, and pictures with Landon and Camille. As I scrolled through her feed, one thing caught my eye.

> Missing Leon right now. I can't believe he is visiting his family and going to a different school now.

I gasped. I wondered what my aunt and uncle thought about this. There was no way they could use this excuse for long. The agency must have paid them off. This wouldn't last for long. Kim and my friends were definitely going to start figuring out what happened. I checked Camille and Landon's pages as well. Nothing out of the usual. They also reposted the same message Kim wrote.

Now it was time to check my aunt's social media page. She didn't use Warble, because it was the latest thing all the teens used. She used an older app called Reinyday. It was basically a forum where you posted about your day or opinions. This was strange. Her page said the same thing. I speculated how much money would make them complacent. Or maybe they were threatened to not say anything. *How far in advance did the agency think about this? What family member was I supposed to be visiting?* I did have family out of town, but we rarely talked to them or visited them. We only spoke around the holidays or if they needed money. I cleared the search history, even though I was sure someone could easily see what I was up to.

The next day, Porter rallied us up to get ready for a meeting. We were all in a car headed to the studio to work on the new album. Audrey sat in the front, blathering about ideas for the album. At least, she was a talented singer, so some of her ideas might be good. But since we were a group, I thought everyone should have a say. Jeff and the audio engineers would probably favor her opinions over ours, like everyone else did, though.

"I can't wait to get in the studio!" Porter said, raising his arms above his head.

"This record has to be different so that we can have more nominations," Jamie said.

"No, it has to be catchy and simple, just like our first album. That one was more critically acclaimed," Audrey told him.

"What do you think?" Porter asked me.

"I think Audrey's idea is good, but we'll have to see," I said.

"I know I'm always right," she said in a sing-songy voice.

"Whatever," Porter said.

I was nervous to go to the studio because only Jeffrey and Audrey knew that I couldn't play the guitar like Vince could . . . *So what would I be doing in the studio?* Maybe all the guitar parts would already be done, or another musician would do it. *How would we hide this from Jamie and Porter?*

The studio was small and roomy. It was way different from what I expected it to be. I imagined the place to be less welcoming, more dull and plain, like the agency. The lights in the room were dim and purple. An antique rug laid on the hardwood floors. A plush-looking sofa was against the wall. Across from the couch was a mixer board and a monitor. The mixer had many knobs on it. *I was surprised by the amount of knobs on the board. I would never be able to remember what all of them did.* In front of the mixer was a glass window and the sound booth. The walls were blue and padded. A mic, with some type of filter on it, stood in the middle of the booth. The producer and engineers were already there, and everyone greeted us.

Audrey made no haste and went straight toward the booth. "I've been working on some things already. Listen to this," Audrey said, grinning widely.

"I'm glad you're ready, Audrey, but just wait one minute," Jeff told her.

"Record this." She ignored him and began to sing some riffs. She seemed so into what she was singing, swaying with her eyes closed. When she stopped, singing the engineer played it back.

When the audio finished, she asked, "So what do you think?" She looked between us and the producer.

"It sounds amazing, Audrey, but I'm thinking of a different tone for this album. We were thinking of more romantic or slower ballads," Jeff explained.

Audrey scrunched her face up. "It should be our choice what we make; we're the artists. Plus, our first record already had a few of those types of songs," she said.

I hate to say it, but Audrey had a point. *Though, I was not going to say anything; if she knew I agreed with her, that would just inflate her ego even more.*

"Here's the demo I want you guys to listen to. Vince will be the main vocals for this track," Jeff said.

What, really? Why? He could of at least told me that earlier or let me hear it first. My stomach gurgled.

"I don't want to be backing vocals on a lot of these projects I'm the best singer here," Audrey huffed her breath, slamming her body down on the couch.

The engineer played the demo. It was a slow, melodic love ballad about a guy that was so in love. It sounded okay, but sappy love songs weren't my thing.

"Vince, step into the booth," Jeff told me. I paused and then, dragged my feet. "Go on," Jeff said, motioning me to enter the booth.

Did they forget that I was not Vince, and that I couldn't sing or play an instrument well?

As I stepped toward the booth, Jeff walked near me and whispered, "Don't worry; we will auto-tune your voice. Just pretend to perform like you did in that class."

I nodded my head. They handed me a paper with lyrics on it, and I went into the booth. *Thank God. So, did the producer and engineer know I wasn't the real deal, too?*

I bobbed my head to the bass line as the song began. After a couple of takes, I got it right. I was glad the booth was sound-proof, so no one could hear how bad of a singer I really was. The remainder of the studio session included Jamie and Porter recording their parts for the drums and bass. I went back into the booth, pretending to know how to play the guitar. I'd gotten better at it, but my nerves still made it hard for me to concentrate. But I did feel cool and enjoyed the experience.

"That was great, everyone!" Jeff clapped his hands.

We must have been in there for hours. I didn't see the time when we left the room; it looked like it was evening. As we walked to the exit of the building, Jeff pulled Audrey and me to the side.

"I know this is going to be strange for you, Audrey, and you probably won't like it, but . . . "

"But what!" she yelled. Her usually breathy voice was full.

"So, to promote the album, I think you and Vince should get back together," Jeff said, taking out a paper and pen from his briefcase.

Audrey chewed on one of her long acrylic nails.

"Do what!?" I yelled.

Jeff hushed us and tried to give us the paper.

"You know I'd rather go back to Omar." Audrey shook her head.

"I know, but I think it will really help the album sell. Especially with the duets that we have," Jeff said.

"No. You said that I could be in a PR relationship with somebody else more famous. I think I'll be better off if I dated an actor or athlete," she said discreetly while Jamie and Porter were nearby.

"You don't have to follow your diet for award season," Jeff said.

Audrey grumbled and snatched the paper, signing her name. She then threw the paper at me. Jeff and Audrey would hassle me, so I had no choice but to sign. *Jeff and Audrey would hassle me into signing.* There was no telling what Jeff would do. This kept getting worse and worse. From the outside in, any guy would want to date Audrey. She was beautiful and talented. But if only they knew the real her . . .

"I think you guys should go out for lunch or a hike. To make your debut as a 'couple' later on." Jeff did finger quotes, and Audrey rolled her eyes. Her upper lip raised and inverted into an 'U' shape.

I gave him the signed paper with my head hung low. *Would I ever have my normal life back?*

"This is completely normal; don't be worried." He tried reassuring me. *Nothing had been normal. How many public figures had fake relationships?* I thought.

"So, later this evening, everyone will know the news. Smile big for the paparazzi, or you can play it off like you don't want to be seen to make you look more realistic," he said playfully.

"Like I told you, I was already talking to someone else online." Audrey started to walk off with her palm on her forehead.

"Come on, Audrey. You can still talk to him after the album and tour; we'll just call it off. You dated Vince before, without it being PR, what's the difference now? Besides the obvious one," Jeff said.

Audrey was already out the door.

"Can't believe she would rather go out with a rapper named 'Little' something or 'Little' that," Jeff muttered lowly. "Do you want a hit or not?" he yelled out the door.

PAPARAZZI

11

THE NEXT EVENING, I was mentally preparing myself to pretend date Audrey. We had planned to hike together. *Did we have to hug, hold hands, or kiss? I was drawing the line at kissing. I couldn't even fathom the thought.* When I first met Audrey, I was completely charmed by her charisma and looks, but now I saw her in a totally different light.

Around 6 pm, Audrey knocked on my door, and I put the game controller down. I was already dressed and ready to go.

"Let's hurry up and get this over with. I don't want to do this just as much as you do. Let's go on a hike," she said. She was dressed in biker shorts, a tank top with a LA cap on, and large dark sunglasses. In her hand, she held Ganymede's leash. He was wagging his tail, happily ready to go on a hike.

"Ugh, take this stupid dog. You know I don't like animals. And don't forget to feed him and take care of him. He's your responsibility now," she huffed, throwing the leash in my hand.

I followed Audrey into the garage, and she unlocked a pink Mercedes truck. I stood in front of the car, stunned for a minute. The garage was filled with two other cars. *Whose are these?*

"You have a car? I just imagined you guys always got chauffeured," I said.

"You know I have to have a car. I just don't want to mess it up." She placed a towel in the passenger seat, and Ganymede hopped in with a toothy grin. Audrey patted him lightly and then turned on the AC. She moved the vents over to Ganymede.

"Let me cool you down, boy," she said.

"So, the dog can sit in the front, but I can't? You just said you don't like animals," I said.

"No, I don't, but Ganymede is the only dog I can tolerate. He's kind of cute." She squished his face in between her hands. Ganymede shook out of her grip.

We drove in silence for a few minutes with only the sound of the wind hitting against the windows and the dog panting. We parallel parked along the side of the street. Palm trees sprung up along the street.

"Do you have any change?" she asked as she pointed at the meter.

"No. I don't have any money. When will Jeff give me my share of the money?" I said.

Audrey snorted hard, shaking her head as she dug into a fanny pack. "I don't know anything about that; ask him. So, you don't have change?"

Once the meter was paid for, we walked along a path through some grass and shrubbery. The street was now a dusty dirt path. As we walked, the ground became more hilly. The hills were patchy with dry shrubbery, rocks, small trees without leaves.

"No, how was your day?" I asked, breaking the silence.

"Like, we don't have to talk if you don't want to," she mumbled, looking up the hill.

"What do you mean? I genuinely want to know. If I'm going to be pretend to be your bandmate and lover, we might as well talk to pass time." I shrugged.

Audrey was annoying, but I might as well try to enjoy being around her.

"About what? And don't ever refer to me as your lover." She stuck her tongue out like she was gagging. "I just went to the spa and got a facial and went out to lunch to catch up with some friends. Lucky for you, Vince is a homebody and mostly invites his friends over. So, you won't seem too suspicious if you don't go out much."

We walked along the trail and scaled higher up without saying anything else. The LA heat sizzled in the air. Nothing but the sound of our feet hitting the dirt path and Ganymede panting.

Where was the paparazzi at?

We made it to the top of the trail, and Ganymede and I were exhausted. We stretched out on a wooden bench. The view was breathtaking and overlooked the city. From the top, we could see the whole city; the buildings were bunched up together. It was dusk, and the buildings were starting to light up the sky. As I admired the view, I imagined all the people that worked and lived in the buildings. The celebrities that lived there or the normal, everyday people. None of this mattered, anyway. However, the thought that we could easily run into someone famous was wild to me. After the breather, we then went to the bottom of the trail. We glanced around to see if anyone was near. Jeff said they'd be here when we get to the bottom.

Moments later, we heard a few clicks.

"Okay, they're here!" she exclaimed, fixing her ponytail and readjusting her tank top. She grabbed my hand as we strolled back on the street and gave me a few quick pecks on the cheek.

"Come on, stop acting so awkward and stiff," she whined.

I relaxed my shoulders and continued to walk. She quickly smooched me on the lips. My mouth hung opened, but I regained my composure for the pictures and began to kiss her back. Our lips interlocked. The kissing intensified as her tongue acquainted with mine. My heartbeat accelerated. I never expected to be kissing Audrey. She must hate this right now, and as soon as the cameras were away, we would pull away, but I closed my eyes and just enjoyed the moment. *Even though I said this was off limits, I couldn't even lie; she was a pretty good kisser.*

We were stopped by Ganymede, who was now galloping down the street toward another dog. It was a small French Bulldog.

Audrey stumbled on the path to catch up to him. "Calm down, boy!" she yelled. He didn't listen; he sped up.

Audrey tumbled on the street, her sunglasses fell on the asphalt, and her knees scraped up against the pavement. The cameras still snapped away.

Ganymede ran down the street. I glanced to see Audrey on the ground, blood covering her knees.

"Don't just stand there! Do something! Get the damn dog," she growled.

I sprinted after Ganymede for a couple of blocks. The other dog's owner was holding him by the collar.

"I'm so sorry about that. He took off and we couldn't stop him," I apologized.

The woman looked up. Her brows were raised. "I'm Heather." She extended her hand.

"Nice to meet you. I'm Vince." I shook her hand.

She giggled. "We met before in Atlanta and New York," the lady said.

"Yeah, yeah. I thought I've seen your face before." I nodded my head.

"But I didn't get a chance to take a picture with you," she said, inching closer to me. I moved back.

Oh great. Here we go again. She was going to ask for a picture while I looked horrible. I had sweat stains all over my shirt and my hair was stuck to my forehead. I know the paparazzi got pictures of me looking bad, but I wanted to get back home as soon as possible.

"Can I take a picture with you?" she asked as her dog was jumping on Ganymede.

"I'm sorry, I'm in a rush. Gany and I have to get back home," I said.

"Come on, just one quick picture won't take long." She pulled out her phone. "You were so much nicer the last time I met you. You seem different."

This lady was crazy. She probably only had a brief interaction with him. How would she know him? She must be a super fan who has met him several times.

"I'm sorry. I really have to go." I snatched Gany away from her and sped walked back to the car.

Audrey was waiting by the car, leaning against the window. She was ready to go home. She opened the back door. "Since you want to be a bad boy, get in the back," she scolded Ganymede. He whimpered as we put him in the backseat. "I can't believe you did that!" she said.

We drove back to the house. I wanted to get back home and get into bed. This evening was crazy. And so was that lady. I couldn't see myself dealing with super fans like that. I wondered if Retro Brite met many fans like her. She probably knows where they live; the thought gave me chills.

If only Ganymede didn't run away. And I kissed Audrey. The moment replayed in my head. Her soft plump lips and her warm breath on my neck. It was amazing. I kissed a few girls before, but nothing compared. I looked over at her. Her jaw was clenched, and she drummed her fingers on the steering wheel. She caught my eyes, and I turned away; my thoughts of the kiss disappeared.

"Oh my god, Audrey! Are you okay?" Elena yelped at the sight of Audrey.

"Yeah, I think so. Ganey decided to chase after a dog," she said.

Elena ran to grab a towel and bandages.

"I hope my legs won't be scarred up for the award show next

week," Audrey said.

"Can't you just choose a different outfit or cover your legs with makeup?" I suggested.

Audrey and Elena shook their heads in disapproval. Elena let out another annoying cackle. *I would never get used to that laugh.*

"This is a custom-designed dress that I already got fitted for. I can't just change it," Audrey said.

The girls then talked about awards season and what outfits Audrey was going to wear. I took Gammy's leash off, and he ran over to his water bowl and started to drink. I went over to the fridge and grabbed a bottle of water.

"So, are you coming? You can be my plus one," Audrey asked her.

"No, I won't be able to make it. Kyle is taking me on vacation." She smiled.

"Who!" Audrey wrinkled her forehead.

"DJ Riff Dub," Elena said.

Audrey screeched. "Really, DJ Riff? You've been seeing an up-and-coming rap star without telling *me?* Get that bag!" Audrey danced around the room.

"You know it. But I think he really likes me. I'm not like the other girls he dates," Elena went on.

"How?" I asked. The girls turned to me as if they forgot I was still in the room.

"Well, look at her. He won't abandon her like the last girl," Audrey said.

"Abandon?" Elena questioned.

"I don't know. I heard he left her stranded on vacation somewhere and while they were dating, he would constantly be with other girls. But you know how blogs are. Plus, the girl could be lying. She didn't have that many followers before she was seen with him. It's nothing. Don't worry. Enjoy your trip," Audrey blurted, hugging her.

I shook my head. *How could Elena think she was any different?* He was most likely with many girls, and she was just in it for the money, it seemed. I couldn't feel too bad for her. I had no idea who DJ Riff Dub even was, and I doubted Audrey's story about him was accurate. I went upstairs to my room for the night.

The next day, we met up at a stage studio to practice our performance for the award show in a couple of weeks.

"This is going to be a long rehearsal. We have to be perfect for next week when we rehearse at the actual venue," Jeff reminded us.

We all took our places on a stage. Jamie counted us in with the drums, and Porter came in with the bass. Then, I pretended to play some riffs, and finally, Audrey started singing.

"No, no, no," Jeff stammered. "More energy. Full out. And Audrey, stop singing flat."

She side-eyed him. "We're still better performers than you'll ever be," she snickered.

"Not now, Audrey!" he yelled, taking off his sunglasses and rubbing his temples.

Jeff was a performer? I wondered if he was an actor or musician. I could see Jeff growing up as a theater kid. How did Audrey know he was a horrible performer? Did she ever hear or see any of his work?

"Vince, you look sloppy!" he shouted. I'm sorry but the heat was unbearable.

"Okay, at this part, there's going to be fire coming out of the stage. So I need more energy!" Jeff said.

Fire, that's cool. I've seen many performers on stage use it before.

We practiced over and over for hours. Sweat dripped down my back. Even though I was pretending to play, I still couldn't keep up. I dropped the guitar; it hung from the strap low on my waist. We practiced so long that the guitar felt like it weighed a ton.

"Can we take five?" Porter pleaded leaning over.

Yes, please. I don't think I can make it any longer. My lungs burned.

"Not yet." Jeff brushed off his comment.

"We've been practicing for hours," he groaned.

"If you think this is hard, wait till we practice with the backup dancers," Jeff said.

"Backup dancers," I murmured and rubbed the back of my neck. *Dang, this performance was a big deal.* There was always more anticipation and expectations from fans during award show performances. I have to get this right. No one can know I'm not Vince.

"It's all rigged, anyway. Does the performance really matter?" Jamie asked.

"It's true, but everyone will talk about this performance, especially if it's bad. Jamie, get back on the drums," Jeff told him.

"Rigged . . . how?" I turned around and raised an eyebrow.

Jeff laughed at me. "You guys are going to win the Music Fans Choice Award. It's already been decided," Jeff explained.

"I t-thought the fans would vote for who wins?" The rest of the group laughed hysterically.

"No, it's all rigged, but we need to focus on this performance," Jeff said.

We continued to practice without a break. During the middle of practicing, we heard a large thud noise.

"Porter!" Jamie hollered.

Porter's body laid limp next to the stage. Jamie and I rushed over to him. His face was flushed, and he was passed out. It was horrifying to see him lay in the grass next to the stage. That could of easily been me. I was lucky I didn't have to sing and perform like they did. I thought he would be used to intense rehearses, but it was hot.

"Maybe he had heat stroke." Jamie pulled his phone out of his pocket.

"I'm sure he's fine. We can practice without the bass. We still have a long way to go," Audrey said. Her tone was cold as if that wasn't her bandmate.

"Yeah, but he needs medical attention," I said.

Jeff waved his hand in disapproval. "He's fine. Let's continue," Jeff dismissed.

We practiced for a little more until Jamie spoke up again.

"Look, this isn't right. We can't get it all right in one day, anyway." He put his drumsticks down and tried to pick up Porter, but was struggling. I put my guitar down and rushed over to help him.

"You're such a follower," Audrey said.

"Can you help us!" I wheezed, lifting Porter up.

Audrey snickered and walked back over to the mic stand.

Jamie and I finally placed Porter in a chair. Luckily for us, he regained consciousness. Jamie and I refused to continue rehearsing. Jeff and Audrey were left with no choice but to stop practicing as well. When we got back to the house, the rest of the roommates were there.

"Are you guys okay?" Elena looked concerned.

"No, we barely made it out of rehearsal. Porter passed out."

As soon as I spoke those words, Porter's girlfriend came running out of nowhere. "Oh my god, are you okay? Let me get you something to eat." She rushed over to comfort him.

"I'm okay," he reassured her.

"I was going to film a couple challenge for our channel," she sighed.

Porter groaned.

"I'm glad everyone is okay, but look at this," the guy with the blonde fade said, holding up his phone. It was the picture of Audrey and me from our walk the other day. We were kissing.

"Explain this," he said, laughing.

"Calix, stop," Audrey told him.

Calix, what type of name was that? At least I now knew what to call him.

"So you guys are back together, I suppose?" Calix said.

"Yeah, we're keeping it low key though," I said.

"Sure, with your tongue down his throat," Elena added in with her signature cackle.

"You guys should stay out of this," Audrey snapped back.

A few seconds passed, and Calix and Elena both began to snicker.

"What's so funny?" Audrey asked.

"This," Calix sputtered, holding up a picture of when Audrey face-planted yesterday on the walk.

"Where did you get that?" she cried.

"It's posted on all the blogs," he said.

Audrey's face turned flush with anger and embarrassment. She got on her phone to call who I assumed to be Jeff.

"Oh, and you're next, Vince," he said. "Some lady that was there yesterday said you were rude and acted differently. Now she's saying how she met you last time and you were so much nicer. 'It's like he's a completely different person.' She's even compared photos of your most recent show to some older ones. Isn't it absurd?"

I snatched his phone out of his hands to get a closer look. "Yeah, it is." I chuckled along, even though my heart was beating out of my chest.

The woman had posted photos of Vince and I side by side. Claiming that his eye color changed and his nose looked slightly smaller. Luckily, most people in the comments disagreed. The Retro Brite fandom was dragging her, saying she was lying and was looking for attention.

Calix took this phone back. *Hopefully, everyone thought this was a hoax, and we could move past it.* But I could see Jeff coaching me and telling me I needed to do better the next time I saw him. *Would he hurt me?*

My mind went back to the guards at the agency and the girl being tased. *Would Jeff want to replace me? Would that be a bad thing? Could I go back home?*

I didn't think so. This seemed to be my new reality. I thought about everything: the woman at the agency, Jeff, and my future. I pulled Audrey to the side to see if she would give me any answers.

"At practice, why did you say that about Jeff?" I asked.

"Say what?" She scrunched up her face.

"That he was a bad performer?"

"Because he was. He used to always talk about how he was a performer and missed it, but had no luck with it. And how his family was disappointed in him. He's a bad performer and not the best manager." She shrugged and walked back to the group.

I wanted to ask her more questions, but I knew I was lucky to get that much out of her.

The rest of the night, I ate dinner with the roommates and retreated back to my room. They urged me to hang out longer, but after today, I needed to rest and clear my head.

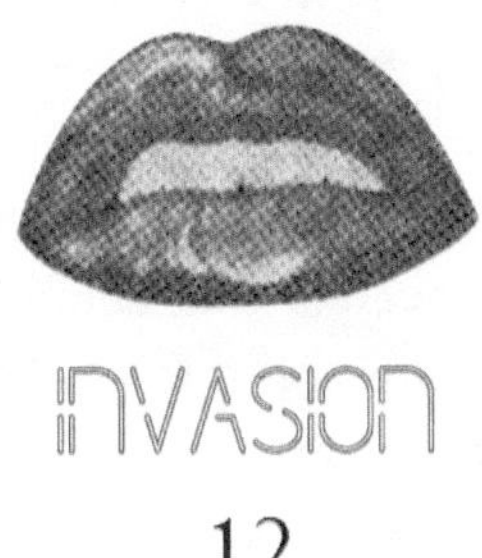

12

THE LOUD SHATTERING sound of glass woke me up out of my sleep. Audrey and the other girls started screaming. I tiptoed down the stairs into the living room but peeked around the corner to watch from a safe distance. A stocky man with a bat was in the living room, dressed in all black.

What was happening? I tried my best to keep my breathing quiet.

"I'm here for my money. Make it quick. I don't have all morning!" he yelled. His voice rattled the room.

"What money?" Elena cried.

"The money your friend owes," the man replied in a gruff voice. He smashed the living room coffee table in. Glass flew in the air like confetti, inciting more screams.

"I'll have your money later, I promise. I don't have it all right now," Jamie said.

"I didn't ask for all of that. I need it now." He hit the wall with the bat, then charged toward Porter and swung the bat straight at his head. Porter ducked just in time.

"Oh my god!" his girlfriend cried.

I saw someone's hand with a phone in it, hopefully ready to call the cops.

"Stop it. I wouldn't do that if I were you." He pulled out a gun, aimed it at the ceiling, and started to shoot. The sound of the bullets cracked in my ears.

This was crazy. I never seen or heard a gun fire in real life. At least no one got hurt. My roommates were ducking behind the furniture. I ducked my head even farther behind the wall.

"So, now, you guys are going to cooperate, right?" The gun was aimed in Jamie's direction.

"I don't have any money on me," Jamie's voice quivered. The man dug the gun into Jamie's head. My stomach dropped and my muscles tightened.

"Sounds like a personal issue. This is the second time, and I need my money now. So you and your little friends can pitch in. Or I can cut this short," the man said.

Porter opened his wallet; he was shaking.

"How . . . how much does he owe you?" His voice undulating up and down like a theremin.

"$2,000," he said, locking his eyes on everyone in the room.

"$2,000!" everyone shrieked in unison.

"Y'all heard me. Get scramming!" the man said. Porter handed him $40. Audrey and Porter ran upstairs.

Man, I wondered how much Jamie bought from him and what. I turned in their direction, ready to follow.

"How about you over there, little guy?" the man said, peering around the corner. I jumped farther behind the wall. *I should have stayed upstairs.*

"Yeah, I see you. Come out." I emerged from behind the wall and stood in front of the man. "Got any money?" he asked.

I shook my head as soon as he spoke. "I'll go look for some." The gun was still held at Jamie's head. Jamie's face was pale and his lip trembled. *We had to find some money, and we had to do it quick. What time was it?* I looked at a clock on the wall. It was 3 am.

My breathing became staccato and my heartbeat synchronized with the clock. *I had to get out of this. Things were only going to get worse from here. I missed my old boring life. Were we being held hostage or in the middle of a heist in our home?*

I rushed off behind Audrey and Porter and went into Vince's room. I tore through the drawers and looked everywhere in the bed and in the closet. I could not find any money. Just a few quarters and pennies. Porter was outside of the room.

"Let's go see if Audrey and the others have some money," he said as I left the room.

Elena ran past us and sprinted up the second flight of stairs. "I have some money I can give. But I'm never lending him any money again!" she screeched. "$2,000, really!? That's about how much we each pay toward rent."

We followed behind her. Calix was outside his room, leaning against the open-door frame vaping. His eyes were half closed.

"So, can you help Jamie out?" Porter asked.

Calix shook his head as he was vaping. "Ask someone else," he said, folding his arms. Calix snorted and exhaled the vape smoke. "What about when I needed money to fix my car?" Calix asked. "Did any of my roommates help? How about the time when I couldn't afford my share of the rent?" he asked, tilting his head. "Who carries cash with them, anyway?"

"Um, I was," Porter said. "Look, there's a gun being held to his head."

"You were—" Calix extended his hand. "Exactly, bro. And I can't help him. He got himself into this." Calix turned around and went into his room.

Elena came down the hall and thrusted the bills at me and stormed back into her room.

"Looks like we have $140. Audrey is our last resort. Let's ask her," Porter said.

"No, I'm staying here," I dismissed.

"Please, I need backup," he whined.

I sighed. "I don't feel like dealing with the wrath of Audrey," I said.

"I know, but she's our only choice. I'm sure she would be willing to help. You'll be fine. Come on, I'll be with you," Porter said, wrapping his arm around me.

Did he even know her that well? I've only known her for about a few months and she isn't the most giving person. I know Porter's trying to be a good friend and help Jamie, but this was a lot. I loved my friends, but I don't know what I would do in a situation like this.

I shook my head and walked down the hall to her room.

Porter knocked on the door. "Look, it's just me and Vince," he said.

No one answered. She was probably dodging him like everyone else was. He then turned the knob. It was locked.

"Leave me alone before I call the police," she cried.

"Hey, watch this," Porter whispered.

He banged on the door and then kicked it. She screeched once again. *I kind of felt bad for her, considering the circumstances.*

"It really is us, Audrey," he said again.

"Ugh. Don't do that to me," she said, opening the door with caution. "And I don't have any money right now."

"Come on, Audrey. Jamie and I will pay you back," he said in a honeyed voice.

"I know Jamie won't pay me back and I don't want to be a part of this." She tried to close the door, but Porter wedged his foot in and pushed his way inside.

Audrey grumbled. "Like I'm not giving him anything. Dig up some coins in the sofa," she said.

"We already did; nothing was there," Porter told her.

I looked around Audrey's room and noticed how spacious it was. I wondered if all the roommates fought over which room to pick. I could see Audrey demanding this room. The room was covered in pink, gold, and white decor. There were a few shelves placed around the room. The top shelves had purses and heels displayed. The bottom of the shelves had a couple of books, crystals, and other knickknacks. I couldn't see Audrey being much of a reader; I bet the books were like the ones in Mikko's house. I tried to get a glimpse of what they were, but they were too far out of sight.

"I'm not helping him out of this. He has to learn to take responsibility for his own actions," she said.

Audrey lecturing about accountability. Things kept getting weirder. I did agree with her. But if she was in Jamie's situation, she would insist that everyone helped.

Footsteps stomped up the stairs. Jolts raced down my spine.

"Who is that? Calix . . . Elena?" Audrey laughed.

"I don't know what's so funny. I need my money!" The man's voice rose with agitation, indicating that we didn't have much time left. He had Jamie in tow, with the gun still pressed against his head. Jamie groaned as the man gripped him.

Audrey gasped and clung onto Porter's arm like a scared child looking for his mother. I got behind them.

"I don't have anything for you. It's not our responsibility. Don't take it out on us," Audrey cried.

This was so terrifying. What if he shot Jamie or us? Could this all be over?

"Well, I need my money now. Oh, this looks nice." He barged in and looked at one of Audrey's expensive handbags from a vanity. He placed his gun into his waistband and let Jamie go. Jamie exhaled and grabbed his chest.

"Well, this, along with the change, should cover all the fees. I bet it's worth a lot." He looked directly at Jamie and said, "I'm done doing business with you. Bye."

But as soon as he grabbed the bag, Audrey clasped onto the strap of the bag.

"What are you doing?" I yelled at her. "Give him what he wants!"

"Yeah, listen to your little friend," he told her while trying to yank the bag from her.

"It's a limited edition and worth $3,000." Audrey was still holding on to the bag for dear life.

$3,000 for a bag? I couldn't fathom paying that much for any type of clothing or accessory. *This was the scariest thing ever. Audrey needed to give him the stupid bag.*

"Even better." He grinned.

"No!" Audrey screamed as the guy tried to pry the bag from her.

He then pulled out the gun and pistol-whipped Audrey with it. She propelled to the floor.

"Audrey!" Porter went over to see if she was okay.

The man made no haste and left the scene.

The rest of the morning, no one was able to get back to sleep. Jamie paced around the kitchen; Audrey had an ice pack to her cheek. Porter and his girl argued about how everyone almost got killed. Elena swept up the glass and cleaned up the damage that was done. Calix, most likely, was in his room, ignoring us. And here I was, pacing from the kitchen to the living room before going back to my bedroom, trying to piece together all these thoughts.

We just got robbed. I never thought this would happen to me. Everyday life felt more like a movie.

My phone rang. It was Jeff.

"Audrey told me everything that happened. I'm glad everyone is okay."

"Yeah, this was terrifying," I blubbered.

"Well, I know you guys can move past this, but I need to tell you about something," he said.

I exhaled.

"Some people—conspiracists—are starting to believe that you're a fake."

"Well, I am. What do you want me to do?"

"Just tighten up; be more careful. I'll give you more material to study."

I murmured in agreement and asked him a question that has

been on my mind. "So . . . when am I getting paid? How much?"

Jeff laughed as if I was telling a joke or had said something charming. "Oh yes, you'll be getting your first paycheck soon. We'll talk about that in more detail at our next meeting."

"Okay, how about my family and friends?"

"What about them?"

"Will I ever see them again?"

"Wow, so many questions for someone who has been up since midnight. Get some rest. You guys are going to be on a talk show tomorrow afternoon."

"A what? I'm pretty sure most managers give their clients their itinerary more than a day ahead of time."

He chuckled again. "Telling me how to do my job now? Get some rest, buddy." He hung up the phone before I could say anything else.

It was not going to be easy to get answers from him or Audrey. I might never get them. Maybe I'd have to tell the other bandmates or even the roommates. They'd probably think that I was crazy and not believe me, anyway.

It was the afternoon and time to get ready to go on the talk show. *What show were we even going on? I didn't watch many of them, so I probably wouldn't recognize the person.* My stomach churned at the thought of being on live television. What if I said something wrong? I still felt unprepared even with the classes at the agency.

My eyes were baggy; I barely was able to get any sleep yesterday. I got dressed in a pair of sweats and a wrinkled old tee. *Audrey wouldn't approve of this look, but we're going into makeup and wardrobe at the show, right?*

I entered the living room; Audrey was already dressed in a long, casual dress. She was sitting at the kitchen island, putting makeup on. Jamie was there, already dressed as well. He seemed like he was pretty put together, even though yesterday morning we were being robbed. He wore jeans and a t-shirt.

"I can't believe I have to go on TV in a couple of hours. Look at this bruise on my face," Audrey complained while piling on more makeup. A dark blue bruise was on Audrey's cheek. She was brushing her cheeks with some sort of powder.

"You're going to have to go to hair and makeup, anyway," Jamie said.

"Shut up. We're still not on speaking terms yet. You owe me a new bag."

"I'm sorry. I'll get you the money for a new one. I didn't know he was going to take your bag. And I'm done with that type of stuff."

"You said that last time. I'm tired of living with a junkie!" she yelled.

"Oh, so you micro-dosing and inhaling herbs is okay?" Jamie piped up.

"It's medicine; it's different," she sighed.

"Stop arguing. Yesterday morning was rough," Porter said, walking to the kitchen. He was also dressed in sweats like me. At least I wasn't the only one that wasn't dressed up.

"Whatever. Let's just go." Audrey got up.

We left the house. Jeff and our driver were in the car waiting for us. Jeff stepped out of the car and pulled us to the side.

"Okay, let's forget everything that happened and be professional," Jeff said.

Yes, back to forgetting and pretending like things didn't happen was the story of my life.

"Now let's see if anyone asks you about you and Audrey getting back together. Don't say anything or try to change the subject," he told me.

"Please, let's change the subject," Audrey added. "How am I supposed to forget about last night? My bag was stolen."

"At least you're okay, Audrey. Material items can be replaced," Jamie said in a soft tone.

"It's a one-of-a-kind custom made luxury bag. It can't be replaced, but you can!" Audrey said.

"Calm down, Audrey. That wasn't nice," Jeff scolded her like a child.

"I can't believe you want to be back with her," Porter emphasized, shaking his head and looking at me.

I pressed my lips together and remained quiet. I didn't know what to do or say.

"Why wouldn't he?" Audrey twirled her hair.

"It's your attitude and the way you treat him and other people," Porter said.

"Let's not go there. Amerie's DMs are full of guys."

Porter turned his head away. His eyes looked like they were tearing up. She must have some insider scoop on Porter and his girlfriend's relationship. She always had a comeback for everything.

We got into a black SUV and drove for a couple of minutes.

"Where are we going?" I asked.

"You'll see," Jeff said.

After what seemed like a few hours of weaving in and out of traffic, we were there. I would never get used to this traffic. There were so many cars, and the highways had many lanes. There were rarely any traffic jams in Crestview, and if there were, it was at most a ten minute delay.

We drove up to a large golden gate. The gate was enclosed by cream and gold-colored walls. Gold letters above the gate read: Kingdom Studios. I gasped to myself as we entered through. Kingdom Studios was a big household name and was known for their many productions. *Man, this place must be a big deal.* We drove past a couple of lots. One looked like a small town. Another one looked like a metropolitan city. The street had store fronts and residential buildings. It was surreal to see these sets and how much detail they had. We drove past them and parked at another lot near a building that had the appearance of a warehouse. 'Lot 24' was written on the side of the building in black.

We exited the SUV, and a lady came out and guided us into the building and through a hallway. On the wall, I saw a red decal that read: The Cherry Show in bold cursive letters. *Was I about to be on The Cherry Show?* I had so many memories of coming home from school and Aunt Mel watching The Cherry Show. It was hard to believe I was going to be on one of the biggest daytime talk shows. Aunt Mel was a big fan of hers and rarely missed an episode. She'd definitely be watching. *Would she know it was me, though? She would have to. I need to know what the agency told her.*

Cherry was known for her vibrant personality and her giving heart. It was amazing to be there in person. The set seemed quite ordinary; it was nothing fancy like I thought it would be. I imagined people running around like crazy trying to make deadlines. A few people, who I assumed were staff members, walked from room to room. The lady that was guiding us introduced herself, but I did not remember her name or what else she said. I couldn't stop thinking about everything I just saw. I felt like a kid at a theme park.

The lady took us into a small room. The door had 'Retro Brite' on it. I smirked. *That was kind of cool.* There wasn't much in the room besides a few chairs, a table, and a gas station sized bathroom. Audrey sat slouched over in a chair. *I guess this room wasn't up to her standards.* Jamie and Porter were talking about how cool it was to meet Cherry.

Moments later, a lady walked in with a rack of clothing. *She must be in charge of the wardrobe.*

"Hi, everyone. I'll be dressing you today. See anything you like?" She motioned to the rack.

Audrey turned her face and snorted.

"Don't see anything you like? Let me bring something else." She turned to leave the room.

"No need. I'll keep what I have on," Audrey said.

"Okay, but I think what you're wearing is a little too

distracting and bold for the camera. How about something more simple?" the lady said.

"I don't do simple and less bold," Audrey said. Jeff looked at Audrey and sighed.

The lady opened her mouth to speak, but Audrey interrupted.

"Fine. This looks kinda of cute." She pulled a blue dress off the rack and went into the bathroom to change.

The rest of us let the stylist pick out outfits for us. The clothes were not bad, but it wasn't something I would normally wear. The dress pants were tight and the button-down shirt was stiff and uncomfortable. We then got placed into another room for hair and makeup. This room, like the previous one, was also cramped. There were two small stations for the hair and makeup. The room was filled with so many kinds of grooming products. Some of them I had never seen or heard of before. Audrey was being her normal self and was telling them how to do her hair and makeup. I didn't think about my appearance much, but all the attention and pampering was nice. I had gotten my hair done more in the last few months than I did in years. The makeup and hairstylist were very friendly and chatty. They talked about their careers and the people they met. Audrey nodded off, half listening, and only responded to them to ask questions about her hair or makeup.

"How did you get this bruise on your face?" the lady asked Audrey.

"Oh, I fell down the stairs." Audrey's voice was high pitched. The woman stopped doing her makeup and was still for a moment.

"Um . . . okay," she said.

Once we were done with hair and makeup, we went backstage to get wired up for sound. We were separated from the stage by a large curtain. Monitors showed us everything that was happening.

This was it. I was about to go on stage and meet Cherry. I rubbed my sweating hands on my pants. Cherry began to speak and introduce the show. Her voice was full of excitement. *I was seeing and hearing her in person. Aunt Mel would kill to be here.*

The closer it got to walking out on stage, the more my excitement turned into nerves. I was thinking about the stiff clothing and all of the cameras watching me. I was so terrified at the thought of this being live broadcasted for millions of people to view.

"Our next guest is a popular band that is making waves in the music industry. Please welcome our next guests: Retro Brite!" Cherry yelled.

As we walked on stage, the crowd cheered. The seats were filled with middle-aged soccer moms. The bright lights mounted above the stage were bright. Multiple cameras on dollies captured our movement from every angle. I couldn't mess this up. Jeff wouldn't be too happy. Cherry hugged and greeted us. Cherry was dressed in one of her signature flamboyant-colored dresses and high heels. We took our seats on a red loveseat. *What! Was I really sitting on the red sofa!*

The set was comfy. There was a bookcase with vases and other decor in the background, along with a fireplace. It felt like we were relaxing in a living room. Some other guest was already on stage. A guy who, I believed, was an actor. He looked familiar, but I wasn't sure who he was.

"So glad you guys are here!" Cherry's red lips widened.

"We are too. How's it going?" Audrey smiled, hamming it up for the camera already.

"Yeah, I love being on the show," Porter said.

"Well, you guys have a new album coming out," Cherry said.

"Yes, we do and we're so excited for you guys to hear it." Audrey shimmied in her seat.

"We can't wait. How about you introduce it?" Cherry looked at me.

Aah, she was talking to me. My eyes darted from Cherry to the cameras.

"W-well, here's our new single 'Wilderness'," I said, biting my lip.

The music began to play. *This must be the song that we were working on earlier. Sounds pretty good.* Audrey sounded great, and no one would be able to tell I was not that talented. The crowd clapped along to the rhythm of the song. They seemed to enjoy it, which was a relief. But it was not like I helped in creating it.

"So now, Audrey, what's going on between you two?" Cherry wagged her finger at Audrey and me.

The crowd laughed. I shifted around in my seat.

"Oh, nothing really." I could easily see that Audrey was uncomfortable with the situation. She looked away from Cherry.

"So, this is nothing?" Pictures of us holding hands and kissing flashed up on the screen for the audience to see.

"Yeah, it's nothing." Audrey tried to shrug it off again.

"So well, there's nothing, I guess," Cherry said, hooting. "Avery, have you met them before? You said you were a fan." She turned to the actor sitting on a couch adjacent from us.

"We're big fans of yours. We watched your films nonstop on tour," Jamie said.

Avery had a flabbergasted look on his face. He was smiling with his hand over his mouth. "I'm an even bigger fan," he said. The audience laughed again.

"We're going to cut to commercial break real quick. After we get back, we're going to play a game of Never Have I Ever." Cherry's smile faded away as the cameras cut off her. She was less enthusiastic and ready for this to be over just as much as I was. It was weird to see. I imagined that her bright, bubbly personality was genuine, and she was like that all time. Maybe she was exhausted like we were. It must be hard to have a big personality and be on for the cameras all the time.

When we returned from break, production came out, handing us paper cut outs that said, 'I have' and 'Never have'. Now I had to answer these questions and think about how Vince would answer. *I hoped I didn't mess up or look too suspicious.* I started thinking about the training videos at the agency.

"Okay, first question. Never Have I Ever hooked up with a fan." Cherry grinned, eyeing each of us.

Porter turned the piece of paper to 'Never have'. Audrey turned hers to 'Never have'. And Jamie flipped his over to 'Never have'. Actor guy flipped his board over to 'I have'. I was the last one now. My fingers trembled. I flipped the board over to 'Never have'. Porter and Jamie side-eyed me. Cherry giggled.

"Is anyone lying yet?" she instigated. The audience giggled once again, like they were being forced to engage. It was probably because Cherry gave them a free month trial to Lumiere Film streaming service.

"Never Have I Ever used a dating app," Cherry asked.

Audrey flipped to 'Never have'. Porter flipped to 'Never have'. Jamie, to my surprise, said he had. I flipped to 'Never have'. I was sure Vince was not the type of guy to ever date online. I was pretty sure he got a lot of attention from women everyday. Actor guy predictably turned his card over to 'I have'. The rest of my band mates side-eyed me once again.

"Let's turn up the heat," Cherry sang. "Never Have I Ever kept a deep dark secret from those close to me."

My fingers twitched as I flipped the card over to 'I have'. Audrey gave me a glare. It was not like anyone would pay attention to this stupid game, anyway. Porter and Jamie hadn't even noticed anything wrong yet. Besides, Vince was the last member to join the band. According to Kim, Jamie and Porter were best friends, and Vince was an outsider. Audrey flipped her board over to 'I have'. Porter and Jamie said they never had.

"Never Have I Ever been skinny-dipping." The audience "oohed" in anticipation.

How should I answer? I'd never been skinny-dipping, so I knew Vince probably had. I flipped the card over to 'I have'. Everyone answered that they had, except for Jamie.

"Okay, that's the end of the game! Thanks to our guests Retro

Brite for coming out, and the great actor, Avery Francest. You can buy Retro Brite's new single 'Wilderness'. It's out now. Catch them performing at the Music Fans Choice Awards."

We left the set and went back home. I was glad it was over; I could finally breathe. It was cool to be on TV, but also nerve wrecking. It was so unreal to meet Cherry. I wondered if Aunt Mel saw the episode. I was so tired from the break-in and the show, but now I could finally rest a bit before we had rehearsal.

THE BIG NIGHT

13

"Time to finally get some rest." Audrey stretched her arms out. Ganymede ran up to Audrey, excited to see her.

"That was fun," Jamie chuckled.

"Yeah, everyone was lying during that game, though," Porter added in.

"Like who?" Audrey's voice rose.

"Vince. You tried online dating several times. Remember when you hooked up with that one fan in Seattle," Porter said, resting his arm on the counter.

"Yeah, it was just a game. I was just playing around." I shrugged it off and went into the fridge.

"You seem different ever since you were sick. I've been telling Jamie. I know we're not that close, but . . . "

Kim mentioned that Jamie and Porter were close, but I really thought that they became close with Vince over the years. Everyone seemed like they were best friends with each other in interviews; even Audrey.

"But what? People change, Port," I said, agitated at his instigation.

"Port," he scoffed. "You don't call me that. And Gany doesn't even recognize you. Are you even Vince?"

"Of course, I am! You know how crazy you sound. Gany." I pat my knees and cooed at him. He trotted past me and went to Jamie. *Was I not convincing as Vince? Were they finally catching on?*

"See," Porter tutted.

"He has been acting strange. He normally follows you everywhere," Jamie said.

"He just likes Jamie. That's all." I sat on a bar stool and ate some grapes.

"Stop fighting," Porter's girlfriend said. "You guys have practice for the Music Fans Choice Awards tonight at the venue and need to get along. Y'all are performing tomorrow."

"We know," Porter snapped harshly.

"What's up with you guys?" Her voice was small.

"Same thing that's up with your DMs," he angrily spat.

"Oh my god, Porter, not this again. It happened once; it's over. Are you putting ideas in his head?" She pointed to Audrey, who sat on a barstool next to me, unbothered.

"No, maybe you should control your own relationship."

Amerie charged toward Audrey, and Audrey fell. The two girls tussled on the floor. Audrey yelped as she got knocked off the barstool, and the stool crashed to the floor. The girls were intertwined to each other, pulling each other's hair. Pieces of hair scattered onto the floor.

"Stop biting me!" Audrey screamed.

Jamie and I struggled to pull them off each other. They kicked and screamed as we separated them. Luckily, no one got injured.

"You're always in other people's business," Porter's girlfriend spattered.

"So, let me see your phone to settle all of this," Porter interrupted.

"For what? You don't trust me?" Her eyes grew wide and filled with tears.

"Yeah, I do, but . . ."

Porter grabbed her phone, which was on the counter. Amerie snatched it back. He tried wrestling it from her arms. The phone popped out of both of their hands and landed on the floor with a thud. They rushed to the ground; Porter nudged her out of the way to unlock the phone. He looked at the phone. His eyes were dull.

"What is this, then? I would love to fly you out to New York?" he read with a deepened voice.

"It was nothing. I stopped replying, Porter. I would never do that again to you."

"You lied. You're right; I can't trust you. Get out."

"I have nowhere to go," she cried.

"Well, go to New York then." He stormed off.

Every single day there was always new drama here. It was so exhausting.

Amerie left through the garage door.

"Don't worry; they have been doing this for three years on and off," Audrey told me. She stood next to the kitchen island. Her hair was tousled all over her head. Her shirt was stretched and hung off her shoulder.

"It's not funny, Audrey," Jamie defended them.

"No one's laughing. It's not like you could keep a girl that long, anyway."

Jamie rolled his eyes. Rehearsal was going to be entertaining, to say the least.

After our little afternoon break, we arrived at the venue. It contained a large stage with thousands of people, much larger than the first show I had played with them. It was bigger than the venue in Crestview. This was going to be a massive show. And it was going to be televised.

Did they think I could handle this type of pressure? The stage was so huge; just standing on it triggered my nerves.

"I know we don't have much practice time, but I'm pretty sure you guys will still manage to have a great performance," Jeff said. "Audrey will stand on this platform right here, and we can raise her up from below the stage. A little bit of smoke will come out," he explained to us.

As we practiced, we stopped a lot because of the bickering that continued.

"Stop; you're singing flat, Audrey. Jamie, you're playing too slow. You're behind," Jeff rumbled.

After a while, we finally got it together. After practicing for a few hours, we made our way to the dressing rooms where the costume designer came to see us.

"Reina, so glad to see you," Audrey gushed, rushing toward her. "I can't wait to try it on!"

"You'll love it," she cheesed. She handed Audrey a dress bag, and Audrey left the stage to get changed.

"So, this is what I brought for the guys." The stylist unzipped a bag, showing us an all black suit. It looked cool.

"I like it," Jamie said, examining the outfit closer.

"I was thinking for the guys, all black army style suits," she said. "I already have everyone's measurements, so everything should fit."

Audrey came back in a pink army-themed leather leotard. I couldn't even lie, she looked great.

"Um, when did we agree to these costumes?" Porter asked.

"Um, remember last time you guys looked like a hot mess? This is a televised event, Porterrr," Audrey yodeled. "We have to look snatched." She placed her hands on her hips and flaunted the outfit.

"Just try on the outfits." She rolled her eyes.

The clothes fit us perfectly. I didn't have to squeeze into the clothing like on The Cherry Show. Recently, I haven't eaten as much so the weight shouldn't come back.

"It's not a bad look, but not something that I would usually wear," Porter scoffed.

After our mini break, we practiced a little bit more and then called it quits.

It was the following night of the Music Fans Choice Awards show. Earlier that day, we practiced all out with the backup dancers. It went well and hopefully the performance would too. Porter, Audrey, Jamie, Mila, and I were now in the back of a limo. The band was dressed in more casual outfits than our performance costumes. Audrey was in a satin pink mini dress. Porter was in a leather jacket with jeans. Jamie wore a colorful blazer and jeans. And I was dressed in a white and black suit. I hated suits. I remembered being forced to wear them to church by my aunt. They were so uncomfortable. Mila was in a long, flowing emerald green dress that complemented her dark hair.

"You look great, Mila!" Jamie cheered.

"Yeah. Where did you get that dress?" I asked.

"The thrift store," Audrey chuckled, clearly jealous that the attention was not on her anymore.

"No, it's actually a Belizzi from the up-and-coming Italian designer that won on the show, Fashion Game."

Audrey sighed and looked away. It was funny seeing Audrey a little threatened by another girl.

"Calm down," Mila's PR agent told us.

"Yes, everyone looks great tonight. Especially the two love-birds," Jeffrey added in, looking at Audrey and me.

"Such a cute couple. They barely look at each other. Is this a publicity stunt or something?" Porter attacked.

"What do you mean? I have always been in love with Leon-Vincey," Audrey stumbled, reaching out to rub my leg affection-ately. I flinched and moved my leg away.

"Leon, who the hell is that?" Porter said. He turned his head around the limo, looking for answers.

I started to sweat. Audrey needed to stop slipping up. You would think that Jeff would train her better. Mila rubbed her temples and looked away, clearly caught off guard by the slip-up.

It was weird to hear my name again, and I bet it was strange for Mila as well. It was the first time she heard it. I wondered what her real name was and if we would be able to reintroduce ourselves.

"It's nobody. Look, we're here. Smile, y'all." Jeff dodged the question.

Mila's publicist and Jeff stepped out of the limo first. I could already hear screaming fans and cameras clicking. Mila stepped out next, and the fans began to scream louder. Jamie and Porter exited next. And Audrey and I were last, holding each other's hands. We were guided to the red carpet.

"Over here. Vince to the right. To the left. Smile, you two!" the photographers yelled.

My head swiveled from left to right, trying to listen to all of them. Audrey and I fake smiled and looked lovey-dovey. We then signed autographs for fans.

"Sign this."

"We love you guys so much." Fans grabbed, hugged, and tugged at Audrey and I behind the roped off barrier.

"Let her go," security warned a girl that was holding on to Audrey. Audrey, surprisingly, could turn it on for the fans. The fake smiles, the manners, and patience. She was a great actor.

"Hey, sign this. I need your autograph," a familiar female voice said, reaching her arm over another fan's head. I peeked over the crowd to see the same lady when I was walking Ganymede. My lips parted, and I shuffled a few steps back.

Audrey reached out for the photo in her hand, which was a photo shoot of Vince. Audrey then recognized who the woman was and her eyes widened. She placed the photo back in the lady's hand, grabbed me, and we moved over to the next section of fans.

I was in awe of how many celebrities I saw on the carpet. Even though I was not into celebrity culture that much, it felt unreal to be in the same vicinity as the stars I watched on TV.

A tall young guy with a beard approached us and waved.

"That's Chas Parker. He's a country singer. He's nominated tonight for an award," Audrey whispered, covering her mouth. I was relieved Audrey was telling me who these people were. I wouldn't have a clue if she didn't.

"Hey Chas, nice to meet you." I extended my hand, but he went for a hug instead.

"So happy to finally meet you guys," he said.

"The album is so good. Good luck tonight." Audrey hugged him.

"Same to y'all." He appeared like he was going to say something else, but he was dragged away by someone on his team.

"Thanks for that. I have no idea who these people are," I whispered to Audrey. She just nodded her head as we entered the venue.

It was starting to get packed. All of the stars were already in their seats. Fans were being seated in the high-rise seats above the stage. I sat next to my fake girlfriend to my left and my fake best friend to my right. In front of us were Jamie and Porter. And in front of them was Omar. I locked eyes with him for a second, then looked away. He then reached back and grabbed my shoulder.

"You better not make Audrey upset. I know who you really are," he whispered as his nostrils flared.

Did he know that Audrey and I were in a fake relationship? Audrey ignored what just happened. *Was her relationship with Omar better than it was with Vince?*

The opening host walked out as music played.

"Who's this?" I asked Mila.

"Do you live another rock, Vince 2.0?" she said under her breath, giggling.

"No, keep it down." These seats were a little too close to be making jokes like that. And Jeff and her PR lady were sitting in front of us.

"It's Ronnie Moore. A multi-talented actress, singer, dancer."

"I knew that," I lied, and Mila chuckled.

Ronnie did an opening monologue. Her jokes were funny. I couldn't believe I had never heard of her before.

"Coming to the stage now, the biggest K-pop group, Special Delivery!" Ronnie bellowed.

"I know who they are." I nudged Mila.

"You better! They're literally the biggest boy band in the world right now."

The only reason why I knew about them was because Camille and my little cousins always talked about the group. Smoke came from the stage, and the main guy in the group dropped down from a crane. They shimmied together on beat. Their moves and formations were so crisp and clean. It was as if one person was dancing on stage.

The country singer, from the red carpet, performed next. I enjoyed his performance and thought he was a great singer despite the fact that I didn't care for country music that much. The crowd was drawn to him; magnetized.

A few more people performed and someone received an award, then it was time for an intermission break. I was having a great time. I had never watched any award shows before. Sometimes, though, I would watch some clips that were posted online for the next few days. Sitting down watching the performances was less nerve-wracking than being on the red carpet and performing. *Oh man, we still had to perform.* I twiddled my thumbs, wishing I could skip to after the performance.

A few minutes later, Jeff turned around and told us we needed to get ready for our performance. My heart started racing. I performed a few times, but I would never get used to this feeling, or over the belief that me, a small-town kid, was trading places with a well-known person.

"Good luck, Vince." Mila pumped her hands in the air with excitement.

I was taken to the backstage room with the guys. Audrey was in another room. She was right once again. The costumes she chose were amazing. We looked like a cohesive group and like we were about to put on a great performance.

"You guys are almost on," the stage director told us. "Where's Audrey?" he then asked.

All of us guys shrugged our shoulders. Man, you'd think she and the makeup artist would have a sense of urgency since this was a major performance.

"Go see if she's ready," he told us. *Wasn't that his job to make sure everyone was good to go? I was still not sure how these things worked, though.*

Porter and Jamie smacked their mouths. Jamie and I walked over to Audrey's dressing room. I knocked on the door.

"Hey, you've already been through hair and makeup. Are you good?" I asked through the door, trying my best to show some concern.

"Yeah. Just one second."

A mumbling sound was emitting from the dressing room. Almost like a chant or song. Maybe she was doing a vocal warm-up. But it didn't sound like any musical scales or exercises. More like a mantra. Her voice croaked with vocal fry and screeched like a siren as it went up and down. She was saying some words, but I couldn't make out any of them.

"Come on now, Audrey. We're ready for you." The stage director got fed up and pushed the door open.

Audrey was contorting her face in concentration. She seemed different. Her face looked paler and more slender than usual, even with the makeup. She was sitting on a stool facing the side wall. Nothing else was in the room with her. And she was already dressed.

She saw the door opening and stopped.

What was all of that chanting about? Was it to calm her nerves? I couldn't see Audrey having performance anxiety.

"I'm ready. Dang, I can't get ready as quickly as the boys," she hissed.

"Um, okay. It's stage time." The stage director looked at his watch and folded his arms.

We finally rushed toward the stage and waited on the wing for the host to announce our appearance.

"What were you doing, Audrey?" Jamie questioned.

"Let's forget about it, Jamie. It's not like she's going to give us answers," Porter said.

"You know, Vince," Porter turned to me.

"No, why would I? You don't even think I'm Vince," I said.

"Coming to the stage, we have Retro Brite!"

Everyone screeched when the host announced us to the stage.

"You guys need to get on stage," the stage director stressed.

"You heard him!" Audrey sashayed toward the stage. The three of us glared at each other but had no choice but to follow.

The stage was completely black. I was scared to death I'd knock something over. We got guided toward our positions. As soon as the lights flashed on, Jamie started playing, followed by Porter, and then me. Audrey grabbed the mic seductively and started to sing. Every note was rich and smooth and glided out of her mouth.

I could not deny the fact that she was talented. I wondered who taught her to sing. Or did she perform magic for her talent? I doubted it. Maybe it was all hoax and Audrey was just being weird.

The first half of the performance went amazing; we flowed from one song into another. Jamie became one with the drum. And Porter made the bass sing. Audrey did what she did best, and I tried to continue to fake it.

Now, it was time for the last song. I had to hype myself up to be able to make sure we closed this performance with a bang. The beat dropped, and Audrey was dancing to the fast-paced rhythm. The backup dancers were now on stage. They wore costumes that matched ours. They jumped to the music. I joined in. As I got closer to the center of the stage, next to Audrey, I scanned the crowd. Everyone was cheering and had their arms in the air. Mila was bopping along to the music. Jeff was smiling like a proud stage mom. *It was such a relief to see him approve. Maybe the group would be more at ease.* Mila's PR agent looked stern and unamused by tonight, though.

Fire effects burst out behind us. It was so neat to see, and I tried my best to not get distracted by it. I closed my eyes and went to the center of the stage, becoming engulfed in the music. I kept getting better and better at performing. I memorized all the lyrics and perfected my dance moves. When I opened my eyes, I noticed one of the giant LED lights hovering over a familiar face. I saw a girl with short red hair and three other people. It was Kim, Landon, Camille, and some other guy I'd never seen before. My eyes widened. I wished I could jump off the stage right now and hug them. They seemed happy and not distraught about my absence. And it looked like they had already found a new member of the group.

I stopped lip-syncing and dancing. Audrey gave me an intense gaze that told me to get my head back in the performance. I tried closing my eyes and shuffling my feet to get back into the groove, but I couldn't stop thinking about my friends. I then did a small jump but slipped. Some of the audience gasped; I didn't need to see Audrey's face to know she was angry. Thank God my audio and guitar tracks were cut off. At least I wouldn't get exposed for lip-syncing and being a phony.

Audrey danced over to where I was and extended her hand out to help me up. I got up, and we finished the song. I caught a glimpse of Jeff's face. He was looking disappointed with his hands underneath his chin. The audience cheered and the stage lights faded to black.

Not even a second after we got backstage, Audrey started to go off on me. We went to the dressing rooms. "The performance was going so well, but you had to mess it up, Vince." Audrey shook her head.

"You mean, *Leon*," Porter emphasized my name.

"No, Vince." Audrey held her index finger up.

"We already know, Audrey. We just don't know why," Jamie

said.

"Why, what?" she asked, taking off her high-heeled boots.

"It's obvious everything about him is so different. Yeah, they look alike, but their personalities are so different. Where is Vince?" Porter continued.

I stood still and watched as they argued. I might as well not have been in the room.

"Keep your voice down," she croaked. "This is about the performance, anyway."

"I-I'm sorry. I got distracted by something," I stumbled over my words.

"It's okay. Let's just relax. We still have to accept our award. And there are more performances to watch." Jamie tried to remedy the situation.

"I'm not going back out there. I can't show my face after that performance. If one of us messes up, then we all do." Audrey grabbed another outfit and walked away.

"It'll be worse if you leave," I said.

"At this point, I'm tired and want to go home. I don't care." She frowned.

"Well, there are more performances I want to see," Jamie said.

After we changed out of our costumes, Audrey left the show.

Great, now when we accept our award, I would have to do most of the talking. What would I say? Jeff should have at least written me another speech like he did at the rally. I changed back into Vince's regular clothes and sat back down next to Mila.

"Don't worry, you guys still performed well despite the fall," Mila said.

"Yeah. At least we won our category," I said.

Mila's mouth was agape. "How do you know that?"

"It's all rigged." I folded my arms and scooted down in my seat.

A few more awards and performances passed by before it was my second time to redeem myself. Two more people walked on stage with the host. A man of a medium stature dressed boldly in a red wine-colored suit and a woman who wore a fuchsia puffy dress.

"There have been many new groups, but these nominees have blown us away with their unique sound, artistry, and style," the woman started.

"But only one has won us over," the man finished.

"And the winner for best rock ensemble group is . . . Retro Brite!" they said in unison.

The cameras zoomed in on us as I covered my hand over my mouth. I probably looked ridiculous. Mila stood up, applauding. Jamie and Porter rose from their seats. We made our way up to the stage. The warmth of the lights caused me to sweat. I got behind the glass podium.

"First of all, I would like to thank the fans," I started. "We would be nothing without you guys. And secondly, thank you to our team. Jeff, you're amazing." I glanced into the crowd to see Jeff cheesing from ear to ear. And Omar frowning.

The crowd cheered. The announcers handed me a gold star-shaped trophy that looked like it was only worth two cents. Jamie and Porter hugged me as I walked off the stage. After a few more awards were presented, the show ended. I had a great time, but I was happy that the two-hour event was over. We walked back to our ride. Fans were still outside, trying to get photos and signatures.

"Step back, they got to go!" security kept telling them.

I then saw them again. My friends. I reached my arm through the sea of fans, even though I knew I shouldn't have. Kim's face lit up.

"Oh my god. I'm your biggest fan. I mean it, please sign this."

I scribbled on a picture of Vince. Before I could look at Landon or Camille, I got swept away.

The agency definitely had something to do with this. Why would they be here of all places? They should know something wasn't right.

DINNER PARTY

14

WE WERE NOW BACK in the limo, just the three of us. Mila was taken away with her agent, and Jeff said he had something to take care of. Jamie was talking about the event while Porter and I sat there nodding along.

"So, you have no idea where Vince could be?" Porter cut through the conversation.

I sighed. I couldn't believe they didn't know anything about the agency. This couldn't be a new thing. "No, that's what Mila and I are trying to figure out. She's just like me."

"So, are they just missing? Vince was pretty sick before you got here," Porter said.

I shook my head in annoyance. I already told them I didn't know anything.

"Mila is just like you. Really?" Jamie's mouth opened.

"I would've never known. Vince had stopped hanging around with her a lot, probably because of Audrey," Porter mentioned.

Maybe that was why Audrey was so hostile to the fake Mila.

To make things seem normal, or maybe she was just the jealous type who liked a lot of attention.

We pulled up to the curb on our street and got out of the limo. As we walked in, we heard pop music playing over a Bluetooth speaker. The girls were chatting and eating snacks.

"How was the award show? Audrey didn't seem too happy," Amerie asked, pecking Porter on the cheek. A few seconds later, he kissed her back. They must still be on the fence about things.

"It was fine. She's never happy about anything," Porter said.

"She said you messed up the performance," Elena said, eyeing me. She proceeded to take out her phone to show me the video.

I cringed as I rewatched myself, tripping and falling. To make matters worse, she kept replaying it and bursting into laughter.

Ugh. Sometimes I hated living in the digital age where everything could be captured in an instant and replayed over and over again forever. It took every part of me not to grab the phone from her hands and throw it to the ground.

"Stop! That's enough!" Calix scolded her.

"Speaking of Audrey, where is she?" I raised an eyebrow.

"She's upstairs getting ready. She said you guys have plans later," Amerie said.

"Plans . . . " I said.

What was going on? And why didn't she tell me anything? I nodded my head and just went upstairs to Vince's room.

There was a note on the bed that read:

PUT THIS ON. WE HAVE A DINNER PARTY TO GO TO.

Next to the note, there was a dressing bag. I unzipped the bag; inside there was a dark pair of jeans and a black buttondown. The outfit was plain and not over the top. I wished I could tell Audrey that I didn't want to go, but I knew it would just be a waste of time.

I put the clothes on and headed upstairs to Audrey's room. Even though this was the second time I was going into her room, it felt like I was going into an unauthorized area. I tapped on the door, and she cracked open it.

"All ready?" She wore a black jumpsuit thingy. Her hair was pulled back into a slick ponytail. It was the first time I saw her without a wild color in her hair. Her natural hair was dark brown, and her makeup was a dark smoky look.

I nodded my head, even though I wanted to stay in and have a regular night. Audrey dragging me to parties reminded me how Camille would always convince me and my friends to go out. I hated being forced to go places, but when I went out with my friends, I always had a good time. But with Audrey, there was no telling what was going to happen.

We said our goodbyes to our roommates, then headed out. Audrey drove in silence.

"So, where are we going?" I finally got the courage to ask.

"You'll see. Just a little dinner date my friends planned." She grinned.

"Where is it?"

She exhaled. "Don't you trust me? It'll be fun." She nudged me.

I looked away. *Why did I even try? I never got the answers I needed. And why would I trust her? Especially after everything that had been happening.*

We weaved through the busy traffic and veered off into a more serene residential area. All the houses were huge and looked identical. They had a modern style, with flat roofs and simple rectangle shapes. The lawns were cut low and kept well-manicured. They looked so perfect; like no one lived in them. It was very different from the houses back in Crestview. The houses back home were decades, even centuries, older. The yards in my neighborhood were never as well kept as the ones here.

"This is such a beautiful neighborhood," she screeched with joy. This place looked like Audrey would live here in a couple of years with her own family. I could see her married to some super famous rich guy with a bunch of kids. All of the kids would probably be forced to work in the entertainment industry as well. I could see Audrey pretending to be a great mother to the public, but secretly doing everything for fame. Meanwhile, I'd go back to being stuck in my small town, making minimum wage. *Or what if I got in trouble for pretending to be Vince? Was this considered identity fraud?* At least I could experience much more pretending to be Vince.

Audrey parked in the roundabout in front of the house. This house was very different from the other ones in the neighborhood. It was older looking and had a more traditional design. The house was made of brick. The slate roof tiles were worn out. I imagined the house was once a vibrant maroon color that became a dusty red over time. The sides were covered in a thin layer of grime. The windows on the second floor were small and looked like they would break if you opened them. The lawn was not as well kept as the others. The grass was taller, and the yard was full of weeds. This house reminded me of Crestview more than the other ones.

Audrey hopped out of the car. *Who lived here? They must have lived here for years.*

"Are you coming?" She looked back at me.

I got out and followed her. Maybe I was overreacting. It could be a normal dinner. We walked on the porch; there were two yellow planters with white flowers on each side of the porch as well as a giant security guard. He took off his dark shades and analyzed at us.

"Go in." He opened the large door for us. As we walked in, a large Greek-like statue was in the center of the foyer. Audrey's heels clicked loudly on the hardwood floors.

"Hey, guys." A girl came out in a black dress with a small cape.

"Hey," Audrey greeted. The girl and Audrey kissed each other on the cheek.

"So glad to see you guys."

The girl took us past a lavish living room. The room was more like a salon filled with antiques. Fine china was displayed in cabinets and the furniture was old-fashioned and covered with a plastic lining. A thick layer of dust coated the plastic. The house had a stuffy smell to it.

This person most likely didn't get a lot of guests.

We passed another room filled with more statues and paintings. I carefully walked through the house. I was afraid that I would knock over an antique or drag dirt on the floors. Soon, we were seated at a long dining table with other guests. The table was set with red napkins and gold cutlery tucked into the napkins. I scanned the table, recognizing a few faces from the agency. I sighed. Audrey told me this was a dinner with friends. All the guests were dressed in black.

What kind of dinner party was this? Was Audrey friends with anyone here? I glanced down the table at a young guy.

"Is that Dustin from Painted Dog? I think he might have been in my class." I nudged Audrey.

"Yes, that's him. The dinner is about to start," she hushed me.

The same girl that greeted us sat at the head of the table. I scanned the room again and noticed Omar was sitting on the other side of the table. I looked away before making eye contact.

"Welcome, everyone, and thank you for coming. I'd like to introduce you to Ms. Gwendolyn Ambrose." She motioned to an older woman with gray hair.

The dinner guests began to clap. Audrey kicked me under the table, indicating I should be clapping along. I clapped softly. I wasn't sure who this woman was, but I needed to fit in and make a good impression.

"Good evening. Those of you who attended the award ceremony, I hope you had a good time."

Her voice, I recognized. My eyes widened. It was the same

woman I saw when I was held captive at the agency. She was my instructor, and she took me out of my cell. My palms started to sweat. *Why was she hosting a dinner?*

"Before dinner starts, let's play a party game," Ms. Ambrose said.

Little chuckles filled the room. My heart began to thump. Audrey seemed careless and relaxed. Hopefully, I didn't have to worry too much. *What was I worried about, anyway?* This could be a fun, normal game.

Ms. Ambrose now had a deck of cards and was shuffling them. The lights in the dining room dimmed. She handed out the cards to the table. As she handed me a card, our eyes locked. Her stare was intense. She had bright-colored eyes and droopy eyelids. I looked away nervously.

What was all this about? She didn't look at anyone else this way.

"Don't look at your cards just yet. Tonight, we are playing a classic game of Murder In The Dark."

"Can we play another game?" Audrey piped up. The entire room craned their necks in our direction. They folded their arms and twisted their mouths in confusion.

"I thought this was one of your favorite games? And you've been the winner a couple times before Vince won last time," the girl from earlier said.

Vince won? It was just a game; why would Audrey care? Though Audrey did want everything to go her way and probably hated Vince for winning.

"What do you suggest, Audrey?" Ms. Ambrose's voice was stern, but she sounded intrigued.

"Um, how about the game we played two years ago?"

"Yes, it was exciting, but I think we should change it up," Ms. Ambrose said.

Two years!? So this weird dinner party thing did happen every year. I was curious why everyone from the agency wasn't invited. *Were Dustin and I the only doppelgängers here, or was that the real Dustin?* I looked over at him. He was tapping his fingers on the table and shifting around in his seat. He must not be the real one. He looked out of his element, like me.

"Everyone, look at your cards. Don't show anybody," Ms. Ambrose said.

I flipped my card over. It read '**Detective**' in bold letters. I looked at Audrey, who was disappointed by her card, and across the table, Omar sat in silence.

"Well, who has the detective card?" Ms. Ambrose asked. I stumbled to my feet.

"Okay, Vince, you will stand outside the room while the lights are out, and guess who the murderer is when the lights come back on," Ms. Ambrose told me.

I nodded my head as she gestured for me to leave the room. I walked down a corridor to the entrance of another room. Someone clapped their hands, and the entire house became pitch black. It was what I imagined the deep abyss of the ocean looks like.

I heard dress shoes clattering on the wooden floor. A thud hit the ground; sounded like someone tripped and fell. A loud squawking sound emitted from the room. *Was someone hurt?* Glass shattered against the floor. Maybe someone knocked over a vase. A sharp scream pierced my ears. I shuddered at the sound. *What the hell was happening? Was someone really getting murdered?* I heard a clapping noise that turned the lights back on.

"You may enter," Ms. Ambrose's voice bellowed. She stood next to the entrance of the dining room with her arms folded.

I tiptoed back in. My palms were sweating even more. I was scared to see what had happened. I wanted this game to be over already.

Back in the dining room, the group was standing still in their last positions. They all were scared and looked like they were beat up. Audrey stood next to an end table near another room connected to the dining room. Her knees were scrapped up and bruised. *Maybe she was the one that fell.* Omar's body laid on the hardwood floor, like a cadaver; with eyes half-opened. His black suit pants were frayed at the bottom.

"Did you do this to him?" I asked.

"No, I was running in the dark from the murder. There's more people to question. Stop targeting me," Audrey scoffed, smudging her lipstick.

Maybe Audrey didn't do it, but she was always a defensive person that deflected everything. I walked away. I believed she wasn't the murderer. It was ironic that I had to be the detective in this game, and in my newfound life. But I was missing my partner-in-crime, Mila. Dustin, from Painted Dog, was sitting at the dining table in the same spot he was earlier. He didn't look as distressed as the others and was smiling. He seemed nonchalant.

"Do you know what happened to Omar and that girl over there?" I pointed to a girl laying near a stairwell.

He chuckled. "I think she slipped down the steps, Vince. I think she's really hurt. I mean, it was pretty dark." He shrugged.

"I thought we were supposed to stay downstairs? People don't follow the rules. So, where were you before lights turned on?"

"Right by the table." He pointed at the table he was sitting at.

"So, you stayed at the table for five minutes?"

"Yeah, I pretty much avoided everyone." He looked down.

"Everyone?"

"Yes. You know, it was pitch black; I really didn't see anyone," he said.

I supposed he had a point. I could barely see my own hands when the lights were off.

"Are you sure you didn't go anywhere?"

"No, I was right here." He slapped his hands against his leg.

"Not even for a few minutes?"

He said nothing at all. His story sounded strange. I wasn't

sure if it was him or not. I still had more people to talk to. He folded his arms and raised his brows, giving me a look that said, "Now what?"

I walked away and went to the next person I saw. I couldn't wait until this was all over and I was back in bed, asleep. I talked to Asha, Audrey's friend, from Mikko's party. She stood next to a fireplace.

"I didn't know you were here," she said, agitated. She probably wanted to leave like I did.

"Yep, Audrey's always dragging me places."

"Let's just get this over with." She smacked her mouth in annoyance.

"Who was the first person you talked to before this?"

"Audrey," she snapped, looking at the ground now. She became flustered and walked away from the fireplace.

"Don't move," Audrey yelled from across the room. "You know Ms. Ambrose hates it when we disobey."

Ms. Ambrose let out a soft chuckle. She shifted her weight as she leaned against the wall, watching us from the entrance of the dining room.

She hated it? This was just a game, right? I knew Ms. Ambrose was important at the agency. I could see her being a strict mentor. She must be if Audrey was so fearful of her.

Asha continued walking. As she moved, a piece of black fabric fell in front of her.

"What's this?" I examined the fabric; it was silky and felt smooth between my fingers. It rustled as I moved it back and forth.

"It's just a snag. Calm down." She waved her hand down.

I looked at the fabric closer and walked over to Omar's body. I placed fabric on the frayed pants. It fit perfectly.

"So, why did you—"

"He attacked me. I was defending myself!" She stomped her foot.

"But why did you?"

She pouted and turned her body away from me.

"Ms. Ambrose, I found the murderer," I announced.

She appeared from around the corner of the connecting room. The rest of the guests started to clap. Omar stood up.

"That was quick. You're one of the best newbies we had. Now, we can celebrate with dinner!" Asha exclaimed, clapping her hands and grinning.

Why was she so happy all of a sudden? I was the best newbie? Did this game even matter?

Her grin faded away when Audrey shot her a look. Audrey's brows furrowed and her arms were folded. Omar rolled his eyes. *Was he mad I won too?* The girl that was laying next to the staircase got up and walked to the dining table.

"Let's enjoy dinner and a toast to our winner, Vince, who was once Leon."

I stiffened at the mention of my original name. *Why were we doing a cheers for me winning a silly game?*

The group lifted their glasses and clinked them. Audrey did not partake in the cheers, but she faked, smiled, and clapped.

Why was she pretending to be happy for me? Everyone here must know that she wanted the attention on her.

Audrey stood up. "Really? We're all so impressed? He won one game. I've had to win so many rounds. And—"

"Enough! He won fairly, Audrey," Ms. Ambrose's voice deepened.

Why was Audrey so upset? This was just a game. I looked around the room. Dustin was also looking confused.

A waiter came over with a silver serving platter and a tall drinking glass. It was placed in front of me. The winner got the first taste of the feast and drinks, they mentioned. The platter was uncovered; it was steak, lobster, and mashed potatoes. I picked up the gold flatware. The food looked delicious, but I was hesitant to eat. *What if they poisoned me?* The aroma of butter and garlic filled my nose. Everyone one's eyes were locked on me, waiting for me to take the first bite. I took a bite of the steak; it melted in my mouth. The food was amazing. Everyone cheered and then proceed to eat. *This was so strange. Even though the food was good, I still wanted to go home.*

"What's going on?" I turned to Audrey and asked.

"Nothing," she said, nibbling on her food.

For the rest of the dinner, the representatives from the agency spoke. Audrey barely touched her plate. She stirred the food around, then she got on her phone and started texting, who I assumed to be, Asha.

"Vince, as the winner, your star power will increase. Everyone at the agency loves you. I can't wait to see what's coming next for you." Ms. Ambrose's stern, harsh voice became more welcoming.

Vince was already well-known. How would they increase his star power? What was the agency planning?

"Ms. Ambrose. What does this all mean?" I asked. Everyone's heads rose from their plates, and Ms. Ambrose's eyes twinkled.

"It means you're the face of the agency," the young girl that greeted us said.

Audrey's eyes narrowed. Her fork scrapped against her plate.

What! What does that mean? I don't want to be. My stomach twisted.

"Time for dessert," Ms. Ambrose said.

Once again, the servers rolled out carts and handed out silver platers. When the plate was in front of me, I uncovered it. I gasped; it was my face.

"It's a cake, calm down. We all get one." Audrey's phone hovered over her cake.

"But why do they look so realistic?" I wrinkled up my face.

"Yeah, they do." She reached over and stabbed my face—the cake. Red icing oozed out.

"It's so good," she said with her mouth full of my cake.

"Try some." She shoved a forkful in my face.

She was so happy to be eating a cake shaped like my face; she garbled it up. Icing was all over her mouth.

Why did she dislike Vince so much? Now she was taking it out on me. I pushed the plate away and refused to eat it.

INCOGNITO

15

I TOSSED and turned in my sleep. The thought of the dark house, the weird game, and the cake kept me up the rest of the night. The sun glared through the curtains. I guessed it was time for me to get up. I hopped in the shower and let the hot water run down my face, then I slipped on some sweatpants and a shirt that was crumbled up on Vince's desk chair. I couldn't remember if it was dirty or not, but I slipped it on without much care.

In the kitchen, I took out a half full quart of milk. Cereal was my go-to. No cooking and no mess.

"Um, what are you doing? I've been letting it slide, but—" Elena pointed at the quart of milk.

"Can I—"

"Nope. The store is just a few blocks away, Vince." She rolled her eyes.

"Fine," I sighed.

I hated shopping. It was my least favorite thing in the world. Not only did I detest it, but I had to do it as Vince. *Would I get recognized? Should I put on a disguise?*

I put on a pair of black sunglasses and a baseball cap. *Was this good enough?* I didn't have any of my own money. I couldn't find anything in Vince's room, but I searched again. I looked in a nightstand and finally found a credit card. *Whew, it was still good, I thought,* looking at the expiration date. I grabbed the keys to the house and my phone. I turned on the maps to locate the grocery store and left.

"Hey," a small voice said.

I glanced over at a young girl, most likely no older than fifteen. I was only a couple of blocks from the house. I couldn't believe I was already getting noticed. Maybe she was just a neighbor or just saying hello.

"Hi," I said flatly.

The girl stared back and scratched her wrist. *Ugh, maybe she was a fan. It was way too early to be greeted by fans.*

"Do you want a picture?" I asked.

"Yes, I'm such a big fan. I can't wait for the album to come out."

I wrapped my arms around the girl. Her eyes lit up. "Yeah, thank you for your support." I smiled, took the picture, and hurried on my way to the store.

A few heads turned when I walked into the market. *Did they recognize me?* I pulled my baseball cap farther down. The sweet aroma of fresh baked goods made my mouth water and soft jazz music played. *I just wanted to get some milk and get out.*

I was underdressed compared to the other patrons, who had on sundresses with floras, button-up shirts, and jeans. *What did I do now?* My aunt did all of the shopping. I went to the front of the store and grabbed a cart. *Okay, let's start with the milk.*

Walking through the aisles made my head spin. Too many options, different percentages, organic, almond. I just wanted milk. Plus, everything was so pricey compared to Crestview. And they had weird products I never heard of, like celery juice. I stuck my tongue out. *How disgusting. Did people really buy this?*

I heard some murmuring, and I looked around the corner to see some teens peering. They shot behind the aisle again. One of the teens pretended to record a video of themselves, but I was obviously in the frame. I grumbled and walked over to them. Their eyes were large, and they scrambled away from the aisle, but it was too late.

"Ask for a picture next time!" I yelled.

The boy was still recording me. I shouldn't have yelled. I needed to control myself better. Everyone was watching me in public. I ran in another direction and continued to shop. Now, these kids were going to post this online, saying, "Look what Vince did," and everyone online would be angry at me. I walked out of the grocery store and back to the house.

I exhaled when I got back home. As I opened the door, I heard some rustling coming from the side of the house.

"Hey, guys," I called out to my roommates. No one answered. It could be them pulling a prank on me. I placed the groceries by the door.

"Gany," I called out, but he didn't come out. I crept over to the backyard where the rustling was coming from. It was the weird lady who was at the concert and that Gany chased. I pressed my index fingers to my temples in frustration.

This woman was insane. What was she doing? Was she trying to break in? I pursed my lips and sighed, pulled out my phone, and called the police.

"Yes, there is a woman trespassing on my property. She's digging in my trash."

The woman heard me. She looked like a wild animal rummaging through the trash. Her hair was wiry like hay. Her eyes were blank, as if she was unaware of her actions.

"What are you doing!?" she boomed.

She rushed toward me, knocking me off my feet. I crashed into the lush grass. Vince's phone fell out of my hands. She ran toward the phone and picked it up. I rushed over to her, and we tumbled backward as I tried prying the phone from her hands. I got up with the phone in my hand and ran toward the patio door. She tackled me and we fell over a pool lounge chair. We tussled for a few minutes. After a few scratches and kicks, I was able to grab the phone and call the police again. My breathing was heavy as I spoke. She then pried the phone away from me again. We tussled on the ground until the police arrived. I was exhausted and out of breath.

"I wasn't doing anything wrong, Officer!" she squealed, as I tried to pull myself up by grabbing the armrest of the lounge chair.

"Calm down, ma'am," the officer instructed.

I gasped for air from trying to get away from this psycho. She was pretty strong; I could barely get up. An officer intervened and pulled her off me. I was scratched up and had grass stains on my clothes.

Would she get arrested? I hope I never had to see her again. She knew I wasn't Vince, but no one believed her. I wondered what would happen if I got arrested. *Would the agency find a way to get me out? Would my identity be known and I'd go back to being Leon? Did I want that?*

"He's the one trespassing! "He's an imposter!" Spit flew from her mouth as she spoke.

"You again!?" a voice yelled. Audrey entered the yard from behind us. "She's been walking past our home all morning." Audrey placed her palm on her forehead.

"No, I haven't!" she hissed.

Audrey approached the woman. "Give me the phone!" She snatched it away with little effort.

Was really that weak or was Audrey that strong? An officer pulled Audrey away from the woman, and Audrey handed me the phone.

"Do you stay in this area?" an officer asked her.

"Yes, sir, I am also a resident here," she pleaded with the cops like she was a victim.

The woman stampeded over to Audrey, but was grabbed by one of the officers. She must be drunk or on some sort of substance. Audrey and the lady continued to argue back and forth.

"Get off our property. You're insane," Audrey said.

"I know them. I was visiting," the woman told the officers.

"She's clearly lying," Audrey said, turning to an officer.

"Both of you, calm down," an officer said as he separated them.

We spoke with them individually. The woman calmed down for a few minutes, but became agitated again, charging toward Audrey.

"They're the liars!" she screamed while running. The cops ran across the yard trying to get her.

A few minutes later, Ganymede came out of the house, barking. The cops were wrestling with the woman; she ran and dodged their attempts. It took three officers to apprehend her.

"The truth will come out!" the woman screamed, and they slammed her against the house and handcuffed her.

When they took her away, I went back into the house. My hands shook; they were warm and sweaty. I put the food away. *What had just happened? I had to tell Kim about this.*

I picked up Vince's phone and opened the contacts. I was ready to call my friends, but realized it wasn't my phone. I set the phone down on Vince's dresser and paced the room. *None of my friends or family would believe any of this, but I wished I could tell them everything that had been happening.*

I glanced at the clock on the nightstand. It was only 10 am; the day was already off to a wild start. I spent the rest of the afternoon sitting around with Ganymede. He, thankfully, stopped whimpering and running away from me. He was starting to warm up to me.

The phone rang; it was Jeff. I rolled my eyes. I didn't have the energy for this. I laid down and let the phone ring. It rang again and again. *Great. I guess I'd have to answer.*

"Yes," I huffed

"He finally answered," I heard Audrey say on the phone.

So, it was a group call, I guess.

"Great, now that everyone is here, we can begin our meeting," Jeff said. "You have to be on set at 6 am."

"At what?" Audrey groaned.

"What set?" I interrupted.

"Let him finish," Audrey scolded me as if she didn't also interrupt him.

"What's the project?" Porter asked.

"It's a pilot for a show called Phoenixville. It's a teen drama with supernatural elements, like vampires and werewolves. Oh, and your roommate, Calix, will be in it. Isn't that exciting? I sent you guys an email about it a few days ago," Jeff said.

Did he? I skimmed through Vince's emails and found a few from Jeff. It would be better if he told me. Too many things were happening, and checking emails was the last thing on my mind.

I blew out a breath and dropped my shoulders. I still couldn't get over the fact I was just on a live talk show. Now I had to act on a TV show? *Would it be hard to memorize lines? It would be neat to on a TV show, I guess. And we would get to see Calix' acting skills. I hope the shoot wasn't long.*

"Ugh, how boring. It's been done before. At least it's on a popular network," Audrey said.

"Anyway, you guys are playing a group of cool vampires who are in a band. I just sent you guys the scripts. There aren't many lines, so you all should be good to go," Jeff said.

We said bye to Jeff. As soon as I got off the phone, I began to read over the script. He was right. It seemed easy enough. *Wow, I couldn't believe I got to be on a TV show.* I wondered how the cast and crew would be. My character's lines seemed simple, but would I choke on set? There would probably be a ton of people and cameras.

My mind started to race.

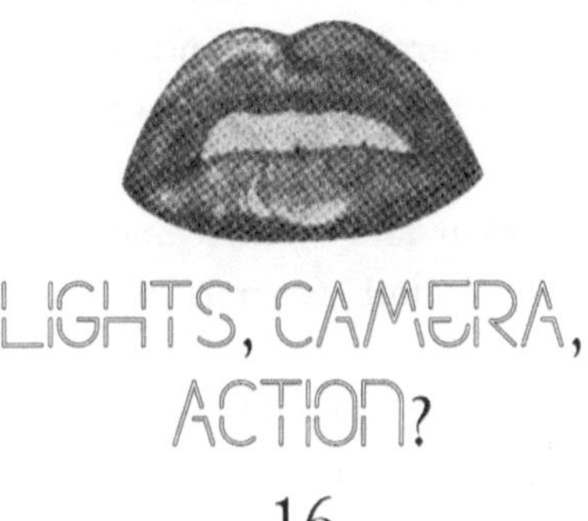

LIGHTS, CAMERA, ACTION?

16

THE NEXT MORNING, I was up and ready in the living room, playing the waiting game. Per usual, Jamie, Porter, and I are ready.

"Are you ready, Leon?" Jamie said.

"Don't call him that," Porter told him. "Cause you're going to slip up one day."

"Well, he's not Vince. We should at least get to know him. And I won't," Jamie said.

"Yeah, if we knew Vince better, we would have known quicker," Porter says.

"If you knew him. I thought you guys were closer? In an interview, you guys said being in a band was like being married to the bandmates."

"We were all closer in the beginning before we got a more popular. But Vince always kept his distance," Porter said. "Were you a fan before all this?" Porter swirled his finger in the air.

"No, not a big fan. My friend Kim is."

"Oh, so you don't like us?" he asked as Audrey and Jeff walked in.

"Of course he does," Audrey answered. "Ugh, I'm ready to go. Hopefully, they have a decent craft service," she whined.

We drove up to the set, which was a high school. The thought of going back to school made me shudder. At least this school was way nicer with its green lawn and three-story brick building. And I got to play a popular kid. I saw a couple of trailers outside of the school on a field. People were entering them.

We got out of the car and walked underneath an awning to enter the building. A tall woman with light brown hair greeted us.

"Hi, I'm Ashlee, the PA. I'm so thrilled you guys are here. I'll take care of anything you need."

"We know. Where's the coffee?" Audrey interrupted.

The PA laughed awkwardly in response. Jeff gave her a sharp look.

"I'l take you guys around the set and show you the trailers. And I'll get coffee for you guys," she added.

She showed us around the school. The lights in the hallway were bright and the floors were so clean I could see my reflection. The lockers were a shiny cobalt. At my school, the lockers were dingy and covered in stickers and graffiti. *The school was probably only clean because of the shoot. I imagined it would be a mess during the day.* The classrooms were spacious, and the football field was well maintained. Unlike the one at Crestview High, which had faded markings. I was surprised that we were filming at an actual school instead of a stage studio. I had imagined a small setup on a stage.

After a tour of the set, we were taken to our trailer, with the coffee, of course.

"We have to share a trailer?" Audrey frowned.

"Yes, it's all we have for you guys," Ashlee said.

"This is great. We are only going to be here for a day," Jamie said, placing a hand on his chest. He thanked her again.

"I'll be back to take you guys to hair and makeup," Ashlee told us.

"Oh, about that. How experienced is this makeup artist? I have to make sure everything is good. I can't have just anybody do my makeup," Audrey said.

"Oh, this person is great. No need to worry," Ashlee said, leaving the trailer. Porter covered his face in embarrassment.

We relaxed until it was time for hair and makeup. This set was vastly different from The Cherry Show. Despite Audrey's complaining, the trailer was a major upgrade from the small dressing room. There was a couch, a small kitchen, a bathroom, and a bed. It was way more comfortable. We also had more time to wait around.

Audrey sat on her phone scrolling away, and Jamie and Porter were talking. Once again, leaving me out. I went over the script again to make sure I had it. The rest of the group seemed pretty relaxed. *Was I the only one who felt unprepared?* Even Jamie seemed like he was calm.

"This is amazing! We get to be in a pilot with Calix," Jamie said.

"Yeah, I guess," I said, lowering my shoulders.

"You don't sound too excited." Porter chuckled.

"No, I just want everything to go by quickly and be okay. I don't know what to expect. This is our first appearance on a TV show."

"It will," he said.

Audrey sat down on a sofa. "I can't wait till this show is over. I'm happy for Calix, but this show will definitely get canceled," she said, burying her face in her phone.

"Can you be positive for once? It might be good," Porter said.

"I'm just being honest," Audrey huffed.

An hour and a half into hair, and ten pounds of makeup later, we were ready for set. Ashlee took us to the first scene, which was the hallway lined with lockers. The director came over to greet us. He was tall with a gaunt face and he wore thick-framed glasses.

"So, in the first scene, I need you guys to walk down the hall.

You guys are the cool kids." He grinned and spoke in a rushed manner. "Like this. Not too fast. Not too slow. Brisk," he instructed while straightening his posture and walking in place, swaying side to side. "Give strong eye contact." He furrowed his brows.

Knots formed in my stomach and my muscles twitched. *This couldn't be that hard; all we had to do was walk. If I could perform in front of thousands of people, I could do this.*

"Action," he yelled.

The four of us walked down the hall. Audrey looked great in her makeup, pink miniskirt, white crop top, and heels. Her character didn't look much different from how she normally did. I could imagine Audrey being the popular girl in high school. Jamie, Porter, and I followed behind her.

Our characters wore clothes that looked vintage and thrifted. The clothes I wore back home were thrifted, but they weren't a cool trend in Crestview. Porter wore an oversized jersey and ripped light wash jeans. Jamie was wearing a striped button-down shirt, jeans, and a leather jacket. I was wearing black-and-white striped pants and a sweater. It was strange to be seen as popular. At my school, I was not popular and blended into the background. It was just me and my small friend group.

"Cut!" the director yelped. "Jamie, more attitude, more power." He balled up his fist. "Action!"

We walked down the hall once more. Jamie straightened his posture and strutted down the hall. I tried my best to stare down the other students as we walked. *I hope I looked convincing enough.*

"Great! Let's get ready for the next scene."

Calix, another guy, and a girl walked down the hall. They were intimidated by us as we stood at the lockers. Audrey nudged the girl as she passed by.

"Watch out," she hissed.

"Cut!" the director screamed. "Stick to the script!"

In the script, Audrey's character wasn't supposed to nudge the girl. But I thought it made the scene more interesting.

"Really? I'm trying to spice up this boring cliche script," Audrey said, running her fingers through her hair.

Look at Audrey, controlling everything as usual. After a few more takes, due to Audrey not cooperating, we finally got the scene done. Our part in this episode was very minor so far. None of us had speaking roles yet, except Audrey.

"Alright, time for a break," the director sighed.

Porter was right, Audrey was so embarrassing. How did anyone work with her?

The actress walked over to Audrey. "Just stick with the script. It's not that hard, but you're not a real actor, so I can understand," she snarled.

Audrey's face reddened. "I've been an actor since I was a child, and I have years of coaching!" Audrey yelled.

The brunette girl raised her eyebrows, intrigued. "So who's your acting coach's most famous client? Have you been in anything people have actually seen?" the actress bashed, raising her chin high and her chest thrusted out. Her eyes stared into Audrey's.

"Yeah . . . " Audrey said. Her voice lowered. *I didn't know much about her career as a child. I wondered if she was in any shows or movies I'd seen.*

"Well, not according to your IMDB page. All your credits say 'appeared as self'. Too bad you can't be anyone else."

"Whats going on? Why are they fighting?" I whispered to Porter.

"Audrey met her at a party once. And they got into it there. And they have been fighting online since then," he said.

Could Audrey at least put her feelings to the side and be professional. I mean, I disliked Charles, but I had tried to get along with him.

At this point, Audrey had her fist balled up, ready to attack. Ashlee stood between the two girls.

"Okay, let's calm down, go to the trailers, and have a snack," she said, sounding like a teacher trying to control her students.

Back in the trailer, Audrey sat on the sofa with her legs

crossed. "I can't believe that girl. Let's make a video to promote the show," she scoffed while eating a carrot stick. She took out her phone.

"I thought you hated the show?" I asked.

"Yeah, but it's for the fans," she said.

"Hey everyone, we're here on the set of Phoenixville. It's coming out soon. And I hope you guys like it. Say hi, guys." She panned her phone over to us. We put on a smile and waved at the camera. Just like that, Audrey put on a happier face for the camera.

Calix entered the trailer a few minutes later. "I'm so glad we get to work together. The show is amazing. I'm sure the network is going to pick it up." He smiled.

"Um, judging from what I've seen, I'm not sure." Audrey shook her head. "How can you work with that diva? Plus, she wants to come for my acting skills. At least people know who I am."

"Great point; you should have said that to her a few minutes ago," Calix said.

I chuckled under my breath. *It was funny to see someone poke fun and Audrey.* Audrey was not rattled by his comment, though. I wondered if he always spoke up to her. She huffed her breath.

After the break, Ashlee brought us to a van, and the driver took us to a building that appeared to be a club.

"So this is where the party scene takes place." She gestured to the building.

We got back into hair, makeup, and wardrobe. In our second scene, our characters were performing a song. It was so surreal; I was pretending to be a rock star, pretending to perform on a TV show. Well, at least, I knew how to act like a musician. We played our fake set then it was time for the next scene. We were mingling with other party guest, when the guy main character became more suspicious of us being vampires. Even though we only had a few scenes, I was getting exhausted.

"I know what you are," he said.

"What?" Porter giggled.

"You do?" I said. I smiled with a toothy grin.

"Then you should be afraid." Jamie popped out his fangs. He then lunged toward the guy, but the brunette girl rushed in and hit him with a folding chair.

Watching this, it was so cool to see the action and the stunt doubles. It all happened so fast. The stunt double fell on the ground, and the partygoers screamed and fled. Audrey then swiped the brunette with her long talons, cutting her on the neck. Calix' character tried punching Porter, who dodged the hit. The brunette girl grabbed a silver knife and jabbed it into Audrey's chest. Blood gushed out as she withered to the floor. Audrey jumped up from the floor like a spring.

"Cut!" the director yelled. "Lay down! Stop ruining the shot."

"Look, hear me out. I just have a few suggestions and questions," Audrey said.

The rest of the crew collectively sighed.

"You should've asked before the take," the director said.

"Listen, I know my character has to die, but why does she have to do it?" She pointed to the brunette actress. "It's annoying that the two female characters are pitted against each other."

The director slapped his hand against his leg.

"Yeah. Can we improvise?" the brunette actress asked.

"Does it really matter? You two were biting each other's heads off a moment ago. Now it's all about girl power? Let's just do the scene," he said, shaking his head.

Audrey's face dropped for a second. The actress closed her eyes and sighed. We continued the scene.

It was strange for me to hear Audrey say that. I understood what she meant, but this was a quick scene and it wasn't that deep. Plus, the director was right; she should have mentioned this earlier.

We finished up our scenes in the afternoon. I truly didn't understand how actors did this everyday. We only had a few scenes, but I was exhausted. We finally returned home for the day.

FANDOM

17

I WOKE up and looked at the clock on the wall. It was 11 am. I was glad the band wasn't super busy, and that I had been getting more downtime. We have had a few days off since we shot the pilot. I was so glad that I could lie around and do nothing. Coincidentally, Vince and I both were introverted and had the same hobbies. Playing video games and watching TV. The stress of being famous was a lot, but I still would choose that over being in class and clocking in and out at Borrowers. The only thing that was missing was my family and friends. I wished that they could be here and experience this with me.

I rolled over and yawned. My phone glowed, indicating I had a text message. It was from Mila.

Hey are you up? Lets get brunch.

I agreed to go out. I once again slipped into some comfortable clothes and put on a cap. Last time the glasses and cap didn't work. It was likely it wouldn't again, but I gave them another try. I called a ride to meet up with Mila. While I was in the car, a man waved at me. I slouched down in the passenger's seat. *He was just saying hi. Why was I becoming so paranoid?*

I arrived at a small cafe. It was a beautiful sunny day; the temperature was 70 degrees. It wasn't too hot or cold. We sat on a patio with lights strung against a mossy brick wall. The seats were close together and separated by small, narrow trees.

Good, so far no one noticed me. I could have a nice, peaceful time.

Mila was dressed in jeans and a tank top. She appeared refreshed and energized as opposed to me with my puffy eyes. We waited for a while after being seated.

"Hi, sorry for the wait. I'm Elise. Here are the menus. Can I get you anything to drink?" she said.

I sighed. It took forever to get the menus.

"I'll take a coffee with cream and sugar," Mila said.

"Um, I'll take an orange juice," I said.

The waitress nodded and left.

"So, how's everything going?" Mila asked, skimming through the menu.

"It's fine. Still can't believe everything that has been happening."

The waitress returned with our drinks a few minutes later. I took a large gulp of the juice.

"It's not cold," I said to the waitress, handing her the glass.

"Sorry, about that. I'll get you another one," she said.

"So, how was the shoot?" Mila took a sip of coffee.

"Alright. Kind of cool. You know, Audrey . . . messing things up."

She laughed.

"So, how's the auditions and dance rehearsals?" I asked.

"It's going well, but the agency could have given us more practice. Speaking of the agency, how was the party?"

I paused for a few seconds, thinking about the confusing and odd events from a few nights ago.

"It was interesting," I whispered, afraid of who might hear.

The waitress finally came back with my cold juice. I took a

large gulp. *Man, that took a while. I hope our food didn't take too long.* We then ordered our food.

"I'll have the quiche," Mila ordered.

"Um, I'll take the waffles and chicken," I said.

"Okay, it won't be long." The waitress smiled as she scooped up the menus.

"We played a murder mystery game," I continued once she was out of earshot.

"Woah, really?" Mila leaned in closer.

"Audrey wasn't too fond of the game and was upset I won. Ms. Ambrose said that my star potential will increase. Not sure what that means."

"Really. Such a weird party game. Maybe you will have some individual projects coming out. I'm not surprised Audrey was mad you won. She doesn't like it when others get more attention. You know she has to be in control of everything."

"Yeah, she does. It was so bizarre. You're lucky you got out of it."

"Not really. I wish I could've come. I had to get to bed and wake up early to shoot a music video the next day. The shoot was long and tiresome," she exhaled.

My stomach rumbled. *Ugh, hurry up.* Mila talked more, but I kept losing focus. Food was the main thing on my mind.

"How is it with the family?" I asked. I glanced around to look for the waitress. She was bringing drinks to a table nearby.

"It's exhausting. Not only do I have to do work stuff, but I also have to be at family events. They boss me around and make me clean after them. It's too much. And we get paid so little. I miss the old life I had," she said.

Family events. I could not fathom having to be around Vince's entire family, but she got paid.

"You got paid." My voice raised.

"Yeah, you didn't?"

"No." I shrugged.

How much was she getting. How much did the bandmates get paid?

The waitress was so slow. It had been almost thirty minutes. *Where was our food? I was starving.* The waitress came back with our meal and another juice. My meal was cold; I frowned. At least Mila's food was good. The waitress apologized once again and went to get me another one.

A group of women a few tables away began to stare, but looked away when I noticed.

"Can we get a picture?" one of the women ran over.

"Can't you see I'm eating?" I huffed.

Mila put her hand on my shoulder. "We can take the picture later." She smiled at the woman, who sat back down next to her friend. Mila leaned in close to me. "What was that for?"

"What?"

"We have to be nice to the fans."

"Yeah, but there needs to be boundaries."

Mila groaned. "They're the reason we're famous in the first place."

"Not really." I shrugged.

Mila was taking this role so seriously, such a method actor. Mila rolled her eyes and continued to eat her meal. The waitress came back with my hot meal. I was so hungry I scarfed it down. I wasn't sure if it tasted good or if I was just hungry.

I knew what Mila meant, but I missed the privacy of being able to walk, eat, or do anything without being bothered.

When we finished, we waited for the check.

"Sorry for the waiting. We're so busy," the waitress said.

"It doesn't look like it. The food was cold and my drink wasn't," I responded.

"I'm sorry, sir. I'll be right back." The waitress dashed off.

"She's not getting anything from me," I mumbled.

"Really?" Mila scrunched up her face in disgust.

"Yes, the food was cold. And she took too long."

"Yeah, but you should give her something."

"The service was horrible."

Mila shook her head. "All this is going to your head. You're the one always complaining about Audrey, and now you're acting like her," she said. She paid for her meal, threw cash on the table for the tip, and stormed off.

Was she right? Maybe I was acting like Audrey.

Everything was happening so fast. I didn't know what day of the week it was. I still was in shock at my new lifestyle. I looked around the patio to see if anyone saw what happened. The women a few tables over were now whispering and glaring. Everyone else continued eating, so I guess I didn't make too big of a scene.

I hunched over in my seat and leaned on the table, stirring my drink with the straw. I left the cafe shortly after, and I went home. I was confused why Mila couldn't see my point of view.

After the cafe, I hung out with my roommates for a bit. Calix, Elena, Amerie, and I were in the living room, flipping through the TV channels.

"So, how has your morning been!" Elena's eyes were animated. She laid on the armrest of the gray sectional. Her feet were dangling over the armrest. She kicked her feet up and down. Dirt flew from her dirty sneakers onto the floor and sofa. Elena always had a lot of energy, but this morning, she was extra talkative.

"Get your feet off the couch. I live with a bunch of slobs," Calix said. He patted some specks of dirt off the gray sectional. Elena emitted a high-pitched giggle. I winced.

"It was okay; brunch was horrible. The food was cold. Mila got mad at me for not wanting to tip the waitress," I said.

"What!? You didn't tip?" Calix said; his refined nose was upturned.

"Mila left a tip," I said, extending my palm, facing him.

"Come on, service work is hard work. Even if the service is bad, at least tip a little. Before I started to get roles, I was a waiter," Calix said.

"You're right," I exhaled and laid back onto the couch. I shouldn't have acted that way. How embarrassing. Aunt Mel would be disappointed at my behavior.

"Speaking of acting, I never want to work with Audrey again," he said.

Amerie and Elena bursted out laughing.

"Look," Amerie said, pointing at the TV. Mikko was on the screen. He was speaking at some event. He was currently in the lead by a large margin.

"People are really voting for this guy?" I motioned toward the TV.

"It looks like it." Amerie shook her head.

"And he's going to take the win," Audrey said, walking into the living room. "Vince, we have to do a livestream."

"For what?" I said, twisting around to face her.

"Just to interact with the fans and talk about the new album."

"Okay, when?" I muttered, rising.

"Now!" she exclaimed. She took me to the outside patio where Porter and Jamie were already seated.

"How's my hair?" she asked, peering into her phone, adjusting a few stray pieces of her lilac wig.

"It's fine," Jamie huffed.

"Let's get started then." She placed her phone on the tripod. "Um, Jamie, why are you in the middle? You know that's my spot." She snickered.

"I'm already sitting here and you said we have to get started now," Jamie said in a low voice.

Jeff was watching from the patio screen door. Audrey stood in front of the middle chair. Jamie laggard to the chair in the back.

"Now, we can finally begin." She turned on the livestream. "Hey, everyone, it's Retro. We're here to answer any questions about our new album."

The first question came in, and Audrey read it. "What's our favorite track so far?"

"My favorite is 'The Crash', it's something you guys haven't heard yet, but it's different from anything we have done." Porter smirked.

"Yeah, I agree." Jamie nodded.

"Of course you would. Next question." Audrey rushed to the next question.

Why was she being mean to Jamie on the livestream in front of everyone? Was she slipping up? Why wasn't she putting on an act anymore?

We answered a few more questions such as: favorite place we traveled to, musical inspirations, and about the new tour overseas. One fan caught us off guard by commenting on me and Audrey's relationship.

"So, are you guys still together? I think you guys make a great couple," a fan wrote in the chat. Several of them then started commenting on our relationship.

"Yeah, we are," Audrey said. She turned around and looked me in the eyes. She told the fans we had to move on. "Okay, I'm going to add some of you to the live," Audrey said.

The first fan that was added could not contain her excitement; she was wiping tears from her face. "I love you guys so much!" she whined through the tears.

"Thanks," Audrey said. Her voice was monotone and her face was void of emotion.

"We love you too," Jamie gushed.

"What's your name?" Porter asked her.

She was too incoherent to answer.

"Okay, we will hear from you later." Audrey disconnected from the call.

We moved on to the next fan. A girl with long blond hair and bangs appeared next. She was calm and quiet.

"Do you have any questions for us?" Porter asked her.

"So, Vince, why have you been lip-syncing lately? Did you damage your vocal cords or have you always done that?" Her expression was now serious and her large eyes were in a deadpan stare.

Audrey chuckled and bit her lip. Her eyes flickered to me.

I was sweating. "Umm . . . " My voice trembled. I kept clearing my throat. *Did someone else besides that crazy lady notice anything? Jeff was not going to be happy about this.* I glanced at Jeff, who was standing at the screen door. I couldn't read his expression. He was wearing dark shades, standing with his feet wide apart and his arms folded.

"Okay, thanks for your question." Audrey hung up. Thankfully, the next few fans were relatively normal. "Let's do a few more," Audrey told the viewers.

The screen flickered on; the camera was positioned to the ceiling.

"Hello, are you there?" Porter questioned.

"Yeah, we're here," a male voice answered. The camera tilted down to three people, two girls and a guy. Camille, Kim, and Landon. Were my eyes deceiving me?

"You guys are my favorite band," Kim gushed. "I've met you guys before!" She held up a photo of her, Vince, and Porter.

"Yep, I remember that night. It was a crazy show," Jamie said.

"People were fighting and everything," Kim said, tucking her hair behind her ear.

"Where are you guys from?" Jamie asked.

"We're from Crestview. We were at the show a couple of months ago," Camille told us.

I was so shocked. *Should I say something to give them a hint?*

"I thought I recognized you guys." I paused. "Didn't your friend enter the contest and win? He looked just like V-me. How's he doing? What he do with the prize money?" I tried my best to make my voice sound like Vince's. His voice was slightly higher pitched.

The three of them shrugged. Audrey and Porter gave me a sharp glance. Jamie's mouth was slightly opened. *It seemed like Porter and Jamie did not know about the contest.*

"I guess he has a whole new life now. He goes to a new school in a different state and is with his family," Camille said, dropping her shoulders.

"Hey, Vince, you sound a little different? Are you sick?" Kim tilted her head.

"Y-yeah, I think I'm coming down with something," I said. I fake coughed and sneezed.

Kim was the only one to notice my voice was different. She was a superfan. She'd notice everything. Maybe I should keep my mouth shut.

"So, you guys have been following us for years. Now it's time for us to follow you back." Jamie took out his phone. Kim was excited, dancing around. At least she got her favorite band to follow her. Porter laughed and smiled. Audrey, however, rolled her eyes. I could tell she wanted this to be over. I was in shock. My eyes bounced from my friends to my bandmates.

"We will see you guys later." We waved bye and ended the live.

I couldn't believe I just spoke with my friends. I wish I could've said more, but Kim was already catching on to me. Jeff stormed outside onto the patio.

"Are you serious? We're going to have a meeting with PR first thing in the morning!" Jeff said with veins popping out of his forehead.

"Should have stuck to the plan." Audrey shook her head.

"What plan? PR? I thought Jeff was the PR agent, manager, and personal assistant," I said.

"But you did this one on purpose. What was that about?" Jeff said. His shades were now on top of his head. His eyes burned into mine.

"I didn't do it on purpose. I just saw my friends," I said.

"Those were your friends?" Jamie said.

"Yeah, they were with me the night of the contest."

"What contest?" Porter wrinkled his forehead.

"Look, that's enough!" Jeff snapped.

The rest of the night, I couldn't brush aside the possible consequences. *Would they send me back to the agency? Could they replace me? Would they let me go? If they did, I could see my family and friends again, right?*

This experience had been terrifying and great. I'd done more exciting things in a couple of months than my whole 17 years of living. But I could never get used to this. It was a lot to deal with and I missed having a low-key life. I missed not having my every move managed or analyzed.

Bright and early the next morning, Jeff was sitting next to a woman with curly hair at the dining room table. I sat down across from the woman.

"This is Leena. A PR agent from the agency. We tried to take a more laid back approach, but now, we have to intervene," Jeff said to me. He seemed like he calmed down from yesterday.

"Yes, from now on, I will prepare detailed scripts," Leena said.

They should have done that the first time. Was Jeff going to be around me more? I began to wheeze. *Was there any way out?*

"I'll be monitoring you. New cameras have been installed in the home." She pointed around the room and waved. "They were expertly hidden. So don't try anything." She crossed her arms.

She was right; I couldn't see any. And when did they install them? It had to be when we were gone.

"And I'll be staying here for a few days in the guest suite," Jeff said. "We have a lot of things to work on before the festival."

"What festival?"

Leena handed me a paper.

I read it briefly. Festivista was one of the biggest music festivals in the US. Millions of fans came together to party and watch their favorite artists perform. I had heard of this festival before. The only thing I knew about it was the tickets cost a lot and every content creator tried to go to it. The paper also had the band's itinerary on it and rules of conduct. They recommended I try to blend in as much as possible. If I got spotted by fans, take pictures, but don't be too talkative.

"Listen, Vince," Jeff started. "We can not and will not have our business exposed. We have been doing this successfully for over thirty years. We've seen every type of behavior from millions of candidates. We have this down to a science." Jeff stared at me.

"Doesn't seem like it," I snickered. A thin, small hand reached across the table. My neck and face twisted to the side like a slinky. I guess that was what I got for trying to lighten the mood. I was sure it was Leena who slapped me, but now I was wide awake.

"Oh, and your friends? They are prohibited from contacting anyone from the band!" Jeff snapped. "And we spoke with the roomies. They know the truth and signed an NDA. Basically, their lives and careers are in our hands."

Leena leaned back and chuckled. "Oh, we have an even closer eye on Mila, too."

I sat back down at the table for a few moments; dumbfounded. *This was all their fault. I bet they gave my friends tickets to the show.*

"You guys were the reason my friends were at the shows and in the livestream," I blurted out.

Jeff and Lenna laughed. "You think we've set you up for failure? We want this process to be easy and the last thing we would want is for you to be exposed," Jeff said in between laughing.

"Whatever." I rolled my eyes. *He was clearly lying.*

"Even if that were true, you still failed to comply with the rules," Leena said.

What rules? It didn't even matter. I felt like I was back at home getting in trouble. No matter what I did, I couldn't win.

Eventually, I was dismissed. Jeff went upstairs to the guest room. I went back into my room to sleep.

Later that evening, I had dinner with my bandmates. I wish I could have sat this one out. Dinner was more insufferable now that I have to deal with Audrey and Jeff on a daily basis.

"So, let me address the elephant in the room, and get this out of the way. None of you are going to be in contact with Vince's 'little friends.'" Jeff air quoted.

My face reddened at him mocking my friends.

"We need a new Vince, anyway," Audrey sang.

"You know we can't do that, even with your little spells," Jeff teased.

"Little spells," I muttered.

Audrey laughed hysterically.

"So, this agency is a real thing?" Porter asked with his mouth full.

"Yes," Jeff answered.

"Is that where Audrey got discovered?"

"No, there is only one me. And I can't be duplicated," Audrey said.

"We knew he wasn't Vince, but where is he?" Jamie brought up.

"He is still on sick leave." Jeff wiped his mouth with a napkin.

"When is he coming back? And why can't we talk to him?" Jamie rambled.

"Why can't we wait till he's better?" Porter asked.

"He is indefinitely out of the group until he gets better. And yes, I'll call him now. And we have so many important events coming up. We can't take a long break."

Porter huffed and looked down at his plate.

Jeff took his phone out of his slacks and dialed a number, putting it on speaker. Jamie, Porter, and I tried to see the number, but he dialed it too quickly. As the phone rang, I moved my leg up and down with anticipation. *Would he answer?* The phone rang once . . . twice. Someone picked up.

"Hello?" a raspy voice whispered.

Jamie and Porter leaned forward. His voice was lifeless sounding. He sounded like he was still sick. *If he was sick, what illness did he have? Why was it taking so long to recover?* These were a few of the many questions I had that would not be answered.

"How are you feeling, man?" Porter asked.

"I'm alright. How's everyone else?" His voice was soft, like he was half asleep.

"Great; can't believe some guy is trying to replace you," Porter sputtered out.

Audrey looked at Jeff, wanting to say something, but he dismissed her.

"Yeah, I'm sure he's great, but I'm coming back soon." He coughed.

"I'm right here," I mustered the courage to say.

"Hey, man, I hear you're great. Keep it up."

Vince's voice grew stronger and more enthusiastic. I didn't think it was Vince. If he was just on sick leave, Jamie, Porter, and the roommates would of reached out and spoken with him. And his voice sounded different and kind of staticky. His accent was different. He sounded robotic; as if he was being forced to answer.

Did Jeff schedule this call? It seemed planned.

Audrey sat with her legs crossed. She had a smirk on her face. Her eyes probed each of us. She was quiet and taking everything in. It was clear to me she knew what was going on. *Did her 'magic' do something to him. Was this another actor? A recording? What number did he dial?*

"I'll talk to you guys later." He hung up the phone.

For the remainder of the night, Jamie, Porter, and I were

stunned. Even when Jeff tried to explain, things never made sense. When Jeff and Audrey went upstairs, we continued the discussion.

"This doesn't make sense. Does Vince have any medical conditions that can leave him sick for so long?" I asked.

Jamie and Porter glanced at each other, then shrugged. "Not that we know of. You're right; he's definitely not sick. Something is up, and Audrey and Jeff are covering this up."

"I mean, he injured his knee a couple of times, but it wasn't serious enough. Only a couple of weeks of recovery," Jamie said.

"But where could he be?" I asked, peering over my shoulder.

"Look, we don't know, but him and Audrey's relationship was rocky before he left," Porter said.

"Like what?" I asked.

"A lot of arguing and fighting. Things weren't good," Porter said, getting up from his seat.

FESTIVISTA

18

A FEW DAYS PASSED. All Jeff and Leena talked about was the festival; what we were going to wear, the set, how to interact with the fans, and the security team. We practiced for so many hours a day, that I lost track of time. The next day, we were leaving for the festival. This event sounded fun and exciting, but I doubted we would be able to enjoy it fully with Jeff being around.

After breakfast, I gathered around the kitchen with the roommates.

"What are you doing?" I asked, looking at Jamie.

"Huh?" He glanced up. He'd been zoned out on his phone, popping in and out of the conversation.

Audrey snatched his phone away. "He's talking to Kim," she squealed.

Jamie attempted to grab his phone away from her, but she was already too far out of reach.

"Wow, is this your real account?" I asked when Audrey showed me his account. "Jeff blocked Kim and the others from our public accounts," I said.

"Shh, don't talk so loud. He's upstairs," Jamie hushed, waving his hand downward.

"He's going to find out sooner or later," I told him.

"You're right. I invited Kim and her friends to the festival."

"What!?" I exclaimed. "Jeff won't be happy with this. He's been watching us like a hawk for the last few days. Does he know about that account? He's been tracking my phone."

"It's a secret one I just made. I'm sure he won't find it. I told them I will figure it out. Kim is cool. I see why you guys are best friends."

"Ugh, Jamie, you don't seem like her type," Audrey teased.

Jamie frowned. "We're just friends, Aud." He turned his head away, blushing.

"Doesn't look like it." Audrey looked at the screen and started reading, "Good morning, beautiful. How's your day? Oh, she sent you some cute selfies," she cooed.

Jamie rushed over and reclaimed his phone.

"Audrey's right; it's looking like more than friends." Porter laughed.

"Looking like what?" Jeff hobbled downstairs.

"Looks like the festival is going to be the best one so far. The lineup is amazing," Jamie deflected.

We suddenly became more tense and quiet when he entered the room.

"Just talkin' about the fest. We can't wait." Porter smiled.

"I know. Reina is coming over for outfit and makeup ideas. So far, I have four outfits planned!" Audrey gushed.

"Isn't that a little excessive?" Porter raised an eyebrow.

"Your breathing is excessive," she countered. Everyone snickered. "And no, it's not. I hope you guys come with the looks. If not, I can't be seen with you guys."

Jeff sat there sipping a coffee. "That's great you guys are excited about the festival. Can you believe the next practice will be on the stage at the festival?" We all shook our head, feigning disbelief. "I have some work to do." He went back upstairs.

Amerie came downstairs with a suitcase in tow. "Can't wait till we leave. We're going to have a great time. My viewers will love it!" she squealed.

Porter snorted. "I know you're excited, but can you go without filming for a couple of days?"

"But my views have been low and this would be a great opportunity to bring them back up. Lots of other influencers will be there. It's important for my career," she continued.

"But what about our relationship!?" he yelled back.

"Are you still mad at that? I thought we got past that?"

Porter stormed off up the stairs. Amerie plopped down on the sofa. She sighed and rested her head on a decorative pillow.

◉

Early the next morning, we were all packed up and ready to go.

"How do I look? I got up extra early to be ready." Audrey's sparkly sequined crop top shined from the sunlight.

"It's cool," Porter scoffed, clearly indifferent.

Audrey rolled her eyes. "I hope you guys are changing." She eyed our outfits.

Jamie wore a sweatsuit. Porter wore jeans and a plain t-shirt, and I was wearing camo shorts and a black t-shirt. I thought there was nothing wrong with our outfits. I was no fashion expert, and always valued comfort over style, anyway.

"I'm going to be comfortable for the ride," Jamie said, motioning to his sweatsuit. "We don't have to look good until we perform."

Audrey waved her hand to dismiss the conversation.

Amerie entered the living room, and everyone sighed at her presence.

"Nice to see ya, too. Look, I won't record anything until tonight. I promise." She gave Porter a peck on the cheek.

"So, is everyone ready to head to the desert?" Jeff asked,

coming down the steps. He was out of his usual attire of slacks and a button-up and was now in shorts and a t-shirt. He looked like a dad taking his kids on a family road trip. He basically was the parental figure of the band.

"What band are we going to see first?" Porter asked.

"We?" Audrey questioned.

"Yes, we are staying together as a group," Jeff said.

"You don't have to watch us that close—" Porter said.

"I do." His eyes shifted straight to me.

Why was he eyeing me? None of this was my fault. I sunk into my seat.

"Okay, the roadies have already packed the gear and are there. I just need to get the rest of the bags," Jeff said.

The van was packed to the brim. I was pretty sure it was all Audrey's clothes.

After five long hours of Jeff briefing us, and Audrey and the guys arguing about who got to control the AUX cord, we were finally at our destination. The dry desert heat took my breath away. It was drastically different from the humid LA climate. We drove into the cul-de-sac of the resort.

"Can't wait to see the penthouse suite." Audrey clutched her bag eager to go in.

The hotel lobby had a very vintage 70s motel feel. I was relieved to be inside the air-conditioned building and out of the scorching Californian desert. The lobby had adobe floor tiles and was relaxing and inviting. Even though I wasn't alive in the 70s, the place gave me a sense of nostalgia. I think it was because the decor reminded me of how Aunt Mel would decorate. The furniture was mustard yellow, and the wallpaper was hunter green with flowers.

We went in the elevator to the penthouse suite. When the elevator rose to the top floor and the doors opened, Audrey flew out. She most likely wanted to get the best pick of the rooms. She giggled in glee as she ran into a large, champagne-colored room. The suite was colorful, just like the lobby. The living room was dark hunter green with rustic orange armchairs. A vinyl record player sat on a bookshelf. This suite was the perfect place to lounge.

"This place looked better on the brochure and online," Audrey commented.

"It's not like we're paying for it," Porter said.

"Still." She folded her arms.

"It's not that bad," Amerie shrugged. "Where's our room, Port?" she asked, turning to Porter, who was pulling his suitcase in the opposite direction.

"Um, there are only three bedrooms. So, it will be better if you roomed with Audrey, and I roomed with the guys," he mumbled, not turning around to face her.

Amerie said nothing and rolled her bag near Audrey. *Maybe he was still upset.*

"Audrey, I think I should take this room," Jeff said.

"There are two rooms left, and I'm not sharing with the boys, and we need more space. Look at this closet and bathroom—"

"As the manager—" Jeff started in a hushed tone.

"As the client, I should choose the room. The other room is just as nice," Audrey said. Her mouth was pinched.

"What do you think, Vince?" Jeff looked at me. *Why was he asking me about this? This was between him and Audrey.*

"Um, I think the girls should have the bigger room." I threw my hands up. It didn't really matter to me.

The three of us guys shook our heads and began to settle into our room. It was a decent size, with two sets of bunk beds. The room was a monochromatic teal.

A suitcase rolled to the room next door. I snickered at the thought of Jeff arguing with Audrey and howling to take the bigger room. Audrey ended up persuading Jeff to let her and Amerie have the bigger room. Jeff was less combative with Audrey than me. If she was on my side, I bet Jeff would be less intimidating to me. After we settled in our rooms, it was time for Jeff to go over the schedule.

"In ten minutes, we have our final rehearsal practice, then we are free to check out the shows, and finally, we perform." He hopped around.

I glanced at the rest of my bandmates, who did not look eager to be here with Jeff.

"We can handle walking around by ourselves. This is supposed to be a fun, relaxed event," Audrey pouted.

"Since when? Our main focus is the performances and press. You guys might be able to see a couple of performances," Jeff said, "but we can have a little fun together." He hugged Porter and me briefly. Porter shimmied out of his arms.

"For once, I agree with Audrey," Jamie said.

"We want some time alone," Amerie said.

"Anyway, let's head to the stage room." Jeff changed the subject.

We entered the practice space, which was an outside stage. The heat was so blazing you could see the air sizzle. I was sweating profusely already. The stage we were performing on was under a large tent, that blocked the sun. Even with the tent, it was still hot underneath.

"All the effects, like the lights and smoke, are set up for you guys to see," Jeff told us. "Audrey, more energy. Jamie, relax," he bellowed while we practiced.

The final rehearsal was long and grueling.

"That's all the time we have now. It was okay, but we need to bring it together for the show. Can't have a repeat." He glared at me, his dark, heavy brows furrowed.

"Well, it's not like I'm a pro or something," I shrugged.

"Now, it's time to party. And an outfit change," Audrey said.

"An outfit change!" the rest of the guys yelled in unison.

I didn't see the point in changing. We would just get sweaty again and we'd have to change again for the performance. Porter folded his arms and Jamie shrugged.

"Yes, we've been practicing and sweating," Porter said.

"I'm not sweaty," Jamie remarked.

"Of course not; all you do is move your arms around, and you guys didn't put in the same effort."

"Okay, so what was the point of this elaborate practice rehearsal outfit?" Jamie questioned.

"What is this? I always look this good," she cheesed, shimmying, as the sequins on her top sparkled.

We made it back to the resort. While Audrey, Amerie, and Jeff freshened up. Porter and Jamie were talking about Kim. It was strange hearing them talk about my friends.

I wondered if they were going to the festival just to see Retro Brite. The tickets to this event were very expensive. How long did it take for them to save up? Landon was the only one that had a job. I missed them so much. But I knew I wouldn't be able to talk to them much

"She's arriving at her hotel now," Jamie whispered.

"Okay, how do we get her to be away from Jeff?" Porter asked.

"We'll figure it out. We have to trap him somewhere."

"So, Kim is really here?" My eyes lit up.

"Shh . . . yeah, but you don't know her," Jamie reminded me.

"Neither do you," I muttered under my breath.

"Plus, you're here with your boo." Porter motioned to Audrey's room.

"Oh great, how could I forget." I shook my head.

"Yes, you are, and you're the lucky one." Audrey posed, leaning against the wall. She was now in an even more extravagant outfit filled with more glitter. She looked very psychedelic.

"Is this what you guys came up with to wear?"

"Yeah, I'm keeping a low profile," Jamie said, pulling his baseball cap down, shielding his eyes. "I came here last year and nobody recognized me." He smiled. "No fans, paps, or other artist."

"Are you sure that's the reason why?" Audrey placed a hand on her hip. Jamie nodded his head. "Not because you're irrelevant, especially when you're not standing next to me?" she hissed.

Porter chuckled to himself.

Jeff came out of the room now with a fanny pack around his waist.

"Eww, take that off," Audrey cackled.

"I thought they were back in?" Jeff said. He adjusted the fanny pack around his waist. His smile wavered when he saw Audrey shaking her head.

"For us youngins. Your generation already had their turn."

"Ta-dah," Amerie said, turning around. She was dressed in a crop top and shorts.

"Ughh, you too." Audrey looked disgusted.

"There's nothing wrong with this outfit," she said.

"It's too bland and outdated," Audrey said.

Outside of the resort, we rented a golf cart. We drove a couple of miles down the road onto the festival grounds. This was my first time in the desert and I still hadn't gotten used to the heat. In Crestview, it never was this hot in the summer. On the drive there, all we saw were cactuses and short, stubby palm trees.

The place was crowded when we arrived, and already full of energy. A large crowd was in front of a stage, dancing to EDM. They were dancing and howling. Not far from the stage were small tents serving food and beverages. People were already stumbling around drunk. There were so many people there, I didn't think too many people would recognize us.

We watched a few groups perform. The groups were up-and-coming artist that I hadn't heard of.

"I wish we could watch Locket perform. It's the first time she's headlining," Jamie said.

"Yeah, but we're performing around the same time," Audrey sighed.

"No one's going to be at our set," Porter mentioned.

"But it's worth missing our show." Audrey looked upset about missing the Locket show.

I was kind of bummed out about it, too. I wasn't the biggest fan of hers, but she was the most iconic pop/RnB star of our time. Many people would say that Locket was one of the most energetic performers and the best vocalist of all time. Locket pretty much performed at every big music event. However, she wasn't at the Music Choice Awards this year.

"Well, time for a snack and bathroom break," Jeff said, walking toward the golf cart. He walked behind us with his head down, looking at his phone.

Audrey grasped my hand as we headed to the golf cart. It still felt so strange. The fake kisses, hugs, and smiles. A few festival goers would glance at us like they recognized us, but they never approached us. Porter was annoyed with Amerie, who was snapping photos every few minutes.

"We have to separate from him, so Kim can come," Audrey teased.

Why would Audrey help Jamie see Kim? I thought she couldn't care less if Jamie or me got in trouble.

"Yeah," Jamie mumbled.

"I can run him over with the golf cart." Her expression turned devious.

I snickered at her joke. *She was joking, right? Though, I honestly didn't know what Audrey was capable of.*

"Um, how about something less dangerous and threatening?" Porter shook his head.

"I got it." Audrey pulled out a tube of lipstick.

"What brand is that?" Amerie examined the lipstick.

"Um, how is that going to help?" I said, tilting my head to the side.

She took off the cap, and a blade was now exposed. *How did that get past security? I knew Audrey was crazy, but damn. My eyes widened. What was she doing with that blade?*

We walked ahead of her while she lingered behind. Suddenly, she jabbed one of the back tires, and the cart sunk into the sand.

"What's going on!?" Jeff exclaimed as he approached the cart.

"What were you doing, Audrey?" He slipped his phone in his pocket.

"The tire is flat. Someone slashed it!" Audrey exclaimed with her hand over her mouth.

Jeff sighed. "The VIP lounge and bathrooms are far away. We better get going." He stepped away from the cart and started to walk away. "Come on, guys."

"That's too far away," Porter said.

"Yeah, it's too hot. Just use the porta potty or walk yourself. And there are some food stands nearby." Jamie pointed out.

"I guess. I really need to use the bathroom." He wrinkled his face in disgust. He entered the porta potty.

"Tip it over," Porter cackled.

"That's too much. Let's just block him in," Jamie replied.

"With what?" I raised a brow.

Jamie noticed a small tree without any leaves and collected a few branches. He looked from left to right making sure no one was around to see. He placed the branches under the handle of the door, locking Jeff in.

"Let's go before he notices," Audrey said, jogging away while holding my hand.

We were finally free from him. I smiled for a moment and looked at all the festival goers fully enjoying themselves. But my smile vanished at the thought of Jeff being angry and berating us in front of everyone.

"Let's meet up with Kim at the Painted Dog set," Jamie said, peering down at his phone.

The festival was so crowded; it took about 10 minutes until we could find my friends. They were in the front row at the stage.

"Hey, guys!" Kim hugged each of us. I wanted to hug her tighter, but knew I couldn't. Camille and Landon walked over, waving.

"This is so surreal." Camille's hand was covering her mouth. She was right; this was so surreal.

Was I really seeing my friends again? It was shocking to see them before, but now I was hanging with them, like they were friends of the band. I thought I would never see them again.

Kim was the most eager to be here. While Landon looked more carefree, slouched over with his hands in his pockets. And Camille was grinning from ear to ear, ready for the performance to start.

"Woah, it's crazy how my friend Leon looks so much like you." Kim turned to me. I did a half-smile. "Your smile is even similar!" Kim exclaimed, pointing at my face.

I turned away from her. My heart beat rapidly.

"Hey, can I get a picture with you guys? I'm so glad you guys are back together!" a girl squealed from behind us. This was the first time a fan had asked us for a photo since we got here. But there might have been thousands of pictures already taken.

"Sure," I said, even though Audrey looked annoyed. My bandmates and I huddled around the girl. Audrey pulled me closer as we faked smiled.

The Painted Dog set was great. *Was it really them performing?* I questioned every performer to the point where it was hard to focus on the show. It was also hard to enjoy myself around my friends. I wanted to tell them everything, like how it used to be. But it was not like they would believe me. The only person that knew what I was going through was Mila. I hoped she still wasn't mad at me. I hadn't spoken to her since I overreacted. I should apologize.

Kim was glued to Jamie's side, like they had known each other for years. And Audrey was glued to mine, like we rekindled a love that we never had. I was shocked to see Jamie drape his arm around Kim . . . was I jealous?

Audrey noticed me staring at them. I tried to look away, but her gaze caught mine.

"Jealous?" She smooched my check.

"No . . . um," I stuttered.

"Have you guys always been just friends?" she whispered.

"No . . . yes. Why do you care?"

Audrey' eyes fluttered, and she looked slightly hurt. "You're right." She shook her head.

"I was never into her that way," I said, moments later.

"Oh, I see," she mumbled.

Kim used to have a crush on me, but I never felt the same way. But it was so strange seeing her with Jamie. I'd seen her with other guys, but this felt different. It was like when two of your friends start dating and it messed up the whole vibe. Even though I don't consider Jamie a friend, yet.

After the Painted Dog set, we strolled around, watching performances and making small talk with Landon and Camille. It was weird to talk to them about small things like the weather, their travels, and what artist they wanted to see perform. I wanted to know more about what they were up to and how they really felt about me just leaving them. Kim pulled a picture out of her backpack and showed it to Jamie. *What was she showing him?* She was a photographer, so maybe it was a picture she took. Or maybe she saw an artist and wanted them to sign the photo.

I walked closer to them to see it was a picture of Vince.

"Don't you think this looks a little strange? It's slightly differ-ent." She held up the photo to Jamie. "Look, compare it to this." She pulled out a smaller photo.

I chewed on my lip. She was looking at the autograph I did at the award show.

"No, I don't see a difference," Jamie said. He glanced over his shoulder to look at me.

"Hey, Vince, look at this!" Kim called me over.

I smiled at her, but the smile faded as I joined them. "Yeah, what's up?" I asked.

"Your signature looks different here." She angled her head to the side, analyzing it further.

I chortled.

"We were in a hurry. Fans were swarming us. It looks like he did that with his left hand," Jamie said. He put up a finger after each point he made.

"Mmhmm," I said.

"I guess." Kim sighed. She clearly didn't believe us, but dropped the conversation.

Later, it was time to perform. Audrey and Porter were right; the crowd was smaller, like we expected. Probably watching Locket's performance. The beat started up. I closed my eyes, swaying from side to side. Audrey's angelic voice bellowed through the crowd. I began to lip sync an 'play' the guitar. I scanned the crowd in search of my friends. Kim was clapping and cheering. I smiled, but it dwindled at the thought of Jeff. *Was he out of the porta potty? Was he somewhere in the crowd, ready to attack us when we got off stage? Or could he be backstage?*

The rest of the performance went by in a blur. We said our goodbyes to my friends and went back to the suite. Porter flickered the lights on; Jeff was sitting at the dining room table. He was now cleaned up and wearing a t-shirt and sweatpants. He gave us a death stare; his eyes fixed on me.

"Don't try this again." His voice was neither angry nor upset, just flat and relaxed. He tilted his chin down and stared at Jamie. Jamie looked away, folding his arms.

"What happened?" Audrey gasped.

"Don't play dumb. Pack up your stuff. We're leaving tomorrow morning!" Jeff yelled. His eyes were opened wide, lips were pressed together.

"But there are still more artist to see," Jamie whined.

"I want to see more performances and I have more outfits to wear," Audrey pouted.

"And we have interviews tomorrow," Porter chimed in.

"Should have thought of that. Get to packing." Jeff placed his feet on the table.

We headed toward our bedrooms.

"This is all your fault. Now I have to give up my weekend," Audrey cried. "All because of that little girl."

"Don't say that about Kim. Lower your voice before he hears us," Jamie hushed her.

"Eventually, everyone will find out," she said, walking to her room.

"This is Vince's fault. He's friends with that superfan psycho," Audrey said.

"She's not a psycho!" I started to yell, but lowered my voice.

"Wait, what's going on?" Amerie's eyes were wide "You know that girl?" she asked, looking at me. "We can't leave now, we just got here."

"Yeah, they're my friends." I shrugged.

"Then why do you hate seeing Kim with Jamie then?" Audrey chuckled.

"I don't. Just leave me alone." I stormed toward my room.

DINNER FOR TWO?

19

BRIGHT AND EARLY THE next morning, we took off back to LA. I was actually glad we were going home early. It was way less anxiety-producing than interviews and possible fan interactions. During the travels back home, everyone was quiet, even Audrey. Jeff was on edge and monitored our every move.

When we got back home, Jeff continued to watch us like a hawk. He rarely left the house or let anyone leave. And if we did, we would be escorted by security. No one was able to visit the house either. It was intense and stressful. This went on for about 2 weeks.

I was a homebody, myself, but it was awful not having the choice to leave. I would rather be back in the desert partying. It had started to feel like I was back at the agency. Audrey and Porter weren't handling it well. She hated Jeff watching her and being escorted out of the house. Porter was bummed we couldn't have any guests. And Jamie was so stressed from Jeff watching him that he'd paced around the house, restless. Everywhere we turned, Jeff was there. And if he wasn't, the cameras would catch us. I mostly stayed in my room.

The days passed by with boring radio appearances and more walking on eggshells around Jeff and the publicist lady. And despite Jamie's stress, he was still secretly talking to Kim, as if he hadn't learned.

One evening, Jeff said he unexpectedly had to go back to the office. This was the first time he was leaving in weeks.

Jamie was in the kitchen making an elaborate dinner.

"I can't believe Jeff left," Calix said.

"I'm glad he's gone. I can breathe a little," I exhaled. I couldn't believe he left either, but the cameras were watching us, so it wasn't like he was completely gone.

"What are you making?" I asked Jamie, peeking into the skillet.

"Steak dinner."

"Who's this for?" I asked.

"It's for Kim," Jamie said.

I looked around for cameras; Jeff might hear us.

"They're low-quality surveillance cameras with little to no sound. We found out this morning when he forgot to lock his room," Calix cackled.

"Yeah, and we will sit outside. The outside cameras are even worse quality and drop frames. Plus, Calix will get rid of the footage."

They went into his room? Wouldn't they get caught? Jeff couldn't be that stupid. He has to know what we were up to.

"Are my friends still around? Is Kim with her parents?" I asked.

"No, they went back home. But I flew her out to visit. She'll be here for a couple of days. She's here along with Landon and Camille. They've been hanging around," Jamie said.

Her parents really let her go alone? I knew they were pretty laid back, but really?

"What!? Jeff doesn't want us to have company. What if he comes home early? What if he sends you away? You'll become the next Vince. They'll lock you up," I sputtered out.

"What!? Relax. Sure, it's been tense around here, but Jeff is full of empty promises. He's always been hard on you guys, but nothing major ever happens," Calix said.

Jamie's eyes met mine. He was biting his lips. Jamie understood my anxiety, but he hasn't seen the worst of Jeff. I don't think any of us have.

"Maybe Leon is right. I should just cancel it," Jamie said. He reached for his phone in his pocket.

"No, it'll be fine." Calix pushed the phone away. Jamie sighed and put his phone back in his pocket.

"Why can't you take her somewhere else?" I asked.

It was way too risky to bring her here. Maybe they weren't afraid of him like I was, because they haven't been to the agency, but being locked up in a dark cell and having your originality stripped away from you . . . They didn't know what Jeff and the agency were capable of.

Footsteps galloped down the stairs; it was Audrey and Ganymede. But I imagined Jeff coming down the stairs to punish us. I flinched at the sight of them.

"Scared?" Audrey smirked at me. Ganymede ran to Jamie, his thick fur shed as he ran.

"What's for dinner, Chef Jamie?" Audrey said, clapping her hands together on the granite countertop.

"It's dinner for two," I said.

"Oh, some new hookup from online?" She stared at Jamie while munching on a piece of cheese from a platter.

"Um, no." He turned away.

"No way," she gasped. "It's Kim. We have to make it a double date! I want to see how this goes down. Get dressed." She waved me to go upstairs.

I felt bad for Jamie, but I wanted to see how things would turn out myself, and I wanted to be around Kim again. But the thought of Jeff lingered in my mind. I didn't understand why Jamie, and the rest of the housemates, felt comfortable doing this. I wish they had believed me when I told them about the agency.

"No, this is just for me and her." Jamie glanced up at the ceiling.

"Let me order some food for us. You like hibachi?" Audrey asked me, opening an app on her phone.

Maybe if I hid in my room all day, away from the drama, Jeff wouldn't punish me. *Yeah, right.* Audrey would just drag me out of my room, anyway. I had planned on eating leftovers and hanging in my room all night, but I did want to see Kim; though, not with Jamie. I couldn't even be myself around her.

Audrey would throw a tantrum until she got her way, so I got out of my sweatpants into jeans and a hoodie. Then, I took to pacing around the living room.

"Anxious to see her?" Audrey was touching up her makeup.

"Yeah. When does Jeff get back?"

"He said he would be gone till the morning. He said it was important."

Important? Did it involve me or Mila? Was it because of what happened at the festival? Did someone see what was going on at the festival? He didn't tell us anything.

An abrupt knock on the door startled me.

"I got it." Audrey ran over to the door. She only wanted to be involved so she could stir the pot and make things more awkward.

"Hey girl!" Audrey embraced Kim.

I gasped. Kim looked great. She was wearing a black spaghetti strapped dress and black heels. And a full face of makeup. The only time I had ever seen her this dressed up was when she dragged me to homecoming. This was a complete 180 from her usual tomboy style. It was weird seeing her dressed up for a date.

"Hey Vince." She waved, and I waved back.

Jamie rushed over. "Hey Kim, let me show you outside." He guided her to the back patio.

"Why are we doing this? Leave Jamie alone," I said to Audrey.

She snatched me by the arm and took me outside. The medium-sized table was set for two. A white candle was lit and a lace tablecloth transformed the patio to a quaint dinner.

Audrey pulled up two chairs up to the table. Kim gave Audrey a half smile and moved her lips as if she was about to speak.

"So Kim, you like California?" Audrey asked, taking the wine glass that was set for one of them.

"Yeah, it's nice. I've never been to a city this big. And the weather is so beautiful here."

Audrey grinned while she talked. It's not that great. Everyone here is hustling, trying to be someone. You know?" Audrey's smile was now gone as she glanced at me. I looked away.

"Well, at least people are ambitious, unlike Crestview. Everyone there goes with the flow and does what they're told. Nothing more," Kim said.

"Will you ever leave?" I asked her.

"Yeah, I want to travel. Be a photographer. Capture performers like you guys. Here are some photos I took." She handed her phone to Audrey, who silently scrolled through the photos.

"Nice! Was this at our show a few months ago?" I asked her. It was a shot of Vince jumping.

Looking at the photo brought back memories of everything. If only I hadn't entered that contest, things would be simpler.

"Yeah, the one with the contest. Can't believe Leon won. Just wish he was around though."

Jamie shuffled in his seat. "Um, let me bring out the appetizer." He hurried back into the house.

"So, how are you and Jamie getting along?" Audrey asked.

"He's great!" Kim's eyes sparkled.

"This lifestyle isn't for everyone." Audrey then shoved her phone in Kim's face.

Kim's eyes shifted from us to the phone. It was a picture of Kim and Jamie at FestiVista. Audrey had pulled it up on Sonder. Kim took the phone, scrolling through the comments.

"'She's with Jamie, ew.' 'She's fat and ugly.' 'He can do better than that,'" Kim shook her head. "This is why I try to stay off social media." The corners of her mouth turned down.

I felt bad for Kim. Those comments were harsh, but I wasn't shocked. People online could be ruthless.

"Yep, as soon as I started dating other famous people, the hate came in. Death threats and hecklers in the streets. It was awful," Audrey told her with solemn eyes, overexaggerating her story. Despite her sad eyes, her voice was very lively and baby-ish. "You'll get used to it." Audrey placed her hand on Kim's.

Jamie came back with a cheese platter, chicken wings, and an artichoke dip. Jamie and Kim started a conversation and seemed to be getting along while Audrey and I sat idle.

"This is so good. Everything looks delicious, Jamie. I didn't know you were a cook." Kim's cheeks blushed as she delicately picked up a cheese cube.

It was so strange to see her eating like that. She must be trying to impress Jamie.

"I tried. I'm not really a cook," he said. "What photos did you take for your portfolio? The shots you got out here were great. You'll easily get accepted."

Oh yeah, Kim was talking about applying to college. She wanted to go to some school in California and one in New York. She had been talking about photography programs since freshman year. so we must have graduated already. Time flew by. I wondered what Camille and Landon were up to. Landon probably got accepted into hundreds of schools due to his academic achievements, and I could see Camille being one of those students that changed majors a hundred times.

Audrey was observing as if she was waiting for something to

happen. The doorbell rang. Jamie stopped mid-conversation, twisting his head around.

"Calm down, it's just the food I ordered." Audrey got the door, and Jamie's phone started to ring.

He sighed. "Sorry, I have to take this," he grumbled. His idea of a perfect date was fading away, but now I was alone with Kim. As much as I didn't like Audrey, and barely knew Jamie, I wished they were here right now.

"You've been quiet, Vince. How have you been?"

"I'm good. It's been a crazy year with our new album."

"Yes, I can't wait. The single is so good." Her round face lit up.

A few minutes of silence passed by.

"Do you really think Leon just took the money and left? I didn't think he would do that," I mustered the courage to ask.

Kim put down her food and tilted her head to the side. "Yeah, but his aunt and uncle always insisted on him doing well in school and going to a better school district. I guess that's why he left," she said. Her brows furrowed, and she placed her hand in her auburn hair.

"Have you heard from him?" I asked.

"A little, but he's been busy with school."

"He doesn't strike me as a good student." I glanced down while taking a sip of my drink.

"He wasn't, but most kids aren't into school." She shrugged.

"Yup, Mr. Williams' astronomy class was the most boring thing ever. Who cares about stars in the sky—"

"How do you know all of this?" Her jaw dropped.

"What—I—" Before I could justify my slip up, Audrey, Porter, and Jamie sprinted through the sliding door.

"Jeff is here," Jamie croaked, grabbing Kim's arm.

"What the hell? What's going on?" Kim asked.

"There's no time to explain—go inside. He's outside, so is Ganey," Porter told us.

We guided Kim upstairs; she was speechless and her eyes

bulged. I felt so bad seeing her so confused. But how would I cover this up? I wondered what was going through Kim's head right now? I couldn't imagine meeting my favorite band and all of this happening.

"Let's go to my room. He won't go in there," Audrey said.

We tiptoed upstairs and down the hall into Audrey's room. We hid in the dark in Audrey's spacious walk-in closet. I breathed heavily as I hid behind a rack of long dresses.

"Hello, where is everyone? Ganey and I are—" Jeff yelled.

Audrey giggled. "I don't know. I think they went out for the night!" she yelled from upstairs. She was near the bedroom door.

"Hmm, not you!" Jeff yelled from downstairs.

"Nope, just have a relaxing night in. You told us to stay in." She let out a high-pitched laugh.

Why did she tell Jeff everyone was out? It was okay; he'd check the cameras and see I stayed in the house. And that this, once again, was Jamie's fault.

"How was work?" she asked.

"Good."

"You guys live with your manager?" Kim whispered.

"Yep, for now. It's a long story," Jamie whispered back.

"What's going on? Are you guys okay? Why are we hiding?" Kim asked, and Audrey hushed her.

"Hmm, everyone is really quiet." Jeff's voice bounced up the stairs. Jamie's fists were clenched and his eyes were closed tight. Porter's arms were wrapped around his body. He sat with his head in between his legs. He made his body small and compact. And I was peeking through the cracked closet door, waiting for Jeff to bust into the closet.

"He's going to know she's lying," Jamie mumbled.

"Why? What's happening?" Kim asked again.

Porter hushed her. "It'll be fine. Hopefully, he won't come in," Porter whispered.

"Everyone's been tired from the past few weeks," Audrey said.

"Whatever. Where's Jamie? He better not be out with that girl." Jeff sighed deeply as he ascended up the first flight of steps. Everyone was silent, trying not to make a sound. He then went up the last flight of stairs.

"Goodnight, Audrey."

"Night."

We snuck Kim out the door.

"I'll explain more later," Jamie told her while giving her a hug.

"I hope you still enjoyed yourself," I said to her. She nodded. I leaned in closer. "About earlier, I'm really Leon. I wasn't supposed to say that stuff. That was just an accident."

Her eyes crossed in confusion. Audrey pulled me away from her as we said our goodbyes.

SEEING DOUBLE
20

THE LAST FEW days were busier than ever with shooting a music video for our new single 'Wilderness'. From interviews for magazines to more talk shows, we had two weeks until the album was released. So the pressure was on.

One day when we came back from press, Mila texted me.

Let's hang meet me at my place.

So I guess she was no longer mad at me. It had been about four weeks since we last spoke. Jeff was now allowing us to leave the house, but wanted us back before the evening. The driver pulled up to her gated complex.

Wow, this area was really nice. Mila did tell me how demanding it was to live with Mila's family. I was nervous and excited to meet them. I wondered how involved they were in the agency. The area was beautiful, but not like Mikko or Ms. Ambrose's. The houses were adobe ranch styled. I imagined most of the people in this neighborhood were blue and white-collared work-ers. The yards were sandy and adorned with cactuses and pebbles. On the side of the house, there was a thin tree that had vibrant fuchsia flowers on it.

I walked up the steps and knocked on the door. Wicker chairs sat to the right and left of the door. My stomach twisted, waiting for an answer.

A tall, slender, dark-haired woman cracked the door open. "You must be Leon," she whispered while peeping behind the door.

I simply nodded as she let me in. Her eyes were hollow. *Was this her mother?* They looked so much alike. She took me to a living room.

The room was small and cozy and had a rustic smell to it. Mila was sitting on a brown leather sofa next to a fireplace. Next to the sofa was a wicker basket filled with magazines.

"So good to meet you," Mila said.

"What?" I chuckled; my mouth twisted in confusion.

The woman sat down next to her on the sofa. "He's here!" she yelled.

A girl with dark long hair descended from the stairs. *What was going on?* The woman and Mila stood up. The girl was wearing yellow rubber cleaning gloves. Her hair was pulled up into a ponytail. Her eyes were puffy. She seemed exhausted.

"Who's who and what's happening?" I was now shaking. *What? Was there more than one Mila double?*

"I'm the real Mila," the girl next to the woman said.

"Yes, and I'm her mother." She motioned to the girl on the sofa. The girl looked exactly like the Mila I met at the agency, so did the one that came down the stairs. They also had a resemblance to the woman that answered the door. *Was this the real Mila and her family?*

"I'm Quinn, the one you met at the agency," said the girl that just entered the room.

I gasped. My eyes shifted from Mila to Quinn.

"Wait, so you're alive?" I inhaled deeply.

The mother's eyebrows lowered. "Why wouldn't she be?"

she said. Her voice was high pitched, and her thin face had a scowl on it.

"Quinn is just contracted to do a couple of stand-ins for me. At panels, meet-and-greets, and smaller events. I've been so busy this year and decided I needed some help," Mila said.

"You needed help? Why not reschedule if you're so booked?" I shook my head.

Her missing a couple of events wouldn't be a big deal. But I was so confused. *They know about the agency?* My mind was racing with so many thoughts, it was hard for me to find the words to speak.

"Quinn told me that Vince might of ran away or been murdered." Mila nodded her head.

"Murdered?!" I screamed. *Who could have murdered him?* It seemed like Quinn told them everything. *Could they really be trusted?*

"Yes, those were the conclusions we came to unfortunately," the mother said. Her face was pale. Mila's eyes became sullen.

"I hope none of this and he really is just ill," Mila said. It was hard for me to see her upset. Vince was one of her best friends. I couldn't imagine not knowing if they were alive or not.

"We'll get to the bottom of all of this," Quinn said as she rubbed Mila's shoulder.

It was beyond weird seeing how much Quinn and Mila looked so similar. Even more so than Vince and I. I mean, even their mannerisms were similar. Their voices were different, but had the same cadence when they spoke. My eyes became flying saucers.

"So, people in the business know about the agency?" I asked.

"Well, yes and no," Mila said. She brushed her hair to the side. "Only certain entertainers do. When you reach a larger status, they contact you. They also do PR, bookings, and other normal things, not just hire doubles."

"Oh, so they don't lock up everyone in cells and hold them captive? And what about Ms. Ambrose?"

Were they not hearing what I was saying? Sure, doubles weren't normal, but this wasn't either.

Mila let out a long sigh and hung her head. "I've heard of horror stories about the agency, but it's all hearsay. There's no actual proof. And Ms. Ambrose is one of the founders of the agency and a well-respected mentor there," she said.

"B-but it's true," I stammered. "When was the last time you talked to Vince?" I extended my hand toward her.

"It was when he was in the hospital. I visited him. He had pneumonia. I got a text from him the other day saying he was still in the hospital recovering."

"Really?" I said.

"Yep, but when I tried to call the hospital, they said there wasn't a patient with that name there," she said.

"What about his parents?" I shrugged. "They came over, and they know I'm not Vince. They said he got sick overseas and was in the hospital there. They're playing along. But why? Can't the band go on hiatus till he gets better? I doubt they would keep all this going if he was murdered."

"They're playing along? You wouldn't understand the heights parents are willing to go through to make money off their kids." Mila side-eyed her mother for a second. Her mother rolled her eyes and looked away. "The show must always go on. No matter what. I tried calling his parents but they wouldn't answer," Mila said.

What was she saying? Did his parents know the whole truth? Was the agency stopping them from discovering what really happened?

"I'm just lost," I said. "Audrey has something to do with this. Do you think she put a hex on him? Is she actually capable of murder?" I asked.

I had seen some of Audrey's rage, and she even joked about running Jeff over, so the idea was not too far-fetched? But why?

The ladies chuckled. They turned to face each other. *Did I say something wrong?*

"Audrey's a quirky girl. Do really believe in that stuff?" Mila snorted. The girls stared at me.

"No—" I started.

"We should go up to the hospital or show up at his parents' house?" Quinn suggested, interrupting.

"Maybe, but it sounds too risky and might make things worse," Mila said.

"What about the other people at the agency? Is Omar okay? How about Arin from Painted Dog?"

Mila's mother shrugged.

"They're fine. I just spoke with Arin the other day. Omar just reinjured himself and needed help as well," Mila said.

I wondered if she really spoke with them. Was she close friends with them? Would she be able to tell the difference? It was a relief to hear that they might be okay.

"I'll figure out our next move," Quinn said.

"But first, you have to finish cleaning the attic," Mila's mother said to Quinn.

"Why can't you guys at least help?" she asked.

"We have to save her energy. She has rehearsal today and a lot of other things coming up. And hurry up, you have an appearance early tomorrow."

Quinn looked at me, dropped her shoulders, and started to go back upstairs.

My phone rang. It was Audrey. "Get back home now!" Audrey squealed. Her voice boomed through the phone.

"What? Why right now?"

"Your crazy friends are here, and Jeff is upset about them being here!"

"Leave immediately. Jamie, you know how I feel about guests! And they were snooping around the house!" Jeff yelled. I could hear the anger in his voice.

"Okay, I'm on the way," I said.

What were they doing back at the house? It seems like every day the unexpected happens.

When I got home and entered the house, my friends were sitting on the couch.

"Can we go now?" Camille said through gritted teeth.

"What's going on, Audrey? What are you guys doing here?" I motioned toward my friends.

"You guys can leave after you sign these right here." Jeff held out a bunch of papers.

"I'm not signing anything." Camille folded her arms.

Kim reached for the documents, but Camille pushed them away. The papers flew to the floor.

"We didn't do anything. And we still don't know what's going on," Landon said.

"Well, if you insist on leaving, you must sign these, or else you're not going anywhere!" Jeff yelled. He yanked the papers off of the floor and handed them to Kim.

The girls signed the papers without reading them while Landon glanced at them and scribbled his signature.

"And you are no longer welcome in this home," Jeff said. His voice was more calm as he eyed each one of them.

"This home isn't yours!" Jamie yelled.

"Hmm, this place was always mine. But now I have to keep a closer eye on you guys! You don't obey my rules. So you will deal with the consequences." His voice rose again as he banged his fist against the sofa.

My friends stood up, and Jeff hustled them toward the door.

"I can't believe you!" Jamie screamed.

"They were going through our stuff . . . your stuff!" Audrey scolded him. "She's just like the last girl."

Porter looked at Audrey. His mouth was ajar.

"The one that used you and stole from you?" Audrey said.

"Wait! Kim would never use him. She's not like that. She was just looking for answers," I said, shaking my head.

"To things that do not concern her at all. This isn't about you, Leon; it never was!" Audrey yelled.

I marched off into my room as my friends left the house.

About an hour later, I heard Audrey crying from her room. I was laying in bed trying to nap, but I couldn't relax. I placed a pillow over my ears; I could still hear Audrey. I got up and went into the hallway where Amerie and Porter were.

"I can't believe this!" Audrey cried from the floor above.

"I'll fix it. You can recover from this," Leena told her.

"No, I'm over. I'm canceled!" she yelped through tears.

"What is she talking about?" Porter and Amerie laughed without any concern of Audrey hearing them.

"This," Amerie said, scrolling on her phone.

"Everyone's talking about Audrey and how awful she is," Porter said.

"Oh, there's more," he continued. "She was at a restaurant and she didn't pay. One of the waiters posted about it. And it's trending online, and it's now a challenge called 'Dine and Dash'. And people are posting videos of them running off without paying," Porter said.

I couldn't believe people were doing a challenge because of what Audrey did. I knew she had many fans, but I didn't know she had that much influence. I thought what I did at that restaurant was bad. *Did anyone overhear what happened and posted about it online?* It could be possible, but if so, I was sure my bandmates and roommates would've told me.

"'With all the money and fame, you'd think she'd just say she doesn't like the food and move on,'" Porter read a comment.

Audrey came down to the second floor, and the snickering and sneering stopped.

"I know you guys were laughing. You don't understand what this will do to my career." She wiped tears from her face. Her eyes were red and puffy. She went down to the first floor, and we followed her.

"I promise I will fix everything," Leena said, trotting down the steps, her heels clicking against the steps. She followed down to the first floor.

"I might as well quit and retire," Audrey whimpered. She balled her body up on the couch.

"And do what?" Jamie asked.

"I don't know. I put my whole life into this!" Audrey wailed.

This reminded me of how Kim told me that Audrey dropped out of high school to pursue music and that she was a child actor.

Jeff entered the living room through the back patio.

"Are Kim and the others returning to Crestview? I haven't had the chance to get back in touch with them," Jamie asked Jeff.

"Stop talking about them. We have more important things to discuss," Jeff sneered while drinking from a mug.

MEET THE PARENTS

21

ONE MORNING, we were in the kitchen having breakfast. Jamie was scrolling on his phone.

"Kim's not answering me back! I even tried calling Camille and Landon, but they're not answering either," he said.

"They're probably busy. They were talking about getting ready for college," Audrey said, while drinking a glass of water.

The idea of going to college or working actually sounded appealing to me. I would rather be sitting in a lecture or getting yelled at by Mr. McKinney. I hoped what Audrey said was true. That they were moving on from what happened.

Jeff walked into the kitchen, and we immediately stopped talking about my former friends.

"How's everyone?" He grinned; his teeth sparkled. Though, he looked unkempt. His hair was feathered out of place and he had bags underneath his eyes.

We mumbled an "okay" in response.

"Okay, the new single is not performing as well as we expected." He folded his arms.

Audrey scowled, making her eyebrows rise up.

"So . . . " she pondered.

"Let me finish. I want all of you to tell the fans to stream the song 24/7 at work, school, and while sleeping. Buy more than one copy of the song," Jeff said.

"So, basically cheat," Porter said, scratching the back of his neck.

"No," Jeff said in a monotone voice. "Bands and their labels do this all the time. Warehouses are full of CDs."

"Really!" Jamie covered his mouth with his palm.

Wow, really? It seemed like everything was fake and manipulated.

"I think it's great. We can't have a release party without numbers or buzz. Oh, by the way, Vincey, we have to go to my parents' for dinner tonight," Audrey said.

"Of course, you're telling me now." I rubbed my temples. "And we're having a release party? When?"

"Sorry, it's short notice. I don't want to go either. I've been putting off visiting them." She glanced away. "Yes, the party is in a few nights."

"Then we don't have to," I said. "Let's stay home. Why do I even have to go?" I stretched my legs out on the barstool.

She took a deep breath. I've been gaffing them off for a while now. And my family has been asking about you. So let's get it over with," she exhaled again.

"Fine." I got up and staggered to my room.

Audrey dressed me up and gave me the rundown.

"Do your parents know this is for PR?" I asked.

"No. They know we're back together, and they think we're dating for real. Just be quiet and let me do all the talking. They're a handful," she said, spraying some cologne on me.

"How!?" I asked.

"Well, for starters, my dad never liked Vince from the beginning. He felt like I deserved to be with someone with more connections, and he hates that I'm part of a band. He wants me to have a solo career. He ignores my little brother and shames him for not being as successful as me." She adjusted the collar on my shirt. "My mother; she constantly will be talking about my career. Asking me all about any upcoming projects. It's kind of sweet, but it gets annoying quick. And my brother is just silently a part of all of this. I'll be ready in a minute." Audrey stepped out of the room.

Woah, that was a lot to take in. I couldn't imagine being a part of a family that forced their kids into a career like this. No wonder Audrey was like this. My aunt and uncle pressured me to make good grades and find a career path, but nothing like Audrey's parents, it seemed.

Thirty minutes later, we were at their home. I was still surprised at how beautiful the homes were here. I thought I would never see houses like these in real life. This house was beige, made out of cobblestone bricks. It reminded me of a villa somewhere in a European country. Small shrubby and flowers covered the yard. Purple flowers were in front of an address plate that was mounted to brick edging; it read: 2874. This house must've cost a fortune.

What did her parents do for a living? Did they take Audrey's money? My stomach churned as I got out of the car. *I had to make it through this evening without causing a scene. At least I got the opportunity to know a little bit more about Audrey.*

A man opened the door. His brown eyes glimmered when he saw Audrey, and dimmed at the sight of my face. He was short and muscular, with dark black hair that looked dyed to cover any gray hairs.

"Hey, honey! Hi, Vince." His voice dropped.

"Hey." I raised my hand.

"Why is he here?" Her dad motioned at me.

"Dad, stop! I wanted him to join us." Audrey giggled.

"Why? Are you with him again?" he asked. He turned around and grumbled as he walked away.

I went into the kitchen, where I presumed from the smell of onions someone was cooking.

"Oh, good, it' you, Audie! You guys came just in time to help me in the kitchen," her mother sung.

Her mother was slim and had light brown hair. Audrey's looks were a perfect mixture of her mother and father. She had the same amber eyes and petite stature as her mother, and her father's nose and mouth.

Audie. I bet she hates that cutesy nickname. I chuckled and glanced at Audrey. She clenched her jaw.

"What are we making tonight?" she asked her mother.

"Fried rice, stir-fried vegetables, and egg rolls. Vince is a great cook, so this should be no challenge for us," she said. She took an egg out of the fridge.

I remembered Kim telling me Vince was a great cook. She showed me a couple of photos he posted online of food he made. I also remembered seeing something about him cooking when I was at the agency. Even though the food looked great in the photos, I couldn't imagine him in the kitchen, let alone creating a meal from scratch. He seemed laid back and more of a guy that ordered take out. I was not a cook at all; my aunt made all of the meals.

"Maybe I can sit this one out," Audrey said, sitting on a barstool near an island.

"Don't ruin everyone's fun," her mother said in a bubbly voice.

Audrey got up to rejoin us. On the wall of the living room adjoined to the kitchen, pictures of Audrey hung. *Where were the pictures of her brother or the entire family? It was awful that she got all of the attention.* The photos captured her at every age. *How old was Audrey, anyway?* She appeared so different, with no makeup, younger, and doe-eyed. A lot of the photos seemed to be promo shots from TV shows, live performance, and modeling headshots.

A few moments later, both of us were assisting her mother in the kitchen. The whole time I was thinking, *Am I doing this right? How do I cut this? How much seasoning do I add?* Between Audrey almost cutting her finger, and me almost burning the chicken, I could say that cooking the meal was a complete disaster.

"I'm going upstairs to freshen up. Come on, Vince." She motioned for me to follow her.

We went back to the foyer and up a spiral staircase. A gigantic chandelier hung above us. I followed Audrey up the staircase and around the corner. She entered a bathroom and shut the door; the hinge clicked behind her.

"Your parents seem nice—" I started to say through the door.

She let out a loud snort. The sink was running. "That's nice of you to say. They're really not, though. All they care about is this Hollywood shit. You see this house? It's mine. I'm the family's national treasure," she sneered.

I was not surprised. She had the typical 'childhood star' trauma. This had been her entire life. She continued blathering on, but I zoned out and peeped down the long hallway to see a door opened. *I'd be quick, and she wouldn't notice.* I crept down the hall, just in case she could hear me. I went inside a pink-walled room. It looked like it hadn't been touched since she was a teenager. Posters of famous actors when they were young, hung on the wall, along with pageant pictures lined up on a dresser. Stuffed animals were stationed on the shelves.

I walked over to a pink fluffy bed with a canopy draping from above. I had to find something of interest. I peered under the bed. Something was underneath, but I couldn't tell what it was. I ran my hand on the edges of the item and pulled it from under the bed. It was a shoe box. It was heavy, but I could tell shoes weren't in it. I pulled it from under the bed and opened it.

Notes flew out from the lid to the floor. Pictures of Vince and Audrey from a photo booth. They looked pretty young . . . maybe teens. *Were they dating back then or were they just friends?* There was one piece of paper with the name Vincent Micheal Continolo written on the entire paper. *Why was his name on this paper?* More pictures with family and friends. Nothing else out of the ordinary.

I rummaged around some more. A lock of dark curly hair was crumpled up in the corner of the box. The texture was similar to mine and Vince's. I put it back in the box and shuddered. *This was weird. I wondered if this was one of Audrey's magic practices.*

"Hey Audrey," a voice said while entering the room. A boy younger, or around the same age as me, entered. "Hey Vince, didn't know you were here."

"Hey, it was last minute."

This must've been her brother. Audrey never spoke about her family until today. She didn't seem too keen of her family, anyway.

"What are you doing in there!?" Audrey's voice softened when she saw the boy. "Hi, Lewis." Audrey had changed into a tank top dress.

"Hey, I'm glad you guys are here!" His lips curved up. Dimples became visible on his cheeks. Audrey grinned back and seemed genuinely happy to see him.

"I'll see you downstairs," he said, and left the room a few seconds later.

"What were you doing in here? Did you tell him anything?" she snapped.

"No, who is he? Your brother, right?" I asked.

"Yes, that's Lewis, my brother. Were you paying attention?" She rolled her eyes. "He's in the background of my shadow and is a failed child star."

"Woah, don't say that so loud." I looked outside the door to see if he was still near.

"It's okay; he's used to it. My parents always bring it up." Her voice dropped. "Let's go back downstairs before we get called down."

We walked back downstairs to the table where the rest of the family was waiting for us.

"So, are you guys back together for real?" Audrey's father asked me before I could sit down.

I glanced at Audrey, who was seated next to me at the small rectangle table.

She chuckled. "Yes, we are. Calm down, Dad. Can we sit down first?"

He folded his arms and went back to eating.

"You guys started without us," she said.

Was he joking, or did he know about the contract? They seemed pretty involved in her career.

"So, when does the tour start?" her mother asked, leaning forward in her seat.

"In a couple of months," Audrey said, her voice was dry.

"The first track is so good. Wish it wasn't a duet though—no offense to Vince. Oh, and your outfit at FestiVista was a killa." Her mom was going on and on. *Like mother, like daughter.*

I thought Audrey liked talking about things, like her career and outfits. *It was weird that it seemed to bother her now. I could see how it was annoying, but I thought she'd loved it.*

"So, what's up with you, Lewis?" Audrey pivoted in her seat. Lewis opened his mouth to speak.

"Nothing much. Just going to community college," the father interjected.

"Don't do this now!" Audrey said, eyeing her dad. "That's great, Lew." Audrey hung her head low. Lewis stared down at his plate and mixed his food around with his fork.

"He's seen and heard worse," the father grumbled.

Worse? What was happening to this family?

After a long and painful dinner of talking about Audrey, it was time to say our goodbyes. Audrey's mother gave me a warm hug.

"Don't be a stranger," her mother said, her amber eyes shining.

Her father pulled me close to him. "This is your last chance. You hear me?" His eyes intensified as they met mine.

"Y-yeah," I stumbled. *What did Vince do? Was it Audrey's word against his?*

We dashed out of the house and got back into the car as if the house was on fire. Audrey was cheesing as we backed out of the driveway. She was more excited to leave than I was. So much was on my mind, I just had to ask Audrey.

"So, your parents don't know about the relationship contract? Do they even know I'm not Vince?" I asked.

Audrey kept her eyes fixated on the road. "No, they don't know about the contract or that you're not Vince."

"Really? They're so involved in your career."

"Yeah, but I'm too busy to talk to them nowadays," she huffed.

"When will this all be over? When can Mila and I go back home? Was Jeff always like this? This can't be legal, right? I was tricked," I rattled.

"Can you hush? Let's go home." She shook her head.

When we got back home, Audrey greeted the roommates and went to her room. Jamie staggered down the stairs.

"I know they're at the agency," Jamie slurred his words. The roommates must have started drinking already.

"Really, how?" My heart started to race. *I couldn't believe it. Was he sure? Were they okay?* The image of them being locked up and tortured, like I was, made my blood boil.

"Yeah, go confront him about it." He hiccuped.

Jamie definitely needed to lay off the drinking. Though, to be fair, there was not much of a difference between drunk and sober Jamie.

"Do it! I need to see this!" Calix exclaimed.

"It's been boring around here," Amerie said.

"Whatever." I headed upstairs to Jeff's room. *They were right. It was time to get answers. I needed to know where my friends were.* As I knocked on the door, my heart thumped.

"Yes, please come in," he responded softly.

I entered his room. It was more spacious than I thought it would be and decorated plainly. A small desk was in the corner.

"So, what's wrong? How was meeting the folks?" His voice was groggy, like he just woke up.

"It was interesting." I nodded.

"Yes, Laurie and Jacob are quite the couple. Anything on your mind?" He gestured for me to sit down at the desk. I hesitantly did. It felt like I was at the principal's office or back when Seth fired me.

"So," I cleared my throat. "Where are Camille, Landon, and Kim? We want to know . . . now! Are they at the agency?"

"What makes you say that? And who is 'we'?"

"The roommates . . . Jamie."

"So you believe anything that fool says? It's early in the evening, and he's already drunk." He looked at his watch. "And look, I really don't know anything about your little friends." He smirked.

"If they're there, then I'll do anything you want to let them go."

He let out a deep belly laugh. He was now pacing around the room. "You really think that? Your friends are pretty useless. Why would we want them?" He threw a hand up.

I balled up my fist and slammed it on the desk. "They're not useless!"

"Why would Jamie believe they're at the agency? They could be anywhere."

"You do know!" Jamie burst through the room and lunged toward Jeff. Jeff hurled him to the floor. His drunk body bounced against the wood flooring. "Get him," Jamie mumbled.

I picked up a desk chair and tossed it at Jeff. It smacked him against the head. He fell to the floor and groaned. I picked up the chair once more and began to repeatedly hit him with it. He winced in pain.

"Where are they?" I gritted through my teeth.

"I don't know. Stop or I'll call the cops," Jeff said.

I grabbed a small vase from his desk. "I'll tell them you kidnapped me and forced me into identity fraud!"

"Tell them," he said, scrambling up from the floor.

I took my phone out of my pocket to call the police.

"Stop, Leon. This doesn't look too good for you." Jamie grabbed my shoulder, then took the vase from my hands.

I pushed Jamie to the side. He stumbled to the floor again. The vase crashed against the wood floor, breaking into many pieces. My fingers trembled as I dialed 911. *What would I say?* My breathing became heavy.

"911, what's your emergency?" a woman answered.

"Yes, I'm being attacked. I've been kidnapped and told I have to be a replacement for Vince Continolo. You know, the singer. They held me captive at Muse Talent Agency," I said, gasping.

"What is the address and what is your callback number?"

"Um . . . I'm not sure. My number is 202-555-0511. Wait, it's . . . " My hands were now sweaty. I gave the dispatcher my phone number. I forgot this was Vince's phone.

"Where is the attacker now?" I looked over at Jeff. He was now standing up. His eyes glared at me as he sprinted toward me.

"He's after me now. He's been surveillancing my family and my friends. I think the agency kidnapped them too," I said, running down the hall to my room. My heart thumped in my chest. My feet clicked against the wooden floors and cold air rushed into my lungs. I slammed the door behind me.

"Sir, this line is for emergency calls only." The dispatcher hung up the phone.

"Hello!" I yelled into the phone. No response. My lungs felt like they were on fire.

Jeff was banging on the door nonstop. I thought the door would cave in at any moment.

"Never try me again! You think the agency was scary? You haven't seen anything yet. If you don't want to go back, do what you're told!" His voice rattled the house.

"Calm down. We just want to know where our friends are," Jamie said.

"They're not your friends. And don't say another damn word!" he said to him.

"But—" Jamie started. He then winced and fell against the wall.

"Go to your room!" Jeff yelled.

I stayed locked inside the room, silent, waiting for the moment to be over.

MISSING

22

I LAID IN BED, shaking from what had just happened. I felt so helpless in this situation. No one believed me. No one thought the agency was bad. Not the dispatcher, Porter, the roommates, or Mila's family. And Quinn didn't help me either. She didn't say much. But I can't blame her too much. This whole situation was crazy, and she seemed to have her hands full with Mila's family. I wanted to escape it all. *Could I leave right now? It wasn't like Jeff and the agency put a tracker on me.* I looked down at my body, flinging the covers off of me. *Did I have a tracker on me?* I examined my body, tugging on my skin. There was nothing. *Calm down, Leon. That would be ridiculous.* I tried to relax and go back to sleep, but I tossed and turned all night.

The next morning, my phone buzzed, startling me. It was a text from Quinn. Or was it Mila?

Look it's from Audrey and Omar.

She then sent me screenshots. It was an email Audrey sent Omar.

Audrey:

> *You always lie to me. This is the last time. I'm for real.*
> *You're so jealous of Vince, but we're done. I have to*
> *work with him. You're both no good.*

Omar:

> *It's not all my fault. Take some accountability. Stay*
> *away from Vince. I don't care if the agency gives you*
> *a PR relationship. I don't want to see it.*

It looks like the messages were from some old email accounts.

Why did Omar dislike Vince so much? Was it just because they dated? Did Audrey cheat on Omar? Were they ever dating?

A hand sat on my shoulder; I jumped around to see Jeff, trying to hide the phone.

"Put that away now! You have to be focused for the event. It's only a few nights away." He laughed deeply, and I shifted in my chair.

"Okay, we need to discuss the release party coming up!" he said as he called the other bandmates into the room.

Audrey talked about how she wanted everything decorated and what we should wear. The usual.

"So, you guys are performing the new singles, and we have some industry insiders, executives, and critics. I need you guys to be great. No problems," Jeff said, eyeing both Jamie and me. "Our singles are streaming number one." Jeff showed us his phone.

I tapped my foot on the tiled floor. *They expected me to behave a certain way. I did get training, but it wasn't enough. It was like Jeff and the agency wanted me to mess up a little to see how I would react.*

After blathering for an hour about the release party, Jeff went back to his office. Jamie approached me a few minutes later and just stared at me.

"What's up?" I asked.

"So you know where the agency is?"

"No, I can't remember where it's at."

"Nothing? Not any details at all?"

"It's a tall skyscraper in the middle of the forest," I said.

Jamie straightened his posture. "A tall skyscraper in the middle of the forest?" he repeated. His forehead wrinkled.

"Yes! That was where it was."

"Really? I'm going to rescue our friends," Jamie said, scrolling through his phone.

"What does the agency have to do with them, though? How do we know if they're there?" I asked.

"I know they're there. I tried to get in touch with Kim, Landon, and Camille, but I haven't been able to."

I rubbed my temples. *That still didn't confirm how he knew.*

"I want to see my friends again, too. But the agency is not a normal place, Jamie! They can and will hurt you! They could be anywhere. Maybe they're busy with school or work. Like normal teenagers," I said.

"Oh, you guys are younger than us. Kim just turned eighteen, right?" he said while showing me a picture of a birthday cake.

Kim's birthday. "What day is it?" I asked, tugging at the collar of my shirt.

"Her birthday? You should know." He chuckled.

"No, today," I sighed.

"June 25th," he said while looking at his phone.

Oh, her birthday was a few days ago. I had forgotten everything. The months had passed by so quickly. *What else did I miss? Has my class graduated yet?* Yeah, they did. School let out on June 10th. Now that Jamie mentioned it, they were talking about colleges at the festival. *If I got back home, would I have to repeat my senior year?* I missed so many days of school. My friends weren't like me; they had much better grades and took school more seriously. They'd leave Crestview, go to college, have great careers, start a new life. And I'd be here, stuck being Vince or stuck in Crestview, working at Borrowers.

"Show me where the agency is." Jamie shoved his phone GPS app in my face.

"I don't remember much. It was traumatizing."

"Do you think it was in Crestview?" He zoomed in on the map.

"No, it was here in California. I was put on a jet."

"So, maybe it's just a few hours away?" he said.

"I don't remember anything. I'm sorry. I can't help you much. Maybe you can snoop around Jeff's room again?"

"I'll figure it out. I don't want to get involved with Jeff again. There must be an agency nearby. I wish I was more help, but I can't remember. I want my friends back just as much as you do."

"I'll search around." He walked off, huffing.

The night of the album release party, we couldn't find Jamie.

"Where's Jamie?" Porter questioned.

"Still not back from visiting family," Audrey answered, shuffling in the room. "We have to focus on the party tonight."

Visiting family? Jamie didn't mention going somewhere. That was weird.

We were in the kitchen; Audrey and her stylist Reina were choosing looks for tonight.

"Let's see what you bought for me!" Audrey cheered as she unzipped a dress bag. "Hmm, do you have anything else?" Audrey asked. Reina shook her head.

I exited the kitchen and went to my room. I had to mentally prepare myself to deal with Audrey, and the rest of the night's events. I had to keep a low profile and listen to Jeff. He wouldn't take anymore of our, or my, antics. I thought about him hitting Jamie a couple of nights ago. I dozed off, laying in bed.

Moments later, there was a sharp knock on the door that woke me up.

"Hey, get up! Everyone is almost ready!" Jeff yelled.

I had to hurry up before he did something.

"Yep, I'm getting ready now." I rushed out of bed.

I skimmed through the clothes in the closet. It didn't matter what I picked. Audrey or Jeff would disapprove and make me wear something else. Speaking of Audrey, she busted into the room.

"Let me give you the outfit we picked out for tonight. Oh, and your hair. Your hair. You should style it like this," she said, running her fingers through my curls.

After I was done being dressed, it was time for the party. We piled into a black SUV. It was dusk outside; the air was cool and crisp. I looked around the SUV; everyone was here except for Jamie.

Where was he? He didn't tell us about a family emergency. Was he out looking for Kim?

Porter and Audrey weren't too distracted by his absence. Jeff was focused on the events of the night and making sure we were on time. He wore dark shades, his arms and legs were crossed, and he had a slight smirk on his face.

Did he know where Jamie was? He was not bothered by his absence at all.

When we arrived at the location, a few cars were already in the lot.

"Okay, everything should be set up. We have fifteen minutes until the event starts." Jeff got out of the car swiftly.

The venue was a cozy lounge. The dim lights gave the place a nice, lush atmosphere. Soft jazz music played in the background. Dark velvet red stools were stationed by the bar. The bar shelves were lit up by a mellow golden light that displayed fancy bottles of alcohol. There were black leather chairs grouped around small round tables.

"Don't ruin tonight." Audrey pursed her lips. "There are industry insiders—" she continued to lecture me.

I ignored her and nodded my head. "Yep," I mumbled.

As the event started, people slowly poured in. They were dressed semi-formal; wearing dress pants and dresses. Porter and I sat at one of the small tables. Quinn came over and gave me a hug.

"I can't wait to hear the new album!" She smiled, her eyes were gleaming.

Audrey sat next to us. "Me either," she said, rubbing my leg.

The three of us made awkward small talk. Audrey was there to stop Quinn and I from saying too much. A few moments later, the host of the event grabbed a mic and invited Audrey to stand next to him. *I was glad she had to do the talking.* I exhaled in relief.

"Okay, Retro Brite is here tonight to premiere their latest album!" the host said in a loud tone.

Audrey took the mic. "Thanks for coming. I hope all of you enjoy it and have a pleasant evening!" she said.

The first track played. The guests were bobbing their heads and swaying. It seemed like they enjoyed it. They cheered and clapped. A few moments later, Jamie shimmied into our section. But I couldn't feel too proud knowing the streams were fake. Jeff told us our song was one of the top streamed since it came out.

"Hey Jamie, where have you been?" I asked.

He looked as if he had just gotten off a long flight or car ride. His eyes were puffy and his clothes were wrinkled. His voice was also lower and more raspy.

"How's it going, Cam?" Audrey asked. She was unruffled. His eyes darted from side to side as his hands fidgeted. My eyes were wide. *Who's Cam? Where is Jamie? Is he okay? What if he's at the agency?*

"It's okay. Vince and Mila are just like you," Audrey said, placing a hand on his shoulder.

"Oh, really?" He slumped over in his chair.

"So, where's Jamie?" Quinn asked.

"Family emergency . . . I don't know. I only do what I'm told." His eyes shifted across the room.

"What else were you told?" Quinn questioned.

"I don't know anything else. I'm just here to do a job!" His voice rose in agitation.

This was a job for him. He comes in and does one appearance, and that was it? While I had to give up my whole identity and life? He was going home to his friends and family, and I was stuck in this madness.

"What!? Really? So you weren't forced to do this, like Quinn and Leon? This wasn't some weird accident?" Porter leaned forward in his seat, intrigued.

I've been telling you, this is real. Jamie's probably being harassed right now," I said. *And if my friends were there, they probably were too.*

"So, did the agency give you classes, like they gave us? I'm Quinn, by the way," Quinn said.

"A couple, but for this gig, I was told just to sit here and not say much," Cam said.

"Let's relax and have a drink or two." Audrey grabbed drinks from a nearby tray It's going to be a good night." She handed Quinn and I a drink. I took the drink and gulped it down. The liquor tingled my tongue and burned my throat.

"Slow down," Cam teased.

"He's coming over." Audrey nudged Cam.

"Who?" I asked.

"The editor of VIBEZ magazine," Audrey said.

A man with a thick beard, dressed in a blue suit, came over and sat next to Quinn. Jeff was watching from afar, monitoring us.

"How's it going? I'm from VIBEZ." He shook our hands.

"Good. Good," Cam said.

"What do you think of the album?" Audrey asked him.

"It's alright. Not the best one, but I'm sure it will grow on me," he said.

Audrey folded her arms. She hated any type of negative feedback.

"Nice meeting you guys. I just wanted to stop by and say hi." He hurried back to his table.

Audrey swatted the air when he left.

"I bet he's going to write a nasty article," Porter said, slouching.

"So, how did you get the role of Jamie? Did you get taken too?" I asked Cam.

"Taken? No, I just went to a casting call. I've been an actor for a while, but I never got to do anything interesting or big. Plus, the pay is decent for this. What do you mean? Are you okay?"

Audrey's eyes went back and forth to the group, and to Jeff, who was sitting at the bar. He was talking to someone but still watching us.

"I was persuaded to be Vince and was taken to the agency. It's a horrible place. They mistreat and exploit you," I said.

He was getting paid? How much? Jeff hadn't paid me much at all.

"It's a normal place. Plus, lots of people have doubles," Cam said.

"Yeah, but Vince has been missing for *months*," I emphasized.

"Months?" Cam tilted his head.

"Yeah, he's been 'sick.'" I air quoted.

"We have no proof he's not sick. His parents even said he was," Porter said.

"You didn't think that call from the hospital was off, man?" I raised an eyebrow.

"Yeah, it was." Porter paused before speaking. "You're right."

Oh, so now he believed me after all the things that had been happening?

"What?" Cam said as he took a large sip of his drink.

Jeff walked over to us. "You guys having a good time?" His

eyes pierced into mine. We nodded. "Smile, you all should be happy!" He grinned and pointed to his mouth.

"We are. Everything is great!" Audrey squealed.

Jeff snickered. The event was wrapping up, and we headed back in the car.

"Thanks for your work today, Cam," Jeff said.

"Wait, that's it? Just a small event for a couple of hours? Will he be back this week? I'm able to do more," he pleaded.

"Yes, he will be," Jeff said.

"Well, can I at least hang around with you guys?" He placed his arm around Audrey and Porter.

Audrey shrugged him off.

"Sure, why not?" Porter half-smiled.

FRIENDS

23

THE FAKE JAMIE stayed over the rest of the night. He even pleaded to stay longer. There was no way the agency would choose him to replace Jamie again.

"Where have you been?" a few voices asked.

I leaped out of the bed and ran to the living room; the roommates were crowded around Jamie.

"Hey," he muttered.

He looked like he hadn't slept in days. He had large bags underneath his eyes and his skin appeared dry and sunburned.

"How's your family?" Calix questioned.

Jamie just nodded his head. Everyone was firing questions at him. Jeff entered the front door.

Jamie looked awful. What had happened to him? Was he at the agency? Did Jeff do something to him? I've never seen him look this disheveled. I doubt he was with his family.

"Glad you're back, Jamie. Anyway, we have to start packing for our tour in Europe and Asia. The album has already been released, and in the following weeks, we will be in London," he said.

My heart was beating fast. *Europe and Asia? I remembered Jeff telling me about the tour months ago when I first met them. Boy, had time flown by. Being in California already seemed like a foreign country to me. Was I really going to London? How much would that cost? My family could never afford that.*

Later that evening, when everyone was in their rooms, I heard Jeff downstairs in the kitchen. Probably getting his third cup of coffee. I went downstairs, and I sat down next to him.

He ignored me for a few minutes, looking at a paper. "Good evening."

"Hey, what are you looking at?" I pointed at the paper.

He peered up from the paper with a vacant gaze.

I shouldn't have said anything. Was he going to be upset?

"Just some numbers." He tossed the paper to the other side of the island and took off his reading glasses.

I grabbed a glass of water from the sink and sat back down on a barstool.

Jeff exhaled.

"How's Jamie? He seems stressed," I finally asked.

"He looked okay to me. Did you ask him?" He shrugged his shoulders.

Of course Jeff wouldn't answer me.

"No—"

"Well then, don't make assumptions," he said, smacking his lips.

"He went to see Kim. What happened to him? Are my friends okay?" I asked.

"Why would I keep track of them?" He smirked.

"I need to see them. Tell me what's going on. I've had enough," I demanded.

"Please lower your voice. You'll disturb the others. And you're already on strike two," he said in a hushed voice.

I folded my arms. *Conversations with this guy never went anywhere.*

"Okay." Jeff stood up and walked upstairs.

I stared at him, puzzled at what might happen next. *Should I follow?* I inched behind him into his room. The air in his room was cooler than the kitchen. I folded my arms and held them close to my body. His room was still tidy, like I had seen it before. Everything was the same except the vase that was once on the desk; he never replaced it.

"You want to see them?" He turned two monitors on at his desk with a big grin on his face.

I gasped. Kim was in some warehouse, lifting boxes and production gear. *Was she at work? Why was he tracking them? Was she okay?* I trembled as I moved closer to the monitor. *Was it her? Could it be a double of Kim just to frighten me? It looked like it could be her. She had the same auburn hair and short stature.*

"Number one, two, and three," he said, switching the camera to Landon and Camille, who were cleaning the floor and washing dishes.

My face reddened, and my nostrils flared. *Why did he have to bring them into this?*

"Can I at least see them!?" I pleaded. I felt sick to my stomach. A lump formed in the back of my throat.

"No," he laughed, "and I can't forget about aunty and uncle," he said, switching the camera onto their house. The house looked slightly bigger, like he actually had them moved. Aunt Mel was sitting on a new couch, watching TV on a large flatscreen.

How much did all of that cost? Were they given money to shut up?

I was filled with rage, but I had to contain it. *I was already on his last straw.* Jeff had his arms behind his head and his feet up on the desk.

I left his room and went back into the kitchen. *Why would they punish them? None of us asked for this. Kim didn't know what was going on. She probably still didn't. He already tried to make her sign an NDA. What else could be done?*

I paced around the kitchen, biting my lower lip. Vince's

phone buzzed. It was from Quinn. I glanced down quickly, but retreated to Vince's room for quiet and more privacy.

I found an interesting message from Audrey.

Really?

Yeah, she texted Mila that she was going to surprise Vince with a trip.

Where?

Mila suggested Cacti Inn. Audrey said it looked great and messaged back a few days later that they booked the location.

Look, I found this picture of them there. It was deleted off of Audrey's Sonder account, but a fan posted it.

The picture showed Vince and Audrey embracing each other. They looked like they were at the bottom of a trail. The sun was a pale orange color. They looked in love, or at least, happy.

Why would Mila text Audrey? I thought they hated each other. And why would Audrey delete the picture?

I don't know. Strange, right? Maybe she deleted it cause they broke up. Let's go check out the location tonight.

I'm too scared Jeff will know

We will leave late while everyone's asleep

Are you sure? Jeff will find out

It'll be okay

What do you think is there?

idk. But maybe it'll bring us closer to the truth about Vince and closer to going back to our normal lives. I don't know about you but I love my life and miss my family. Mila's family is too demanding of me. This isn't for me. And Audrey definitely did something to Vince. She might've dumped his body out there

Do you really think so? I'm sure someone would've found it by now

I don't know. It could be possible

See you tonight

See ya

As soon as I was done texting Quinn, I deleted the messages. I could sense Jeff watching me, even though the door was shut.

Did he put the cameras in the bedrooms? What about the bathrooms? Jeff would know that I was not home. He'd check the cameras. What would happen if we got caught? Would we be banished from the outside world and stuck as celebrity doubles? Or would we go to the agency and rot away till the end of time?

The thought of both of those outcomes sent chills down my back. I could see why Quinn wanted to go back to her old life. She came from a nice, middle class family. She had endless options and opportunities. I bet she was a better student than me and would go to some prestigious college and live a successful life. Even though my life before this was lousy, I missed it compared to what it was now. I missed Crestview. The anonymity of being an everyday person. Going shopping and eating at a restaurant in peace.

I sat on Vince's bed, deep in thought. I might finally be close to finding out what happened to Vince.

I exhaled.

GHOST TOWN
24

For the rest of the day, I anticipated tonight's events. *Would we find anything there? Had Audrey and Vince been taking a normal vacation?* Jamie still wasn't himself. He was even less talkative, groggy, and spaced out a lot. I decided to go to his room and speak with him alone about what happened to him.

I knocked on the door. There was no answer, so I knocked again. The door then opened. Jamie poked his head from behind the door. His hair was tousled and his clothes were wrinkled like he had just woken up.

"What is it, Leon?" he asked in a soft voice.

"You were at the agency, right? Did you see my friends? Jeff showed me surveillance footage of them there; I know it! He also showed my family. My house looked so much nicer."

Jamie's head swiveled down the hallway. He then pulled me into his room. The place was a mess. Clothes were dispersed on the floor. The bedding was crumpled up. Food wrappers sat on the bed, along with empty beer bottles. On the walls, canvases with abstract paintings hung.

Had Jamie painted those himself? I didn't know he was into art.

After a moment of silence, Jamie spoke. "I did find the agency, but I didn't see Kim, Camille, or Landon. I asked about them."

"What did they say?!"

"They kept asking if I needed any help or if I was looking for someone. When I asked about our friends, Vince, and about the doubles, they escorted me out and security beat me up," Jamie said, lifting up his shirt, exposing a purplish bruise on his ribs. "Jeff really showed you videos of them? How much is the agency paying them?"

"I don't know. Probably more than us. I still don't know where our friends are at. But if the workers at the agency kicked you out, they might've suspected you know the truth."

"I don't know, man. Let's talk about something else," Jamie said. His left eye twitched as he spoke.

"Okay, I'm just glad you're okay," I said. I left his room and retreated back to Vince's before someone saw me.

It time for Mila and I to embark on our journey. Vince's phone buzzed. She must be outside. I crept down the hallway and down the stairs, step by step, hoping the wooden floors wouldn't creak. Sneaking out of this house was scarier than sneaking out of Aunt Mel's house. She would be mad and disappointed, but I never feared for my life. My heart raced and my breathing was heavy, but I tried my best to not make a sound. I touched the doorknob; it was cold as ice. I slithered out the door and saw a black car parked down the street.

Was it her? It could be that someone from the agency had discovered our plan and was out to get us. The windows rolled down a little, revealing a hand motioning for me to come over. I paused for a moment, then moved toward the car.

Quinn rolled the dark tinted windows down further. I got in, and she sped off down the hilly road. *How did she get this car? Did Mila's family let her borrow it, or did she sneak out as well?*

We drove in silence for a few minutes; we were going to be secluded away from civilization. *What if Quinn left me out here like Audrey might have done with Vince? I really didn't know her.*

She seemed like was ready for this trip, even though we were walking into the unknown. She was humming and drumming her fingers on the steering wheel.

"Was it hard to find the location?" I asked.

"No, it was easy. As if they wanted us to figure it out." She glanced at me briefly, but then put her eyes back on the road.

"Figure out what? Why are we doing this exactly?" I shrugged.

"To scope out the area and ask the locals if they recognize Audrey or Vince."

"I hope no one is following us." My eyes darted up to the rearview mirror, but the road was deserted.

"Relax. If they are, what will they do? Make us go back home?"

"I don't know about your manager or Mila's family, but Jeff is capable of hurting us. He beat Jamie up. I'm out of chances with him."

"Hmm . . . really!?" Her voice rose and her eyes became wide. She still didn't seem too convinced.

Instead of asking for more information, she turned on the radio. A Retro Brite song played. Audrey's angelic voice filled the car. We both reached out to change the station.

◉

After about three hundred miles, the scenery switched from buildings and cars to desert and emptiness.

"We're almost here."

We saw a few small, decrepit buildings. Most shops were

boarded up. Signs had faded paint that made them illegible. The paint on the buildings was chipped. It was obvious the town was once booming and full of energy, but now it seemed like it never had any visitors.

"Looks like no one is here," I said.

"Yeah, like a ghost town. I think this is the inn they stayed at." She parked behind the building.

The sand scratched against my shoes. The cool desert air gave me goosebumps. I shriveled at the thought of us being here alone early in the morning. Anything could happen to us. We walked up to a small wooden inn, resembling a western styled saloon. It put me in the mind of an RPG game that I played.

The door creaked as I opened it. This didn't seem like a place Audrey would vacation at.

A middle-aged man was at the reception desk. The lobby was decorated with cactuses and taxidermy animals. A mountain lion was displayed near the entrance. Quinn jumped back and grabbed on to me.

"Don't be scared. Are you guys lost?" the man asked.

Quinn readjusted her hair and regained her composure. "No, we need a room," she said.

"A romantic quiet getaway, huh?" the man asked.

We looked at each other, taken aback for a moment. "No," we both said in unison.

Quinn held out her hands and shook them. "A room." Quinn paused. "Do you know if Audrey and Vince from Retro Brite stayed here? What room?" she asked.

"Who?" The man tilted his head to the side.

"They're in a band." Mila pulled out a picture from her pocket and showed him. His eyes shifted from the picture to me.

I turned away, embarrassed. For a moment, I forgot that I was pretending to be Vince.

"Isn't that you?" He pointed at me.

I nodded. "Yes," I mumbled.

"You were here a couple of months ago?"

"Yeah, I loved it so much here I had to come back," I said, nodding my head.

"Didn't seem like it. You and the other girl kept arguing. She left without you. So, is this your new girl? She came back from the hike upset and said you took off."

"Really? Where did they go? I want to see the hike." Quinn turned to the man. "What was the trail called?"

"Dusty Pike," he responded.

"Well, we will be back. I want to look at the other shops," Quinn said.

The man shook his head. Quinn grabbed a map of the trails off the counter as we exited.

We walked a few feet from the inn, entering a bar. It was shabby and cozy. The balmy heat warmed me up. The place had a variety of scents that ranged from earthy, sweet, and floral. There were lanterns hanging above a light brown wooden bar counter. Behind the bar, many glasses were stacked up. The soft lighting exposed dust floating around and sticking to the glasses.

"You're back," a gruff female voice said as I walked in. "Do you need a drink?

"Sure," Quinn answered.

The bartender filled up a glass of beer and slid it on the counter. Quinn took the drink and went over to a slot machine and put a quarter in.

"Last time you were here, your friend was mad at you for spending and drinking too much. Surprised to see you back again."

"Yeah," I sighed.

Quinn slapped her thigh and groaned. She must of not have won.

"This is going to sound crazy, but he is not the guy that was here earlier," Quinn said when she came back.

The woman squinted her eyes. "You were here a couple of months ago?" the woman asked.

"No, it's not him. We're looking for the guy that was here."

The woman shook her head and turned around to place a glass on the shelf behind her. "So, you're telling the guy that looks like him, isn't?" She chuckled.

"No, that's my twin brother. He's missing," I told her.

"Go to the police." The woman turned around, dismissing our presence.

"But we did." Quinn's voice dropped low.

"Unless you want another drink, don't bother me. I came to this town to get away from city folk drama."

"I just want you to tell us anything about your encounter with him."

The woman seemed uninterested and continued to clean the glasses. Quinn walked over to the counter and placed a crisp $100 bill on the counter. The lady spun around, smiling.

Where did she get that money? Did she have more?

"Your brother came in with a girl. She had a crazy hair color . . . red, maybe purple." She waved her hands near her head. "They were having a good time, but had too much to drink and were arguing." She tutted her lips. "Something about talking to other girls . . . who were fans. And something about the band. I don't know. She said she was a part of some famous group." She shrugged.

"Thanks. Let's go." We left the bar.

"Now what?" I questioned.

"Let's hike the trail," Quinn suggested.

"Now!?" I exclaimed. The dry air caused me to cough.

"Yes, we might get some new insight."

I exhaled and slapped my arms to my side. We drove a couple of miles from the buildings.

"Come on." She waved getting out of the car. I followed up a winding sandy hill.

"This doesn't look so bad," she said.

"It is," I huffed, already out of breath.

I had never been a good student or athlete. I barely participated in gym and only played soccer to appease my uncle.

After fifteen minutes, we were close to the peak of the hill. A loud rustling sound came from some bushes. Quinn hopped behind me and yelped. A coyote sprang out, growling. It snarled at me. Its eyes were golden and his teeth were razor sharp. I began hyperventilating.

What should I do? It lunged forward more. I slid back, causing the dirt and gravel to loosen up underneath me. I picked up a medium-sized rock and chucked it. It bounced off its eye; the coyote jumped and nipped at my feet; ripping my jeans.

Quinn began to launch more rocks, and the coyote stepped back and retreated.

"That was close," she exhaled.

"Yep," I said.

We made it to the top of the peak.

"This was a steep climb. Someone could have easily fallen off, gotten hurt, or been pushed off." She eyed me.

Why was she looking at me like that? What if she just pushed me off now? She wouldn't do that. I shook my head.

"We still have no proof of this happening. There's never any answers," I said.

I followed her down the path. *How did she still have energy?* We were back at the bottom of the hike, about to get back into our car, when a black SUV pulled up. It was, of course, Jeff, Quinn's manager, and Lenna.

"Hurry, get in!" Quinn jumped into the passenger seat. She tried to speed past them, but Jeff sped up and got in front of us, blocking us from leaving.

"Stop now!" Jeff yelled with the windows down and a megaphone.

"Ugh, so extra." Quinn rolled her eyes.

"Let's just follow through," I said. She nodded.

Leena got out and opened the door to our vehicle. She motioned for us to get out. We complied and got into their SUV.

"What were you guys doing?" Jeff snapped.

"You already know." Quinn folded her arms. "How did you even find us?"

"You guys forgot to turn off the phone . . . so stupid." Jeff sneered as he turned to Leena, who was in the passenger seat.

I took out Vince's phone. *Damn, it still had reception. How could I do something so dumb? I was sure they would of found us anyway, though.*

"Why did you bring the phone?" Quinn asked, slapping her leg.

"What were you guys doing here!" Jeff yelled.

Quinn and I did not answer him.

"You guys think this is a game?" He chuckled.

We were quiet once more.

Jeff asked us what we were doing here again, but his time, through gritted teeth. He zoomed down the dirt road. The car bounced up and down as we drove over the bumpy desert road. Quinn and I held on tight in our seats.

"No, we don't, Jeff," I said.

"It seems like you two don't know how to listen." His voice rattled the car. He made a sharp right turn. Quinn and I jolted to the right, and Quinn shrieked.

"Please, stop!" she pleaded.

"What do you guys know?" Jeff asked. His eyes were red.

"Nothing," I said. He made another sharp turn. *Oh my god, would he calm down. I don't want to get into another accident.*

"We know Audrey and Vince were here. That's it. We want to know if Aud—" Quinn spoke.

"If Audrey what?" Jeffs voice croaked.

"We want to know the truth, Jeff. That's all!" Quinn yelled.

"Why? So you can run and tell everybody?" He took one hand off the steering wheel and made a running motion with his index and middle finger.

"No one would believe us anyway," I said.

"I'll make sure of it," Jeff said. He was now driving even faster.

My body pressed against the door as we sped uphill. *Where were we going? This wasn't the way Quinn and I drove on the way here.*

"What the hell are you doing!?" Leena asked.

Quinn and I screamed at the top of our lungs. My eyes widened and my stomach dropped. This was the end. We were going to die; all of us. And maybe the cycle would start over. The agency would eventually find out and just replace all of us. I closed my eyes. The tires screeched.

When I opened my eyes, we were at the edge of a cliff.

"Ae you crazy?" Leena jumped out of the car.

"Get back in!" Jeff told her. He got out of the car. His button-down shirt was soaked in sweat.

I panted, trying to regain my breath. Quinn got out of the car and was leaning against it, heaving. Her face was flush. *What had just happened?*

I was right about Jeff. He was insane. And just like that, he was back in the driver's seat, smiling, like nothing happened. Like it was the first day I met him at the concert.

LONDON

25

A MONTH HAS PASSED by as we were focused on the tour and practiced for hours a day. Jeff wanted everything to go perfect for tour.

Every day, I wondered if Jeff would tell Audrey what happened. I didn't think he did. If so, Audrey would have been furious.

Today was the big day; we started our tour in London. Even though I was on edge from Jeff's antics in the desert, I was excited to go. Over the last few months, I experienced more than I could ever imagine. My first plane ride, music festival, and, of course, performing as Vince. I was exhausted, but traveling had been one of the only plus sides of this weird experience.

Over the past week, I had been looking at pictures of London. The city seemed like it was massive. *Would Jeff let us see or do anything? I bet he wouldn't. We'd be confined to our hotel suite.*

We got on our jet, and ten hours later, we were in London. I got used to flying. I felt more at ease, and was even able to peek out the window at the fluffy white clouds. It was hard to imagine my fear subsiding from the the first flight I took.

When we landed at the airport, millions of people were there. Despite this, the place was clean and bright. There were tons of shops and restaurants. The shops ranged from cafes, bars, gift shops, to even, luxury clothing stores. My eyes shifted nonstop. There was so much going on. People chatted away on phones. The wheels of luggage slid across the tiled floors. As I walked through, I was greeted by the smell of coffee and baked goods. We were ushered to baggage claim where, unfortunately, a large group of fans and paparazzi started flashing away with their cameras.

"I love you, Vince!" a young girl shrieked.

I waved and nodded in her direction. She squealed even louder. I squinted my eyes at the flashing cameras. I bet those pictures were really unflattering. *Could we hurry up and get to the hotel?* I combed my fingers through my hair and readjusted my shirt.

"Sign this!" a boy yelled.

Audrey stepped forward to sign the poster, but he bypassed her and went to me. Audrey looked away as if it didn't happen, but I could still see the agitation through her thick, framed black sunglasses. After our bags were placed on carts, we got into the car to go to the hotel. Fans followed us out, still screaming for pictures. The paparazzi continued to flash until we drove off.

I couldn't be too annoyed at the fans; they were the reason I was in London. Audrey had a stone-cold expression the whole time.

The sky was overcast and a dull gray. The sun tried to peek through the clouds, warming the air. We drove on the highway for about thirty-five minutes until we got to a residential area. The highway was overgrown with lush lime green trees. It was hard to believe that me, a small town kid from Crestview, was in a different country. Everything fascinated me: the accents, the fact that we were driving on the left side of the road, the Londoners even dressed so different from people from Crestview. People in Crestview dressed like they didn't care how they look; wearing shorts, t-shirts, and PJs. While Londoners dressed like they didn't care about what people thought; wearing bold and quirky clothing. They wore mixed patterns, like plaids and polka dots, but still looked well-dressed. They seemed like they were in their own worlds. I felt like such an outsider.

The city was so massive and made me feel like a tiny ant. The roads were congested. I thought LA traffic was bad, but this was worse. Cars honked and swerved in and out of traffic. Pedestrians ran across the streets. Shops on the street had display windows showcasing fancy clothing brands I have never heard of. When we arrived at the hotel, my mouth was wide open. The building was sleek and rectangular looking; it looked like it had been here for many years.

"The Stonebridge Hotel," I read out loud as we pulled up.

"Nice, innit?" Audrey cackled in a horrible English accent.

I nodded my head and rolled my eyes. *That actress that we worked with was right . . . Audrey was a horrible actor.* But this hotel was incredible. A couple of large flags hung above the entrance.

We were immediately valeted and escorted inside. The interior took my breath away. The floor was a beautiful rosewood, and pictures of regal looking people hung on the walls. The furniture was antique, but modern looking at the same time. And, of course, a place couldn't be elegant without mirrors and chandeliers.

We went to the front desk and got the keys to our penthouse suite. We were then taken to our rooms by the bellhop. When we entered, I gasped again. Audrey spoke about how this place was a common vacation destination for celebrities and royalty, and she wasn't kidding. The room had golden curtains draped over a huge window. A tiny gold vase sat on a shelf. A large gold chandelier. Comfy-looking cream-colored sofas framed the edge of a cream and dark green rug. Next to the living room, there was a long, dark wood dining table with a dark green table runner.

This place was too nice. What if I messed something up? I examined the floors as I took each step so I wouldn't scuff them up.

"This is amazing," Porter said, glancing around the room, taking it all in.

"Right?" Jeff said.

A man, dressed in a classic tux, greeted us. "I'm Alexander; your butler. I will be accommodating you during your stay."

Audrey grinned. Jamie plopped down his luggage the bellhop brought up and sat down at the piano. A ruckus erupted from the instrument.

"Stop! You're messing up the vibe. Stick to playing the guitar." Audrey turned her nose up.

"The drums," Jamie said, rising up from the piano.

"Mmm, yeah," Audrey mumbled.

We spent the next few hours unpacking and settling in. I was glad that we all had our own rooms and didn't argue over them. I felt sorry for the butler having to be ordered around by Audrey. It was his job, but being around Audrey was exhausting. And she probably would order him around a lot.

"Let's get ready for dinner. We have a lot to discuss, and a performance tomorrow," Jeff said.

As I got ready, I could not stop thinking about how I didn't deserve all this luxury. *I was an imposter. I should, at least, try to enjoy these moments.*

The dinner was thankfully at a more laid-back location. Not much happened, but Jeff briefed us about the performance and press we had in London. Of course, Jamie already had a few drinks too many. Jeff and Audrey cut him off before it was too late. When we returned to the hotel, everyone retired to their rooms early due to the full schedule tomorrow.

The sun cut through the giant windows. As I looked to my right, a figure stood next to me, and I jumped.

"Jeff, couldn't you just knock!"

"I did. You were out cold. Breakfast is being served."

The butler was setting up the table. We were served a standard English breakfast: fried eggs, sausages, tomatoes, mushrooms, beans, toast, coffee, and tea. It was a little different, but a good change. I wasn't the biggest fan of tomatoes and mushrooms, and found it kind of strange that people would eat them for breakfast. We then were off to rehearsals. With only a few hours until the show, the pressure was on.

"More energy. Stop. You guys are off. People pay for this!" Jeff scolded.

After we got it right, it was less than an hour till the performance. I was now dressed up and ready to perform. The performance was phenomenal, and the crowd was wild. After the performance, we signed autographs and took pictures. Arms were grabbing me left and right. Porter warned me that the international fans were more intense.

Back to the hotel, we were able to decompress. Porter and Jamie watched TV in the living room, and before I could do anything, Audrey spoke.

"I need to talk to you," Audrey said, dressed in a luxurious designer robe. "It's so relaxing here." Her face was dewy and glowing; the scent of vanilla lingered on her skin.

"What do you want?" I cut straight to the point.

"In private," she said.

I followed her into her room and onto the balcony. She pulled a cigarette from out of her robe pocket and lit it. The humid air made my shirt stick to my skin; it was drizzling. She leaned on the rail, her hands dangling over it. She flicked the cigarette ash over the balcony.

Audrey smoked? I imagined she never did it in public due to the agency making her the darling of the group.

"Isn't it beautiful?" She nodded toward the courtyard below.

I nodded.

We were high up in the penthouse, but the garden below was

beautiful. The roses were a vibrant mixture of red, pink, and white. I hadn't had the chance to check it out since we've been here.

"It seems like you're getting used to all of this," she said, exhaling smoke. Her eyes were locked onto mine. She leaned against the railing, and it creaked.

"Yeah, this is the only good thing about this lifestyle." I motioned out of the balcony.

"You don't like it a little bit?"

"Sometimes, but it's a bit much. And now the agency wants to push my image even more," I said.

Audrey's gaze shifted down to the rose garden. I leaned on the railing, causing it to squeak again.

"Okay. Well, you don't have to worry about that anymore. Vince will be back soon, and you won't have to worry about that. The agency and the fans will have their attention back on me."

I looked at Audrey. Her face was serious, but I didn't know what she was talking about. She paced back to the balcony door.

"Will he? And you can have all the attention back. I didn't ask for this," I said.

Audrey's gaze refocused on me. *Why did I just say that?* My mouth started to get dry.

"Do you want to go back to that crappy little town Crestview that bad?" she said. Her head tilted to the side.

"I actually do."

"What, really? And give up all of this? You should be grateful for this opportunity. Most guys your age would kill to be Vince."

Hearing her say the word 'kill' made me shudder. *And she was partially right. I would miss the traveling and not having to worry about making my family proud.*

"Why do you think he's not coming back?" Her voice shifted higher. She stubbed the cigarette out on the floor. "You're such a bad liar . . . just like Vince."

I turned my head. *Did she know Quinn and I were at the desert looking for Vince?*

She was right. I was a bad liar.

"So, it's cool to be in London?" I changed the subject.

"Yeah, it is. I've been here before. What are you hiding?"

I slouched over the balcony and hung my head low. The railing wobbled. Audrey walked over from the other side of the balcony.

"I don't know anything, I swear!" I extended my arms out and shrugged my shoulders.

"Tell me now!" She clenched her teeth; she was so close to my face. Her breath was pungent with the smell of smoke.

My body shook. *I guess I had to tell her.* I cleared my throat. "Quinn and I were at Dusty Pike last month . . . " I began.

"For what!?" Audrey pushed me against the railing. It squealed and teetered back and forth.

"We know you took Vince there. We know you left without him."

"So? That means nothing." Her teeth ground.

My heart pulsed. "Audrey, I know he's not coming back. I know you have something to do with it. It's obvious, but why?" My voice trembled as I spoke.

"I don't." She leaned against me again.

I wiggled my way around her. She was now leaning her side against the railing.

"No, he's not coming back. What's it to you? You're good at being Vince, but I'm the real star . . . " she continued blathering on, but I could barely hear what she was saying.

The railing wobbled back and forth.

"Audrey . . . Audrey!" I yelled, but she didn't listen.

A loud snapping noise pierced my ears. My eyes and mouth widened as Audrey tumbled over the balcony. I reached out to grab her, but it was too late. She let out a bloodcurdling scream. My hands were trembling. This all happened so fast.

"Audrey!" I called out. I peered over the balcony. Her body laid on a bed of roses. She didn't move. *Was she okay?* Her house slippers were thrown off a couple of feet away from her body. My stomach churned. Tears poured down my face as I screamed for help.

REVIVAL

26

WE STAYED in London for a few days, then went back to LA. Audrey was severely injured after the fall. She was in critical condition. We informed the public that we were canceling the tour due to her injury. The fans were devastated but at least they got a refund.

Within a few days Jeff informed me that Audrey didn't pull through. The funeral arrangements were tomorrow. Jeff told her family that the railing was faulty and she slipped off of it. And that it was the hotel's responsibility.

I paced around the room. *Wow. Was this all my fault?* No, it was the balcony. *I was not the best person in the world, but I was no killer.*

The house was now emptier even though the rest of the roommates were still there. I hadn't been able to eat or sleep. On TV, every channel was talking about her injury. None of them said anything about her death. *Why wasn't it reported yet? Did Audrey's family want her death not to be disclosed yet?*

I laid in bed until the next morning. The sunlight burned my eyes. It was time to get dressed for the service. I was in the same black suit I wore to that party, but this was not a celebratory event. Jamie, Porter, and the rest of the roommates got into the car and we drove to the agency.

Why was the service being held here? The auditorium was packed with guests from the agency and her family was sitting in the front row. My stomach churned. Ms. Ambrose and Jeff were standing at the front of the auditorium.

"Thank you everyone for coming," she sighed. "Audrey was such a treasure to represent at the agency and loved what she did. Such a great talent was taken too soon." Her usually stern voice was now somber.

This was so crazy. Funerals were the worst. This was the first one I've been to since my parents passed away. I looked at Jamie and Porter; they both seemed unbothered and like they wanted the service to be over.

It was so strange. I imagined Jamie would be sobbing. They didn't like Audrey that much, but she was their bandmate.

Jeff stepped forward and took the mic. "Yes, Audrey Noelle Menna was quite the character," he chuckled. A few people chuckled along. "She came to the agency at the age of 3. So excited to be an actor and singer. She was extraordinary, but she was also like many of you here. She was a doppelgänger."

My jaw dropped to the floor. Photos of Audrey were playing on a slideshow. Some of them showed her as a 3-year-old toddler. *So, she was a doppelgänger too? She thought she was different from us . . . from me. Audrey would be livid to find this out.*

I chuckled at the thought, but stopped when I remembered I was at a funeral. *Why would her parents sell her out like that?* I scanned the room. Everyone, as a collective, was confused. We didn't know whether to cry, laugh, or what. Audrey's mom was in shambles. They should be ashamed.

"But she won't be missed for long. She's here with us in spirit and can be with us forever." Jeff clicked a button on a remote.

The slideshow faded to black. He hit another button, and a figure appeared in the middle of the stage . . . a hologram? Everyone in the room gasped. Audrey's parents were smiling.

"She will still be performing with us." He hit another button. The hologram started dancing. The motion was so fluid and life-like. It felt like she was really there.

"My Audrey!" her mother yelped as she ran to the hologram. Jeff turned the hologram off. She kneeled on the stage, sobbing. Her son, Lewis, grabbed her off the stage and they exited the auditorium. The father trekked behind. The service concluded with a few more people giving their condolences.

This was so cruel. Why would they show her family that? Why didn't they get a replacement for her? Of course, they were thinking about money.

As people exited the auditorium, Audrey's grandmother lagged behind. She approached me. She didn't seem as distraught as the rest of the family. *I know everyone grieves differently, but it was weird.*

"I'm so sorry for your loss." I patted her shoulder.

"It's okay,;Audrey is still alive," she said.

" . . . what?" I raised my eyebrows. "Then, why are we having a service for her."

"She is dead to the agency. Jeff and Ms. Ambrose are no longer working with her. They can't deal with her antics anymore. Jacob and Laurie are devastated. There's nothing they wanted more than to have a famous child."

"She can still get signed by another agency, right? So, she's not returning back to the band, but they're using a hologram of her?" My eyes were wide.

"Yes, Jeff and Ms. Ambrose are full of theatrics." The grandmother looked like she was about to say more but was whisked away by another family member. This was crazy. That was why Jamie and Porter had no reaction.

Was I the only one that Jeff told Audrey was dead? It seemed like it. I wondered if she was recovering. Jeff probably wanted me to feel guilty and bad. What about Vince? Jamie and Porter found this whole situation weird as well and thought I knew Audrey was still alive.

COURTSIDE

27

THE NEXT DAY, we were in the studio, as if nothing happened.

"We just finished the last album not long ago. Are we going back on tour soon? What about Audrey?" Jamie questioned.

"Yes, Jamie, and if she's not the lead on a song, you guys will still perform them." Jeff was irritated. "Time is money," he said, folding his arms.

We recorded the song. *It was weird to be in the studio without Audrey. And now that she was gone, I had to be the lead vocalist. At least I could let my guard down around Porter and Jamie now. I didn't have to pretend to have talent.*

Later that evening, Jeff had a photographer come over to take promo shots. The process was quick, easy, and . . . somewhat enjoyable. The vibe was so much different than when Audrey was around. We got the shoot done without any arguments or tantrums. We laughed and joked around. This would have never happened with Audrey in the group. When the shoot was finished, we posted some photos online.

Ugh, boring. I wish Audrey was back.

Finally, Vince getting the shine he deserves.

Most of the comments were positive. A lot of fans wished Audrey a speedy recovery.

We woke up bright and early to practice. Jeff was hard on us and critiquing our every move. I hoped no of us would pass out like last time.

"Jeff, can we take a break?" Jamie rubbed his temples.

"No, we have to work harder now that Audrey is not a part of the group anymore. Do you guys want to be out of the agency, too? Do you guys even care about your careers?" Jeff questioned us.

"We do. I just think we need a break. Tensions been high. Can we at least wait till Audrey recovers more? I know she's not a part of the group anymore," Porter started.

"You guys didn't even like her. I'm so glad I don't have to deal with her anyone." Jeff smiled. "She was spoiled and disobedient. This is the best decision for the group. It gives you guys a. chance to shine for once. The fans will miss her in the group, but her hologram will replace her."

"Why not get another doppelgänger?" Porter asked.

"It's a new technology that will save us money, time, and effort. Now let's get back to practicing," Jeff said.

Later that evening, the PR team filled us in on the next event, which was performing at the halftime of a basketball game. This event seemed so stressful. We were coached on who was going to be there and how to interact. This was my first time performing at a sporting event. I always steered away from them for the most part, except for when my uncle would drag me along or when Landon had a game. The game was tomorrow and Audrey's hologram would also be performing.

I shuddered at the thought. *Could they just let her recover in peace? All the agency cared about was money and their image.*

We spoke more about the costumes and performance, and then, Jeff entered the room.

"We will have someone else joining us on the road. A photographer." A girl stepped from behind him. "This is Daniella, our photographer."

"Hey, Jamie, Porter . . . Vince," she paused when she saw me.

"Hi," I said softly. The girl nodded. *Was that . . . Kim?*

I gasped and hugged her.

"I missed you so much!" she squealed.

"Enough of that. Yes, she is your little friend, *Daniella.*" He emphasized the name. "She will no longer go by the other name."

Kim's naturally red auburn hair was now jet black like ink. Her hazel eyes were now darker and her skin was more olive. Jamie walked over to embrace her.

"Where are Landon and Camille?" I raised a brow.

"Back where we left them. She's more useful. And we're on a budget," Jeff answered.

"So, how much will I get paid?" she asked.

Jeff scoffed. "We will figure that out later."

Kim hung her head low. Kim and I then caught up. We spoke about the agency, the fake duplicates, and our families back home. Jamie stayed nearby, comforting her.

It was exciting to have Kim here . . . I mean, Daniella. She snapped photos of us dressed up to perform at the basketball game.

"This is exciting!" Porter yelped.

Kim cheesed from behind the lens.

We sat courtside with a front row view of all the action. We were so close I could touch the players. I couldn't imagine how much these tickets cost. Kim sat behind us. It felt like old times. We were laughing and joking like we used to. Jeff sat close by, giving us a death stare if we were too loud.

"Look, Mikko's here." She pointed him out.

I glanced at him, and he glared at me. I wonder how he was doing in the polls. Last time I checked, he was leading.

It was hard to believe that people were voting for him. He might become one of the youngest mayors. Why was he staring at me like that, though? Did he think I was the reason Audrey got hurt?

The game started, and I zoned out. The guys were watching every move. They were jumping and cheering. Kim was just happy to be there.

"Now, what we have all been waiting for is the debut performance from Audrey, the hologram," the MC announced. The crowd howled. They seem pretty excited to see Audrey, even though it was just a hologram of her. *I wondered if any of them thought it was weird.*

Jamie and Porter gave me a concerned look. The hologram rose up from the stage. The lights dimmed and the music started to play. She grabbed the mic and began to sing. Her voice was sweet and delicate. She swayed back and forth. Two backup dancers came on stage. They gyrated to the beat as the tempo increased. Audrey dropped down low and rocked her hips. The crowd cheered and whistled. Audrey always had a sexy side, but it was now more exaggerated.

Sex sells, so I guess the agency knew what they were doing.

The audience still seemed to enjoy it. I got chills from seeing how realistic the hologram was. If they didn't tell them it was a hologram, it could have easily passed to be the real Audrey. I needed to get out of here. I stood up and started to walk away.

"Where are you going?" Jeff asked. He didn't want to take his eyes off the performance.

"To the bathroom."

"Well, hurry up. You got five minutes." He sighed.

I walked out and went outside for a breather. The cool evening air relaxed me.

THE FINAL ACT

28

"Leon, come here," I heard a voice say. I craned my neck but didn't see anyone. The voice came from a car nearby. The windows rolled down; it was Mila and Quinn. I gasped. *What were they doing here?*

"Get in quick," one of them said. I got in the back seat of the car. We drove out of the parking lot. A woman with short hair was in the front seat driving.

What was going on? Who was she? We better drive fast; Jeff was going to look for me.

"We need to go to the police immediately. I know they didn't believe you, but Mila and I told them everything," Quinn said.

They believed them? What did they say?

"I'm sorry for everything. I should have never agreed to have a double." Mila turned around in the passenger seat.

"And they believed you!" I said. My eyes were popping out of my head.

"Yes, Leon. This is abuse and labor trafficking. We were tricked. I thought I was at the mall and was promised money for modeling. I was a broke college student. I didn't know any of this would happen," Quinn said.

"Oh, and this is agent Vera Fox. We have been working with her for a few weeks." Mila said.

They hired an investigator. What evidence did she find? We drove for a couple of minutes until we reached a police station. *It was finally over. I could go back to my old life. No more fans or paparazzi. No more Jeff and Audrey.* I bit my lip. *Was it finally here? It couldn't be that simple.*

The station was a gray square-shaped building with tiny windows on the second floor. Police cars were parked outside, and a large American flag fluttered in the wind.

Vera got out of the car. She was wearing a pinstriped suit. Her short, heeled shoes clacked against the concrete. "We have a lot of things to discuss," Vera said.

We walked into the police station, and Vera guided us past waiting area. A man sat in a chair with his arms folded.

"Wait here," Vera said to the girls, and they sat down. We walked past a man typing away at a counter. We were in an open space filled with cubicles. It was quiet except for the clicking of mouses and keyboards. Officers were busy working away. No one looked up as we walked through. The room smelled like coffee.

We went into a hallway. The doors needed keycards to be opened. Vera stepped in front of one of them and reached around her neck to pull out a card that was on a lanyard. A green light flashed, indicating we could enter. We were now in a more secure and isolated part of the station. We walked down around the hall. As her heels clicked against the floor. My heart skipped beats. My breathing became heavy. I craned my neck back toward the entrance.

There was no turning back. I knew I was in a police station but I did not feel safe. What would she ask me? I wish Mila and Quinn were here. As we continued walking, I expected Jeff and the agency workers to come from behind the corner. I was breathing louder.

"You're okay, Leon. You're safe now." Her voice was soothing. She stopped in front of another door. There was a monitor above the door that showed the inside of the room. She took out her keycard, unlocked the door, and she gestured for me to enter.

I shuffled my feet on the smooth concrete floor. I looked up and in the corner of the room was a small camera swerving from side to side.

"Please have a seat. I haven't formally introduced myself. I'm Vera Fox. I'm just going to ask you a few questions." She pointed to a metal chair that was bolted to the floor. The metal seat was cold to the touch. I laid my forearms on the table in front of me.

Vera sat across from me in a comfy office chair. "So, how did you find out about Jeff and the agency?" She cleared her throat.

"My friends and I went to a Retro Brite Concert, and I entered a look-alike contest. Audrey interviewed me. It was a weird interview."

"Hmm. What day was this?" Her eyebrows raised. I glanced at the swiveling camera from the corner of my eye. I started to sweat as it watched my every move.

"I don't remember; it was months ago . . . in April." I turned my head to the side, trying to jog my memory. I went on to tell her everything I knew. From the abuse at the agency to Audrey falling off the balcony. Her face was expressionless while I spoke.

What was going through her mind? I felt hesitant to tell my story. But if Mila and Quinn trusted her, so could I.

"Well, the evidence I have supports your story. I gathered DNA samples and photos."

Over the next few weeks, Vera continued her investigation. They held Mila, Quinn, and me at a hotel. We were protected from Jeff and the agency. It was strange to talk to Quinn without having to be discreet. I could finally be myself, Leon, and she didn't have to be Mila anymore.

LIFE GOES ON

29

So I GUESS you guys are wondering what happened to me. Well, Quinn and I stayed at the hotel for a few months while Vera found more evidence. The band permanently separated, and the agency was busted. The case had now become public, and the media was eating it up. Every channel covered the story. My face was plastered on TV, news articles, and social media. I was now getting attention as Leon. I was glad it was all coming to an end.

It turned out Audrey was found guilty of murdering Vince and was now spending the rest of her life in prison. I felt a little sorry for Audrey; she was thrown into this lifestyle. It seemed like she didn't really have a choice. Of course, what she did to Vince was unforgivable. Jeff, Ms. Ambrose, and the other workers at the agency were also imprisoned.

"I'm just glad everything is over," I said, leaning back into an armchair.

"I bet you are," Cherry said. She leaned in closer to me, speaking in a hushed voice. The audience was quiet and listening to every word that was being said.

"We're so glad that he's back," Aunt Mel said. Her voice was breaking. Uncle Dan rubbed her back. I knew they were happy to have me back, but they still chose money over me. Though, I wasn't sure how much they were paid.

"Well, it looks like you can go back to your normal life in Crestview, right?" Cherry asked.

"No, we won't be back. It was too much for Leon and us. The constant questions from neighbors and the the media. We're leaving," Aunt Mel said.

"And where are you guys going?" Cherry glanced at the three of us.

"Somewhere more secluded," Uncle Dan said.

After I returned home, I tried to reacclimatize to my old life but couldn't. I was taking courses online to finish my senior year and mangaged to get a job as a dishwasher at the diner my aunt worked at. Every day people from all over traveled to meet me; it was overwhelming. I felt like Vince again.

My friends went off to college and moved on. Kim got into her dream photography school. Landon went to college in a bigger town a couple of hours away. He still had plans to run his father's business. Camille stayed in town and went to cosmetology school. I still wasn't sure about my future and was taking it one day at a time. All of us stayed in touch, but the relationship was not the same.

When I reunited with them, they constantly would ask me questions like: "How was it being famous?" "How were the bandmates?" "Did they really torture me?" I understood that the situation was unbelievable, but it was annoying.

Eventually, Kim stopped listening to Retro Brite and talking about them. She was still talking to Jamie. It was strange; Retro Brite was a big part of our lives for the past three years. It was all she would ever talk about, but she had moved on and started talking about other musicians. Hopefully, the attention would soon die out and I could start a fresh slate as Leon.

"Now that we heard Leon's story, let's bring out our next

guest, Quinn," Cherry said. The audience cheered as she walked out.

"So, Quinn, you were just a regular college student that wanted extra money. You thought you were modeling?" Cherry said.

"Yeah, Leon and I were tricked. I never thought this would happen. But I knew things would work out and go back to normal eventually," Quinn said.

"How?" Cherry asked.

"I wasn't stopping until I got answers," Quinn said.

I wish I had been as optimistic as she was. It had seemed like being Vince would last forever. Quinn had transitioned back to her life easier than I had. She didn't have thousands of people stalking and questioning her. Other doppelgängers from the agency were also guests at The Cherry Show. Like Omar and Aaron. The Cherry Show was my last public appearance.

Had I wanted all of this to happen? No, but I was glad it did. I got to do more in life than I could have ever imagined. I had met many people and seen a ton of things. And learned not to take my life for granted. I used to hate my mundane life and wished for more. I never appreciated my aunt and uncle and what they did for me.

I still wasn't sure what the future held for me. I might not become a doctor like my father aspired to be. But I could live my life as Leon Halloway the III, and I was okay with that.

AUTHOR'S NOTE

This book's idea was inspired by my love of music and pop culture. Growing up, like a lot of young people, I was fascinated with celebrity gossip. I would check every blog and read many magazines. I wanted to know every detail about my favorite singers and actors. I wanted to hear about other people's opinions and their conspiracy theories. Over the years, my interest in these topics has decreased. I am not as obsessed with these topics, but I am interested in how celebrity culture has changed from my generation and where it is going.

In this story, one of the topics I explored was the idea of anonymity and being a public figure. Once someone is a public figure, people feel like every detail of their life is now an open book. Another topic I wanted to explore was self-identity. Whether it be a person still finding their identity or losing it in a newfound role. The outlook on these themes is constantly changing, and I wonder what the perspective will look like in years to come.

ACKNOWLEDGMENTS

I had this idea for this novel years ago. I never thought that I would finish yet publish it. This process was hard for me. It took a while for it to come together, but with Chelsea Lauren's coaching, the process was much easier. Her coaching and feedback motivated me to keep going. I would also like to thank my family for nurturing my creativity and supporting me.

ABOUT THE AUTHOR

Felícia Jones was born in Georgia and currently resides on the coast of North Carolina. Her love for music began when she started piano lessons at age five. She later began to write songs. Felicia's love of writing also began early when she was in school. She started writing stories about her favorite TV shows, movies, and characters. She is currently continuing to express herself through writing and hopes to work in different creative mediums.